Games for Dead Girls

Also by Jen Williams

Dog Rose Dirt

Games for Dead Girls

Jen Williams

HARPER
Voyager

Harper*Voyager*
An imprint of HarperCollins*Publishers* Ltd
1 London Bridge Street
London SE1 9GF

www.harpercollins.co.uk

HarperCollins*Publishers*
Macken House
39/40 Mayor Street Upper
Dublin 1
D01 C9W8
Ireland

First published by HarperCollins*Publishers* 2023

1

ISBN: 978-0-00-838384-8 (HB)
ISBN: 978-0-00-838385-5 (TPB)

Set in Sabon LT Std by Palimpsest Book Production Ltd, Falkirk, Stirlingshire

Printed and bound in the UK using 100% renewable electricity
at CPI Group (UK) Ltd

MIX
Paper | Supporting
responsible forestry
FSC
www.fsc.org FSC™ C007454

This book is produced from independently certified FSC™ paper
to ensure responsible forest management.

For more information visit: www.harpercollins.co.uk/green

For everyone in that caravan with me

Prologue

Six months ago

There was a seagull on the damp sand ahead, fat and solid and grey.

Every time they came to the coast on holiday, Cheryl was surprised at how large and bolshie seagulls were up close. And this one was mean-looking too; its tiny yellow eye was full of fury. As she watched, it pecked violently at a cigarette butt someone had left on the beach. She thumbed the camera awake on her phone, but by the time she had it trained on the bird, it had dropped the fag end and hopped away from her.

'Shit. Suit yourself.'

Instead her eye was caught by a small gathering further up the sandy beach. At this end, the place was nearly deserted. Cheryl's own family, like most visiting the beach that day, had set up their towels and picnic bags closer to the small fairground that crouched above the concrete breakers. There were small wooden booths down there too, selling ice creams and freshly fried doughnuts. Down this end, there was just the sand, the stones and the persistently grey-brown sea. To Cheryl, already tired of her whingy cousins, the quiet end of the beach had looked very attractive.

And it seemed she wasn't the only one to think so. Just ahead was a complex of brightly coloured windbreaks, the pink and blue material slightly tattered at the edges and snapping in the strong sea breeze. A tall man stood with a hammer, rhythmically whacking the poles into the damp sand. Cheryl was immediately fascinated. He was taller than her dad, so at least six foot four, and he was old; somewhere in his late sixties, from his iron grey hair and deeply lined face. He wore a clean long-sleeved white shirt, buttoned neatly up the front and at the wrists, and a pair of beige slacks. On his feet were brown leather sandals. It was a peculiar outfit for the beach. She wandered over towards the windbreaks for a closer look.

Despite his age – to Cheryl, who had not long turned fifteen, he was impossibly ancient – the man was hitting the poles firmly and without hesitation, and she sensed a great deal of coiled strength in his wiry arms. Spotting her approach, he stopped.

'What are you after, girl?'

Cheryl jumped. The voice came not from the man, but from behind the windbreaks. She stepped forward, peering around curiously. This family were very keen to avoid the wind, by the looks of things. The tall man had set up what was essentially a fort, with walls on all sides and a small gap at the front to grant a view of the sea. Inside it were two old-fashioned stripy deckchairs, and several towels laid neatly on the sand. There was a huge, traditional wicker picnic basket and a long dark blue tarp wrapped around something bulky – but Cheryl's attention was taken by the woman lying on the nearest towel. She was the one who had spoken.

'Nothing, sorry. Just wandering about.' Cheryl pushed a

2

wild strand of hair behind her ear and slipped her phone back into her jeans pocket. 'It's nice down here,' she finished.

The woman shifted on the towel. She was wearing a vintage-style swimsuit with a navy and white floral pattern, and her long legs were so tanned they looked almost leathery. Her toenails were painted red, and she was rubbing greasy-looking sun-tan lotion into her thighs. Cheryl could see little of her face; it was mostly obscured by a huge floppy sun hat.

'It's nice for young people, this beach.' Her voice was leathery too. 'That's why we come here, isn't it, dear?'

Cheryl blinked. Neither the woman nor the man with the hammer could be mistaken for 'young people', even if you were feeling particularly charitable.

'My family seem to like it,' said Cheryl, mostly to fill the silence. 'We all get dragged down here every year.'

The woman tilted her face up towards Cheryl, and the girl got a brief look at the lower half of it, split into a dizzying smile; bright red lipstick, the colour of poisoned apples in a Disney film, and a sharp, unforgiving chin. She got a glance at skin that looked wrong, stretched somehow, and then the woman had bent back to applying lotion to her legs.

'The beach, the sun,' continued the woman. 'The sea. Candyfloss, hot dogs, ice cream. There's nothing else like it. Everyone should get to see the beach, don't you think?'

'I guess.' Cheryl thought everyone should get to see Disney World, not a poxy seaside town on the south-east coast of England, but the woman seemed very taken with the idea.

'Even bad girls get to go to the beach.'

Something about the way the woman said 'bad girls' made Cheryl frown, but her attention was taken by the tarp. It seemed to twitch, as though suddenly caught by the wind. Except it was safely behind the windbreaks.

'What?' said Cheryl, distracted.

3

The woman snapped the lid back on her sun-tan lotion. For the first time Cheryl noticed that there was a box open by her leg. It looked a little like a larger version of the sewing kit her mum kept in her crafting box, only messier. There was a large pair of scissors with orange plastic handles, several bobbins wound with black and yellow thread, a rusty-looking thimble. It struck her that this was an odd thing to take to the beach, but perhaps that was how the woman relaxed; with embroidery, something like that.

'I expect you think yourself too old for the beach,' said the woman. She glanced up again, smiling, and Cheryl found herself smiling back. 'Too old for sandcastles and crabbing, sweetheart?'

'I guess so.' Cheryl shrugged. 'My cousins still like it, but . . .'

'How old are you, dear?'

'Fifteen.'

'You'd rather be on your phone, looking at grown-up things?'

Cheryl bristled slightly. This was too close to the regular complaints she endured from her dad about how much time she spent glued to her phone, but the woman was chuckling warmly to herself, as though she were fond of Cheryl and her quirky ways.

'You have no idea how very young you really are. That's one of the gifts of the very young – you don't know that the sand is even in your hands, let alone that it is running through your fingers.'

'Okay.' Cheryl glanced over to the tall man, who still hadn't spoken. He was looking off down the beach, as if he'd heard the conversation many times before. 'I suppose I should go back to my family, they'll be wanting to get started on their sandwiches—'

Suddenly the tarp began to thrash back and forth, so violently

4

that Cheryl felt herself take an involuntary hop backwards. There was a muffled moaning sound.

'Hey! What—?'

'You see?' The woman looked up, her red lips creased with displeasure. For the first time Cheryl could see her entire face, and every bit of warmth seemed to drain out of her body. 'You see what thanks I get for my generosity? I get shenanigans! Malarky! Disobedience!'

Too late, Cheryl realised that the tall man had vanished from his spot by the windbreaks. She had a moment to look back at the tarp – still thrashing, still moaning – and then a pair of strong arms closed around her from behind, and she was lifted, kicking, into the sky.

Chapter 1

Now

When I saw the old sign for the caravan park – big brown cartoon letters and a colourful cartoon parrot, of all things, as if parrots were native to the chilly south-eastern coast – it was like being kicked in the gut, and I had to pull over, a cold sweat breaking out across my forehead and back. Katie, safely buckled up in the back seat, leaned forward far enough that I heard the seatbelt click.

'What's the matter, Auntie Charlie?'

'I'm fine, I just need a second . . . to think.'

Immediately I could see how stupid this sounded. We were parked up around a hundred feet from the turn-off that was our destination, nothing but thick hedges on either side of the road. On the other side, I knew, were rows and rows of caravans, hidden by foliage. The bleak early winter sun was leaching rapidly from the sky; soon it would be completely dark. There was absolutely no reason to stop so close to the park, but here we were.

I turned around in the seat to give her a smile. She was

always such a solemn kid, and the look she gave me was close to rude, glaring back at me like I was the worst person she'd ever met. In the gloomy light her skin looked too white, and the splash of freckles across her nose looked grey, some accident of the shadows. Her hair, which was cut into a severe fringe at the front and left loose over her shoulders, was dark brown and a touch greasy – that last brought me up short. Greasy hair meant she was edging towards being a teenager, and something about that made me uneasy.

'Hey. This'll be fun,' I said, in the tone of all adults everywhere trying to convince themselves of something. 'Just the two of us for a few weeks. You can do whatever you like – play games, do your drawings, go down to the beach. Anything you want to do. And I'll get on with researching my book. You can help me, if you like.'

'I know,' she said flatly. 'You've already said that.' She shuffled her feet in the footwell, oversized pink and turquoise trainers, rainbow laces. She was wearing a pair of frayed denim shorts that came down to her knees and a baggy T-shirt, and for the first time I felt a stab of concern. Those were the wrong clothes for January. Still, it was warm in the car, and the caravan would have an electric fire. 'Can we just *go* now?'

I nodded, some of my false cheer leaking away into the car seat. For a long moment, it felt like I was frozen in place, reluctant to take this final step. This was a bad idea, wasn't it? And then I thought of the letter, and without another word, I started the car and turned into the car park.

Tall evergreen trees on either side ate us up, and the sound of wheels crunching over gravel rose to meet us. The lamps weren't quite all lit yet, so I navigated mostly by the pale line of the road, rolling slowly past the small blocky buildings that were the site shop and the little place where you could rent televisions and extra heaters. There was a phone box there, too, an old red one, but I doubted it still contained a working phone. Along from there was the swing park – climbing frame like some industrial skeleton, slide with a pile of dead leaves and mulch at the bottom – and the shower huts. Then, the first of the caravans, long capsule-shaped things, neatly lined up and inert.

At these, I felt something inside me wake up. They were exactly the same as they had always been. At first glance, they looked identical, but if you trained your eye you could see all the things that set them apart from each other – and if you were a little kid, left to run riot around the site all day, it was vital to learn these differences. Otherwise, you might never find your way home again.

'What did you say?' asked Katie suddenly. 'You said something then.'

'Nothing,' I said, my eyes still on the road. 'Just thinking out loud.'

'I'm hungry,' she added. 'Are we having tea when we get in?'

I nodded, glancing at her in the mirror. 'Absolutely. Spaghetti hoops? Toast? It feels like that sort of evening, doesn't it?'

She smiled, and some of the chilliness eased from her posture. I looked back at the caravans.

They did all look the same, but there *were* differences. The patterns on the side, for example; different stripes of brown, ochre, yellow, pale pink, olive green, dusty red, blocks of colour and cream, all very discreet and tasteful. They were different shapes, too, some very boxy and square, others rounded off at the edges. Some were so huge and sprawling they were basically bungalows, and the biggest and fanciest had wooden steps leading up to their doors, painted white and decorated with flowers. These ones often had old satellite dishes too, the ultimate sign of luxury when I was a kid.

As we crawled along, the headlights sending beams of soft glow into the rapidly darkening night, I saw that perhaps some things had changed after all. Spots of rust here and there, weeds thick around the supports of some of the caravans, windows empty of curtains or nets, or covered over with cardboard. I looked away, telling myself I needed to concentrate on getting us to the place we were staying. There'd be time to look around later.

We turned a few slow corners, and here at last some of the lamps began to flicker into life. All at once I just wanted to get inside, away from the petrol and leather stink of the old car.

'There we are, look.'

It wasn't *the* caravan, of course. That was long gone, for all sorts of reasons. This one was relatively new, but still quite cheap. It looked long and grey and boxy in the twilight, but I could see snowy white net curtains at the windows, and someone had swept around the bottom of it at some point in the last few weeks. It made me feel surer of myself, so I parked up and got out, Katie following close on my heels. I bent down to the blue gas canister and retrieved the keys from underneath it, and I stepped onto a set of slightly wobbly metal steps to open the door. Katie shot through it ahead of me, making loud *BRRRR* noises.

'Yes all right, let's get the heating on, warm things up in here. I'll get the tea on, shall I?'

Katie nodded and plonked herself down on the narrow sofa that ran around this end of the caravan. I flicked on the electric heater, waited for the grey coils to turn a deep orange, and then began unpacking some of our bags. In no time at all, the place felt like the caravan always did when I was a kid – a small, cosy place, full of yellow light, the smell of toast. The windows beyond the net curtains looked too black, so I tugged the curtains across them. Eventually I sat down at the small table, sliding into the booth to sit opposite Katie, and we began to munch our way through our tea. As a treat, I had sliced up some cheese on top of the spaghetti and melted it under the grill.

'That's better, isn't it?' I watched Katie carefully, her head bent over her food, only looking up to take sips of her chocolate milk. She lifted one shoulder in reply.

Afterwards, I switched on the telly and gave Katie the remote. She flicked around the channels for a bit, her small face intent, until she finally settled on some reality show that seemed to involve awful tattoos. I had a moment where I wondered if this was appropriate viewing for a pre-teen, but the idea of me, of all people, instructing Katie on what was morally correct was so laughable that I did just that – a small, congested chuckle escaped me. She looked up, visibly irritated.

'What?'

'Nothing.' I waved at the telly. 'I just hope this doesn't give you nightmares.'

She snorted at that, but at the same time she seemed to lose interest in the TV. When I sat down, she turned to face me, pulling her legs up onto the sofa so that her feet rested against my leg.

'This book,' she said. 'How will you do research for it? What sort of stuff do you need to know?'

'Well, it's a book about folklore. Specifically folklore of the area. Do you know what folklore is?'

She rolled her eyes and shoved me with a foot. '*Duh*. Stories and stuff.'

'All right, smarty-pants.'

'God you are so *old*.'

I laughed. 'Yeah, stories and stuff. I used to really love that type of thing when I was your age, and I particularly liked

11

stories about this place.' My smile suddenly felt cold and wrong on my face, so I grabbed Katie's foot and squeezed it. She shrieked and kicked me again. 'So I wanted to put all the stories together. What I'll do is spend some time here in Hithechurch, talking to people about the folktales of the area, maybe visit a few other places, and write down what people tell me. And then eventually, I'll stitch it all together into a book. Probably a very short book.'

'You'll just be wandering about talking to people?'

'That will be a lot of it, I think.'

Katie rolled her eyes. 'I don't see why you can't just do all this on the internet, like a normal person. I don't see why you had to come all the way down here at all.'

'That wouldn't be the same.' I smiled. 'The past is important, Katie. I want to immerse myself in it. This place is important. To me, I mean.' I could see this wasn't winning her over, so I squeezed her foot again. 'But you don't have to do what I'm doing all the time. You won't get bored, will you?'

Katie scrunched up her face, thinking about it. Eventually she shrugged one shoulder. 'I brought loads of books to read. And I want to go down to the sea and collect seashells – I got a guide for them out of the library.'

'Good. I know it's cold and quiet here at the moment, but I'm glad I've got you for company. We'll have fun, won't we? And it's better than school, right?'

As Katie went back to her TV programme, I went over to the door and opened it a crack. A sliver of cold night air slipped into the caravan, and I heard Katie tut behind me, but I only opened the door wider, seized with a need to breathe in the dark. The light streamed out around me, revealing the caravan opposite in shades of grey, and the line of trees to the right, black and unknowable at this time of night. All was still. Without really knowing why I was doing it, I slipped my hand into my trouser pocket and pulled out the letter. It had been folded and refolded so many times in the last couple of weeks it had become soft and pliable in my hands. I unfolded it and held it up to the light, although I knew perfectly well what it said.

IF YOU WANT TO STOP HER, FIND WHAT YOU BURIED TOGETHER. IT WILL RUIN HER.

The handwriting was simple and somehow terse, scratched into the page with jagged strokes. It had arrived at my door in a plain brown envelope, dangerously anonymous. It wasn't signed, had no return address, and I didn't recognise the writing. A perfect little mystery.

My imagination supplied a host of eyes watching me, enemies waiting just out of sight. I folded the letter and put it away again, although I could feel it there, burning against my leg.

Who are you? I thought, not for the first time. *And how much do you know about me?*

I stepped back inside and closed the door, locking it with a quick twist of the handle. Katie glanced up at me, but if she wondered what I was doing, she didn't ask. Without another word I sat down next to her on the sofa, and trained my eyes on the ludicrously small television screen. Exhaustion settled over me like a heavy coat.

Chapter 2

July 1988

The jangling discordant music of the amusement arcade – sewn together from a hundred different blaring slot machines and video games – was almost loud enough to drown out the clattering alarm. Almost.

Charlie took a step backwards from the tuppeny pushdown, her foot still throbbing from the sturdy kick she'd just given it. The prize she had spent a whole three quid of her holiday money trying to get was still wedged in the tube, but a few coppers had made their way out into the tray below. She scooped them up quickly and shoved them in her pockets.

'Here, what did you do?'

It was the woman who worked on the change desk. Although Charlie and her family had only been down here for a couple of days, Charlie had already identified her as a potential source of trouble; she spent much of her time in a padded seat by the kiosk, watching everyone coming or going, her beady eyes narrowed suspiciously. The ends of her fingers were stained a deep grey from handling all the coins.

'I didn't do nothing,' said Charlie.

'Why's the alarm ringing then?' The woman had her arms crossed over her chest. 'Where are your bloody parents? You shouldn't be in here unaccompanied.'

'There was a man in here, a fat man with a beard. He kicked the machine, just kicked it really hard and ran away again. I don't know why.'

'Bloody nonsense. You can't come in here causing trouble! Have some respect, you little—'

'What's going on?'

It was Charlie's older cousin, Darren. At seventeen he was practically an adult, and at the sight of him Charlie felt a flood of relief. Darren would sort it out.

'This old bag is shouting at me.'

'Is this your little sister, young man?' The woman drew herself up to her full height, which was still a whole head shorter than Darren. 'You want to keep her on a leash!'

'Yeah, all right.' Darren dropped a heavy hand on Charlie's shoulder and began to turn her away from the machine. 'Keep your knickers on.'

'How dare you! Get out! Your whole bleedin' family can get out and don't come back.'

Darren nodded as though this were a request he heard daily, and herded Charlie towards the big double doors.

'Nice going, *Charlotte*.'

Outside it was a flat, hot day, and Charlie stood on her tiptoes for a few seconds while her eyes adjusted from the perpetual gloom of the arcade.

'It wasn't my fault. There was a gang of older kids in there, and they were messing about with all the machines. I think they must be relatives of that cow because she just let them get on with it, but I suppose when they broke something she had to find someone else to blame.'

Darren fixed her with the same long, cool look that most of Charlie's family summoned when she was spinning a particularly ridiculous story. Behind them, a tall figure stepped out of the amusements and glared at them both, his arms crossed over his chest. Charlie had clocked him in the slots before too: he was the man that fixed the machines when they conked out, and she was scared of him. He wore a stained shirt, and his greasy hair was swept back from his forehead, almost long enough to reach his collar.

'Come on.' Darren took hold of Charlie by the arm and began to steer her down the street, away from the tall man. 'If they've barred us from those slots your mum is going to be well cheesed off.'

'It wasn't my fault!' Charlie was already distracted. Hithechurch was a tiny seaside town, always busy in the middle of the summer season, but today it was practically heaving, and the main street had been shut off to traffic. Coming down the road towards them was an odd procession – a string of people riding horses, surrounded by a crowd of holidaymakers. 'What's that?'

'I don't know, do I? Some sort of fete.' Darren was already looking around, probably seeking out another family member to dump Charlie on.

The crowd came closer. At the front was a huge black horse with a splash of white across its nose, and riding it was a strange, bedraggled figure. It had its arms held out straight to either side, hands dangling limp at the ends, and it wore a collection of brown and yellow rags. The face, though. It was the face that caused Charlie to blink, her stomach doing a single slow somersault.

The woman – they were close enough now to see that the figure was a young woman – had a mask over her face. It was bone white, with ragged triangles cut for her eyes and nose, which had been painted black, and rather than a hole for her mouth there was a long straight line, punctured with thick stitches. Her hair, the colour of straw, hung untidily to her shoulders.

'What is it?'

Charlie thought she hadn't spoken loud enough for anyone to hear, but next to her Darren tutted loudly.

'It's a scarecrow, you benny.' People were giving out pamphlets, so Darren plucked one from a passing lady and gave it to Charlie. 'It's something to do with an old story that happened around here.'

'What do you mean, a story that happened?' Charlie glanced at the pamphlet, but she couldn't look away from the scarecrow for long. 'Stories don't *happen* anywhere. They're made up.'

'You know what I mean.'

Behind the scarecrow, the other men and women on horse-back were more readily identifiable. They were dressed as pirates, complete with silk shirts, eyepatches, cutlasses and a few unrealistic beards. These riders were interacting with the crowd, laughing and calling out to the kids and brandishing plastic hooks. Coming up behind them was a small marching band, playing a jaunty tune. As Charlie stood there, watching the scarecrow figure move away on the back of her horse, she noticed that there was a wooden stick shoved through the sleeves of the woman's ragged jacket. This was what was keeping her arms so straight.

'Come on,' said Darren. 'I'll walk you back to the campsite.'

For the moment, Charlie didn't move. The crowd had mostly passed them, leaving behind a confetti of creased pamphlets and sweet wrappers on the street. A woman trailing at the back came over to Charlie and pressed something into her hand.

'Have a great Pirate Week!' She beamed at Charlie, and then hurried to catch up with the others. Charlie looked down at her hand. It was a tiny felt figure of a scarecrow, a piece of cardboard in it to keep it stiff. Now that she looked, a few of these had been dropped in the road too; the woman had been giving them out to all the kids. Normally, Charlie might have turned her nose up at such a thing – it was clearly aimed at little kids, and she, at eleven, was beyond such things. But the odd little white face, split into pieces with fat black stitches, immediately seized her.

'Come *on*.' Darren tugged at her shirt. 'Or I'll leave you in the road.'

They walked back. It took about fifteen minutes, along a long country road which at night had no lights, and on either side there were blank fields; one filled with grass, the other with crops. Keeping Darren's red shorts in her peripheral vision, Charlie trooped on behind him, reading the pamphlet.

The Story of Susan Cartwright

In 1842, little Susan Cartwright lived with her father in a fisherman's cottage in Hithechurch. It was a hard life, one of deprivation and hunger, and survival often hung on the whims of the sea. To keep food on the table, Susan's father became a wrecker – on dark and stormy nights he would use lights to mislead passing ships so that they would founder on the rocky shore, and then Susan's father and his brothers would claim the cargo as their own. When little Susan was old enough, she was brought into the family business: at night, she would lead her donkey along the beach paths, lanterns hung on the side of its makeshift saddle.

Then one night, a pirate ship narrowly avoided being smashed to pieces on the famous Hithechurch Jawbone. Realising what had happened, the pirates came ashore and sought out the lights that had so nearly spelt disaster for them. Susan's family fled, leaving her behind with her donkey. Desperate, she fled into the fields, where she found a ragged old scarecrow. Standing next to it, she pulled the hessian sack over her face and the pirates passed on by. Eventually they found Susan's father and her uncles, and the pirates had their bloody revenge, but brave Susan Cartwright survived.

Charlie stumbled over a loose stone in the road, and looked up, but her mind was still in the field with Susan Cartwright. The dead of night, a cold moon looking down on you, and pirates coming to cut your throat . . .

'What are you grinning at?'

Darren had turned to look at her. Up ahead, the sign for the campsite peeked out from a row of evergreen bushes.

'This!' She waved the pamphlet at him. 'It's so messed up. This scarecrow woman used to help wreck boats so they could steal the stuff on board, but apparently . . .' She looked at the jolly red writing on the back. 'Apparently they have a festival day in her honour every year. She was a thief!'

'And a murderer,' Darren added cheerfully. 'I doubt everyone got off those sinking ships alive.'

'Wow.' Charlie pulled the little felt scarecrow out of her pocket to look at it again. A thief, a criminal and a murderer, but they handed out little toys of Susan Cartwright with her stitched-up face to kids. In truth, Charlie was delighted. At home she spent much of her time trying to access the horror films her older cousins got to watch. She hung around the video shop looking at the covers of VHS tapes in the horror section, the ones with titles written in drippy blood, with haunted houses on the front, or murderous clowns. In the library she sought out books about unexplained phenomena, like spirits and yetis and spontaneous human combustion, and periodically she would try her luck borrowing a Stephen King book. In her rucksack there was a dog-eared copy of the Usborne book *True Stories of Ghosts*, which she'd managed to get from the school book club, against her mother's tired arguments. Yet here was a grisly story, one that involved pirates, murder and a spooky disguise, and adults were actually handing it out to kids in the street. 'Brilliant.'

'Look, you know your way from here, don't you?'

Charlie dragged her attention away from the little scarecrow. They were well inside the campsite by now, and Darren had spotted a bunch of teenage boys standing over by the climbing frame. Being seen with his eleven-year-old cousin was no longer tenable. She nodded distractedly, and he jogged off towards them, his lanky frame moving with surprising grace across the scrubby grass. Charlie wandered in the other direction, towards the caravan packed with members of her family.

She was still so absorbed in the story of Susan the scarecrow, her mind full of the stealthy tread of a pirate boot, the blood-curdling cries as Susan's father had his throat opened by the rusty edge of a cutlass, that she didn't notice she had wandered towards the wrong caravan until the loud thump of a car door being slammed made her jump. She was standing to the side of a caravan that looked a little like theirs – brown and yellow – but this one had a broad white stripe around the middle, and a car she didn't recognise was parked outside. It was a tan colour, touched with rust in places. The back window had a piece of silver tape across it.

'Emily, get your bags. Now.' The man who had just slammed the car door was stocky, wide across the shoulders, his brown hair held in place with gel that was shiny under the sunlight. He looked angry, with a flush of colour across his cheeks like he was running a fever. There was a thin gold chain around his neck, and hanging from it, a tiny golden cross.

A girl that looked to be about Charlie's age appeared from the other side of the car, a heavy travel bag in her arms so that her chin rested on the top of it. Her hair was black, and shockingly short, and on her feet she wore a pair of trainers that looked like they were falling apart. She was followed by a tall skinny woman in a yellow sundress. She didn't look especially old, but her black hair was streaked with grey.

'Emily, what are you doing?' The girl was moving towards the door of the caravan, but apparently not fast enough for her father. The man stalked over to her and grabbed her by her skinny arm, half lifting her off the ground in an attempt to get her to walk faster. Charlie heard the woman murmur something, some tiny protest, but the father took no notice. He yanked on the girl's arm again, and Charlie winced as the travel bag fell from her arms and its contents spilled onto the ground.

'For *fuck's* sake.' The man jumped away from her in apparent disgust and stepped up the little stairs to the caravan door, which he unlocked jerkily before stepping inside. Charlie felt a moment of pure fury against the injustice of it all; the man had made the girl drop the bag, but now he was blaming her. The woman murmured something again, but instead of stopping to help the girl gather her things, she too stepped around her and went inside the caravan. With a sigh, the girl dropped to her knees. A pair of battered jelly sandals had fallen out, some folded underwear and a pair of balled-up socks. She began to gather them up.

Hesitantly, Charlie took half a step forward, meaning, perhaps, to help the girl, or at least express some sympathy regarding the poor behaviour of adults, but at the movement the girl looked up sharply. She had wide, dark green eyes; the colour, Charlie imagined, of the sort of sea that pirates roamed across.

The girl fixed her with a scowl. 'What are *you* looking at?'

21

Chapter 3

Now

In the morning I got up and shuffled into the tiny bathroom, trying to shake off the vague disorientation that comes with waking up in an unfamiliar bed. While I brushed my teeth, I noticed just how obvious my roots were – a good inch or so of ginger hair was peeking out from under the dark, brownish black. When I was dressed I poked my head into Katie's room to check she was still asleep, and then I drove the short distance into town. In the small chemist on the narrow high street I bought a home dye kit and brought it back to the caravan. Katie had got up in the meantime and had a book open on the table, so I let her get on with it and went back into the bathroom. The colour I'd chosen was another dark brown; close enough, I hoped, to match up with the previous dye, and warm enough not to look too weird against my freckled face. I covered my hair in the foul-smelling muck, covered that with a piece of clingfilm, and went back out into the living room to let it percolate. Katie looked up, wrinkling her nose.

22

'You're dyeing it again?' she asked, her thumb held against the page to keep her place.

'Just doing the roots,' I said, trying to sound breezy. 'Do you want a bacon sandwich?'

'What are you doing that for?'

'Bacon sandwiches are delicious.'

She gave me the long-suffering sigh of a ten-year-old vexed by adults. 'I meant the hair.'

I turned to the stove and switched on the grill. 'Changing your hair colour whenever you like is one of the very few bonuses of being an adult.'

I remembered Katie's hair, at another time; how fine it had been, how I had picked a blade of grass from it, and we had laughed. I took a knife from a drawer and pierced the plastic pack of bacon.

By the time I'd cooked the sandwiches and we'd eaten them, my hair was done, so I went into the bathroom and washed it all off with my head over the sink. Through drips of water I could see the dye running away down the plughole, suddenly looking much more like blood than it had before; blood running over a rusted blade, perhaps; blood sinking into sand. I went into the bedroom and rubbed my hair dry with a towel I'd brought from home, before taking a hairdryer to it. When it was done, I stood in front of the long mirror set into the narrow wardrobe and felt suddenly cold. With my hair so short and so dark, I looked just like—

'What are you doing today?' Katie had appeared in the doorway to the bedroom, leaning her whole body against the frame like it was a huge effort to stand up.

'That depends. What would you like to do?' I smiled at her, ignoring the ghost in the mirror. 'Go to the beach? Get some sweets from the shop? I think we should settle in a bit before I throw myself into research.'

23

Katie turned away and bent her knees so she slid down the frame a little. 'I don't wanna go out at all. It's too cold.'

'Are you sure? You could go to the little park here, all the swings will be free.'

The look that met me was verging on belligerent, so I turned back to the mirror. A pair of scissors I'd brought in from the kitchen drawer were on the bedside table. I picked them up and snipped at my fringe, which had grown out a little since the last cut. Pieces of nearly-black hair fluttered to the carpet like the feathers of some dark bird.

'You don't have to go out,' I said to the mirror. 'I'll go to the campsite shop and get some supplies in. Any requests?'

But Katie had vanished back into the living room.

Outside, the day was still grey and cold, and I didn't really blame Katie for wanting to stay indoors. The campsite shop was back near the entrance, a small boxy building that sold basic groceries, newspapers, replacement gas canisters if you needed them. I had half expected it to be closed in January, but on my way to the chemist that morning I had noticed someone moving around inside it, and when I arrived there was a tall man behind the counter, whistling as he filled up a tray with chocolate bars. I averted my eyes and moved along the shelves, pretending to be interested in bottles of laundry detergent, but in truth I felt faint, and oddly light, as though I might float away at any moment. The shop was almost exactly as I remembered it from back then, down to the sun-bleached, peeling posters for tourist attractions and the humming freezer full of ice creams. It was as though by stepping into the shop I had fallen backwards through time, shedding decades in a second. A crawling sense of panic began to bite at my insides, but I forced it down. I picked up a packet of cereal and a carton of milk.

'Just these, please.'

The guy behind the counter smiled, and then began poking at the ancient till as if he had never seen one before.

'Sorry, our other till conked out so we've replaced it with this antique. Haven't a bloody clue about this thing.' He had a mild Welsh accent, so I looked up at him curiously. He was skinny, with narrow hips, and he wore a black jumper with sleeves pushed up to the elbows that revealed tightly muscled arms covered with an energetic explosion of tattoos; I could see skulls, ravens, scantily clad women, all caught in a network of ink. His eyebrows were thick and dark, and leapt up rakishly as he tried to make the till do his bidding. 'You'd think it'd be bloody obvious, wouldn't you, a thing like this? It's out of the bloody ark.'

I leaned over the counter slightly to get a better look, as if I knew anything about shops, or working in them.

'I reckon you put in the price, then press item?'

He picked up a packet of Frosties, read the price ticket, and punched it in. He grinned, and rang up the rest of it.

'Now subtotal,' I said, feeling both embarrassed and proud of myself.

'Ah, you're a lifesaver, you are.' After some searching about behind the counter, he came up with a flimsy plastic bag that clearly wouldn't last the trip back to the caravan and then began to pack away my things. 'Staying in one of the caravans, are you?'

'I'm here with my niece Katie for a couple of weeks. My sister is going through a rough time at the moment, so I'm giving her a break from the little gremlin. And Katie could do with a holiday too.'

'Well the weather's crap, but it's quiet. I'm Joseph, by the way. Joseph Bevan.' To my shock, he stuck his hand over the counter, and after a moment, I shook it. His skin was warm, and I felt something like an electric shock travel through my whole body.

'Hi.' I hadn't expected to have to do this yet. 'I'm Sarah Hewitt.' To cover the fact that I didn't know what to say, I brought out my purse and passed him a fiver. The till crashed open and he took a step back to avoid it, muttering 'Shit' under his breath. 'I'm here researching a book.'

His eyebrows leapt up again. 'Really? Wow.'

I laughed nervously. 'It's not that exciting. Just a personal project about folklore in the south of England. There's always loads of information about stories from the north, or the west country, but down here . . .' I shrugged. 'I just felt like there could be some interesting stuff to explore.'

'I'd love to hear more about it. Anything to liven this bloody place up a bit.' He stood straighter, as if sensing he might have said something wrong. 'Although I'm sure you'll find lots of interesting things. You should talk to my uncle's friend, Stan. He's well known for spinning tall tales down the pub, you know the sort.'

I clutched at my shopping and nodded. This was an unusually long conversation for me and I felt like I was losing my grip on it; a rollercoaster car about to shake itself off the track by going too fast.

'Does your uncle own the shop?'

'Yeah, he does. But he's never here, you know.' Joseph passed me my change and leaned back against the wall, crossing his arms as if readying himself for a long chat. 'I'm sort of the jack of all trades in this place. I keep an eye on the grounds, clean the bloody shower huts, you know.' He laughed, and I laughed a little too. I could still feel the remainders of that electric charge in my fingers and cheeks. 'If you've got any sort of problem with your caravan, you let me know, all right? Actually . . .' He reached under the counter and came up with a piece of paper with a number scrawled on it. 'That's my number, in case of a caravan themed emergency.'

'Oh there's really no need . . .' I looked down at the bit of paper in my hand with a growing sense of panic.

'You'll be doing me a favour! Honestly, Sarah, it's so quiet here at the moment I'm going out of my mind, to tell you the truth. I'd welcome the opportunity to unblock a toilet, that's how bad it is. Oh, and if you want to talk to Stan, he's usually at the Smuggler's Cove. I'm sure he'll be happy to bore you rigid.' He smiled at me. He had brown eyes. I slipped the number into my pocket.

'Well. Thank you. If I have any toilet issues, I'll let you know.' *What?*

Mortified and desperate to get out of there before I said anything worse, I headed towards the door, only for my eye to be caught by a display of that day's newspapers on a rack against the front window. One headline, in stark black letters, felt like it had been placed there especially for me.

BEACH GIRL STILL MISSING SIX MONTHS ON

Of its own accord, my hand reached out and picked up the paper. It was a local one called *The Lighthouse*, covering several nearby coastal towns. Dread filling me up like poison, I read the article beneath the headline.

Police today mark six months since Cheryl Yates went missing from Folkesholme beach with a fresh appeal for witnesses. Cheryl, 15, was on holiday with her family and was last seen walking up the sands towards Hithechurch. Cheryl's father, Antony Yates, 47, has stated that Cheryl was happy at school and home, and had no reason to run away. Police are treating the disappearance as suspicious. Previous appeals to the public led to the police asking for owners of blue vans in the area to come forward, and in September of last year a mobile phone belonging to Cheryl was recovered, although police have not revealed any further details. Cheryl's mother, Sharon Yates, 45, has recently accused the police of not taking the disappearance seriously enough, stating to this newspaper that: 'if Cheryl were a year or two younger, they'd be tearing the place apart.' Hithechurch itself has a history of . . .

I looked away from the article to the photograph of the missing girl, Cheryl. In the photo she was wearing a white school shirt, and she had blonde hair and gold hoops in her ears. She looked happy, and posed, the picture clearly taken from her Instagram account. Meanwhile, Joseph had spotted what I was looking at, and over a great ocean of white noise I could dimly hear him speaking again.

'. . . bad business, lots of rumours but the police seem to have their heads up their arses. No one will say it outright but the council are worried it'll affect tourist numbers this summer. The bloody vultures.'

I nodded absently. My eyes skittered to the bottom of the page, where there was another, shorter article: CONTROVERSIAL BOOK DEAL NOW LINKED TO POSSIBLE TV SERIES. I blinked. Abruptly, my feelings of fear curled up and withered away in the face of a boiling fury.

'Thank you,' I said, and without looking at Joseph, I dropped the newspaper back on its rack and left the shop. Outside, the sky had grown dark, and it was spitting with freezing rain. It was barely midday, yet it felt like the daylight was already draining away somewhere, as if it couldn't bear to waste its energy on this cold, unloved January day. I stalked back to the caravan, my fingers turning white as the plastic bag handles twisted around them, and just as I got to the door, my phone trilled from my pocket. I snatched it out, already dreading what I would see. Who could be sending me a message?

Half leaning on the door, I unlocked the phone and a picture message flashed up at me. It was a photograph, alarmingly clear, of Hithechurch High Street. It was filled with weak wintery morning light, and in the middle of it, a woman with short messy hair was stepping up to the entrance of the chemist, her arm raised to push open the door. It was possible from the angle to see a section of her face; she looked pale and stern, and her gaze was down, as if in preparation to avoid direct eye contact with anyone inside. I looked tired, too. No surprise there.

Underneath the photo was a message.

Why are you wasting time?

I stood on the steps for a long moment, looking at the picture and its short, icy little message. And then from inside the caravan I heard Katie call out to me, and I put the phone back in my pocket, my hand only shaking a little.

That night I woke up with my heart pounding, curled into the foetal position in the very middle of what served as the double bed. I lay there for a few seconds, frozen in place, my breath caught in my throat as I tried to figure out what had kicked me out of a very deep sleep, when I heard it again. A series of loud knocks against the outside of the caravan; a tinny *donk-donk-donk* followed by a shrill of laughter; the sound of small feet running. It was both deeply familiar and enormously unnerving. How many times had my cousins and I run around the caravan, banging on the sides and shouting to each other? Never at three o'clock in the morning, though.

I sat up, drawing my knees to my chin. The noise came

again, from the other side of the caravan – more banging, more laughter. I thought of Katie, asleep in her own room, and I frowned, my fright crystallising quickly into annoyance. I slipped out of bed, wincing at the chill beyond the safe warmth of the duvet, and padded quietly out into the open space. Katie's door stood open a few inches, and for a long moment I stood and listened intently, trying to figure out if she was already awake. If she was sleeping through the nuisance, I didn't want to wake her up with my own blundering about. From outside, I heard more laughter, a half-whispered conversation.

I poked my head in the door. Inside the narrow room I could just make out Katie asleep, the dark splay of her hair across the pillow. Quite unlike me, she slept with her arms flung to either side and her head back, her mouth slack. After a moment I caught the soft fluting noises of her snores, and I smiled. *Sound-o.*

And then another loud bang, this time very close to my head, and I jumped half out of my skin. Abruptly furious, I stormed away from the bedrooms into the living room, and I yanked back the curtains from the window. I could see no one out there, but a brief flash of shadow on the frosted grass caught my eye – someone running, and on the tail of that, the distant sound of laughter again.

'Fucking kids,' I muttered to myself, furious with the way my heart was thumping again. 'Kids with nothing better to do messing about.'

But as I tugged the curtains back into place, I thought of the text message with its watchful photo. I thought of the letter, with its very specific advice. Perhaps I wasn't really alone out here after all.

Chapter 4

July 1988

When the hesitant knock on the caravan door came, Charlie shot across the tiny living room to open it before anyone else got there. Standing on the step, looking deeply unsure of herself, was Emily, the girl she had met the day before. She had combed her black hair into a neat parting and put on her jelly sandals, and she wore a T-shirt that almost came down to her knees over a pair of faded pink shorts. Cautiously she peered into the caravan, but Charlie was already shouting over her shoulder.

'Going out for a bit Mum, see you later!'

'Hold your horses, young lady.'

Reluctantly, Charlie hung in the door while her mother extracted herself from the dining table. She, Charlie's nan and two aunts were crammed round it playing a raucous game of Yahtzee, but they all stopped at the interruption, lit cigarettes sending thin trails up to the ceiling. Charlie's Auntie Marj, seeing an opportunity, got up to put the kettle on.

'Mum, I'm just going to the swings, all right?'

'Are you now?' Charlie's mother was a tall woman with

broad hips. Where Charlie's hair was a barely controlled mess of ginger curls, her mother's hair had a soft wave, and it was more truly red than carrot-coloured. 'And who's this?'

'ThisismyfriendEmily,' Charlie muttered, gesturing briefly at the other girl. Emily, for her part, looked bemused. On the narrow sofa that ran around the inside of the living room, Charlie's grandad sat, fast asleep with a newspaper on his lap, and Darren slouched at the other end, an electronic puzzle game held up in front of his face. Carol, Charlie's older sister, was painstakingly applying mascara to her lashes, her eyes intent on a small hand mirror. 'I met her yesterday.'

'Emily, is it?' Something in her mother's face softened, and she waved her fag end at them. 'Go on then, sod off. Be back before it gets dark. And you can take Jenny with you.'

'What?' Immediately Charlie began backing towards the door, pushing Emily behind her. 'Jenny won't want to come, you can't just . . .'

But her mother was already calling to the back bedroom, and presently one of Emily's other cousins appeared. Twelve years old but young-looking for her age, Jenny wore thick prescription glasses and had a continual cold. She had been in the bedroom with her My Little Ponies, and she clutched one in one hand, her sleeve thick with balled up tissues.

'*Mum . . .*'

'Go on, fresh air, the lot of you. Keep out of trouble.'

Outside it was another hot, flat day, tempered by a cool breeze that smelled faintly of salt. The three kids wandered, as kids wander. Jenny trailed at the back, her big glasses reflecting flashes of sun, while Charlie and Emily kicked up sods of grass and shared a packet of Refreshers.

'You have a big family,' said Emily. She had a quiet, scratchy sort of voice, as though she had been shouting for hours, or had never spoken before at all.

'Yeah. Ten of us crammed in that caravan. Me, Mum, Nan, Grandad,' Charlie counted them off on her fingers, 'my sister Carol, and then also Darren, Jenny, Auntie Marj, Auntie Beverly and Uncle David.'

Emily was impressed. 'How do you fit them all in?'

'That's not half of it!' Charlie crushed another sweet between her teeth. 'Sometimes my uncle comes down with his kids for a few days, and they sleep on lilos in the living room! And also,' she added, getting into the swing of it, 'I have more cousins, and they'll sleep in the cupboards and on the roof.'

'That's not true,' said Jenny from behind them. 'You're making that bit up.'

Charlie shot her cousin a look, but Emily seemed unconcerned.

'There's just me,' she said. 'I don't have any cousins.'

'No brothers or sisters?'

'Just me.' She rubbed at her thin arms as if they were cold, and Charlie caught sight of a large purple bruise just under her baggy T-shirt. 'And my dad. And mum.'

'Hey, do you want to go to the climbing frame?' The small swing park had just come into sight, and the big structure in the middle, built from red and yellow metal pipes, was free of other children. 'We can sit on the very top.'

Emily nodded, and the two of them ran across the grass and started climbing. Jenny followed on behind, blowing her nose. When she reached the climbing frame she stood at the bottom, looking up.

'I don't want to climb up there,' she said. Her nose was red.

'Don't then!' Charlie scrambled up the pipes, her trainers slipping against the metal. Emily was a couple of rungs ahead of her. 'Go and jump in the sea!'

The girls laughed and got themselves seated on the uppermost rungs. From here, they could see all of the swing park and the shower blocks, and even the caravans looked a little smaller. Charlie glanced down; Jenny had seated herself on the dusty dirt underneath the climbing frame and was playing with her plastic pony. Warm, summer sounds drifted over to them: children laughing on the swings, the buzz of a lawnmower, the shrieks of seagulls.

'Oh, look.' Emily placed her hand on the red pipe between them. A brown garden spider the size of a penny was making its way across it. Charlie cringed back, but Emily let it walk onto the back of her hand and lifted it up.

'Aren't you scared of spiders?'

'No, not really. They don't hurt you.' Emily put it down on the side furthest from Charlie. 'We probably destroyed its web climbing up here and now it has to go and make a whole new one.'

'Huh.' Charlie suppressed a shiver, wondering if she was covered in tiny invisible spider threads. 'My mum's friend went on holiday in Spain, and when she came back she had this really painful spot on her cheek, and it kept getting bigger and bigger and sorer and sorer, and then eventually one day the spot burst and hundreds of tiny baby spiders came out.'

Emily looked stunned. 'Is that true?'

Charlie nodded happily. 'It's a good story, isn't it?' She had read it in one of her all-time favourite library books, *Scary, Gross and True! Spine Tingling Tales* – a book her mother regularly cursed the existence of. If the title of the book said it was true, that was good enough for Charlie.

'Do you know any others?'

Charlie grinned.

Over the next half an hour or so, in between climbing up and down the frame, hanging from the struts by their hands, or swinging across the rungs, Charlie went through many of her favourite gruesome stories, from the old lady who put her

34

poodle in the microwave to dry it off after a rainy walk, to Bloody Mary, the story of the ghost girl who appeared in a mirror when you summoned her. At this, Emily grew quiet.

'Yeah.' Charlie was in her element. She swung her legs back and forth. One of her trainers was getting loose. 'In the girls' toilets at my school. She hates the school because she was murdered there, and the school covered it all up and she never got justice.'

'Justice,' murmured Emily.

'So if you go into the toilets at night, and say "Bloody Mary" into the mirror thirteen times, she will appear in the reflection, all soaked in blood. And if you turn away because you're scared, a bloody hand will reach out from underneath the toilet door, and if it catches you it will drag you to hell.' Charlie nodded. She was especially pleased with that detail, which she had added on herself.

'This is all rubbish, you know.' It was Jenny. She was standing up, her pale round face turned towards them. Her lower lip was trembling, and Charlie realised with a mixture of guilt and pleasure that her stories had frightened her cousin. 'She makes up stories all the time, it's all lies. You shouldn't listen to her.'

'Oh, shut up, Jenny.' With the toe of her other foot, Charlie pushed her loose trainer off, and it fell neatly onto Jenny's upturned face. There was a thump, and a cry, and then her cousin was running across the swing park, sobbing loudly.

'Shit. Come on.' Charlie began to climb down. 'She'll go and tell her mum, she always does.'

'Will they come and get you?' Something in Emily's voice made Charlie look back up at her. She seemed tense, her small shoulders up near her ears.

'What? No. Well, Auntie Beverly might come and shout at me, so it's probably best if we're not here.'

They climbed down and once Charlie had retrieved her shoe, they ran off across the park in the opposite direction to Jenny. Soon the pair of them were pleasingly lost amongst a sea of caravans and cars.

'So what happened to Bloody Mary?'

'What?'

'The girl in the mirror. Did she ever get out? Did she get the person who killed her?'

Charlie considered. People didn't normally want to hear more of her stories, and she wasn't used to testing their logic in this way.

'Nope, she's still there. The person who killed her has never been back to the school, so she can't get him.'

'Who was it? Who killed her?'

'Ah. Well. A teacher. They ran away afterwards though.'

Emily nodded slowly at this, as if teachers murdering children was fairly standard and to be expected.

'It's a waste. If I was a ghost, with ghost powers, the person who hurt me would never get away.'

'Here, look at this place. Full of weirdos.'

They had arrived at one of the landmarks of the caravan site, a place referred to by Charlie's mum and aunties as 'the Ranch'. It was a caravan, but a sprawling, ancient one, with multiple extensions so that it took up twice as much space as the others around it. There were sheds attached to it, a pair of gazebos, a tent, and a small, wild-looking vegetable garden. Despite the evident work that had been put into it, the place still managed to look run-down; there were patches of rust on the caravan, and the gazebo fabric was bleached yellow-white from the sun. Someone had hung bunting all over the thing, and in places it had broken, leaving bedraggled lines of dirty flags. A couple of the windows were patched up with cardboard.

'What is it?'

'People *live* there, not just for holidays. They're there all year round.' As they stood looking at the Ranch, Charlie thought she spotted a face behind one of the net curtains. It was too gloomy inside to make it out. 'There's always people coming and going.' Charlie's family had all sorts of rude names for the family that lived at the Ranch, but she didn't want to say them so close to the place. At that moment, a dark shadow fell over them both. Charlie jumped, sure it would be one of the people from the Ranch, furious with them for staring, but it was the man who had dragged Emily from the car the day before.

'Dad!' Colour dropped from the girl's face like it had been slapped out of her. 'I was just . . .'

'I want you back indoors. Now.' He looked between them both. His face was an alarming pink, like bacon fresh from the packet, with two blanched white spots on the tops of his cheeks. Charlie felt a strange prickle of alarm run down the back of her neck. 'What are you doing out here?'

'We were just having a walk,' Charlie said, wondering even as she spoke what she was playing at.

'A *walk*.' He sounded just as sceptical as the rest of Charlie's family when she was telling a story. 'You shouldn't be out unsupervised, Emily. What are you looking for, aye? Who are you looking for?'

This only confused Charlie further. 'Er . . . nothing? We were just playing . . .'

'I promise, Dad, we went to the swings, and then we had a walk over here. We haven't done anything. I haven't spoken to anyone else, I swear.'

'What have I told you, Emily?' Emily's father turned away, his hands on his hips. He looked around and then pushed his long hair out of his eyes. 'What have I *said*?'

'Dad, honestly . . .'

He grabbed her so quickly that Charlie had barely registered it before Emily was being dragged away. The girl stumbled, her feet not quite able to keep up with her father's pace. Charlie had one last glimpse of her new friend's face, her mouth turned down at the corners and her eyes squeezed shut, and then she was gone, lost around the corner of a caravan.

Charlie stood still, trying to ignore the urge to cry. She didn't really understand what had just happened, but she felt deeply frightened. When she had herself back under control, she began to walk slowly back to her own caravan to face the inevitable wrath of Auntie Beverly.

Chapter 5

1949

Derek's first memory of the house in London, or at least the clearest, was the pile of rubble at the bottom of their garden that had once been a neighbour's house. The end of the war was four years in the past by then, and although Derek had been born the year before the celebrations and street parties, he still felt the presence of the war very keenly – it was like a very noisy person had passed through the room on their way to somewhere else; he could still hear the echoes of their shouts, smell the remnants of their aftershave and cigarette smoke.

Flowers and grass had grown up through the rubble as their garden slowly took it over, and Derek would spend happy hours sifting through the broken bricks for hidden things, clues to the identity of their missing neighbours. Derek knew that some of the family had been in the house when the bomb had hit the street, because Nanny still spoke of it in hushed tones; they hadn't liked the shelters since the youngest child had picked up fleas after a visit. *Fools*, Doctor Grafton would murmur from behind his newspaper, and that was usually all he would have to say on the subject.

The ghosts of war lived inside their house, too, although this was a distant, older war, one that Derek thought of very specifically as His Father's War. It was during this war that Doctor Grafton had come to his profession. Doctor Grafton kept in his study an archive of all his work and research over the years, and sometimes, he would show it to Derek.

For Derek, these occasions were a confusing mixture of exciting and dreadful. His father was a distant, controlled man, who left the day-to-day management of his small, and now, only, remaining son, to the nanny and the cook and the tutor, and he rarely addressed his son directly, let alone spent much time with him. A visit to his father's study was special. But it was also terrifying.

'Sit here, boy,' Doctor Grafton would say, and he would let Derek climb onto the chair at his desk, thoughtfully padded with cushions so he could easily see. 'It's important you know what I do for a living. Do you understand?'

Derek would nod, and Doctor Grafton would begin to place cardboard boxes and folders on the desk, and he would sift through their contents, placing grainy photographs and browning sheets of paper on the blotter. While he did so, he would speak.

'In the Great War, we found ourselves facing terrible new weapons. Machine guns, poison gas. Heavy artillery. The enemy would fire shells filled with shrapnel, and when they exploded they would fling hot pieces of metal in all directions. Often directly into the faces of the men in the trenches.'

Photographs of young men were passed across the desk. Derek would try to look at their eyes only, to stop his own from wandering to the ravaged landscape of their faces.

'My colleagues and I were faced with an unprecedented

number of facial wounds, wounds of such severity that these men would be unable to live normal lives. And so we worked to find ways of fixing them.'

Here, Doctor Grafton would open another box, and Derek would see more faces; these ones he could bear to look at, although they made him feel strange. Here the faces were swollen, bulbous, smooth or rigid with scar tissue. Men with noses that appeared to have been smeared to one side, men with deep dents in their foreheads, eyelids pinched or drooping.

'You see, Derek, when the pieces of hot metal tore through the flesh, they would leave these huge gaps where the skin had been blasted away.' Doctor Grafton's voice would become livelier as he spoke, as he warmed to his subject. Derek craved those moments. 'And if we just stitched one edge of the wound to the other, it would pull the face too tightly.' Often, Doctor Grafton would trace a finger across Derek's cheek or forehead, demonstrating where the hot metal had carved away the flesh, which would make him giggle. 'So we would take a flap of skin from here,' another stroke of the finger, 'and pull it down over the wound. With this method, we were able to give these men some semblance of their faces back. Do you understand, boy, why this was important?'

At this point Derek would usually start to panic. He wanted to give his father the right answer, but the faces from the Archive were watching him too closely. Derek would fidget in his seat, and Doctor Grafton would sigh.

'Listen to me, son. It was *ground-breaking* work. With their faces came their lives. They could go back to their mothers, their wives, their families, and be welcomed.' Here, often, Doctor Grafton would pause, and the eyes behind the steel-rimmed spectacles would grow distant. 'Or, at least, not turned away. Not shunned, like something monstrous.' He would turn back to the boy and give him a brief shake. 'Doctoring was

41

often a butcher's job on the front lines, but *we* made it something else. We crafted it into something *higher*. You get that, don't you, boy? You will be a surgeon like your old man, won't you?'

Derek would nod vigorously, glad to finally be sure of the correct answer, and sometimes – so rarely but treasured all the more for it – Doctor Grafton would kiss his small son on the temple.

At night, though, when Nanny had tucked him into his small bed and all the lights were out, Derek would be joined by the faces from the Archive again. He would see them in the moonlit folds of his own clothes, stacked neatly on the sideboard, or in the damp spreading from the corner of the ceiling. And worse, he would see them when he closed his eyes too, and here they could move and talk, calling his name while their faces melted and stretched, or split apart with the force of white-hot pieces of metal. Often, when Doctor Grafton had shown Derek the Archive during the day, Derek would wake up in the early morning with the cloudy stench of urine in his nostrils, and then it was only a matter of time before Nanny found out.

On these occasions, when Derek would be standing by the back door, stripped bare and shivering while Nanny briskly rubbed him down with freezing cold water, he would often see his father watching. Doctor Grafton would seem distant then, and although Derek would cry out and reach for him, he would not come to his son, or give him a comforting word. Only when the boy had been thoroughly soaped, washed and dried, would Doctor Grafton speak to him, and he only ever said one thing:

'You have to be stronger than this. Don't shame me, boy.'

Chapter 6

Now

'You all right in here? You need anything?'

Katie was lying on the sofa with her head in a book, and she barely spared me a glance over the top of it.

'Can I put all the bars of the heater on?'

'Of course you can, you numpty.' I flicked the bars on, then stood looking down at her with my hands on my hips. I felt like I wasn't doing my job properly somehow. 'You sure you don't want to come outside? I'm going for a walk around the site.'

She drew her feet up underneath her. 'I just want to read. I *like* reading.'

I knew this was true. I had been the same when I was a kid, after all. 'All right. Well, keep that door locked, and don't answer if anyone should knock.'

I wasn't sure why I said that – Katie was no idiot – and she rolled her eyes at me as I left. It was the newspaper, I told myself. The missing girl had made me twitchy.

Back out in the chilly air I went to the boot of the car

and got the spade and trowel I'd brought with me. Although the rain had come to nothing much, it was still cold, and I pulled my hood up as I headed back out into the gloomy afternoon.

The phone message had unnerved me too. So far it had felt like I was managing to keep Hithechurch at a safe distance, like I wasn't really *here*, not in any sense that mattered. I skirted around the edges of my history, not looking directly at any of it and Katie was helping to keep me distracted. Who can dwell on the past when you've got a whiny kid to feed, to entertain? But the questions still circled uneasily in my head: who had sent me the letter? And more to the point, who was here taking photos of me now? They had to be the same person. Did they *know me*? None of these questions had good answers as far as I could tell, so I had decided to ignore the message. If I didn't respond, perhaps they'd assume they'd sent it to the wrong number. If I didn't engage, they couldn't hurt me. Right?

At the northern edge of the campsite was a sizeable clump of woodland, meant, I suppose, for holidaymakers to take strolls in, but even when I was a kid it was slightly too over-grown for that. The woods had been quiet then, and when I got there I found them to be much as I remembered, only darker, wilder, and dripping with wet. I hesitated on the edge, the spade held loosely in one hand, the trowel in my pocket.

'It won't take long,' I said aloud. I turned back to look at the caravans behind me, half imagining faces peering out between net curtains to look at me, but the place was still, no movement anywhere at all. The clouds overhead had started to break apart, and a patch of sunlight touched my face, almost warm, like a ghost of summer, or the premonition of one. 'Over and done.'

I stepped into the treeline and let my feet take me where I

needed to go. As overgrown as it all was, the familiar dirt paths were still visible, and after about fifteen minutes I came to a clearing, one of several scattered throughout the place. It was much smaller than I remembered, and for a few moments all I could do was stand there, disorientated. *I'm just taller than I was*, I told myself, *or the woods have been creeping in over the years*. That's all. Nothing strange about this. The smell of the place was sharp and green in my nose, conjuring a thousand memories I didn't want to have to deal with yet. To distract myself, I pulled a battered old diary out of my pocket. It was a little girl's diary, pink, each page printed with the faint watermark image of a kitten. I let it fall open to the page and glanced down at it.

Eleven paces east from the big chestnut tree. Seven paces north. X marks the spot!

There was a very rough map, scribbled in biro. Next to it I had drawn a face with its mouth and eyes stitched up.

I looked down at my own handwriting from decades ago. I didn't need to read it – I had had years to memorise those words, after all – but I had a sense that these things should be done . . . correctly. The big chestnut tree was still there, much larger and grander than I remembered, even in January – *Charlie the Chestnut*, I thought, feeling slightly sick – and it didn't take me long to spot the big oak too, and the silver birch. I went over to the chestnut tree and placed my back to the trunk. For a flickering, unstable second I was back *there*. My fingers brushed rough bark, and the skin on the backs of my arms was tight with sunburn. Someone was with me: a high-pitched laugh, the smell of Polo-sweetened breath . . .

'No. Just get this done. Come on, for fuck's sake.'

I shook my head briskly, and took eleven paces east, seven paces north. I tried to keep in mind how much shorter I would have been back then. Little legs, little paces. When I got to the space I stared down at the mixture of grass and mud and dead leaves. Was this right? I had half expected it to be calling out to me, a beacon leading me into the past, but I felt nothing.

Using the broad head of the spade, I took a square chunk of grassy dirt off and lifted it away. I caught sight of a worm, pale brown, vanishing into the wet earth, and then I set to with the trowel, digging down through mud that was annoyingly packed with stones. Had it been like this before? How could the earth have got stonier? How far down had I dug, when I was eleven and my arms were so skinny? Despite the freezing January air a layer of sweat broke out across the back of my neck, while a little pile of dirt and grass and stones grew next to me.

'Shit.'

I kept expecting to see it, but there was nothing; only more dirt, more stones. I started a side excavation, broadening the hole in case I had missed the spot by a few inches, or half a foot. Still nothing. As I dug, perhaps inevitably my mind turned to Cheryl Yates, the missing girl on the front page of *The Lighthouse*. I've always had a slightly morbid imagination – some might say that was a massive understatement – and it occurred to me that I was digging around in a place that someone might well hide a body. Wouldn't that be just my luck, to find a dead girl in the woods when I was looking for something else entirely? As rueful as the thought was, I immediately felt a huge stab of guilt. I was already picturing this girl Cheryl Yates as a corpse.

'I guess that's why I'm so popular,' I muttered at the broken earth. 'My endless generosity and sunny disposition.'

I stopped digging where I was, and tried in the other direction, making a mess of the clearing about three feet wide, but the earth remained stubbornly empty. I sat back on my haunches.

Was I just in the wrong place? It would be easy, after decades away, to miscalculate. Maybe I was looking at all of it from the wrong direction. I turned around to orientate myself with the chestnut tree again, and that's when I saw her.

I fell back into the mud, making a noise in the back of my throat. The grass under my hands was wet, but I could barely feel it. My fingers were numb, tingling.

No no no, I told myself. *She wasn't real* then, *and she isn't real* now.

There she stood, though, pressed close to the chestnut tree, half hidden in its shadow. Her hair was long and matted, coming down over her shoulders and tangling with the buttons on her dirty cardigan. It was too gloomy to see much more, but I could make out a section of her face, and that was all I really needed. Still sitting in the dirt, I bent forward at the waist, a sound somewhere between a laugh and a sob stuck in my throat.

No no no.

What do you do when you're faced with the absolute, unswerving evidence of the sickness of your own mind?

I picked up the trowel again and stood, holding it in front of me like a weapon.

'You're not real!'

The words tore out of me, and the ragged woman on the other side of the clearing seemed to startle, as though she hadn't thought me capable of speech. The air around her shimmered, like a heat haze. And then she stepped back into the shadows and was gone.

'You're not . . . you're not real.'

'Charlie?'

My heart gave a sick lurch in my chest, but it was just Katie, standing some feet behind me. She was wearing her shiny blue raincoat, and her hair was pulled back into a scrunchie.

47

'Bloody hell.' There were clods of mud stuck to my jeans; I brushed them off hurriedly. 'What are you doing out here? I thought you were staying in the caravan.'

'I'm bored,' she said, although she didn't look bored. She looked worried. 'Can we go into town?'

'Katie, you shouldn't go wandering off in the woods by yourself . . .' Except of course that *we* had, when I was her age. We had done it all the time. 'Anyone could be out here in these woods.' For a second, that strange combination of laughter and tears was in my chest again. I shook it off. 'Okay, look. What do you want to do?'

'Get some ice cream,' said Katie, her voice firm. 'I want to eat ice cream for lunch.'

I rubbed my muddy hands together, brushing off the muck. The thought of getting out of these woods was suddenly irresistible. Besides which, I had clearly miscalculated the place where I had to dig. This needed more thought.

'If you want ice cream, you shall have it.' I held out my hand to her. 'Help me carry this stuff back, will you? And I need to change out of these clothes.'

Chapter 7

Now

When I was a kid, the ice-cream parlour in Hithechurch had been one of the busiest places in the town, all of the booths constantly packed with holidaymakers, while a healthy queue was always evident at the little service window. When we arrived, I half expected it to be closed, this deep in the off season, but the door was open, and a woman in an apron stood just inside it with a mop, trying to expel some dead leaves that had blown in. She gave me and Katie an affronted look, then morosely plonked her mop back behind the counter.

'Can I help you?'

'A banana split, and two scoops of salted caramel and chocolate, please. With a wafer.'

She gave me an odd look then, and I smiled and glanced away, reaching up to tug at my newly dyed hair. I wondered if she could smell its sharp, bleachy aroma.

'Go and sit down,' she said. 'I'll bring them over.'

Katie chose the booth right at the back of the shop, the furthest from the counter, and when the woman had brought our ice creams over she got straight to work, her head bent over her bowl of bananas and whipped cream. I had a spoonful of the salted caramel. It was good.

'What were you doing? In the woods?'

Katie hadn't looked up from her bowl, and her voice was very quiet. She hadn't mentioned the woods on the way here at all, and I had hoped that it wouldn't come up.

'I was just having a look around, kid, you know. It's a shocking fact, but ancient people like me enjoy a bit of fresh air now and then. It's good for you.'

'Is it?' she said archly, and I remembered again how close she was to being a teenager. A couple of years and it would be wall-to-wall sarcasm from this one.

'Yeah, yeah, all right.' It occurred to me that sugar was exactly what I needed. On the tail of that, I thought of my mum; it was always her way to make us sugary tea when we'd had a shock. I put my spoon down. 'That's what we're here for, isn't it? Get you out of yourself for a little while.'

'Mmm.' She didn't sound convinced.

'It's nice, right? To be beside the seaside? Tiddly om-pom-pom, all that.'

'I don't see why I have to be here at all.'

I sighed and sat back, tapping my spoon against the dish. I wanted so desperately for her to be enjoying herself, but you can't force kids to have a good time.

'We talked about this, didn't we?'

She shrugged one shoulder at me, mashing her banana into a paste with the back of her spoon.

'Katie?'

'Can we get some sweets from the shop before we go back?'

'Sweets?' I raised my eyebrows at the half-demolished banana split. 'Haven't you had enough sweet stuff?'

She shrugged, still not looking at me, and I decided not to

argue the point further. The kid was on holiday, and there are few people as easily swayed as a guilty aunt. When we were done, I took her to the sweet shop and she shot inside to look at all the big glass jars of sherbet and bonbons. I went to follow her into the shop when a poster stuck to the window caught my eye. There was a photo of Cheryl Yates in the middle of it, with the stark word MISSING printed in caps above it. Underneath was a short caption: 'Cheryl Yates, 15, has been missing since 8 July. Last seen on Folkeshome beach. If you have seen Cheryl or have any other information, please call . . .' And there was a phone number and, underneath that, an email address. The photo of Cheryl was different to the one I'd seen in the newspaper, and I wondered who had chosen it; if one of her parents had gone through a family album, or looked through the files on their computer.

'Wotcha, Sarah.' I jumped, and turned to see Joseph, the man from the campsite shop, smiling behind me. 'How's the toilet?'

He raised an eyebrow to show that this was a joke, and I laughed a little, caught off guard.

'No problems yet, I promise. We just came out for ice cream.'

He was wearing a black rain jacket over dark jeans with paint flecks on them, and his dark hair, shaved close at the sides and left long on top, had been pulled into wild spikes and whorls by the wind. His cheeks were ruddy with cold.

'Ah, right you are. Good choice.' He lifted up a plastic bag that looked like it was filled with maintenance equipment. 'Fixing a fence that blew down. You know, there's a shrine for her on the beach here, just at the top.' Seeing the expression of confusion that passed over my face, he nodded to the poster in the sweet-shop window. 'For Cheryl Yates. Wasn't far from here she, uh, went missing, so there's a little place up at the top of the sands for people to leave flowers and notes and that. It's all very sad.' His lively eyebrows sketched a sombre expression.

'A shrine? I mean, they don't know . . . Maybe she just ran away.'

'Oh. Yeah.' He looked flustered at that and ran a hand through his hair. 'I suppose it's really a place for, I don't know, people to show they're thinking about her. There's another at Folksholme, I think. Listen, uh . . .' He looked rueful again, and it occurred to me that he had a lot of lanky charm. 'If you're bored in the evenings, you know, I'm usually around the shop, if you wanted to say hello. There's a little kitchen out the back, with a little hob, so I make myself baked beans there some nights, when it's cold.' He grinned suddenly, laughing at himself. 'I'm a shit cook, but I can usually manage to get the beans on top of the jacket potato, if nothing else. You're very welcome, you and your niece.'

I blinked. I had completely forgotten about Katie.

'Thank you. We might take you up on that.'

He looked pleased. 'Did you speak to Stan yet? I told him there was a writer in town eager to talk to him, so I imagine he's insufferable at the moment.'

'It's on my list,' I said. I felt a slight tremor of panic at the idea that Joseph was telling people I was a writer. It made me feel like a fraud.

When he'd wandered off again, hunched against a sudden cold wind that was blowing down the street, I ducked into the sweet shop. When I had been a kid, the place had been a proper confectioners, with a long wooden counter filled with glass jars, and chocolate bars laid out in a colourful display. Now, I saw that it had partly become a newsagent, with bottles of alcohol behind the counter, and cigarettes. It made me sad, for some reason. Katie I found around the back behind a freezer unit, out of sight of the shopkeeper, which was handy because she had opened a packet of Polos and had carefully been arranging the tiny white hoops in a pattern across the floor.

'What do you think you're doing?' I hissed.

She glanced up at me, apparently unconcerned by the anger in my voice.

'I'm just playing,' she said.

I took her arm and lifted her up, scooping her out of the shop without looking over at the counter. Once we were outside I took a few deep breaths, trying to control my temper.

'Hey,' I said eventually. Katie was standing, staring off down the street at nothing. 'Hey, I know. Let's go up to the beach, yeah? That wind will knock all the miseries out of us, right? You can run around, see the sea. It'll be good. Get some fresh air.'

Katie looked at me like I was losing my mind.

'It's freezing,' she said.

'Then the air will be at its freshest. Come on.'

We walked across the street and up the small hill until we came to the wide concrete steps to one side of the old amusement arcade. From there we walked up onto the promenade, where the whole expanse of Hithechurch Sands was spread before us. I had to admit, it was a bleak sight. The sky was thick with pale grey clouds, and although the sea was relatively calm, it was the colour of beaten steel. Even the sand didn't look especially inviting; dark from the recent rains, the stretch of beach was almost entirely empty, save for a distant figure walking their dog. At the shoreline, a rim of white foam and spray moved restlessly back and forth, and up the coast, standing in the sea, was the Hithechurch Jawbone – four weathered points of rock, looking deeply unremarkable in the watery light.

'Go on.' I gave Katie a little push towards the steps that led down to the beach. 'Go and have a bit of a run about. It'll make you feel better.'

I thought that she would protest again, but instead she took a few stiff steps, then seemed to relax, as if some tension had gone out of her body. Once she was down on the sand, she began to skip towards the sea, her brown hair whipped back and forth by the wind. Belatedly I wondered if I should have told her to stay out of the water, but she wasn't stupid.

I looked down the beach in the other direction and spotted the big green stones that marked where the outfall had been. The hairs on the back of my neck stood up. You don't see them around much these days. It's a tunnel that leads from the sea to an industrial works of some sort, and wastewater is discharged through it into the sea. And by wastewater, I mean sewage. Or at least, some of the time it is. It had been filled in since I was a kid, of course – covered over with cement and sand so that only a few of the old stone blocks remained, like tombstones.

I forced myself to look away from it, and I walked along the promenade, noting how the wide beige paving stones had not changed. There were wrought-iron benches here with shelters over them, and on one of these I found the 'shrine' Joseph had been talking about. The missing poster of Cheryl was here too, and around it people had left flowers, notecards and soft toys. I stopped in front of it and read a few of the messages: people praying for her, pleading with her to come home. The whole thing was looking a little bedraggled; the wind and the rain had snuck in under the shelter, turning paper damp and warped, shaking away the petals on the flowers. Some of them, though, were fresh, and I wondered if Cheryl's family were still in the area. They had been on holiday in Folksholme, but how strange it must be to have to go home without a member of your family . . .

A huge wave of sadness moved through me then like a tide, and I sat down heavily on the part of the bench not covered in tributes. I thought again of my musings while I'd been digging in the woods – the idea of finding Cheryl accidentally, uncovering her body. That had been a horrific idea, but now I wondered if there wasn't some way to help instead. I was here, after all. I was already snooping around the town. Couldn't I also ask around about Cheryl Yates? I allowed myself a brief daydream, imagining myself finding an obscure clue, something I could call the police about – anonymously, of course – which would in turn lead them to finding Cheryl, safe and well. It would be one small good thing, one tiny glimmer of *good*, in a life that had been such a litany of painful mistakes.

I lifted my head, meaning to look for Katie's small form down on the beach, but instead I was brought up short by something else someone had left on the bench. In amongst the flowers and the tattered pieces of paper, someone had left a big pair of scissors – huge, old silver ones. I frowned. Perhaps someone had left them there accidentally. Perhaps they had brought them to cut fresh flowers. I stood up, no longer keen to be so close to the shrine. There was someone walking along the promenade towards me too, and for some reason I didn't want anyone to see me here, reading these sad notes. They tore at my heart.

Because no matter what I had said to Joseph about the girl running away, or my hopeful daydreams of finding her alive, I knew how these things usually ended. Cheryl Yates, that blameless kid with her hoop earrings and her hopes for the future, was dead, and likely had been for some time.

Abruptly I felt chilled, and the urge to speak to someone

– anyone – was suddenly overwhelming. I fished my phone out of my pocket and opened the picture message. Whoever this person was, they knew a lot about me. Perhaps they were the only person I could talk to. I tapped out a quick message and pressed send before I could think twice.

Who are you? What do you want from me?

Chapter 8

July 1988

The hot weather was holding.

Each little rock pool Charlie planted her feet into was a cool blessing. She wriggled her toes in the water, watching the little clouds of sand poof up between them. There were crabs around here, but only tiny ones – you had to go to the big walls of the outfall to catch any worth the effort, which was where her sister and cousins were currently gathered. She and Emily were stalking the rock pools with a bucket and a net each, but so far had only caught a few tiny transparent shrimp, which was fine because Emily wasn't interested in the sea life anyway.

'Tell me another,' she said.

Charlie straightened up. She'd never met anyone with such an appetite for her stories, and much to her own bemusement she was starting to run out.

'Did I tell you the one about the man with a hook for a hand?'

'Yep.'

'Hmm. The one about the murderer and it turns out the calls are coming from inside the house?'

'Yep.'

Emily had been quiet when she knocked on the caravan door that morning, her eyes just a little redder than they should have been, but down on the beach, with just Charlie for company, she had brightened up. She wore the same baggy pink shorts over a neon yellow bathing suit. The ghosts of old bruises, yellow and green, were visible on her arms and legs.

'Oh well then. What about . . .' Charlie stepped out of the pool onto one of the rocks, which was covered in slick green seaweed. She looked up the beach for inspiration, and spotted the brown and black shapes of donkeys in the distance, each with a child on its back. It made her think of the horses she had seen on the high street with Darren, and the figures with their plastic swords riding them. 'Oh! I know one. And it's a really good one because it actually happened around here.'

'It did?'

'Yes! In Hithechurch. Listen . . .' She recounted the story of Susan Cartwright more or less as it had been printed on the pamphlet – which she had long since memorised – but when she got to the part where Susan was hiding in the field, she decided to change the details. Years later, Charlie would look back on that moment and try to find reasons for it. Perhaps if she had left the story as it was, everything that came after might have been avoided. But whenever she thought of that day, she could find no sinister intentions. There was only the slight doziness that came with blistering heat, the faint prickle of the beginnings of sunburn on her shoulders, and the pleasure of sharing a story with a friend. 'The only place she could find to hide was in a field, and so she went and stood with this scarecrow, right? Her arms sticking out to either side.' Charlie held her arms out, bucket dangling from her fingers. 'She was

58

hoping that the pirates would see the shape of the scarecrow and not look any closer. But she was unlucky, because the pirates spotted her, and caught her. The captain, whose name was Captain Bloodbeard, thought that the scarecrow disguise was pretty funny, so he had the ship's surgeons stitch up her mouth and eyes, and then they dressed her in the scarecrow's old coat and hung her on the pole. And finally they put the scarecrow's old bag face over her head and cut her belly open.'

Emily had gone a little pale. 'And she died?'

'Of course she died,' said Charlie, cheerfully enough. She stepped over to the next rock pool. She had spotted a crab the size of her thumb. 'Her guts were all over the ground, like uncut sausages. But because of the scarecrow disguise, the villagers didn't find her body for ages. In fact, they only found it because someone noticed all the crows were flocking to the field – because they were eating her guts, you see. Look, I'm going to get that crab.'

Emily wasn't looking at the pool. She was staring at the sea, an odd expression on her face.

'It's not fair,' she said. 'All she was doing was what her dad told her to do. It was his fault, and she . . . It's not fair.'

'I suppose not.' Charlie shook some blobs of sand from her net. The crab had disappeared into a crevice in the rock. 'Grown-ups, huh? Bastards.'

'Every night, leading that donkey by herself in the dark. Just doing what she was told, and in the end her dad didn't even save her.'

Charlie looked up. Emily was still looking at the sea. At some point she'd dropped her bucket. Belatedly Charlie realised she might have upset her friend.

'Yeah well. But the thing is, Susan haunts the beach, up by the rocks. People call her Stitch Face Sue, because her face is all riddled with these big stitch marks, you see, but she cut the ones on her eyes away with a pair of scissors. So now she stalks Hithechurch, looking out for bad people, and if you do something bad, she cuts up your belly with her scissors.'

'She does?' Emily turned to look at her. There was a fine sprinkling of sweat on her forehead.

'Yep. Only bad people though.' A small inspiration occurred to Charlie. 'Like dads that are nasty to their daughters. She especially hates those.'

Emily smiled suddenly, bashfully, and Charlie grinned back.

'And it happened here?'

'It totally did. I have a pamphlet about it and everything, it's a historical *fact*.' Charlie turned and looked back up the beach. 'You see those paths up there, above the sand? Where those green bushes are? That's where Stitch Face Sue used to lead her donkey every night, with the lamps. Up and down those paths. And at night, if you're down on the beach, you can see those lights sometimes, still trying to lead ships to their doom.'

'Can we go and have a look?'

Charlie stepped down from the rock she was standing on and shrugged. They dumped their buckets and nets with Charlie's nan, who was snoozing in her deckchair, and headed off away from the sea. They climbed the stone steps that cut up through the sea wall, and from there walked along a grassy verge until they came to the sloping area of grass and stone that ran parallel to the beach. The paths underfoot were roughly clad here and there with large flat pieces of grey stone, and were dusted all over with dry sand. Tall grass, yellow and green, sprouted everywhere, and bushes with long, thin, tough-looking leaves threatened to overrun the stones. From where they were, they had a good view of the beach and the sea. There were lots of people in the water, close to where the surf broke against the shore, and Charlie thought she even recognised her sister and her cousin Darren. They were wrestling with an inflatable killer whale.

'Was it here, do you think?'

Charlie blinked. She'd forgotten all about Stitch Face Sue. 'Oh yeah. All along here. Look.' She spotted a rounded indent in the dirt. 'See that there? Do you think it looks like a donkey's hoofprint?'

They crouched down to examine it, and both agreed that it did. Emily pressed her fingers to it thoughtfully.

'Every night, she did what she was told, even though she knew it was wrong. What was she supposed to do? Refuse to do what her dad told her?'

'And she gets murdered for it.' Charlie pulled up a handful of grass and scattered it across the path. 'Stitch Face Sue, some grass for you,' she sang awkwardly. 'I'm sorry that your life was poo.' She laughed, and Emily smiled a little, but she looked confused.

'What are you doing?'

'Oh, you know,' Charlie shrugged. 'Ghosts like it when you leave them things.'

Emily straightened up and fished around in her shorts pocket until she came up with an open packet of Polos. She took one of the mints and placed it carefully on the stone part of the path, before looking nervously at Charlie.

'Do you think that will do?'

They walked along the paths a little way. Every now and then they passed other holidaymakers, using the paths as a kind of shortcut, but the further they went the quieter it got. Charlie was starting to get hungry, and she was about to suggest going back to the beach to get some sandwiches when Emily stopped, her hand shading her eyes as she looked up the bank.

'The field where she hid as a scarecrow . . . wouldn't it be close by here?'

'Yeah,' Charlie thought quickly. 'It's got to be, hasn't it? Because she wouldn't have been able to run far, in the dark, with the pirates looking for her.' Charlie scrambled up the bank, directly across the paths. 'Come on, it's got to be just up here!'

They climbed up the bank, laughing and filled with energy again, until they reached a low wooden fence at the top. This far down the beach they had reached the part of the town that gave way to farmland, and sure enough, there was a field beyond the fence. It was filled with lush green grass, and the odd brown hump that Charlie took to be cowpats. It was easy to imagine that once, a hundred years or so ago, this field had been filled with bright wheat or barley, or something similar, and at its heart, the ragged figure of a scarecrow once stood.

'This is it,' said Charlie with all the authority she was capable of – which, as an accomplished liar, was quite a bit. 'This is the field where they caught up with her and found her hiding with the scarecrow. Look, it's just over there.'

Roughly in the middle of the field was a set of three rocks, leaning drunkenly against each other. The girls ran over to them, a little breathlessly.

'These rocks mark the spot,' said Charlie confidently. 'The villagers buried her body in a secret location, because they were ashamed of Sue and her family, since they were criminals, but some people who liked her put these rocks here, as a sort of memorial. On the exact spot where the pirates cut her stomach open.'

Emily looked solemn. Together, they examined the rocks. There were a few discarded beer cans under the rocks, and graffiti on the side of one; black and red shapes that almost looked like letters. Charlie was pleased; it made it look like a place of witchcraft. She bent down to examine the dirt around the rocks.

'So much blood here. I think you can still smell it.'

They knelt together on the ground, and for the first time that day, a cloud passed over the sun.

'Imagine hiding here, in the middle of the night.' Charlie thought of her own imaginings, of the pirates approaching with their rusty cutlasses, the sound of their breathing, their stealthy footsteps. 'Imagine knowing that someone wanted to *kill* you.'

It felt colder than it had done. It was easy to imagine this place in the middle of the night.

'Imagine,' continued Charlie, 'the needle *piercing* your *eyelids*. The sword against your stomach, cutting through your flesh.' She glanced at her friend, worried she might have upset her again, but Emily wasn't looking at her. She had her hands in the dirt, as though she were trying to feel the blood that had been spilled there, so many years ago.

'Charlie,' she said, 'I have something I want to show you.'

Chapter 9

Now

The brisk beach weather did appear to cheer Katie up, so when she had run off all the sugar, I suggested we visit the Smuggler's Cove and this time she agreed readily enough. Her cheeks were red from the wind and her hair had blown itself into a tangle.

The Cove was a new place to me – there had never been anything so slick or exciting in Hithechurch when I was a kid. It was tucked up on the corner of the high street, its big colourful awning depicting swaying palm trees and treasure chests planted in golden sands, which I felt was a bit optimistic for the south-east coast of England. Inside it was dark and gloomy, and I thought I had misunderstood what the place was; the first thing I saw was a bar, with bottles of spirits stacked along a dirty-looking mirror, and a fishnet pocked with plastic lobsters hanging over it. Great – a couple of days into our holiday and I had brought Katie to a dodgy pub. But as my eyes adjusted to the dark I saw that beyond the bar there was a larger, better lit space full of the sorts of games machines where you won tickets to exchange for prizes, and even further back, there was a miniature bowling alley.

'Oh!' Katie squeezed my hand once. 'Can I go and have a look?'

'Go on then.' I fished a fiver out of my bag and gave it to her, thinking that if I'd been given a whole five pounds at her age I'd have lost my mind. 'Go and see what you can win.'

The place was quiet, with a couple of adults hanging around the bar. I could see how it worked, though – bring your children in here of an evening, let them entertain themselves within shouting distance while you have a well-earned drink. I went over to the sticky counter and smiled at the barman, who looked to be about twenty.

'I'm looking for Stan?'

'Oh yeah.' The lad looked relieved, as though he suspected me of being the sort of person who wants a really complicated cocktail. 'He's over at the prize desk.' He nodded to the section squeezed in next to the bowling alley.

I sauntered over, taking a moment to pretend that I was interested in the prizes. There were big cuddly toys, a variety of plastic swords, a whole display of plastic keyrings – all the sort of tat I had coveted as a kid. There was an older man sitting behind the desk, a newspaper across his knees, but when he spotted me he quickly folded it away and stood up, a warm smile on his face. He was short and a little hunched at the shoulders, and he wore a very neat baby blue three-piece suit, with a canary yellow shirt underneath it. His skin was brown, and he had a black goatee beard – the word that immediately occurred to me was 'natty'.

'Stan? Joseph sent me to have a chat with you. I hope that's all right?'

His eyebrows leapt up and he beamed all the brighter.

'Sarah! There you are. I've been waiting. This place has been like a politician's soul these last few weeks – entirely empty.' He flipped up the partition on the desk and gestured to a small folding chair next to his. 'You want to join me? I got tea here, or I can get you something stronger if you like? You're my guest today. Joe said you had a little girl with you?'

'She's already playing the games.' For a long second I stared at the folding chair, oddly overcome with panic. The idea of sitting in an enclosed space with someone else made me feel strange. I thought of the picture message I had received, from someone watching me go into the chemist. But then Stan was brushing imaginary dust from the seat of the chair, and the idea of refusing became unthinkable. 'Thank you, a cup of tea would be great. It's bloody cold out there today.'

I sat down, and as I did Stan waved at the bar across the way. 'Jerry! Two fresh teas please, when you have a moment!' He sat down, pinching the knees of his trousers as he did so. 'I've almost got him trained, you'll see.'

'How long has this place been here? I don't remember it from my holidays as a kid.'

'Oh, must be five years or so now?' Stan tugged at his goatee. 'It gets busy in the summer, let me tell you – basically a circle of hell in the summer, if I'm honest with you, and I wouldn't do this job alone for all the tea in Surbiton, etcetera, but in the winter it gives me something to do and somewhere warm to sit. Usually someone to talk to, as well.' He grinned at me. 'So, a *book*!'

'Yes, well, I hope Joseph didn't talk it up too much.' I glanced over to where Katie had disappeared. Distantly I could hear the wails and sirens of some sort of video game. 'It's a personal project. I'm looking for old stories about Hithechurch and the general area, I'm sure you know the sort – like the mysterious black dogs they have up north, or monks haunting a ruined abbey. Joseph said you were the guy to talk to.'

Stan looked pleased at this. The barman appeared with two mugs of tea, filled right up to the top. He placed them carefully on the counter, then vanished back off to his bar.

'Sugar?' Stan reached under the desk and retrieved a small tray with a couple of plastic bowls on it – there were packets of sugar, sweetener, little plastic cups of milk, and a collection of battered-looking teaspoons.

'Two please.'

When the tea was sorted we both sat back in our chairs, and I felt a wave of unreality break over me. Here I was, in an arcade, drinking tea with an old man I'd never met, like this was the most normal way to spend an afternoon. Was this what it was like to be a writer? With that in mind I pulled a notebook and pen from my bag. It was important to look the part.

'You don't mind if I make notes, do you?'

This only seemed to please him more.

'What sort of stories would you like?' asked Stan. 'I'm afraid that a lot of my stories won't be suitable for a book . . .'

'Any stories you care to share,' I said, smiling.

'Well, you might have noticed we have parakeets down here now? Noisy green buggers – they even give the seagulls a hard time, you know.'

'I hadn't noticed that.'

'They've come all the way down from London, you see. Back in the 60s, a pair of parakeets escaped from Jimi Hendrix's flat. Decades later, and the south of England is covered in loud green birds.'

I smiled again and made a note, but my heart was sinking. I'd heard this urban legend, of course, but it wasn't really the sort of thing I was after. As if sensing this, Stan leaned forward and tapped me on the knee.

'Going back further, there were pirates too, you know. And

smugglers. Very much the area for that, the south coast. This place is riddled with caves, all great places for hiding *booty*.' He laughed, pleased with the word. I sat very still, feeling a chill settle over me like a shroud, but Stan didn't seem to notice. 'No one likes to talk about pirates so much these days, which is a disappointment to the tourist board here. Smugglers, you can just about get away with . . .' He gestured to the inflatable palm trees bookending the bar.

'Any ghosts?' I asked.

'Oh yes.' He took a sip of his tea. 'The public toilets on the high street are said to be haunted. Did you know that?'

That surprised a laugh out of me. 'Really?'

'Back in the 40s and 50s, there was a well-known family in the area who, well, let's just say their business wasn't entirely above board. Someone got on the wrong side of them – snitched to the police, I heard – and that was it, for them.' To my surprise, he lowered his voice, as though afraid someone could be listening to our conversation. 'This family were in the building trade, at least on the surface, and they built those toilets. Supposedly the body of the snitch is buried in the foundations.'

'Wow. And people have seen his ghost?'

'Not as such, but visitors have reported toilets that flush when there's no one in the cubicle. And it's cold in there. Very cold.'

I laughed. 'I wouldn't have picked Hithechurch as the setting for a Sopranos-type hit.'

'Oh, a lot of darker stuff goes on around here, believe you me.' Stan seemed to draw into himself then. He looked down into his teacup, frowning slightly. 'People think seaside towns are all harmless, but they only ever see them on their sunny days.'

He grew quiet, and a small silence spread between us. In it

I could hear the wails and jangles of whatever game Katie was playing.

I cleared my throat. It was time to push this along a little. 'Such as?'

'Hmm, well.' He brightened up again. 'There was the story about the beauty queen?' When I nodded, he continued: 'Rosa, her name was. Very beautiful. She wanted to move to America and try her luck with Hollywood, the whole thing. She worked at the funfair and saved up all her pennies to enter beauty competitions, all along the coast. But her mother hated it, hated the very idea of her flaunting herself.' He leaned forward a little, catching my eye. 'It was a different time, you see, and her mother, well, she was of a different, harder generation. She had no time for it.'

'What happened to her?'

'There's a haunted house in the funfair, you've probably seen it yourself. Full of ghost puppets and leering mirrors, that sort of thing.' I nodded. 'It was Rosa's job to keep it clean and tidy, which is not an easy task, with the floors all uneven and the pretend cobwebs everywhere. Well, the story is that her mother sneaked in there one night, knowing that Rosa would have to clean it in the morning, and she rubbed grease all over one of the crooked stairwells. The next morning, in the gloom, Rosa came to those stairs and fell, naturally, crashing all the way to the bottom.'

'And she died? Broke her neck?' I knew how these sorts of stories worked. Stan gave me a slightly odd look before he continued.

'Oh no. But she became a recluse after that.'

'Wow,' I said again, half laughing. 'You're right. That is dark. And is there any evidence that this actually happened? Was Rosa a real person?'

Stan looked vaguely offended by the very suggestion of

69

fabrication. 'Her mother was well known in these parts, and they built the funfair, after all. Rosa though, I never met her. No Hollywood starlet future for her.'

'Blimey. That's quite a story.' I made a few notes in my notebook for the look of the thing.

'Oh! Ghosts.' He tapped his finger firmly on the counter. 'I almost forgot. There's the sightings of the Grey Woman. That will be much more up your alley, I imagine.'

My fingers felt abruptly numb, so I let the pen rest in my lap. 'The Grey Woman?'

'Yes, I can't believe I almost forgot about it,' he said. 'She's been seen all over Hithechurch, always at night or at dusk. She has long untidy hair that covers her face, and ragged clothes, like a tramp. I think the last sighting was, oh, only a few years ago. People swear blind they've seen her in the woods on the edge of the town, or even down on the beach at night, and she *moans*, apparently. A horrible, muffled sound.'

Stan looked pleased with himself and nodded towards my notebook.

'That's a good one, isn't it? The rumour is that she's one of these girls that have gone missing over the years.'

I looked up, a nest of snakes in my stomach. 'Like Cheryl Yates?'

Stan pressed his lips together and turned away slightly. 'Poor girl. I dare say she'll turn up, though. A runaway, most likely.'

'Let's hope so.' I thought of the shrine, up on the sea wall. 'Did her family come in here last summer? Do you remember them?'

'Oh yes, I remember them a little. It's so hectic in here in the summer that I have a lad, Jack, who helps me during the busiest periods, but I saw them often enough myself. The girl spent much of her time on her phone, as young people do these days, but she had some younger cousins that became very set on winning one of our kites.' He gestured to the display above them; there were several brightly coloured kites hanging there, their long tails neatly folded and bagged. 'So I remember them. They got really good at the skittle ball machine and would come back with armfuls of tickets.'

'Do you remember the parents?'

Stan raised an eyebrow at me, as though I had suggested something off. 'Young lady, I know that these days people always suspect the mum and dad first, but not those two. I don't remember them from the summer as such, but once she disappeared? I saw them all over town, asking whoever they could get their hands on if they'd seen their girl. They were distraught.' He shook his head sadly. 'A real mess. Besides . . . Well.'

He took a sip of his tea that felt like he was pausing for dramatic effect.

'What?'

He sighed. 'Like I said, this can be a dark place. I'm sure, with all your research and whatnot, you'll find that out yourself.'

I filed that away as something to think about later. 'Your helper, Jack, who works here in the summer. Is he around? Can I talk to him?'

Stan gave me a puzzled look. 'Well, he's just a boy, he doesn't know any stories worth telling.'

'Maybe not, but I'd like to get a view from all generations.' I smiled intently to cover this obviously weak argument. 'Just to build a broad picture of the place.'

He shrugged. 'Jack's mum runs a little coffee morning for the greatly aged in the church on Mondays and Wednesdays. Jack often gets dragged along to help out – you'll likely find him there.'

At that moment, my phone buzzed and I remembered with a rush of dread that I had replied to the anonymous text message. I didn't want to look at it, but my traitorous fingers danced across the screen, opening the notification.

Meet me at the Happy Harvest. Tomorrow, 2 p.m. Ask for Watkins. Come alone.

'Are you all right, dear?' Stan was looking at me with concern. I forced myself to smile.

'You've been so helpful, but I think I shall have to make a move now. Katie will be wanting some real food for lunch.'

'Oh. Well. You'll come back, won't you? I have so little to do here.' He got to his feet and retrieved a large stuffed animal from the row of prizes. To me it looked like a massive yellow hamster with red cheeks. 'Please, take this for your niece. I'm sick of looking at him.'

Outside, the day was overcast and bleak, but Katie seemed to be in a better mood. As we walked back down the road, I gave her the toy to carry.

'There. Enjoy your lurid yellow hamster.'

'Oh my *god* Charlie, it's a Pokémon. Don't you know anything?'

'I suppose I don't, no.'

Across the road a van had parked in front of the funfair. A tall man with wiry arms was loading boxes into the back, and at the sight of him a chill crept down my back.

The funfair man, I thought. *The one who nearly chased me out of the slots that day.*

Despite the cold he wore an open-necked polo shirt, and as he turned away I saw his face in profile, just as I had on the beach all those years ago. All at once I felt as though I were walking through treacle, and I was deathly afraid that he would turn around and see us, and I would be pinned in place.

It's him, I thought. *He was there.*

And then Katie grabbed at my sleeve and shook it.

'It's cold,' she said. 'Can we go home?'

I smiled down at her and quickened my pace. I kept my head turned from the van across the road.

'Come on, before we freeze our arses off.'

Chapter 10

Now

The Happy Harvest restaurant was a few miles outside of Folkesholme, a sprawling one-storey building with a cheerful red tiled roof and an old combine harvester parked out the front and painted white. They had nailed their menu to it. I steered Katie inside, who was looking around with interest, and found a slightly hectic corner that was apparently the children's 'stay and play' area. It was surprisingly busy for January; there was a clutch of mums drinking coffees together and their kids had all been dumped in the corner with the colouring pads and slightly sticky toys. Katie looked deeply sceptical, but I set her up with an 'all-you-can-eat' ice-cream pass and she settled in the corner with a book, side-eyeing the other kids, who were all a good few years younger than her.

'I won't be long,' I said. 'Okay?' Katie shrugged.

Moving out into the wider restaurant, I soon caught the eye of a waiter, who clearly wanted to stop me from wandering about.

'A friend has booked a table,' I said, hoping he wouldn't

expect me to pick them out myself. I had no idea what this person looked like, or even what gender they were. 'Under the name of Watkins?'

To my relief he immediately led me off to the quieter side of the restaurant, far away from the yummy mummies, and nodded to a small table in the far corner. There was a person sitting there, facing away from me; a woman, judging from the hair and the jacket. I forced myself to smile warmly at the waiter.

'Oh, there they are – thank you so much.'

When he'd scuttled off, I took a moment to gather my thoughts. This was, I reminded myself, an enormous risk. I really didn't know anything about this person; in fact, all I did know was that they knew I was Charlie, not Sarah; that they apparently knew where I lived, and knew my phone number – information I gave out to barely anyone. Everything about that suggested they could be ready to make an awful lot of trouble for me.

But what was I going to do? Turn around and walk out, without knowing?

Taking a deep breath, I walked straight up to the table and stood behind the other chair. I smiled again, a little harder this time.

'Hello. You're waiting for me, I think.'

The woman in the chair startled badly, and she looked up at me with a hunted expression. She was a little older than me, maybe seven or eight years into her forties, and she had dark hair in an outdated frizzy perm. She wore tortoiseshell glasses with big, blocky lenses, and had a dash of coral blusher on each cheekbone that only seemed to highlight how pale she was. As she watched me sit down, she took a nervous sip of water from a glass on the table.

For a few seconds we sat in silence. I cleared my throat.

'I suppose that you . . . know who I am?'

The woman nodded once; an odd little birdlike dip of her head.

'And you are . . . ?'

She grimaced. 'I'd rather not give you my name, actually.' Her voice was soft enough that I had to lean forward slightly to catch what she was saying.

'Well, that's a bit rich,' I said. When she didn't reply to that, I sighed. 'Watkins, isn't it? That's the name you gave to reserve the table.'

It hadn't seemed possible, but the woman turned a shade paler, and shifted in her seat.

'Look,' she said. 'I don't want to get involved. I just want to make sure that the . . . wrong person doesn't come out of this smelling of roses.'

'Okay, Watkins. How did you get my address? My phone number?'

The woman looked away. 'Do you want to know why I wrote to you or not?'

At that moment, the waiter reappeared, so I ordered some toast and coffee. Watkins shook her head and took a few more sips of her water. When he was gone, she seemed to suddenly loosen, like the strings holding her up had been cut.

'I work for Pine Cone Press. You probably haven't heard of it.'

'I'm sure I wouldn't have, except—'

She looked me dead in the eye then. 'Except that they have signed a high-profile book deal with the woman who used to be known as Emily Haynes.'

I sat back a little. It still made me very uncomfortable to hear her name.

'Aren't there laws against that sort of thing? I mean, profiting off the back of other people's suffering, and so on?'

'Sort of, yes.' Watkins curled both hands around her glass of water and looked down into the top of it. 'But it's all been very cleverly done. She has a literary agent, and they've sat down with the publisher and worked it all out. The proceeds will go to a victims charity. Each part of it has been checked and cleared with psychologists and lawyers. I wouldn't, by the way, advise you to go to a lawyer – they've got it all tied up so neatly that it could cost you a fortune. It's become quite the project. Pine Cone have put so much into it, every other book is practically on the back burner. We're only a small independent press, really, and this isn't something we'd usually have the resources for. But . . .'

The waiter reappeared with my coffee and toast. When he was gone, I took a nibble from the corner of a slice, but I had no appetite at all. I barely had any money of my own. Of course I couldn't go to a lawyer.

'But?' I prompted.

'The pre-orders are already through the roof. People *want* to read this book. And that's half the battle won.'

'Vultures,' I muttered, although deep inside I felt a quick shiver of shame. Wasn't it exactly the sort of book I would have loved as a kid? 'So if you work there, why didn't you stop it?'

Watkins shook her head. 'I'm just an assistant editor. I have no say in this stuff. Which is why I . . . wanted to talk to you. If anyone can stop her, it's you.'

It was my turn to shift uncomfortably in my chair. The last thing I wanted was to have anything to do with Emily. The very idea turned my insides cold.

'I would like nothing better,' I said. 'But you're wrong. I'm the last person who should get involved. How much sympathy do you imagine anyone has for me?'

'That's exactly the thing.' She leaned forward over the table, clattering her knife and fork against the empty side plate. 'It's why I wanted to talk to you. Because in this book, Emily *destroys* you. This is her side of the story, and she's painted you to be the monster.'

I sat very still. 'What? But it was her—'

'It doesn't matter. This is her book, and she makes you out to be the villain in every way, and everyone is going to be reading it. There's going to be a documentary series. Do you realise how this will change things for you?'

For a long moment, I couldn't say anything at all. I knew this was going to be bad, but having someone say it out loud somehow made it all the more damning. I felt sick. I felt furious. How was it that Emily got to say what happened that summer? Emily, of all people?

'I don't see why that should bother you,' I said eventually. 'Most people would say this is exactly what I deserve.'

Watkins frowned and shook her head slightly. 'It's all wrong. We shouldn't have bought this book. *That* is what bothers me. So that's why I wrote to you. If something terrible came out about her, just before the book was published, well . . . they'd probably have to go back to the lawyers.'

'What, something more terrible than what everyone already knows?' I couldn't quite keep the sarcasm from my voice, and Watkins winced.

'Yes, but, you see, all of that, it's *old*. People can tell them-selves it was all a long time ago. But if you found something new . . .'

'Yeah. Speaking of which, how do you know about . . . what we buried?'

The woman pushed her glasses up her nose a little. She could barely bring herself to make eye contact with me.

'I don't know what it is exactly. And I don't *want* to know. I heard Emily's agent speaking to our legal team about it, and what I do know is that it would cause a lot of trouble for them if it was suddenly unearthed.'

From somewhere on the other side of the restaurant, I heard a sudden peal of laughter: the yummy mummies at their coffee morning. I wondered what they'd think if they knew they were sharing space with Charlotte Watts, and the thought turned me cold. I took a sip of my coffee, barely tasting it. All at once I felt like I had run out of words.

'So you're . . . doing it? Looking for the buried thing?' Watkins glanced at me through her thick glasses. When I didn't say anything, she leaned forward, forcing me to look at her. 'I can show you the manuscript.'

'What? Have you got it with you?'

Watkins shook her head. 'Not with me, no, but I can get an advanced copy. If you meet me again, I can show you what she's been writing. Maybe then you'll realise how important it is that you keep looking.'

'All right.' I took the coffee and had a few quick gulps. Then I put the cup down and stood up. I suddenly needed to be back in the part of the world that didn't know who I was. 'You can get this, yeah? Not all of us get book deals and I'm short on cash these days.'

Chapter 11

1954

By the time Derek Grafton was ten, he had overcome his fear
of the faces in the Archive.

In fact he had come to see them as friends, or at least,
colleagues. People he saw daily as part of his 'work'. Doctor
Grafton now allowed him to come to the study whenever he
wished – as long as he himself wasn't at work in there – and
Derek spent much of his free time absorbed in his father's
notes, getting to know the language of skin and flesh and bone,
the music of needle and thread. Doctor Grafton brought out
other boxes, ones that contained wax models of men with
their skin pulled back to expose the redness beneath; they were
tattooed with instructions on what could be moved where,
how skin from the neck and chest could be used to reconstruct
the chin and jaw and so on. One of these wax models his
father nicknamed 'Harry', and Derek came to think of it fondly,
even with its skin all stripped away from its face.

At school, Derek applied himself. His teachers spoke highly
of him and noted that the boy was attentive and thoughtful

in class, showing a particular enthusiasm for mathematics and the natural sciences. Of less importance but also praiseworthy was the boy's ability in art – Derek had a particularly good eye for anatomical sketching, and could copy out scientific diagrams to a high standard. When Nanny came in to speak to his teachers at the end of term, Derek waited outside a classroom, his head close to the crack in the door.

'Bright as a button, that one,' his maths tutor said. 'He'll be a doctor, just like his father. A surgeon even. A boy that bright, he can do anything he turns his hand to.'

Out in the corridor, Derek flushed with pride.

In the long hot summer after Derek turned eleven, he found himself at something of a loose end. His father was working on an article for a London magazine and therefore had no time for their usual studies together. Nanny had a day off, and Cook did not want him under her feet in the kitchen, so he took himself off outside.

The part of London where he lived had largely been rebuilt, but there were still areas where it was possible to find the sort of rubble that had fascinated him as a small child. Half-demolished houses and factories crowded together in overgrown clumps, wild weeds and even small trees transforming them into places of adventure. He knew a group of boys his own age and they prowled the rubble together, poking at things with sticks, scavenging materials for hideouts, breaking glass. They called him 'Doc', half affectionately, because of his quiet and studious attitude.

On that day they wandered further than they normally did, and came across a wide stretch of wasteland. There had been buildings there once, but the rubble had mostly been swept away, save for one broken structure off to one side. It was a shell of a house, one side of it sheared clean off, the insides standing open and exposed. Derek could see scraps of damp wallpaper curling in the wind, and under his feet there were shards of blue and white pottery. Plates, probably.

''Ere, Doc, do you reckon we could get up to that top floor?' asked Tommy. Tommy was a lad a year or so younger than Derek. He always had a dirty face and what Nanny would have called 'rough manners', but he held Derek in high regard and often consulted him before carrying out some plan.

'Stairs are all blasted out,' said Sid, a tall boy with ratty features. He was busily rolling a cigarette. 'It'd be a right bloody palaver.'

'But you'd be able to see for miles,' said Tommy. The building was three storeys high, or at least, what was left of it was. 'And I bet no one else has been up there yet. Could be anything in that room.'

'I doubt it,' said Derek, thoughtfully. 'It's been here for years. And I reckon this isn't even bomb damage.' He cast about the broken wasteland around them. 'They're just clearing this place to build more houses, new houses. They just haven't done this one yet.'

'Ha,' said Tommy. 'Then it's a piece of luck for us, i'n't it? This is probably our last chance to explore it. Come on, let's have a look at least.'

They ventured inside the wreck, passing the now lit cigarette between them. The place smelled of wet plaster, and there was little in the way of furniture or fittings left. Derek saw pale patches on the walls where pictures had once hung, and a discarded iron poker. The stairs were at the back, and they sagged dangerously under the weight of debris and damp. Even so, Derek could see a path up it. He grinned.

'Sod that,' said Sid. 'I'll stay here and look after the fags.'

Tommy mocked him mercilessly but Sid wasn't to be budged, so in the end it was Derek and Tommy who made their slow way up the broken stairs – Derek leading, testing each step with his weight as he went. They passed up through the first floor, the walls of which had been painted a sickly green, and then to the second. Derek paused, looking out across the wasteland to the cramped rows of houses in the distance. He could see thin streams of smoke moving lazily up through the thick London air.

'Come on, Doc,' said Tommy, from behind him. 'We ain't got all day.'

The next portion of the stairs was more hair-raising; big portions of the structure had fallen away, so that Tommy and Derek had to take long, awkward strides to pass safely over the gaps. More than once Derek found himself glancing down through the broken steps to see the shattered floorboards, far below. It was dangerous enough that it took all their concentration, and Derek was surprised when they found themselves at the end of the stairs, looking out at the third floor.

Tommy walked across the sodden carpet, his thumbs hooked into his trouser pockets. He shouted out to Sid.

'How are you doing down there, you big softy Mary? Do you want my sister to come and hold your hand?'

Sid shouted a flurry of swear words back, and Tommy walked out to the edge. The floor ended in an irregular, shattered portion of floorboards, and beyond them, there was nothing, just a dizzying drop. Derek edged out after him, still smiling but feeling a little knot of tension in his chest.

'Watch it, Tommy,' he said. 'There's not much holding us up, here.'

'Don't you start.' Tommy bent over at the knees, looking over the edge. Below them Sid's face was turned up, a white patch against the rubble. 'I bet I can spit on him from here. Just you watch.'

Derek laughed, and took a step forward. He was aware, for

a brief second, that the floor underneath him was moving – tipping up, even – and then he heard a panicked shout from Tommy, right in his ear. The world turned upside down and he had a quick, confused glimpse of rotting wallpaper followed by a terrible sense of falling into space. A sharp white pain split his head in two and everything turned red.

To Sid, Derek seemed to fall like a rag doll, turning at least one complete circle before he hit the ground with a crunch. The boy dropped his cigarette and ran forward, all the colour draining from his face, yet when he got to Doc the kid looked okay – he was just lying on his back, his eyes closed and his mouth slightly open. He couldn't even see any blood.

'*Jesus, Mary and Joseph* . . . Doc, you've scared me there, I don't mind saying.' He knelt by the boy and shook his arm. Behind him he could hear the scrambling of Tommy making his way back down the stairs, going a lot faster than was sensible. 'Come on, I can see you breathing, stop pissing about and open your eyes.'

Tommy appeared at his side, his breath whistling out of his nose.

'Is he all right, Sid?'

Sid shook the boy's arm again, but he still didn't open his eyes or speak. 'Shit. He's knocked himself silly, that's all. Come on, help me get him up and we can carry him back to mine. Best we keep him out of the sun for a bit.'

The two boys moved to grab him – Sid went to take Derek's shoulders, while Tommy grabbed his ankles – but when they lifted him up, his head moved oddly, and too late Sid spotted the length of thin rusted pipe protruding from the back of his head, just behind his ear. Sid gave a little cry and dropped the boy, but by then the pipe had come out of its own accord, and with it came a flood of bright red blood, spreading swiftly

84

all over the dirty broken stones. It was more blood than either boy had ever seen, and for a long handful of seconds they just stood and watched, paralysed with horror as everything that had made Derek 'Doc' leaked out onto the jumbled mess of the wasteland.

Chapter 12

'I lied to you before. About my family, I mean.'

Charlie raised her eyebrows, wondering where this was going. Emily had taken her back to her own caravan, and she couldn't help noticing all the differences. At hers, the place was constantly noisy, filled with family members; the kitchen was always in the middle of some sort of meal preparation, the kettle was always steaming. There would be crossword puzzle books strewn across the seating area where her nan had left them, little white paper bags of raspberry ruffles or lemon sherbets; a pile of everyone's shoes by the door. Everywhere, half-finished cups of tea.

Emily's caravan was neat, and cold, and quiet. The sink and stove were pristine. Crucially, her mother and father were out.

'What do you mean, lied?'

'Come on. Here.' Emily led her into the back bedroom. There was a small double bed, and a fold-out bed lying alongside it. It had a number of brightly coloured sheets and blankets thrown over it, and next to it, Emily's bag, which Charlie recognised from the day she had arrived.

86

'You sleep in here?' Charlie frowned slightly. There was another small bedroom, as well as sofas that became beds in the front room. 'In the same room as your mum and dad?'

Emily shrugged as if that didn't matter. Instead, she sat on the big bed and pulled her bag up onto her knees. Charlie sat next to her. From inside a zipped section of the bag she pulled out an old, battered-looking brown envelope.

'I have a sister too.'

She tipped the envelope up, and a number of photographs came slithering out, which she passed to Charlie. All of them showed a girl about the same age as Charlie's own sister, around sixteen or seventeen. She looked very much like an older version of Emily; the same bone-white skin, the same raven-black hair, but her eyes were blue. In most of the photos she was smiling and, often, posing with Emily, and together there was a kind of glow to the younger girl that Charlie hadn't seen before. In one of the photos, they had matching baseball caps with their names on. The older girl's said 'Louise'.

'She's five years older than me,' said Emily, solemnly. She took the photographs back from Charlie and began flicking through them. 'She likes music, and dancing. She used to dance with me, all the time. It was our favourite thing to do. Louise would buy a single and then when she brought it home, she'd make sure I was there too, so we could listen to it together.'

'Where is she? Why isn't she on holiday with you?'

Emily had come to another set of photographs. These ones were smaller, and had thick white margins around the square images. Later, Charlie would know these were Polaroids – the sort of photo you didn't have to take to a chemist to get developed. Emily passed the first one over, her face entirely blank.

It showed a quite different Louise. Here, she wasn't smiling, and her white face and bare white arms almost seemed to glow against a dim background. There was a dark bruise on her cheekbone, and her lip had been split open. She looked as though she'd been crying, but she didn't look sad; she looked furious. Another Polaroid, a similar scene; here, Louise was holding up her arm, a portion of which was bright red. It looked as though she had been scalded. In another, there were small round burns on the top of her thigh; in another, a black eye.

Charlie frowned. She wanted her mum.

'Emily . . .'

'Louise made me take these. She said it was our insurance.'

'Who did it?'

Emily looked down at the photographs. Outside, Charlie could hear children shouting, playing some sort of summer game like forty-forty. It felt like they were a million miles away.

'My dad gets so angry, all the time. Over small things, weird things. With Louise it was the way she wore her hair, her clothes, the people she was friends with at school. And then it was how she cooked the dinner, or left her washing in the basket, or her shoes in the hall. There was always something. They were always shouting at each other, screaming really, and then . . .'

She seemed to run out of words.

'Your dad is a massive arsehole,' Charlie said hotly.

'It was awful but it was okay because Louise was there. Do you see? I had Lou, and she had me, and we could get through everything together. And then one day I came home from school and Dad said that Lou had packed her bags and left. Had run away. I didn't have anyone anymore.'

'What about your mum?'

Emily shook her head, a sceptical smile on her face that briefly made her look even more like her older sister.

'Mum? Mum doesn't want to know. If Dad and Lou were arguing, she'd find reasons to be on the other side of the house, or in the garden, or round the neighbours. If she couldn't see it or hear it, it didn't matter.'

'Where did your sister go?'

'I don't know.' Emily grasped the collar of her own T-shirt and twisted it between her fingers, an odd, nervous gesture. 'She never phoned, or anything. And I don't think she would run away like, not without taking me with her, because why would she leave me behind, with *this*?' She took a watery breath. 'Lou wouldn't. She wouldn't just . . . leave me.'

'Well.' Charlie thought rapidly. She felt out of her depth, lost in the face of her friend's sorrow. 'Listen. Listen, if your dad was hurting your sister, you have to tell someone. Like, tell my mum!' She felt a surge of feeling then; her mum would help. That's what she did. She would be sensible and take no nonsense, and that included any nonsense from Emily's dad. But Emily had turned a shade paler, and she grabbed Charlie's arm and squeezed it hard.

'No! I can't, and you can't either, okay? You have to promise me right now, Charlie. Promise me right now you won't tell anyone!'

'But . . . if you think . . .'

'No. I trusted you, Charlie, I trusted you.' Emily's eyes were full of tears now. 'If we tell on him . . .' She made a noise in the back of her throat. It sounded like a trapped animal. 'Do you promise? Please?'

Charlie swallowed hard. She looked down at the photos of the girl, the glint of anger in her eyes. It was difficult to believe that this girl had run away, or that she'd left her little sister to take the brunt of their dad's anger. And if not, what had happened to her?

'I promise,' she said, although she felt sick. 'I won't tell.'

Chapter 13

Now

I've never been an early riser, but the next morning I got up with the first shreds of light showing through the curtain, and I washed and dressed quickly, pulling on a red knitted hat over my newly darkened hair. Katie was up and about already herself, eating a bowl of cereal that was perched on her lap. The TV was showing cartoons.

'What are you doing?' she asked.

'Just going for an early-morning walk. Get some fresh air.'

'Can I come with you?'

I stopped shrugging on my coat. 'Do you want to?'

She looked at me for a long moment. 'I don't like the woods.'

'How do you know that's where I'm going?'

On the telly, a cartoon cat yowled as a cartoon mouse slammed a book down on its paws. Katie stirred her cereal, pushing puffs of rice under the milk. 'The woods are *boring*,' she said.

In the end, I left her where she was and slipped out of the caravan with my spade under one arm.

Just get it done, I thought.

On my way to the woods I passed by the caravan and its collection of outbuildings that we had called the Ranch when I was a kid. A caravan that was bigger than all the other caravans, this one had sprouted extensions – if anything it was even bigger than I remembered. Sheds and gazebos and washing lines, a vegetable garden, a fence, chicken wire, bunting. There were two dented cars and a van parked around it, and I thought of that old Wild West phrase, 'circling the wagons'. I wondered if it was the sort of thing that I could put in the book – my family had certainly had all sorts of stories about the Ranch, and they were, in their own way, a kind of urban legend, and urban legends are only a generation or so away from folklore.

There was a silvery, lavender quality to the dawn glow, and it drew bright lines around everything; the edges of the caravans, the leaves and the dew on the grass. The morning was nearly silent too, without even the chatter of the dawn chorus, and the closer I got to the woods, the less certain I became that I knew where I truly was, or when.

I slipped in through the silent trees, and made my way back to the clearing. I examined my diary entry again, and counted out the steps again. Again, I dug a hole in the ground, turfing up clods of earth and stones, and again I found nothing. I gritted my teeth and thought about my strange meeting with the woman who called herself Watkins. I thought about Emily's book, and how what we had buried was the only thing that could stop it.

It's fine, I told myself. *The note in your diary isn't accurate, that's all. It's just going to take longer than you thought.*

I tried a second time, and a third. By the sixth attempt I could feel the very edges of panic. The morning was beginning to feel like a nightmare. I stopped and looked at the holes I had dug, ugly brown disturbances in the grassy covering.

Perhaps I wasn't digging deep enough? Or was this entirely the wrong clearing? I didn't believe either thing was true, but I decided to dig one more hole and then go and get some breakfast. Food in my stomach might shake off the nauseous sense of unreality that continued to cling to the day.

Instead of counting out the steps I just chose a random spot. The edge of the spade sunk easily into the ground there, and I had a moment of hope, but again, there was nothing. I was just lifting the spade out, thinking that I would make a full fried breakfast if Katie was up for it, when I spotted long, brown strands sticking to the metal. I pulled the spade up further, feeling a cold sensation move down through my chest.

Hair. There was hair in the ground here. I dropped the spade.

'No,' I said aloud. 'No, no.' My mind went instantly to Cheryl, to the posters and the lonely shrine on top of the beach. And then I saw what was actually buried in the dirt. I got down on my knees and pulled out a plastic doll's head. The thing had mud in its eyes and much of the painted face had been scraped away, but I could still see what it was easily enough. 'Her hair is *blonde*,' I said, saying it firmly to try and chase some of fear away. 'Cheryl is a blonde. You know that. And this is just a bloody doll.'

I attempted to pick the synthetic hair off the spade, but when my fingers moved over the slippery strands, my stomach abruptly heaved, and I stumbled away, one hand pressed tightly to my mouth to stop myself from being sick.

'All right, that's enough.' After a moment I straightened up, my eyes watering. I felt idiotic, ashamed of myself. It was time to get some perspective. 'I just need to—'

There was a crashing noise, the sound of something moving heavily through the undergrowth. I remembered the ragged figure I had seen, but right on the heels of that awful thought

I realised it wasn't that at all; it was Joseph, the handyman from the site shop. He hadn't spotted me yet, thankfully, but I could see him well enough. He had a plastic bin bag in one hand, and the hood of his parka was down. Quickly, I dropped my spade into a nearby thicket, and headed off at an angle to intercept him. I didn't want him seeing the holes I'd dug, or the doll's head I had excavated.

'Hey! Morning!' I forced a smile onto my face to meet the startled expression that passed over his. 'You're up early.'

His face broke into a grin. 'Yeah. Got a dead tree round the back, been slowly taking it apart.' He briefly held up the bin bag, which I assumed held tools of some sort. 'You don't need anything from the shop, do you? I don't normally open up for a couple of hours yet.'

'Oh no, just out for a walk. In the, uh, early morning . . . light.' I had mud on my hands, so I stuck them in my pockets. I realised, with a crawling sense of horror, that I didn't know what to say next. My experience of small talk isn't so much limited as almost non-existent.

'Your niece not with you?'

'Nah, she prefers to sleep in, that one,' I lied. 'Lazy bugger.'

'You should take her up to the funfair, you know? In town. Believe it or not they are open at this time of year, it's just that they don't turn the gate lights on during the day. The owner is a skinflint. And the offer of lunch is still open, by the way. Or dinner! You can both come, I've got plenty of baked beans.'

I laughed a bit. My heart was thumping oddly. Minutes ago I had been frightened beyond all reason, and now I was struggling not to blush.

'Sure.' My mouth seemed to be saying words without my permission. 'That would be great.'

'Brilliant. Seven? I'll meet you at the shop then.'

He wandered off, and I made my way back out of the woods. Back at the caravan, Katie was lying across the sofa, arms flung out to either side like a dying damsel.

'I'm bored.'

'How about the funfair? Rides, ice cream, doughnuts, more rides, a high possibility of throwing up? You won't get a better offer than that.'

She swung her legs around and looked up at me. She still looked a little too pale for my liking, but I found that my chat with Joseph had lifted my spirits an alarming amount.

'Come on. We'll put some colour in those cheeks, grotbags.'

Chapter 14

July 1988

In the evening it was largely quiet in the shower block, and Charlie and Emily had found it a great place to avoid their respective families. It had been another long hot day, and even this late in the evening it was still hot outside, but the shower block, with its white tiled floor, was pleasingly cool underfoot. The girls sat in the corner under the sinks, playing top trumps and talking. Emily was working her way steadily through an entire packet of Polos.

'Okay, my Frankenstein has a scare factor of seven. Does that beat yours?'

'It's Frankenstein's monster, really,' said Emily. 'And my werewolf has an eight, so there.'

'Hmph.' From outside came a flurry of shouts as some kids playing a ball game made their way past. 'I reckon a monster made of dead bits of people is scarier than a . . . a big dog.'

Emily snorted. 'I dunno. Have you ever seen a big dog that's really angry? It's pretty scary. Our neighbours had an Alsatian that bit my ankle once.'

'Really?' Charlie looked up from her cards. 'Do you have any scars?'

'From that? No.' Emily crunched another Polo between her teeth.

'Was it, like, the scariest thing you've ever seen?'

Emily put her cards in her lap, her black hair falling over her eyes. A certain sort of silence grew between them, a silence Charlie was beginning to recognise.

'It's all right,' she said eventually. 'You don't have to answer that. Look,' she nodded to the wall to Emily's left, where a daddy-long-legs was crouching just above their heads. '*Gross.*'

'A crane fly,' said Emily. Again, as with the spider on the climbing frame, she didn't appear to be alarmed by the insect.

'I used to catch them, crane flies, and I used to throw them into spider's webs so that the spiders would come out and eat them. It was interesting to watch, because they were so fast. They would just pounce, right, and then spin the daddy-long-legs all around so their legs were all tucked up and they were stuck in this cocoon. And then they'd eat its insides and that.' Charlie flicked a card against her chin. 'But my mum caught me doing it, and told me I wasn't to do it anymore, because it's cruel.'

'Well that's daft,' said Emily. 'It might be cruel to the crane fly, but you're actually *helping* the spider. And the crane fly might have ended up in the spider's web anyway.' She paused, and then, 'The scariest thing I've ever seen is my dad, or like, the shadow of him. When he's out in the hallway at night, he would just . . . stand there and wait, listening. And sometimes he would walk on by, and sometimes he would go into my sister Louise's room. Sometimes I would force myself to stay awake and listen until I knew he'd gone to bed, because then I could sleep. Because it was safer then, you know?'

Charlie nodded, although she didn't know, not really. Her

dad was a loud, boisterous man who was often away for work. When he was back in the house you knew it, because he liked to talk to everyone about what he'd missed, usually at the top of his voice. It was hard to imagine him standing outside a bedroom door, lurking in silence.

'I don't like your dad,' she said quietly. She glanced up at the shower cubicles, just in case Emily's dad had chosen that second to go for a late wash.

'He's . . .' Emily dropped her voice to a whisper. 'I think that it would have been better if *he'd* gone. I think that would have been fairer. If Louise had stayed with me and Mum, and Dad had just gone away somewhere. We'd all have been happy, then.'

'Have you ever wished for it? Wished him . . . away?'

Emily put her packet of Polos back into her pocket. Outside, the sun was finally giving in, and the pebbled windows above them were flat orange squares of dying light.

'I do,' she whispered. 'I wish that *every day*.'

The dripping of water echoed in the small space. Charlie could smell the metallic scent of the steel sinks hanging above their heads. It was in her nature to distract with stories, to retreat into them in the hope that the world would make more sense, which is why she said what she said next.

'Let's leave another offering to Stitch Face Sue.'

Emily's face lit up, brighter than it had been since she'd told Charlie about her missing sister.

'And I can ask her for anything I want?'

'Yep. But let's make it a good one.'

They spent the next hour in a flurry of inspiration, collecting things for their 'offering' that had been scavenged from all around the campsite. Charlie brought a joker from one of the many packs of playing cards that were scattered around her caravan; a strawberry bonbon filched from her nan's bag of sweets; a blue hairclip stolen from her cousin Jenny. Emily brought a handful of fat daisy heads, picked from someone's flower box; a paper hat she'd folded herself; and a pinch of brown pungent-smelling stuff that Charlie initially didn't recognise.

'What's that?'

'Some of my dad's tobacco,' Emily replied. There was an odd, set look to the grim line of her mouth. 'So she knows who he is. Stitch Face Sue.'

When they had all their pieces together, they set off for the edge of the caravan park, where the little patch of woods began. It was dark by now, and Charlie knew they were starting to push their luck – sundown was 'going in' time, by the basic laws of the site, and soon various mums would be standing at caravan doors, bellowing for their kids to come in and have tea. But it had been another long, balmy day, the air still warm and full of all the indolent scents of summer. That night, it felt like they could have stayed out until dawn.

'Will this be the right place, do you think?'

Charlie looked into the dark trees. Behind them, the caravan park was still a source of light and noise; a radio playing somewhere, the lights on someone's pushbike whizzing down a path. Ahead of them though, was a pool of silence, and that felt right. She fished her little torch out of her pocket and shone its weedy little beam between the tree trunks.

'Yeah, this'll be perfect. Let's find a good spot.' They wandered along the most obvious path. 'Stitch Face Sue knows all the wild places of Hithechurch, because that's where she most wants to be, as a ghost. She won't like noise, or too many people, so this will be a place she can visit. Here, look at that tree! It's perfect.'

Her tiny light had picked out a great fallen tree, just to the left of the path. It had clearly been dead for some time, the bark all broken away to reveal the smooth white underneath, like bone. There was a small clear area in front of it, and Charlie thought she had never seen a more obvious location for witchy business.

They trampled their way over, laughing breathlessly in the dark, until they sat cross-legged, the white tree trunk looming just behind them.

'So,' said Emily. 'What do we do?'

'Here, look, it's easy.' If there was one thing Charlie was good at, it was making things up on the fly. 'We put all we've collected on the ground and draw a circle around it.' She picked up a likely stick and dragged it through the dirt around their small pile of things. 'That way, Sue knows that everything inside is hers, which we have gladly given, right?'

Emily nodded. She had taken custody of the torch, and her small pinched face was very white.

'Now look. I'm going to speak to her spirit, okay?' Charlie held out her hand, and the other girl took it. She felt a flutter of something in her stomach – an emotion somewhere between fear and excitement. The longer they sat there, the darker the woods seemed, and the further away the caravan site felt. She had thought the woods were quiet, but there were noises all around them; wind tugging its way through branches; the unknown crinkling patter of small animals moving; the last songs of the day birds. 'Susan Cartwright, if you're there, we want to ask for your help. We are friends of yours, and we've brought you presents to show you we mean it.' She squeezed Emily's hand, then let go of it. 'Now I'm going to light the match.' She pulled a box of matches from her pocket and extracted one, then held it poised over the striker strip. 'Turn off the torch, and then when the match burns, ask Sue for what you want.'

'Me?' Emily looked startled. 'Do I . . . do I have to say it out loud?'

Charlie pursed her lips briefly. If it had been anyone else, she would have insisted they speak their intentions in a loud and, if possible, spooky voice, but something about Emily made her more amenable.

'No, just say it in your head, but really mean it. Are you ready?' She pressed the head of the match to the strip. 'Remember, think it while the match burns. Turn off the torch.'

With a tiny plastic click they were plunged into darkness, and they both giggled nervously for a second before Charlie struck the match. The light was back, but it was an old, orange light that moved and jumped and turned the woods around them into an entirely different place.

'Oh,' said Emily, and then she looked down at the offerings in their circle. Her lips moved silently as she spoke her wish to the night. Charlie watched, feeling shivery and strange, and then the heat of the match was unbearable, biting at her fingers. She dropped it.

'Ow, shit!'

The dark was back, and Charlie's vision was crisscrossed with a trail of green after-images from the match light.

'Did you finish it?' she whispered to Emily. 'Did you think all of the wish?'

Silence. Charlie blinked rapidly. She couldn't make out anything much with her light-startled eyes. It was as if the other girl had vanished, eaten up by the woods somehow.

'Emily?'

'I'm here.' The other girl took her hand in the dark. 'I've dropped the torch, can you see it—'

The silence of the woods broke into pieces as something large crashed through the bushes near them. Charlie let out a shriek and was on her feet in moments, and then, running on instinct more than sight, the pair of them scrambled out of the little clearing and back onto the path. In the wild panic of it all Charlie thought she heard a low, human noise – someone laughing, maybe – and then they spotted the lights of the caravan park ahead. They scrambled out of the woods, not stopping until they were back on a gravel path, a tall fluorescent lamp attracting moths over their heads.

'What do you think that was?' gasped Emily. 'Do you think that was *her*?'

'I dunno.' Charlie looked back at the woods. Normally she would have leapt at the chance to give extra credence to her stories, but the scare felt much too fresh for that. She rubbed a hand against her cheek uneasily. 'My cousin Darren goes in there sometimes with his mates, you know. They take cans of beer in there . . .'

But Emily wasn't listening. She was staring at the woods too, and her eyes were alive with some new knowledge.

The next morning, Charlie had just finished her bowl of Coco Pops when there was a hammering at the caravan door. She looked uneasily over to her mum, who hadn't been best pleased with Charlie being 'a dirty stop-out' the night before, but she was too absorbed in the daily logistical nightmare of serving up several fried breakfasts at once to take much notice of what her daughter was up to. Charlie slunk over to the door and opened it. Emily was standing on the doorstep, her face bone white save for two bright points of colour on the tops of her cheeks.

'Charlie, it worked.' She held up one hand, red to the wrist in blood that was already drying. '*It worked.*'

Chapter 15

Now

The funfair, which crouched just under the inland side of the sea wall, was much as I remembered it, only smaller. There were the dodgems, the magic carpet, the twirling teacups ride for the little kids, the big carousel with its elaborate prancing horses and its gaudy chariots. At the back was a low building with glass doors, and from inside I could hear the clanging and wailing of various fruit machines and video games. I bought some tokens from a bored-looking teenager in a booth, then followed Katie from ride to ride as she dithered over what to try first. The day had warmed up a little as the sky clouded over, and I wondered vaguely if it was going to rain. As far as I could see, we were the only customers in the place.

'This one!' Katie had stopped by the carousel, and in seconds she was seated on one of the huge, leaping steeds. I eyed it warily. Had these things been this sinister when I was a kid? The horse's lips were pulled back from its huge, chomping teeth, and its eyes were wild, a blue pupil surrounded by a thick circle of white. It looked terrified, or mad. The man running the ride shouted at me to stand back, and off they went, tinny calliope music winding its way out into the cold air.

I stood and watched, my arms crossed over my chest. Every so often, Katie would come back round on her carousel horse, her arms flung around its neck as though she was holding on for dear life, and then she'd be gone again. The music played on and on. Inevitably, I thought about when I'd been here before. That had ended badly, of course. Everything about that holiday had ended badly. As if it had been waiting for me to think about the past, I spotted the funfair's old van, parked to the side of the building housing all the slot machines. It was painted differently now, but I recognised the style: the sort of poorly rendered copyright infringement you always saw at funfairs and on ice-cream vans. The characters painted on the side of it now were all from comic books and their hugely successful movie adaptations. I spotted a somewhat cuboid Incredible Hulk, and a shifty-looking Iron Man.

After a couple of minutes, the back of my neck began to prickle. I looked around. There was no one else here – just the teenager in the booth, who was peering avidly at their phone, and the man in charge of the carousel had vanished from sight. Still. I was getting a strong sensation of being watched.

I looked back at the carousel. Empty horses, empty chariots. Katie must have just passed me.

I caught movement at the very edge of my vision, and I turned again. There, far above my head, a figure was standing at the sea wall, looking down. I narrowed my eyes against the glare of the sky. Was it her? The shape was just a silhouette, but I thought I could see long, unkempt hair and thin arms, but then the carousel was slowing down and I heard Katie calling me. When I looked back again, the figure – if it had been there at all – was gone.

'I want to go in the Haunted House next,' Katie said in a matter-of-fact tone.

'Of course you do.'

'But I want you to come in with me.'

'Katie . . .'

'You promised I could do whatever I wanted while we were in this place!'

The Haunted House was built to look like a slumping, crooked little cottage, painted white and black in that mock-Tudor style that was everywhere in the 80s. I handed my tokens to another teenager, who looked at me like I was mad.

'Are you sure you want to . . . go on this?' Underneath a padded windcheater she was wearing a faded 'Hithechurch Funfair' jumper. I smiled at her – she was much too young to have any idea who I was.

'Oh, I think I'll be fine,' I said, attempting to sound breezy. 'If my niece can handle a few plastic skeletons, then so can I.'

The teenager shrugged. 'Yeah okay. Whatever.'

Inside it was dark and awkward, with wonky staircases that leaned dramatically to one side as you moved from room to room. There was low, distorted organ music playing, which I thought was a nice touch, and whispery fake cobwebs hung from the ceiling and trailed ghost fingers through my hair. Katie seemed entirely unfazed by it all, stomping away ahead of me like she'd been born and raised in a haunted house. I thought of the story Stan had told me, about the beauty queen who had slipped on greasy stairs, supposedly inside this very haunted house. It would have been decades ago, if it had even happened at all, but still.

'Oi, slow down,' I called to Katie. One of the wonky stair-cases had me half slumped against a wall, and for a hairy moment I thought I might fall backwards. 'Be careful on these stairs. Don't get out of my sight, okay?'

She shouted something impatient back at me.

In the first room there was a somewhat humorous tableau of a family of skeletons sitting down to a meal. Each plate had a small skeletal fish in the middle of it, and each of the skeletons – two big, two little – clutched knives and forks in their fleshless fingers. Somewhere, a string was making the largest skeleton's jaw creak up and down, as though he were asking the children how their day had been.

'What do skeletons even eat, anyway?' asked Katie.

I smiled at the question, sure the answer was in some Christmas cracker joke somewhere. The next room was more impressive and significantly gorier – apparently this upper room was home to a scene from the French Revolution. There was a makeshift guillotine, with the blade flying up and down, while a headless body slouched on a platform, clothed in voluminous skirts. The head in the basket was wearing a curly white wig and the eyes in its waxy face were open. Fake blood glistened everywhere, and for the first time I felt a real tremor of unease. I thought of the ragged figure I thought I'd seen in the woods. *Grey women everywhere. Are you watching, Stitch Face Sue?*

'This is stupid,' said Katie.

'It was your idea to come in here.' As soon as I said it, I felt bad. Katie didn't reply. We went out into the corridor again and spent some time banging around to the third floor. Here, there were a few automated mannequins that jumped out of the walls, and both of us gave small shrieks.

'All right, okay, maybe we should just go now.' My heart was beating rapidly, and despite feeling enormously stupid, I didn't want to be in the Haunted House anymore. But Katie just shook her head, and we made it into the final room.

At first, I didn't believe what I was seeing. I froze, one hand clutching the door frame as though that could keep me rooted in reality.

This last room had a large scarecrow in it, pinned, arms spread wide, to a wooden post. Its clothes were ragged and spattered with more fake blood – it's fake, my mind insisted, all of this is fake – and its face was a pale piece of battered leather, with rough features stitched into it with thick black thread.

'I . . . this is . . .'

In front of me, Katie was standing with her arms crossed over her chest. 'Huh, a *scarecrow*. What's scary about that?'

'Come on.' I grabbed her little shoulders. They were as cold as ice. 'Let's get out of here. I don't even know why . . . Just, come on.'

Together we tumbled our way down the crooked stairway, ignoring the portraits on the walls with eyes that shunted back and forth, until we came to the final section. Here, there was a collection of funny mirrors, and I caught sight of myself twisted into monstrous shapes; one moment I was a thing so tall and thin I was all bone and sinew, the next, I bulged as though something inside me were forcing its way out. At the last mirror, I saw, peeking out from beneath its frame, a pair of battered, old-fashioned boots. Ahead of me, Katie had found the door and was out, letting in a brief shout of cold January air and light, but I stood for a second longer, looking at the boots. There was a smell too, something sweet and sharp and half familiar. Not a funfair smell, but something else that made me think of children. Was someone behind the mirror? Was *she* behind the mirror?

It's another mannequin, I told myself. *One final bad joke.*

I turned away from it and headed for the door, but not before I caught movement out of the corner of my eye. As I stepped into the cold afternoon, I clasped Katie's hand in mine and we left the funfair without speaking.

When we were on the pavement outside, the weirdness of the funfair felt less powerful. My phone buzzed, and when I checked it, there was another text message from Watkins. There was a picture attached.

'Is that Mum?' asked Katie, a little hopefully. She was pulling her hair out of the folds of her scarf and not looking at me, so she didn't see the expression that passed over my face. The picture was of me, from the back, staring at the carousel. I thought of the figure I'd thought I'd seen, watching from the sea wall. The text simply said:

Why are you still wasting time?

And why are you watching me? I thought, surprised by how angry I was. I felt a spike of anxiety. This woman might be trying to help me, but I knew nothing about her.

'Just a spam text,' I said, putting the phone away. 'Come on, let's get back in the warm.'

Chapter 16

1954

Derek spent around two months in hospital, for the first three weeks of which he was unconscious. When he did begin to open his eyes again, he felt as though he were at the bottom of a deep well filled with water, the faces of doctors and nurses floating somewhere above him. Their voices thundered around his head – sometimes he thought he heard his father, too.

Eventually this sensation left him, and he was able to sit up a little in bed. Derek's head hurt fiercely, and a thick wad of bandages made him feel heavy and slow, but the nurses seemed pleased with his progress. One of them brought him a glass beaker of water, but it slipped through his fingers and soaked his bedsheet.

'Not to worry, love.' She snatched up the empty glass before he had a chance to grab it. 'I'll get another, and hold it for you this time.'

Derek's days were long and uncomfortable, with sharp pains lancing through his temples every time he moved his head, but at night he fell easily into a deep, almost suffocating sleep. He would dream about his father's study, and the Archive. The model they had nicknamed Harry would be sitting on top of the desk, his skin all rolled back to reveal the red meat beneath, and sometimes Harry would talk to Derek: his voice was an insistent, low whisper, making Derek think of the ground when there had been no rain for weeks. It was a dry, dead sound.

The nurses brought him his dinner on a tray. Derek picked up his knife and fork to cut up his pork chop, but the cutlery slipped through his fingers. The nurses exchanged a look, and then one of them leaned over him, her soft arm brushing against his shoulder.

'Here, let me cut it up for you,' she said. 'That'll make it easier, won't it?'

But things did not get easier for Derek. Over the weeks he taught himself to hold the knife and fork, and even to hold a cup to his lips, but it took fierce concentration and his hands still trembled constantly. One day his father came and stood just outside the room with the doctors for a long time, talking with them in a low voice. Derek watched, trying to sit up as straight as he could, and when his father came back into the room he forced himself to smile.

'Will I be going home?' he asked.

His father held his hat in his hands, and spun it around his fingers pensively.

'Soon, Derek,' he said. 'You'll be going home soon. Your doctor tells me you might have some neurological issues, which will hopefully go away with time.'

'What does that mean?'

His father's face was very still. Derek couldn't tell what he was thinking or feeling at all.

'Your hands don't always do what you tell them. Is that right?'

109

Derek shrugged, a response that would normally earn him a clip round the ear. His father looked away.

For the next week or so Derek practised as hard as he could, holding the glass beaker to his lips, turning the pages of a book, or using his knife and fork. The concentration made his head ache even more, but gradually he did get better at handling objects, until he was sure that he must be back to normal. At night he still dreamed of Harry; the wax figure stood in the middle of his father's desk in a patch of moonlight, his tiny whispering voice filling the whole room.

Eventually he was allowed to go home, and Nanny became like a nurse to him, which he hated, and he was desperate to get out of the house – to get back to school, where he could be one child among many again. The wound on the back of his head had healed into a rigid swirl of scar tissue, and he let his hair grow slightly long in an attempt to cover it.

When he did go back to school, though, he found he was unable to concentrate on his lessons, and the words in his books seemed to mingle and shiver, becoming unreadable. Things that had been easy for him before the accident – mathematics, drawing graphs, writing essays – became so difficult that he spent each school day in a simmering rage. Despite all of his careful practice, his fingers would still tremble at odd moments, and out of the corner of his eye he caught his teachers watching him with sad, pitying expressions. This only made him feel worse, and he lost his temper frequently, until the other children knew to keep out of his way.

The Archive, he felt, had to be his salvation. Everything else had been lost to him, but there was always the study with the papers and models he knew so well. This would still make sense to him, he was sure of it, yet when he went to the study he found that it was locked.

'Where is the key to the study, Nanny?'

Nanny was busy darning Doctor Grafton's socks, and she spared him one, harried glance over her glasses.

'He's had it locked up while you were in hospital, my dear.'

'I want to go in there. There are things for me to read. Where's the key?'

Now Nanny looked actively uncomfortable. She pursed her lips at the sock in her hands, as though it were giving her particular trouble.

'He keeps it with him these days. Now then, let me be. I have things to do.'

But when he found his father and asked to be let into the study, Doctor Grafton just looked at him for a long time, his face very still.

'What is it?' Derek asked. The frustration and fury of his day at school felt close to the surface, and although he had never in his life lost his temper in front of his father, it was becoming harder and harder to avoid it.

'Derek, do you know why I let you sit in my study and go through my archive?'

His archive.

'Because it taught me things. I was learning.'

His father nodded slowly. They were in the dining room. The used plates and tureens for that night's dinner were still on the table, and it occurred to Derek that the maid was avoiding the room.

'Learning, yes. Because it was my plan that you follow me into my profession. For you, I wanted a future of service, of helping people. Surgery is an honourable profession. Pass me that glass, will you?'

Without thinking, Derek reached for the wine glass, and as he did his fingers trembled again, his fingernails briefly tapping against the crystal. He looked up and met his father's eyes. It had been a trap.

111

'There's no real need for you to be in my study now, Derek.' He sniffed and looked away. 'We'll speak no more about it, as I'm sure it breaks both our hearts.'

Derek stood for a second longer, frozen in place by his father's words. And then he turned and left the dining room. Deep inside his head, Harry's whispering grew a little louder.

Chapter 17

July 1988

The blood was Emily's father's, although there wasn't nearly
enough of it, in her opinion.

'What happened?' Charlie steered her friend away from the
caravan, very aware that if her mum caught sight of it she
wouldn't be seeing Emily again any time soon. 'Is he . . . ?'

'It was a dog. It bit him!' Emily's eyes were wide and glassy
with excitement. 'Come on, I'll show you.'

Together they ran across the caravan site, weaving their way
around parked cars and holidaymakers, until they came to the
site entrance. There was a narrow strip of pavement there, and
Emily skidded to a stop next to it.

'Look. There.'

A splatter of dark red across the concrete. Charlie stared at
it. She had seen blood on the pavement before – when she'd
fallen off her own bike – but never this much. It made her
feel strange, as though she were about to come down with a
fever. Emily was scuffing the blood with her trainer, but in the
heat it was already dry.

'You said there was a dog?' Charlie looked around uneasily. When her mum took her to the video rental place, she liked to hang around in the horror section until she got caught and shooed away. One of the videos that held the most fascination for her depicted a huge St Bernard, its jaws slathered with drool and its eyes running with blood. This is what she pictured coming around the corner to see who else it could bite.

'My dad comes out here in the mornings to smoke,' said Emily. 'He likes to do it away from the caravans and all their gas canisters and because he likes to be by himself in the mornings. Says me and Mum make too much noise. But this morning, there was a stray dog walking down this road, and it came over to my dad, who went to stroke it. But it bit him.' She grinned, and then looked down at her blood-covered hands. 'Bit him right here.' She poked a finger into the fleshy part of her hand just below the thumb. 'He came back into the caravan hollering.' She shuddered then, a full body twitch that Charlie didn't think she was aware of at all. 'He bled all over the table, and then Mum made him wash it, and she drove him into town to go to the emergency GP. He had to have an injection in case the dog had diseases. They came back, but Dad was in such a bad mood that Mum told me to go out, stay out as long as I like.'

'They're back?' Charlie asked, but she was looking at the dried blood on Emily's hands. She was wondering why neither of her parents had made her wash them.

'Don't you see, though?' Emily turned around. There were bloody fingerprints on her T-shirt. 'It *worked*. The ritual called Stitch Face Sue and she did something.'

'Let's go back to the shower block. I need the loo.' They began walking. 'Is that what you asked for? A dog to bite your dad?'

'No, not really but . . . it's close, isn't it? It's like we almost got it right.'

'Like we hexed him.'

'Hexed?'

Charlie pushed her hair out of her eyes. If anyone deserved to get bitten, it was Emily's dad. 'Yeah, it's a curse witches do. A bad spell.'

When they got to the shower block, Charlie took Emily to the sinks and made her run her hands under the hot tap. She squeezed some pink soap out of the dispenser and rubbed the other girl's hands in her own until they both had foam up to the wrists. Emily let her do all this without comment. Now that the initial excitement was over, she seemed to have drifted into a quieter, more thoughtful mood.

When their hands were clean they rubbed them dry with green paper towels.

'We should do it again,' Emily said eventually. She looked down at her hands, now very pink and clean. 'I want to do it again. But maybe slightly differently.'

'You want your dad to get bitten by a dog again?'

'Yes. I mean, no. Something else. I don't know.'

'All right. What I think is, we need to find better things to leave for her. Stuff that's really properly valuable or important.' They were wandering through the site now, and Charlie could feel the top of her head getting hot. It was another blisteringly clear day, with nothing between them and the full weight of the summer sun. 'Gifts for her.'

'And maybe we should do it somewhere else? Like, I was thinking that place we found, where she died?'

'I guess so.' Charlie frowned slightly. Technically she wasn't allowed outside of the campsite without at least one older family member, but also, how would they know? She and Emily would go to the field, leave their offering, and

115

be back again before they got called in for tea. It would be easy.

That day was a beach day for Charlie, and she didn't see Emily for much of it, but she kept an eye out for things to take to the field that evening. In a zipped pocket in her rucksack she put the best shells she could find, a few of the shinys from Darren's football sticker collection, and a small plastic horse she'd stolen from Jenny – she felt momentarily bad about this, but her cousin had tons of the brightly coloured toys. She still had the packet of matches, which no one had noticed were gone.

Later, when they had all trawled home from the beach, tired and windblown and slightly sunburned, she announced to the rest of the family that she was going out to play with Emily.

'She's out all the time lately,' observed her nan, who was already propped on the sofa with her shoes off and a cross-word puzzle book on her lap. 'Barely seen hide nor hair of her.'

'She's made a little friend, haven't you, Charlie?' Her mum smiled at her as she wiped her hands on a tea towel. Behind her mother she could see her sister Carol making a face and mouthing '*a little fwend*'. 'It's good, keeps her out of trouble. And Emily looks like she could use the company. Never seen a lonelier looking kid.'

'Yeah all right, see you later.'

'Tea's in about an hour, okay?'

Outside there was still plenty of sunshine to be had, and the campsite swing park was full of kids. Charlie met Emily by the slides, both carrying rucksacks and both grinning with secrets.

'Let's see what we've got.'

They found a quiet spot on the edge of the wooded area

and shared the contents of their bags. Emily had brought more of her dad's tobacco, and even a navy blue sock of his. Then to Charlie's surprise she brought out a small jam jar, empty save for something spidery and grey.

'Ugh, what's that?'

'A crane fly. See?' Emily held it out to her. 'I caught it in the shower block. I thought that maybe Stitch Face Sue would want something . . . alive. I don't know.'

'Like she's a spider,' Charlie said uneasily. The crane fly buzzed angrily inside the jar. Holding it, it was just possible to feel the faint vibrations through the glass.

Feeling extremely daring, they left the campsite together, holding hands. By that time the sun was easing its way towards the horizon, and the day was starting to feel cooler. The sky was dotted with clouds dipped in orange, and Charlie and Emily became two small shadows on the road. The liquid sound of blackbird song seemed to leak from every hedge.

Uncertain how to get there otherwise, they walked all the way up into the town of Hithechurch, then down onto the beach and up the rough path along the sea wall. Earlier in the day the beach had been heaving with holidaymakers, but now there were only a few people left – mostly adults and teenagers, enjoying the sunset. Charlie felt a strange thrill. No one knew where they were. They had their own business to do tonight.

By the time they found it, the sun was heading down. To their left, the sea was a vast glittering strip of movement, but the field was quiet and still. The rocks with their squiggles of graffiti were just where they'd left them.

'How about a pentacle this time?'

'A what?'

Charlie grabbed a stick and began to draw a large and slightly wonky star shape in the sandy dirt. She had seen diagrams of pentacles before in *The Braeburn Book of Ghosts*.

'Do you have the matches?'

'Yep.'

They put their treasures into the middle section of the star. Charlie stole a quick glance at the other girl's face. Emily's lips were drawn into a thin line and her brow was furrowed, as though she was in the middle of an exam. The sun had vanished into the gathering of clouds waiting at the horizon, and darkness was settling over the field. For the first time, Charlie's excitement was replaced with unease. She pulled a larger plastic torch from her bag (this one 'borrowed' from Darren) and clicked it on. It only made the field seem even darker, so she pointed its light onto their pentacle with its odd collection of items.

'The sun's gone down, so I suppose now is the time.' Her voice sounded very small. She cleared her throat. 'Do you know what you're asking for?'

Emily nodded.

Charlie got the matches out of her pocket and sat poised with the match against the striking pad.

'Stitch Face Sue, we're calling on you once more . . .' She paused and cleared her throat again. The breeze had picked up, blowing in colder air from across the sea. 'We're calling on you for help. Please, accept our gifts and listen to our words. We have come here, to the place where you died, hoping that you'll be able to hear us more clearly.' She cast around for something else to say. 'We, your humble servants, ask for your help.'

She struck the match. This time, out in the open, its light looked puny and uncertain. Opposite her she saw Emily's lips moving as she said her own silent prayer, and then suddenly the girl leaned over and snatched the glass jar out of the pentacle. In one jerking motion she yanked the lid off and tipped the crane fly out against the rock. Charlie saw it move, long legs almost appearing to float over the stone, and then Emily's hand squashed it flat.

A bare second later, the match burned Charlie's fingers and she dropped it.

'Ow!'

'Are you all right?'

'What did you do that for?' Charlie rubbed her sore fingers on her shorts. 'You killed it.'

Emily looked down at her hand. In the torchlight it looked very white, but it was possible to see a smear of something grey and unpleasant across her palm. She frowned.

'It seemed like the right thing to do. Like Stitch Face Sue would want it.'

'Why would she want a dead bug?' Charlie lowered her voice. She wasn't so much annoyed by the crane fly sacrifice as she was frightened by the suddenness of it. Emily had made her jump, and she was already on edge. 'It's just gross.'

To her surprise, Emily's face began to crumple. Hurriedly, Charlie leaned over and squeezed her arm.

'No, I think you're right. Like we said before, it's like feeding a spider. This gives Sue a sort of starter before the main meal. Before . . .' She skirted around saying it. *Before she gets rid of your dad*. 'Let's bury this stuff, okay?'

Emily rubbed at her eye with the heel of her hand. 'Why?'

'Because it'll be closer to her. Think about it – when she died here, her blood soaked down into the ground and that's where her ghost comes from now.'

In the end, they only managed to cover the items with a small layer of sandy mud, but Charlie pronounced it good enough. By that time it was full dark, and the beach was empty. They took each other's hands again and began to walk back.

That night, Charlie could not sleep. She shared a room with her cousin Jenny and her Auntie Beverly, who were both snoring merrily away, but every time she lay down and closed her eyes alarming images spun around her head; the photos of Emily's sister with her bruises; the pale shape of Emily's hand against the stone, and the flat noise it made as she slapped the crane fly into oblivion.

Eventually, she sat up. The slim cot she slept in was crammed up against the window, so she pulled the net curtain aside and peeped out. Outside she could see the strip of grass between their caravan and the next, all lit with bright fluorescent lights that leached the colour from everything. There was no one in the caravan opposite, so the curtains were open in their windows, showing a flat, black nothing.

She thought about the dog that had bitten Emily's dad. Where had it come from? Was it really just a stray wandering down the road, or did it belong to someone on the campsite? Or maybe it really was a kind of ghost dog, sent by Stitch Face Sue to do her bidding. For a time she amused herself by breathing onto the window and drawing in the vapour. She drew a dog's snarling face, big long fangs and a spiky collar.

Something moved outside. There was a person walking around the corner of the caravan opposite. Automatically, Charlie ducked out of sight – she didn't want to be caught spying on any drunk adults making their way back from the local pub – and she watched from the very edge of the window.

The person was moving slowly, and they wore a long skirt that came all the way down to their ankles. And perhaps they *were* drunk, because they were shuffling and lurching, as though they weren't used to using their legs. It was a woman, and her hair was very long and untidy, covering her face, and now she was turning and coming towards the window. Everything about her was grey.

Charlie had been truly frightened a few times before. When her grandad had been angry with her, or it was 3 a.m. and she'd been reading scary books before bed. But those were scary things with boundaries; deep in her heart, she knew she wasn't in danger, not from her grandad and not from the scary things in her book. This was different. It gave her a cold, terrible feeling in her chest, making it hard to breathe.

The figure shuffled forwards, inch by inch. Charlie crouched, frozen in place. Now the woman was closer, Charlie could see that she was wearing a ragged, stained cardigan, and there was dust in her hair. Dust, and something else.

A crane fly.

Charlie bit down on a shriek. As if it heard her anyway, the figure outside lifted its head. Its face, if that's what it could be called, was a jigsaw of strange, disjointed pieces, crusted and held together with wide, ugly stitches. It looked in at Charlie with eyes lost in thick ridges of scar tissue, and it smiled.

Charlie screamed the place down.

Chapter 18

Now

At around ten to seven I found myself walking slowly up towards the small campsite shop. It was a little like being in a dream; my head was making all sorts of reasonable arguments as to why this was an enormously bad idea, yet my legs were moving, taking one plodding stride after another regardless. It was full dark already, and the lampposts that lit up the path gave off a yellow light that seemed to hang in the air like a solid thing, holding the night unnaturally still. My mind kept returning to Emily's book, which Watkins had offered to show me. Every day, I knew, was a day closer to that book being out in the world, and then . . . And then my life would effectively be over. And I still hadn't found what we had buried. I resolved to put it out of my mind for the evening. *Try to enjoy yourself*, I thought firmly.

Katie, unsurprisingly, hadn't wanted to come, and I couldn't blame her – at that age would I have been interested in spending the evening watching two adults make small talk? Absolutely not. In the end I'd made her tea early and left her reading a book; she had a tablet too – a thing that seemed almost magical to me – and with that she could text me if she wanted anything.

When I got to the shop I stopped. The lights were off in the front part, but I could see an open door in the back, and I could just make out a small stove, a pan on top of it leaking steam. It looked very cosy, but now that I was there, it was like my feet had taken root. The idea of taking those last steps and knocking on the door felt ludicrous. Who did I think I was, exactly? Much better to—

'Oh, Sarah, there you are!'

A figure appeared from behind me. For an alarming second, I couldn't see his face, but then he stepped out of the shadows and there was Joseph, smiling like it was the middle of a summer's day and not a pitch-black night in the middle of January. He was wiping his hands on a cloth. I swallowed hard on the strangled noise that threatened to leap out of my throat. My heart was pounding.

'Am I early?'

'What? No, just a couple of things I forgot to sort out. No fear, dinner is cooking. Come on.' He unlocked the shop door, and we stepped through. Once inside, I could smell something rich and warm, something with spices.

'I thought you said jacket potato?'

'Ah, well.' Joseph looked rueful as he waved me towards the back room. 'Baked potato is good for me on a lonely night doing nothing, but when I have company I like to show off a bit. You caught me out. I hope you like curry? Christ, you're not vegetarian, are you?'

Despite myself – heart still skipping along sickly in my chest – I laughed.

'I'm not, don't worry. Curry sounds brilliant.'

The room out back was nicer than I was expecting. There

was a stove, a sink, a small fridge, a battered but clean looking kitchen table, and three mismatched chairs. The lino on the floor was old but very clean, and there was a framed Guinness advert on the wall.

'All right, first of all, don't look at that,' said Joseph, pointing at the picture. 'I bloody hate it but my uncle thinks it's hilarious. Sit down. What do you want to drink? There's tea, coffee, squash, wine, beer – no Guinness you'll be glad to hear – I think there's a Coke in the fridge . . .'

'A glass of wine would be great.' This, I felt immediately, was a mistake, but Joseph just nodded and filled two glasses. He paused to poke at the pan on the stove, then came and sat at the table.

'Your . . . niece, was it? Your niece didn't want to come?' He sounded neutral, neither surprised nor especially interested.

'Yeah, Katie, she wanted to watch a film on the telly . . . You know what kids are like.'

He shrugged. 'I've got four brothers, so I feel like I know far too much about what kids are like.'

'*Four* brothers?'

'Aye, I'm the second youngest.' He shook his head, as though wondering how he'd ever ended up with so many siblings, as though brothers were athlete's foot or parking fines. 'It's not bad being one of the middle kids – you get away with a lot because no one takes much notice. So . . . do you have a brother, a sister?'

'A sister. Older.' What could I say about Carol, exactly? 'Old enough that she didn't take much notice of me, either. When we were kids.' I paused. The last time I had seen Carol we had both been very tense. *Oh yeah, I have an older sister, she went a good five years without speaking to me and once pretended not to know who I was on the street.* I tried instead to think about what *Sarah's* sister would be like; that was easier somehow. 'She's a teacher. Very clever. She was the clever one, I was the likeable one.'

Once the curry was dished up – along with fluffy white rice and a store-bought naan bread – we sat for a couple of minutes in a slightly awkward silence. I ate a few mouthfuls of curry, barely tasting it through my own terror. Joseph seemed unconcerned though, and I stole small glances at him up through my eyelashes as he ate. He was wearing a clean white shirt with the sleeves rolled up, and I could see tiny bits of other tattoos peeking up behind his loose collar. He had long fingers, clean hands with the small scars of someone who worked outside a lot. He'd obviously shaved for the occasion, but even so there was a bluish shadow to his jaw. It was all alarmingly appealing.

'So,' he said eventually. 'Did you . . . go to uni? Study marine biology in the Antarctic? Spend your twenties in the Cayman Islands for tax reasons? How did you get into writing?'

I laughed, but inside a trapdoor had suddenly dropped open. I'd thought about this, of course; had considered every possible part of Sarah's identity on the off chance someone in the street demanded to know my work history or whether I'd flunked or passed my GCSEs, but now, faced with a real person wanting to know, everything I'd conjured up sounded ludicrous. I cleared my throat and, buying myself some time, took a big gulp of the wine.

'You don't have to answer if you don't want to,' Joseph said apologetically. 'It's been so boring here lately I'm desperate to hear from anyone who isn't from Hithechurch.'

I saw my opportunity and clutched after it like a drowning woman.

'You're not from here though, are you? Do you have family in the area?'

'Oh, I've family all over.' He reached over to top up my

wine glass. 'In Swansea, mostly. A couple of my uncles are big in caravans, if that doesn't sound too daft, and we've ended up having a more active hand in a few little parks like this. Mind you, it's mainly me who's doing the active bit these days, and that usually seems to involve mud or cutting grass or fixing fences. In the summer it's not so bad, plenty of people around to chat to, plenty of work to do, but in the off season? I'm really just here to make sure kids don't get in and tag the caravans. The language on the little bastards, honestly.' He broke off, and smiled. 'It's nice to have company for once.'

'Do you find it gets spooky here, in the winter?' The question was out before I even had time to think about it. 'I mean, it gets dark so early, and . . .'

'You mean the stuff that happened here years ago?' He looked away from me for a second. 'Yeah, this place has a slightly dark history. My uncle is always trying to stop us talking about it. He thinks if everyone shuts up people will forget.' He shrugged. 'I reckon you go back far enough, everywhere has a dark history.'

My throat felt frozen solid, as though I'd been eating cement instead of curry. I could feel the colour draining from my face. *Any second now, any second now and he'll look at my face and this time he'll see it, he can't not see—*

'Jesus, are you all right?' He put his wine glass down, his lively black eyebrows crawling up his forehead. 'You're not going to be sick, are you?'

'No!' I managed to gasp, and smile. 'No, sorry, I've been feeling a bit under the weather lately, I probably shouldn't have even come over here.'

He waved that away. 'I'm a tough lad, I can take it. Can I get you a glass of water or anything?'

His apparently genuine concern calmed me, and I made

126

myself smile at him. 'I'm fine, honestly. Thank you, by the way, for leading me to Stan. He was very entertaining.'

'Oh, he is that!' Joseph laughed into his glass of wine. 'Did he give you plenty of material for your book?'

'He did. I'll probably go back and bother him again before we leave. There are so many stories, you know, hidden in every small town.' I curled my hands around my wine glass. The alcohol was doing its secret work, making me relaxed, even drowsy. 'I think it's incredible. All these stories people carry around in their heads. He told me one about a beauty queen who had a terrible accident in the funfair. Do you know that one?'

He nodded. 'I do. Technically that family still owns the funfair.'

I sat up, a little surprised. 'They are real then? I mean, the beauty queen was a real person?'

'Yep. Old Rosalind Stimpson. She became a recluse, I think. No one has seen her for years. It makes the story even more impressive, doesn't it? Her face got torn off, so she became, I don't know, the Phantom of the Opera of Kent, or whatever.'

I snorted into my curry. 'You must know everyone here. Are there any more people like Stan? People who've been here forever, I mean. Old timers who have all the stories. The more people I can talk to like that, the better.'

'I can scare up a few names, I reckon.' Joseph drained the last of his wine, and poured us both some more. 'But if you don't mind a bit of friendly advice?'

'Not at all.'

'Don't be surprised if some of them aren't inclined to tell you all that much. This stuff with Cheryl Yates, it's made people skittish. Defensive, I suppose you'd say.'

'Why is that?' Cheryl's name brought some of my disquiet back.

127

'Like I said before, dark histories.' He sighed, looking down at his empty plate. 'People don't want to believe terrible things can happen in little seaside towns like this one, but the history proves them wrong, doesn't it? People have gone missing before.'

I nodded, suddenly unable to meet his eyes. I had finished my curry too, and I placed my knife and fork carefully across the plate.

Joseph stood up, reaching over to clear the dishes away. 'Look, I've got a lemon meringue pie for afters. Do you fancy it? It's probably shit but I got some squirty cream to cover it up.'

Later, he insisted on walking me back to the caravan, which I was actually rather glad about, since by that point I had had more wine in one night than I'd ever had before in my life. It was a strange, detached feeling, as though if I didn't concentrate on the path ahead of us I might just float off into the night.

It also distracted me from the fact that I was walking, alone, in the dark, with a man who had asked me to dinner.

'Thank you,' I said. 'For the curry. And the pie. It was good actually.'

'Can't beat Tesco's Finest range,' said Joseph, and then we sniggered about that for a bit. 'Really, though,' he said eventually, 'I should thank you. I wasn't kidding about it getting boring here in January. You've been a great distraction.'

My face felt very hot suddenly. Up ahead, I could see the lights of our caravan. With every other one around it dark, it looked strange, like a film set, or something out of an Edward Hopper painting.

'Listen,' I said, and then, 'Look.' I stopped and looked up at him. I felt dizzy again, but in a slightly different way. 'Do you want to come in for a nightcap?'

He looked down at me. I wondered if he was more sober than me, because he suddenly looked quite serious.

'Well . . . What about your niece?'

'Oh.' I looked over to the caravan, as though Katie might be peeking out through the net curtains, and when I turned back he took my hand and kissed the back of it. His lips were warm against my cold skin, and I felt suddenly full of warmth myself, as though he'd passed it on to me. It was such a quaint gesture, and all the more charming for it.

'Maybe another time, yeah?'

When I got back inside the caravan, Katie had changed into her pyjamas and had eaten an entire packet of Pop Tarts; the debris was spread all across the dining table in sugary bits.

'What are you grinning about?' she asked me.

'Shut up,' I said. 'And go and brush your teeth.'

Chapter 19

July 1988

'It serves you right, doesn't it? Staying out late and putting the wind up everyone. Of course you had nightmares. Overstimulated, that's what she is. It's all those weird books and cartoons.'

Charlie kept her head down, letting this lecture from her nan pass over her head – she knew it was largely directed towards her mum, anyway. She was drinking sweet hot tea, a bowl of Coco Pops untouched in front of her. Luckily for her, the focus of the family had moved on to a different drama: Auntie Marj and Auntie Beverly had had a row, resulting in one of them locking themselves in the toilet and crying that morning. Now the caravan was simmering in an uncharacteristic silence, and Charlie's mother especially looked exhausted by it all.

Later that morning, when Darren proposed going to the funfair in town, she looked relieved – an uncomfortable silence was always worse the more people were sharing it. So Darren, Carol, Jenny and Charlie were shooed out of the caravan door into another blisteringly hot day. When Charlie asked if they could knock for Emily, her sister and Darren exchanged a look. As the eldest, Carol shrugged agreement.

'One more brat makes no difference.'

Hovering outside Emily's caravan, Charlie had felt nervous. What if Emily's father answered? What if he didn't, because Stitch Face Sue had come for him in the night, snipping open his belly with her vicious scissors? She thought of the figure that had slipped past her window in the night. By the time the adults had looked out of the window – Auntie Beverly got there first, her hair sticking up on one side – there had been no one out there at all, and it had been dismissed as a night-mare. But it hadn't felt like a dream. Not at all.

When the door opened, it was Emily. She looked even more forlorn than ever, and for a second or two she hung in the door frame, looking blank. It frightened Charlie; it reminded her of Emily's dad.

'Hey. Can you come out? To the fair? We're all going.'

Emily looked up slowly, taking in the small group standing off to one side. She nodded once, leaned back in to grab her backpack, and they left. Charlie noticed she didn't call out to either of her parents to let them know where she was going.

When they were out on the road, they fell into pairs; Darren and Carol at the front, Charlie and Emily at the rear – and Jenny in the middle, walking by herself. When they were a sufficient distance from the other kids, Emily spoke, her voice flat.

'It didn't work,' she said. 'My dad's fine this morning. Although his hand is sore and still bandaged up from the dog bite.'

Charlie considered this in silence for a few moments. Serious introspection was not easy for her, but she was dimly aware of an inner conflict. She knew, deep down, that many of the stories she spread around her family or made up on the spot were not real, or were only a version of the truth. Yet she also knew what she had seen outside the caravan in the early hours of the morning. She felt like an unexpected tide had come in, lifting her up and away from the usual rules and depositing her on some new ledge, where the view was very different.

'Listen,' she said quietly, her eyes on the road. 'I think it *did* work though. Sort of.'

'What? How?'

'I saw her. Stitch Face Sue.' To avoid meeting Emily's startled glance, she pulled a green baseball cap from her rucksack and fitted it firmly on her head. The sun was fierce. 'I saw her outside our caravan.'

'Are you making this up?' Emily sounded suddenly close to tears, so Charlie grabbed her hand quickly, and squeezed it.

'I promise I'm not.'

'What happened? What was she like?'

Ahead of them, Darren and Carol were laughing about something, trying to elbow each other into the ditch.

'She had long hair, and there was dust and cobwebs all over her. Her face was like . . .' Charlie's mind seemed to slip over the face. It was too close to something that would appear on the cover of a horror film videotape. 'Her skin was weird. And there was a crane fly in her hair too.'

Emily's eyebrows shot up. 'The crane fly we gave her!'

'Yeah.'

'Then we are doing it right – or at least, we've got part of it right.' All the life had come back to Emily's face. Her cheeks were flushed. 'We've just got to try again, but change things a bit.'

'Are you sure you want to?' When Emily frowned at her,

132

Charlie shrugged. 'You didn't see her. She was . . . I don't know. Really scary. I thought she was going to reach in through the window somehow and drag me out.'

'That's daft,' said Emily mildly. 'We're her friends, aren't we? We're the ones giving her stuff. She wouldn't hurt us.'

'But your dad . . .' Charlie trailed off, not quite sure what she intended to say.

'My dad.' Emily rolled up the sleeve of her T-shirt. At the top of her arm was a trio of fingertip-shaped bruises, clearly fresh ones. Charlie pursed her lips. 'My dad should meet her,' said Emily. 'He definitely should.'

Just ahead of them, Jenny tripped up and went crashing down onto the concrete, the small plastic horse she'd been carrying flying off into the grass. There was a single second of stunned silence before she began to wail. Darren and Carol came trotting back, their faces set in identical expressions of rueful guilt. For the rest of the walk, they walked together, and Charlie and Emily kept their plans to themselves.

When they arrived at the funfair, Darren and Carol peeled off towards the slots, and Charlie, Emily and Jenny began to wander around the rides, weaving in and out of clumps of families and feeling the full force of the summer sun on the tops of their heads. They pooled together some twenty-pence pieces and bought a bag of pink candyfloss from one of the booths, and were soon giddy with sugar, their fingertips and tongues bright pink.

Round near the back of the amusement arcade, Charlie spotted a brightly coloured van. The back doors were open, and the tall man from the slots was crouched to one side of it, painstakingly painting a cartoon character. It was Donald Duck, but Donald Duck if his face had melted a little. She and Emily wandered a little closer, Jenny trailing behind as usual.

She had the last bit of candyfloss clutched in her hand; it had turned into a wad of pink crystals.

Silently, Emily raised her hand and pointed to the character above Donald Duck, a kind of warped yellow boy. She and Charlie exchanged a look and giggled behind their hands.

'*Bort Sormpson*,' said Charlie, in a wobbly high-pitched voice. The man stood up slowly. The look he gave them was not friendly.

'What do you kids want?'

'You need to check your spelling,' said Emily brightly. Charlie looked at her in surprise. 'It's cowabunga, with a "u", not cowabooonga.'

The man's brow pulled slowly downwards into a frown. The hand that gripped the paintbrush curled into a fist. Charlie glanced over her shoulder at the wider funfair; although they stood out of the way of the main crowd, there were still plenty of people about. It was too bright and sunny a day for anything bad to happen. Out here, with the taste of candyfloss in her mouth, the memory of Stitch Face Sue outside her window felt much less vivid.

'I don't need no brats telling me my job,' hissed the man. 'Now go and play in the sea.'

Charlie edged away and glanced into the back of the van. The inside of it was much less colourful than the outside. She saw grey and brown offcuts of carpet on the floor, all of them stained, a bunch of old plastic bags, and, oddly, several big tubs of face cream. Charlie recognised it as the same brand that her nan always slapped on her face before bed – thick and greasy and white, she said it kept her wrinkles at bay, despite evidence to the contrary.

'Oi, you!' Suddenly the man was in front of her, pushing her away with a sharp poke in the chest. 'Nosey little sods.

Aren't you the kid I chased out of the slots the other day? Yeah, some little ginger brat.'

'Watch it!' Emily stepped up next to Charlie, her pale face pinched with fury. Abruptly, Charlie felt more afraid of her than the man. Behind them Jenny was whining, insisting that they go and find Darren and Carol. 'You leave us alone, we're only looking!'

'Get out of it, the lot of you.' The man slammed the van doors, making them jump. 'Or do you want me to drag you out of here, too?'

'I said watch it!' Emily made an odd movement, and there was a small penknife in her hand. Charlie blinked, then turned to see if Jenny had seen it, but her cousin had her back to them, no doubt looking for other family members.

'Emily . . .' She placed her hand hesitantly on the other girl's shoulder. 'Let's just go.'

'He needs to watch it or we'll hex him!' said Emily. The tall man's demeanour had changed, however. He was looking at the knife, and he was smiling.

'Oh, that's a pretty little piece you have there, girl,' he said. There was a soft, dangerous tone to his voice Charlie didn't like. 'Where'd you nick that from? Your brother? Your dad?'

'Come *on*.' Charlie pulled on her shoulder, and the expression on Emily's face flickered, as though she'd walked into a room and forgotten what she was there for. Once Charlie had persuaded her to come away from the funfair van, the other girl made the penknife vanish again. Jenny had wandered off some distance and was blowing her nose.

'Where *did* you get it from?' asked Charlie nervously. 'Having a knife is . . .' Her words trailed off. She often got into trouble with her mum, usually for lying, but sometimes for other things; breaking stuff that wasn't hers, stealing biscuits out of the cupboard before dinner. But having a knife was a whole new magnitude of trouble.

'I've had it for ages,' said Emily, and when she glanced up at Charlie her expression was back to its more usual bashful smile. 'I brought it with me for our next *ritual*. It's important to me, so I thought it'd be a good, you know, gift. For her.'

'Yeah,' Charlie said, trying to sound more certain than she felt. 'Good idea.'

The three girls made their way to the teacup ride, and all the way round it, that knife was weighing on Charlie's mind. A boy Darren's age carrying a penknife, that she could imagine. But Emily? The thought of it was slippery, unnerving somehow.

When they got off the ride, all feeling a little ill from the swirling and the dipping of the teacups, Emily seemed a little more herself. They wandered into the amusements, all blinking as their eyes adjusted to the gloom. Jenny went over to the grabbing machine to stare at the plush unicorn toys inside, and Emily and Charlie moved to the back wall, where all the video games were lined up. Walls of brightly coloured pixels flashed at them rhythmically.

'What shall we do next? For Stitch Face Sue?' asked Emily.

'Well.' Charlie leaned against a tall arcade console, slapping the red and yellow buttons with the palms of her hands. 'We've got her attention, haven't we? Like we've almost got it right, these last two rituals.'

It's a game, she thought to herself. Press the right buttons, win the game. Don't think about figures outside your window, or the knife in your friend's backpack.

'So,' she said, 'we got a dog to bite your dad, and we got Stitch Face Sue to . . . appear. We know she likes presents, things that are important to us.'

'And the match,' said Emily thoughtfully. 'And the pentagram thing. So, a little fire, presents in the pentagram.'

'And us, thinking summoning thoughts,' said Charlie. She grinned. 'Maybe we need to think harder.'

'Or we need more of us,' said Emily. 'More of us believing at once.'

'I was thinking about that,' added Charlie, although it had only just occurred to her. 'This is the best time to do it, isn't it? It's *Pirate* Week. Everyone in Hithechurch is thinking about Stitch Face Sue. It's the anniversary of it all happening, so her ghost will be at its most awake, and it'll want to do justice. Probably if we were here at any other time of year it wouldn't work at all.'

Emily's eyes lit up. 'Do you really think so?'

'Yeah,' Charlie nodded. 'It makes sense, doesn't it? Ghosts always remember when they were killed. So we've got to do it again tonight, I reckon, so we don't miss out. *And,*' she added, glancing over at the claw machine, 'we'll get Jenny to come too.'

Emily looked sceptical. 'Your cousin?'

'I know she's a div, but she'll do whatever we tell her to. And she's good at believing in ghosts and that. Maybe it's the push we need, to get Stitch Face Sue to . . . do what we want.'

'All right.' Emily rubbed her arm where the fresh bruise was. 'Let's do it. And I'll bring my knife.'

Chapter 20

Now

The coffee morning was well under way when we got there. It wasn't taking place in the church itself, but in a small cosy building to one side of it. The foyer was covered in posters advertising local services, and pictures drawn by schoolchildren that encouraged you to recycle and pick up your litter. In the main room, there was a number of tables and chairs dotted about, and along the back, a trestle table heaving with home-made cakes and several coffee urns. A number of older people were seated at the tables, sipping steaming teas and carefully holding slices of lemon drizzle cake with napkins. There was a low-level buzz of chatter. Somewhere, a radio was playing BBC Radio 2.

I gave Katie a couple of quid to buy us some cakes from the stall and headed over towards a woman standing next to a table covered in leaflets. A lanky boy of about seventeen or eighteen was furiously typing away on his phone. I thought there was a good chance this was Jack.

'Hello, Jack is it?' I smiled at the boy, who looked startled, and then his mother, who was glaring at me with open suspicion. 'My name is Sarah, and I'm writing a book about the area. I've spoken to your work colleague Stanley? From the Smuggler's Cove?' I glanced between them, hoping some of this was making sense. Jack looked entirely nonplussed, his thumbs poised over his phone screen. 'I wondered, Jack, if I could ask you about working at the Cove?'

'What for?' snapped his mother, before Jack could speak.

'A bit of local colour, that's all,' I beamed at her, trying to project 'harmless' and 'good-natured' through my very eyeballs. 'It's good to hear from different age groups.'

The woman glanced at her son. 'It's up to you, Jackie.'

The kid shrugged, and we wandered a few feet away from the table.

'So, Jack. How long have you been working at the Smuggler's Cove?'

He looked up at me finally. He was a good-looking kid, with an artfully tousled mess of black hair on top of his head, a tiny gold hoop in one ear. Had earrings become fashionable for boys again? I had no idea. He had that slightly gangly, all knees and elbows look of a boy that was still growing, but one day when his shoulders filled out he would be a real heartbreaker. The look he was giving me was flatly hostile.

'Just the last two years,' he said. 'During the summer.'

'Do you enjoy it?'

He shrugged. 'It's a job, innit.'

I nodded as though this were a fascinating observation.

'And will you go back there this summer?'

At this he glanced back at his mum, who was pretending not to be watching us.

'I dunno,' he said. 'Mum thinks . . . Well, after this last year, she thinks I should get a proper job. Out of town, maybe. The big B&Q is always looking for people in the summer.'

I shifted my weight slightly so that his lanky frame hid me from his mother. I lowered my voice, just a bit.

'Is that because of the girl who went missing, Jack? Cheryl Yates? Stan said he remembered the family coming to the Smuggler's Cove.'

'Yeah, well . . . Yeah, she was there. With her little cousins.'

I nodded. Of course he remembered. She was a pretty blonde girl, and I imagined that one of the few excitements for a teen living in a seaside town was checking out the holiday talent.

'Did you see her there a lot? Did you ever see her talking to anyone outside of her family?'

I saw immediately that I had pushed it too hard with the questions. His face closed up, and his eyes flickered back to his phone. He was frowning.

'I already spoke to the police, all right?'

'I know, but—'

At that moment, a small figure stepped in between us, and I found myself looking down into the face of a diminutive old woman. Her hair was a clear bright white, no hint of yellow, and it was cropped into an elegant pixie cut. Her eyes twinkled up at me as she inserted herself into our conversation.

'Are you talking about that girl? Oh god it's *terrible*, isn't it? *Disgusting*. No one is safe now, not even people on their holidays – mind you, you'd think we'd know better than that around here, wouldn't you? I remember when we didn't lock our doors, when people were in and out of each other's houses day and night, but even then things were going wrong, weren't they? Oh yes, lots of *disgusting* things going on everywhere, but no one talks about them. I'm Joan, nice to meet you, did you say you were writing a book?'

I blinked rapidly. Jack looked appalled, and had even taken

half a step back, but my heart was racing. This was what I wanted. This was what I needed. But did I have the guts to do it?

'Yes,' I said, 'a book about the local area. It's nice to meet you, Joan. I'd love to hear more about it, if you have the time?'

'Sweetheart,' Joan fixed one freezing cold hand around my wrist and squeezed. 'All I have is time! What do you want to know? About the girl and her family? They were down from Chelmsford, the parents hadn't long got back together after splitting up, and you know that causes all sorts of tensions, and supposedly the girl was a bit of a so-and-so at school – you know the type.'

'Cheryl,' I said, feeling a spike of annoyance. 'Her name is Cheryl.'

'Yes, but she isn't the first, is she?' Joan sounded oddly triumphant now. She had dropped my wrist and crossed her arms under her tiny bosom. 'Not the first *at all*.'

'What do you mean? Who else is there?'

'Well. There was a local girl, her name was Natalie. I don't rightly remember the year – no, wait, I was pregnant with my second, I do remember that, so it must have been 1968. Her mother is still in that Terrarium Home on the seafront, poor woman, the stress of it quite scattered her marbles. Gawd, she must be in her eighties by now . . . Mrs Price, that was her name. And then there were two other girls, Sophie and Alison, both on holiday, both vanished. I remember because my girls were small at the time, and it scared me silly.' She caught the look on my face and raised her eyebrows. 'See? I bet you didn't know all that.'

'When was this?'

'In the 70s, both of them, don't remember rightly which years, but my Marie was still at infant school so that would have been . . .' She trailed off, defeated by the maths of it, then regrouped. 'And there was all that stuff a few years later, in the eighties. Now that was *disgusting.*'

My heart seemed to stop in my chest, a cold lump of foreboding.

'What was that?' I had to force the words out, like little stones between my teeth. 'What happened?'

'Oh, you can't have missed it, love, it was all over the news!' Joan was opening her handbag and retrieving a slice of cake she had apparently hidden inside it earlier. 'Very nasty business, but can't have been related to what's going on now. Still, makes you wonder, doesn't it? And it's all in the news again now, which no one round here wants, believe me. They want to forget about it.'

I thought about Emily's book, and Watkins' letter. *If you want to stop her, find what you buried together.*

'Were you here? When it happened?' My face felt very hot, and the back of my neck was prickling. I imagined that everyone in the room had turned to look at us.

'Actually I wasn't, my love. Those were the years when Bernie and me started to go to Florida for our holidays. Three weeks of glorious sunshine, it was *fantastic.* Heard all about it when we came back though, didn't we?'

'Do you know . . .' I cleared my throat. 'Do you know if there's anyone I can talk to about it? Who was actually here when it happened?'

'*Hmph.*' I realised I had annoyed Joan by suggesting that her testimony wasn't good enough. 'Not as many as you might think. A lot of people moved away in the early 90s, you see. And I've heard that *her* family still lives in Allcot, which isn't far from here. The Stimpsons, that's who you want, although now that I think about it, they're mostly all dead, as far as I know. Harald though, he's still around, he used to work for them . . .' She trailed off, and a lot of the cheer seemed to drop out of her face. 'Yeah, that one's still around.'

'Where could I find him?'

'Oh he'll be around the funfair,' she said. 'You'll have seen him, with his ugly van. Hard to miss. Or at the caves – he does a bit of maintenance up there, too.'

My stomach pitched a slow roll, like a ship at sea when the storm is coming in. The funfair man. I had no reason to think it, but somehow I knew it was the same person.

'Thank you,' I said. 'I'll definitely—'

'Who are you, anyway?' said a sharp voice. Jack's mother had reappeared, and she was looking at me in a way that turned my blood to ice. 'What business is it of yours?'

'She's writing a book, Paula,' said Joan, helpfully. 'About Hithechurch.'

'Thank you so much for your time, all of you,' I said, already backing away. Paula was still staring at me, and it felt like at any moment I would see her eyes widen slightly in recognition, see her mouth open with fury . . . 'I must be going, I'm afraid, but you've been so helpful. Katie? Time to get lunch.'

Chapter 21

Now

'I don't know why we had to come all the way here for Chinese food.'

'It's an all-you-can-eat buffet, Katie, that's why. Are you going to eat that spring roll?'

Folkesholme was essentially a larger version of Hithechurch, with more high street shops and a few chain restaurants, and I was glad to be there. After my unsettling conversation with Paula and Joan, it was a relief to be away.

'When I was a kid, I'd have killed for an all-you-can-eat Chinese buffet.' I speared the last spring roll with a chopstick.

'The one round the corner at home is better.'

When we'd eaten as much as we physically could, we took a slow walk down the high street. The rain had cleared away along with the heavier clouds – the weather always did change quickly on the coast – and it had become bitterly cold instead. I pulled my hat down over my ears as I waited for Katie outside a Claire's Accessories. I was hoping that she wouldn't ask to have her ears pierced – this definitely wasn't something

I was qualified to be responsible for – when an old lady in a thick padded coat handed me a flyer.

'We haven't given up hope on our Cheryl,' she said. 'There's a phone number on the flyer, my love, if you've seen or heard anything.'

There were two photos of Cheryl on the flyer, one of which I recognised from the newspaper coverage. The other was a school photo, where she wore a dark blue blazer and a striped tie. Underneath it was a short paragraph about where and when she had gone missing, along with a phone number and an email address.

'Are you a family member?'

'Oh no, love, bless you, I'm local – I'm just helping out.' The old woman nodded to a stall further down the pedestri-anised street. 'That's her family, there. They've been here since she went, poor sods. They say the police have done bugger all so they're looking for her as best they can.'

When the old woman had wandered off to press a flyer on another shopper, I folded the piece of paper and put it in my pocket. Katie appeared at that moment, pulling her hood up over her head.

'Can we go to the slots now?'

'Hold on, there's a few more places I want to visit.'

The front of the trestle table had a big banner across it, reading 'BRING CHERYL HOME' alongside a blown-up photo-graph of the girl. The table itself had more flyers and posters for people to take and put up in their shops, as well as a petition. Sitting behind the stall was a frail-looking woman with sore, red eyes; she sat with her hands folded neatly in her lap, while two larger blokes stood and spoke with anyone that would listen. As I lingered there, one of them, a big man with ruddy cheeks, held out the petition towards me.

'Would you mind signing this, love?'

I took it. 'What's it for?'

'We want to get a permanent space in the market that's here on Saturdays.' The man gestured up the road. 'The council won't have it, because they think it'll put people off their shopping or whatever, but it'll help us reach more locals. And the more people we reach, the better chance we have of finding Cheryl.'

'Oh, of course.' I took the offered pen, and I had written the first letter, a big looping 'C', before I realised I was actually going to write my real name. My heart skipped a couple of beats, and with some difficulty I turned the C into a very lopsided S. 'Anything I can do to help. I'm not from the area but I don't suppose the council looks closely at every signature.'

'Thank you, darling,' said the woman with the red eyes. The look she cast up at me was both brittle and defiant. 'We've not had as much help from the local area as we'd have liked, frankly.'

'You haven't?'

The ruddy-cheeked man looked uncomfortable. He offered me a smile that was closer to a grimace. 'I'm Simon Yates, Cheryl's uncle. This is Sharon.' He nodded to the tearful woman. 'It's these seaside towns, innit? Much quieter in the winter, a lot of the businesses shut, just fewer people to look around generally.'

'You've had no leads at all?' I thought of the lonely bench up on Hithechurch seafront, the wilted flowers and the cards warping in the salty air.

'I'm afraid not.' Simon Yates shook his head wearily. 'We've been staying in a hotel up the road, taking it in turns to go home, and come back. There's the van police want to know about, and supposedly there was a pair of scissors found on the beach. It all feels a little insignificant, if I'm honest with you.'

146

Sharon Yates sniffed noisily. 'Lots of rumours, plenty of those,' she said. 'The locals seem quite happy to share those, at least, but not anything useful. To them I suppose it's just a sad story in the news.'

'There are rumours?' I glanced to one side quickly. Katie was still in sight. She had paused by the window of a Greggs and was peering in through misted windows.

'We're from Chelmsford,' Simon Yates said heavily, as though this explained something. 'People round here, they're odd, you know? Full of strange ideas.'

'There's one man,' broke in Sharon Yates, 'came and told us all this nonsense. It made me quite angry, I don't mind telling you.' She took a hanky from her bag. 'Who has time for that sort of thing? Not us, that's for certain. They should have arrested him for wasting our time. Preying on vulnerable people, that's what it is.'

Simon Yates cleared his throat. I wanted to ask: what nonsense? What things did this man say? Did he tell you Cheryl was taken by a shambling figure, a grey woman with long hair and thick black stitches across her mouth? I imagined saying it, imagined how their faces would change. Instead I nodded sympathetically.

'Who was he? A local?'

'Oh, as local as you can get,' said Cheryl's uncle. 'He runs the second-hand bookshop down the road from here.' He nodded up the street. 'From what we've gathered, he's a, uh, *local personality.*'

'A local nutjob is what he is,' said Sharon Yates hotly.

'He means well, I expect.' Cheryl's uncle moved a paper-weight from the table onto a pile of signed petitions. 'But his sorts of wild theories are not really what we need at the moment. We need answers.'

I wished them well again, saying that I hoped Cheryl would

turn up soon – knowing even as I said it how ineffectual that sounded – and wandered away up the street. *Where are you, Cheryl? What happened?*

Katie joined me a few seconds later.

'Are we going back now?'

'In a minute,' I said. 'There's a bookshop I want to look at.'

Katie brightened up a little at that – she liked books – but when we reached the second-hand bookshop I saw her face fall again. It clearly wasn't going to be crammed with Harry Potters and the latest David Walliams – this was the *old* kind of bookshop, one with dead flies in the windows and a table out front stuffed with yellowed paperbacks. The missing poster of Cheryl Yates was displayed prominently, just as it was in all the shops down the street. I already knew how it would smell inside; papery and musty, a hint of old teabags.

'Do you want to come in?' I asked her.

'I guess.'

A bell tinkled. Bookshelves loomed on all sides, almost appearing to lean over the taller they got, and the path through the shop was narrow, winnowed away by boxes of books with yellowed pages and tiny, handwritten price stickers. Katie trailed off down one of the narrow passages, running her fingers over a line of Narnia books.

At the back of the shop was a desk, mostly hidden underneath an enormous and antiquated till that made Joseph's one at the campsite shop look state of the art. Also partly hidden behind the desk was a diminutive old man sitting with his legs crossed, a battered copy of *The Secret History* in his lap. He was wearing orange corduroy trousers and his long white hair was tied back in a loose ponytail. At the sight of me, he put his book down, peering over the tops of his reading glasses.

'Can I help you?'

'Just having a browse.' The desk had a small pile of Cheryl

148

Yates pamphlets too, so I touched my fingers to the top of them. 'It's so scary, isn't it? About this missing girl.'

'Oh yes.' The bookseller stood up, took his glasses off and polished them on the edge of his pale yellow shirt. 'You're not from Folkesholme?'

'I'm not.' The question caught me off guard slightly. 'I'm on . . . holiday. Sort of. I'm actually here researching a book on folklore. Stories about the area, basically.'

He put the glasses back on, letting them perch on the end of his nose. 'Are you now? That's interesting.' He gave me a sceptical look over the top of his lenses. 'You'll have to forgive me, but if I had a pound note for everyone who came in here and told me they were writing a book . . . Even better, if I had fifty pence for every time someone tried to get me to *stock* a book they've printed out at home.'

I laughed. 'I promise I'm just here for research. Have you lived in the area for long?'

'I moved here fifteen years ago. Quiet place, I thought, crying out for a proper bookshop. Looking out at the sea puts people in a reading mood. But there's an edge to it. To this whole bit of coast. Doesn't surprise me that something like *that*,' he tapped the pamphlet, much as I had, 'happened here.'

'It doesn't?' I'd wanted to get him on the subject, and I was slightly taken aback that I'd barely had to try. 'You don't think maybe she just ran away?'

'Who runs away from their family in the middle of a hot day on the beach in July?' said the bookseller. 'When you run away from home, you run away from *home*, not holidays.'

'Yeah,' I said. Despite all my well-earned cynicism, I felt my heart sink a little. Somewhere deep inside I had been hoping that Cheryl had just made for the hills of her own accord. 'I suppose so.'

'Did you ever hear about the Beaumont children?' The

bookseller came out from behind the desk, heading towards an especially tall and narrow bookshelf in the corner of the shop. As he went, I noticed there was a little pile of bookmarks on the desk next to a small 'Please take one' sign. I picked one up, noting the small header and the picture of a seashell underneath it: Kastner Books.

'Uh . . . I don't think I have, no.' I put the bookmark in my pocket.

'Here.' He pulled a large volume down from the shelf. It had a clear plastic cover and looked like it had once belonged to a library. Seeing the title, I felt a sudden surge of vertigo. *Top Fifty Most Mysterious Disappearances.* I had borrowed it, or something very like it, when I was a kid. Mr Kastner was taking no notice of me, though, and was swiftly flipping through the pages to the chapter he wanted. 'There.' He held it up to me, and somewhat reluctantly, I took it.

There was a black and white photo at the top of the page, showing three almost-smiling kids; two girls wearing white cardigans, and a little boy, looking cheeky. Behind them were rocks, and a strip of grey sea.

'Jane, Arnna and Grant Beaumont,' said Mr Kastner. 'Took the bus to the beach one day, never came back.'

'Bloody hell.' I scanned the page. 'This was in the 1960s. In Australia.'

If he caught the incredulous tone in my voice, Mr Kastner didn't react to it.

'One of Australia's most infamous and enduring missing persons cases,' he said. 'The children were seen at the beach by multiple people, bought a meat pie from a pie seller, and then just vanished off the face of the earth. No sign of them ever found.'

'Someone will have taken them,' I said. 'It's not like there's no rhyme or reason behind it. *Someone* hurt them.' I swallowed hard. No wonder the Yates family had taken against Mr Kastner, if he'd immediately started dragging up ancient tragedies from the other side of the world.

'My dear, children go missing from beaches all the time. You do realise that?' The bookseller took the book back from me, closed it up and stroked it once, like it was a sleeping animal, before putting it back on the shelf. 'On busy summer days, it's so easy to lose track of them. But there's more to it than that, I think. Any place where the sea meets the land is strange, if you'll forgive me a bit of poetic licence.'

I nodded reluctantly. 'That's why I wanted to put this book together, I think. Places like these have strange stories attached to them.'

'Of course! They are shifting places, difficult to pin down. Even the shape of the coast must be an approximation, you see? Where exactly does the sea meet the land, when the tide is going in and out?' He smiled up at me over his glasses again. 'Seaside towns are inherently strange, I think. Little limpets of human civilisation, looking out at a vast expanse of untameable nature.'

'Do they know for certain that Cheryl didn't wander into the sea? It can be more dangerous than people realise.'

Mr Kastner shook his head. 'She wasn't dressed for paddling. Had her phone with her. You know of any teenager that will risk their iPhone in saltwater?'

I nodded, conceding the point, but Mr Kastner was turning away from me, pulling down a book from another set of shelves.

'And I happen to think that Folkesholme, and Hithechurch, are both a little stranger than usual. Do you know about the caves around here?'

'Caves?' There was a light crash from one of the aisles, and Katie's voice piped up with a 'sorry!' I looked at Mr Kastner but he appeared to be politely ignoring it.

'Here.' He opened the book he had in his hands, which looked to be some sort of small press geography book – definitely *not* something I'd have got out of the library as a kid. On the page he showed me was a black and white map that looked to me like random squiggles. 'If you're writing about the local folklore you'll have to put something in about the caves. You see this? It's south of Folkesholme, but not that far. A whole network of caves and tunnels, in the chalky cliff faces – not as famous as the ones at Botany Bay or Kingsgate, but you can bet they were used by smugglers too. Dark places, secrets, hidden things. This part of the coast is riddled with them. I asked the family – you know, the Yateses – if the police had been down and looked around the caves. I don't think they took me seriously, but they should, you know. All sorts could be hidden down there. All sorts *has* been hidden down there.'

I thought of the girl's body, concealed in a dark and shadowy place. Of course the Yates family were angry – they didn't want to hear about bodies stashed away in caves. They wanted to believe Cheryl was still alive.

'Girls have gone missing before, on this stretch of coast,' Kastner continued, and I felt a little trickle of unease move down the back of my neck. Joseph had said something very similar, and Stan too, with his tales of the Grey Woman. The old woman at the cake sale had told me their names: Natalie, Sophie and Alison. I opened my mouth, daring myself to ask about it, even as my own fright reached up to close my throat, but Mr Kastner was back to looking at the shelf of books.

'Here.' He slid another, much slimmer volume off the shelf and passed it to me. Again it looked like it had been produced by a local press, but it was glossier, and had more pictures. It was called *The Magical Caves of Kent*. 'Why don't you take this? It will give you a good working knowledge of the whole lot. Plenty of good material in there for your book, no doubt.'

I realised, belatedly, that I could hardly walk out without buying something, so I handed over a fiver. The chance to ask about other missing girls appeared to have gone, and I just wanted to leave.

'Thank you,' I said, my lips feeling slightly numb. 'Local history is so interesting.'

'Come back any time!'

On the way back, my phone buzzed as it sat on the seat next to me. Katie was in the back, fiddling about with a small electronic game she'd brought with her, and didn't spare me a glance. At some traffic lights, I scooped up the phone and looked at the message. It was from Watkins.

I have a copy of the book. Can you meet me? You will want to see it.

A cold sensation moved down through my chest. Emily's book, the one that exposed our story – only she had twisted it to make *me* into a monster. The lights turned green, and after a couple of seconds a flurry of beeps from the cars behind us brought me back to myself. I put the phone back on the seat, face down, and drove on.

Chapter 22

1959

Although Derek was locked out of the study, he never did forget its contents – especially not Harry, the wax model with its skin all peeled back. He couldn't forget Harry, because Harry continued to visit him in his dreams.

In the dreams he would be in his father's study. One wall of it had fallen away, and it looked out across a blasted waste-land of jumbled brick and virulent weeds. He was high up, three storeys at least, and the wooden boards under his feet weren't to be trusted. Harry himself was on the desk, the red wax of his stripped face glistening in the moonlight, and the grin he gave Derek was too wide and toothy; he had no lips, after all.

'I'm not allowed in here,' Derek said. 'Not anymore.'

Even so, he went over to the drawers in the cabinet behind the desk and pulled out the one where his father's old knives lay, neat and clean against dark blue velvet. He would run his fingers over the blades, and in his dream they stayed steady and did not tremble. In his dream he knew exactly where he would cut, and where he would sew, to make everything better again.

And then he would hear Harry's voice, just behind him. Somehow the wax figure had climbed down from the desk to stand at ankle height.

'There's a hole in your head, boy. And all that was good about you leaked through it.'

By the time he was fifteen, Derek Grafton had all but abandoned his schooling, and his father had essentially abandoned him. Derek spent his days out on the pavements and cobbles and grass of London, roaming around with a new group of boys who had dropped out of school even earlier than he had. Tommy and Sid had drifted away from him after the accident, either because they felt guilty or because what had happened to him had frightened them off the streets, but Derek didn't mind. He was the oldest of his new friends, and they looked up to him – or perhaps they were scared. It was difficult to tell. He knew that they listened to what he said, and his orders were followed, and that was enough.

On a cold February afternoon, when the light was already fading from the sky, Derek and four other boys were playing cards in a butcher's basement. The butcher's belonged to Barry's dad, and as long as they tidied up after themselves, they were allowed to come and go as they pleased. It was damp and stank of old blood, and wicked-looking instruments hung on the concrete walls, but these were not the sorts of things that put off teenage boys.

They were the type who teased each other, little rounds of insults that would often lead to a brief scuffle and the odd bloodied nose, and on that particular day it was a boy known as Nedry who was getting the treatment from all of them. He was small and slight and quiet, a prime target for teasing, and he had a large port wine birthmark on his left cheek.

'I'll have to tell my dad to clean up better down here,' remarked Barry. 'Looks like Nedry got some old pig's blood on his face again.'

The boys sniggered and elbowed Nedry, who glowered down at his cards.

'Yeah, good one,' he muttered.

'Nah, that's just where his mum kissed him,' put in Geoff, a kid with thick ginger curls and dirty hands. 'She likes to kiss him long *and* slow, don't she, Ned?'

'Fuck off,' Nedry said shortly.

'I reckon it's where his sister slapped him,' added Barry, laughing. 'After he tried to look up her skirt.'

Nedry had turned pink, his face flushing closer to the colour of his birthmark. 'Yeah, aren't you all so fucking clever.'

'We're not the clever ones,' said Geoff, cheerfully enough. 'That's Doc. Doc, what do you reckon that thing on Ned's face is?'

Derek looked up from his cards, taking pleasure in how each boy's attention was now focused on him. The boys' dads were butchers, coal men, rag and bone men. Derek's father, they knew, was a famous doctor, and therefore anything Derek said had weight.

'What I reckon is – I reckon I could fix it.'

They all laughed at that, save for Nedry, who shook his head.

'No, I mean it.' Derek put on his most serious face. 'I learned how to do it in my father's study. You take a flap of skin from somewhere else, you see, and you use it to cover over the unsightly bit. It would be easy, especially as the muscles and bones on Nedry's face aren't damaged.'

'Ha, go on then,' said Barry. 'I wouldn't mind seeing that.'

Derek stood up. He had been eyeing up the knives on the

156

wall all afternoon, and he picked out the longest, slimmest blade; one that perhaps wouldn't look out of place in his father's drawer. Nedry jumped to his feet, dropping his cards on the table, and the other boys, laughing, jumped up with him. To them, this was another joke, a natural extension of their usual teasing. Barry grabbed the smaller boy's arm as he turned to go up the basement steps.

'Come on, Ned,' he said. 'Won't take a minute, will it?'

Geoff had grabbed the other arm, and the two of them easily pushed him against the wall. Nedry was effing and blinding at the top of his voice, but this only made them laugh more.

Derek advanced, the knife in his hand. He knew that his friends were joking around. They imagined that he would threaten Nedry with the knife, hold it up to his face perhaps, and then give him a good hard pinch or a Chinese burn instead. But deep inside his own head, he could hear Harry whispering. He could see the diagrams of the Archive, and beyond that, some glittering golden future where he proved himself here, in this dank basement; proved that he could hold the knife steady and perform the delicate, intricate operations that his father had during the war.

'Hold him still,' he said. His voice was tight in his throat, but the others didn't notice. 'He mustn't move an inch.'

Barry, always the first to throw a punch in any of their fights, pushed one big meaty hand against Nedry's forehead, holding him in place. And in that second, Derek could see exactly where he needed to cut – a flap from his neck would work nicely, he was sure of it, and then pieces stitched together over the gap . . .

Noise hit him like a hammer. Nedry was screaming and grasping at his neck, blood pouring from a cut there, while the other boys had jumped back, their faces ashen.

'Fucking *hell*, Doc!'

'He needs to keep still,' said Derek, although he could already see that this was pointless. The boy was screaming like the animals that had once passed through this basement room, and the emotion that jolted through Derek was a strange mixture of fury and pleasure. He wanted to cut him again, wanted to force him still and work without interruption, just to see what he could do. He wanted to—

At that moment the basement door crashed open and in came Barry's father, a broad man in a dirty apron.

'*What the bloody hell do you think you're playing at?*'

Chapter 23

Now

The address Watkins had texted me was on the outskirts of Folkesholme again, but this time it was in a quiet residential street. Katie had campaigned to be left at the Smuggler's Cove, so after a quick word with Stan to keep an eye on her, I had set her up with a pocket full of twenty-pence pieces and cash for lunch. She would be fine. I sat in the car for some minutes, just looking out of the window and going over things in my mind. It was a cold and rainy afternoon, making everything look darker than it was, and the houses on the road were shabby and neglected; the grey clouds hanging overhead didn't improve their prospects.

Speaking to Watkins still felt like a huge risk. She knew exactly who I was, and she knew that I was in Hithechurch. If she wanted to, she could cause me all sorts of trouble. But the chance to look at the book before anyone else saw it was too tempting to resist. I had to see what Emily had written about me.

Eventually I got out of the car and walked swiftly across the pavement to the house, grimacing slightly against the rain.

The house was squat and grey, with an overgrown front garden, and the paint was peeling off the windowsills in long, white curls. I pressed the doorbell, and when nothing happened, I knocked briskly at the door. Almost immediately, it opened, and Watkins glared out at me.

'Come in then. Wipe your shoes, please.'

I did as she asked, although there seemed little point. The carpet in the hallway was clearly old, the pile flat and grey and even shiny in places from years of footfall. I followed her into the back room, which apparently served as a kind of dining room: there was a table there with four chairs around it, and a dresser with some old crockery against one wall. I looked around but there were very few details to take in, so I sat at the table. Aside from a pair of horse brasses on the dresser (one of a horseshoe and one of a crucifix) the place was devoid of decoration, and something about that nagged at the back of my mind, but then Watkins was hovering over me, her frizzy hair hanging in her face.

'Squash? Tea? Coffee?' She smiled hesitantly. 'I can put a fresh pot on.'

'Squash would be nice, actually.'

She went back into the narrow hall, and for a little while I listened to her moving about in the unseen kitchen. Outside, the rain grew heavier, and it seemed to me that the gloomy little house creaked all over with the effort of keeping it out. When Watkins came back in with two glasses of orange squash, I nodded at the window. Through slightly dirty glass I could see a narrow garden with a swing at the bottom.

'Rotten weather out,' I said.

Watkins glanced at the window as though she'd never seen it before, then went to the dresser and opened one of the bottom drawers. She pulled out a fat brown envelope and put it in front of me on the table, and then sat down herself.

'That's it,' she said. 'You wanted to see it. I can't let you take it away with you. Normally we're giving out advance copies of books all over the place, but this one they're keeping a close eye on. For legal reasons.'

'Yeah, this one is *special*,' I said, not bothering to keep the acid out of my voice. I opened up the envelope and slid out the thick wad of A4 pages. They were loose, and the top page read '*PINE CONE PRESS: A MOST DANGEROUS SPELL – not to be shared, sold or reproduced.*' I turned it over, and my eyes slid over the first few lines.

> *I was a lonely child. My father was strict, and although my mother was around, she could hardly be said to be present. One summer, on our only holiday of the year, I met another little girl – a little girl who wasn't like me at all. She had a big family who loved her, cherished her, and listened to her stories. I wanted everything she had, and I wanted to be her friend. But what I didn't realise about my new friend was that above everything else, she loved to lie. And her lies would ruin both our lives, and end the*

I slapped the page back on top of it, hiding the words from view. I felt sick, punch drunk, and the gloomy little dining room seemed to spin around me like I was back on a funfair ride.

'The absolute *cow*!'

'There's much more, just like that, and worse,' said Watkins. She was watching me closely. She paused to gnaw at her lip, a quick nervous gesture. 'That's just the introduction.'

'I can't believe you're going to publish this.'

'Not me,' she said quickly. 'I would never have signed this up. Are you . . . Are you going to look at the rest of it?'

I didn't want to, but I did anyway, flicking through the pile of pages to glance at short sections. I could never read more than a paragraph or so before I was too angry or upset to continue – I saw a section that claimed I bullied my cousin Jenny, who was too meek to stand up to me; I saw her talk about all the gory stories I liked to tell, how I had taken a particular pleasure in those that involved murder, revenge or knives. I read enough to see that she painted me as the one who had created Stitch Face Sue and the rituals that asked for her favour . . . which was true, in a way, but hardly the point.

Finally I came across a section towards the end that described a night on a deserted beach:

I could barely see for crying, but I could hear the surf crashing against the shore. It is a sound that has haunted me all my life

Quite abruptly I stood up, swaying on my feet slightly. 'Where's your bathroom?'

Watkins looked panicked, but she nodded to the door. 'There's a downstairs loo opposite . . .'

I stumbled back out into the corridor. Luckily the loo door was standing open, and I fell to my knees in front of the toilet just before I threw up.

'Are . . . are you all right?'

Watkins' voice came from just behind me. My hands were shaking and my head thumped steadily, but I managed to croak out a response. It seemed to me that there was a banging noise from somewhere above our heads, but when I got back on my feet it had stopped. I wiped my mouth, then flushed the toilet.

'Sorry,' I said. I still felt very shaky. 'I don't know where that came from.'

Watkins said nothing. We went back into the dining room,

and without needing to be told she picked up the pages of the manuscript and tidied them away into the bottom of the dresser. I was glad to have them out of sight.

'So. Do you see what she's doing?' Watkins was back to gnawing her lip. 'She gets to have her say, and thousands of people will read it, and then even more will watch it on television when the documentary comes out. And where does that leave you?'

I gulped down the orange squash, trying to get the taste of vomit out of my mouth. I was thinking about my family; those of them that were left, anyway. The last thing they would want would be the whole awful business in the public eye again. And Emily was building me up to be the villain.

'It's wrong to publish it, but no one will listen to me,' Watkins carried on, 'so you see, you have to find this thing, whatever it is. Because she doesn't want it found, I'm sure of that, and that's got to be a good enough reason to find it.'

'How do you know about this again?'

Watkins looked away, staring fixedly at the door behind me.

'Like I told you, I overheard them talking. Pine Cone's legal team – well, we have a lawyer and her assistant, which is about all we can afford – they said we had to have a list of anything that could cause *A Most Dangerous Spell* to be pulled at the last minute. If we put a load of money behind it, and some court decides we can't publish it after all, the whole company will probably go under. So Emily Haynes – you know she doesn't call herself that anymore – her agent had to provide a list, and like I said, I heard them talking about it. There were a few things, but this was the one that made me sit up. Something buried. That could ruin her. Something you buried *together*.'

She dragged her eyes back to mine, and for a second I realised that she looked as sick as I felt.

163

'What is it? What was it you buried together?'

I looked away. 'I'd rather not talk about it, actually.'

She shook her head slightly, frustrated. 'You have to find it. Do you see? You have to find this *thing*. You have to find it *now*.'

I nodded, but I felt deeply uneasy. I hadn't found anything so far, after all. And time was running out.

It had stopped raining by the time I left, and I turned back to look at the house. I saw a curtain twitch on the second floor, and hesitantly I lifted a hand in a wave, but if Watkins was watching me go, she didn't wave back.

Chapter 24

July 1988

To Charlie's surprise, Jenny barely took any persuading at all. She brought up the idea of the 'ritual game' with her cousin in the morning, after breakfast, and Jenny just shrugged one shoulder, half sulkily.

'You always leave me out,' she said. 'You and Darren and Carol and all of you. It'd be nice to be included for once.'

Charlie decided to ignore that. 'So you need to find stuff to give to . . . the ghost. Presents, like. Little ones.'

'Okay.' Jenny pulled a handkerchief out of her sleeve and folded it over and over between her hands. Charlie could tell that the mention of the word 'ghost' had made her nervous, but she had clearly decided she wasn't going to be scared off. 'I'll find something.'

It was the first properly overcast day of the holidays. Charlie, Jenny and Emily met up in the afternoon and went back to the field by the seafront – Charlie had reasoned that it was too soon to try another late-night excursion.

By the rocks with their scattering of graffiti, the girls began placing their gifts inside the pentagram Charlie had drawn with a stick. Emily had brought more of her father's tobacco, another crane fly in a jar, and a postcard; the beach on the front of it had a sea bluer than anything they'd seen at Hithechurch. Charlie turned it over, looking at the spidery biro handwriting on the back.

'It's from Louise,' said Emily, glancing briefly at Jenny. 'She went on a school trip to Jersey a few years ago and sent it to me.'

Jenny wasn't paying attention. Instead she was mournfully turning over a small plastic horse in her hands. It was pink with yellow hair.

'Are you giving that over or what?' said Charlie. Having Jenny there was making her nervous. 'You have to put it in the circle.'

'I *am*,' said Jenny sulkily, but it was still a few more seconds before she placed the pony in the pentagram. She followed it up with a handful of other small objects: three strawberry bonbons, a yellow colouring pencil, a tiny plastic troll with stiff purple hair and a small eraser shaped like a pineapple. Charlie was actually quite impressed with the haul, and after she'd added her own offerings – a page from a Yahtzee pad, a tiny plastic car from a Kinder egg and a glittery pink pencil sharpener – it occurred to her that there was something quite different about the things that Emily had brought. It made her uneasy, for reasons she couldn't put a finger on.

'All right, so there are three of us.' Charlie sat up straight. It was colder than it had been; all three of them were wearing jumpers or cardigans, and the wind off the sea was throwing Jenny's long blonde hair into her face. Periodically she had to untangle it from her glasses. 'Three is the best number for magic. It's why there are always three witches.'

'Are there?' asked Jenny. She sounded dubious.

'Yes,' said Charlie firmly. Emily was watching her seriously. 'Three of us, three lots of offerings.' She took the matchbox out of her pocket. 'So I'm going to light three matches.'

'You're not allowed to have those!' said Jenny immediately, but Charlie silenced her with a look.

'And you have to think about Susan Cartwright while the matches are alight. Think about how we need her help.'

'Do we?' asked Jenny.

'Jenny, do you want to play this game or not?' Charlie shifted on the grass. 'You can't just be asking questions all the time.'

'We need to do this *right*,' added Emily. Charlie saw Jenny dart a quick look at Emily, her blotchy face unreadable under her thick glasses. Her cousin pulled her cardigan tighter around her shoulders and shrugged.

'*Sorry.*'

'Stitch Face Sue,' Charlie began in her most solemn voice. 'We're asking for the justice of your scissors. Blood has been shed, but it's not enough.' Jenny made a small noise at that, and Charlie felt an odd uncurling of triumph in her chest. No one ever believed her stories, but Jenny would. Emily would. There was a power to knowing her words were affecting her listeners. So she decided to push it a bit further. 'We ask you to try again. We gave you a small life before, and now we do so again.' At this she caught Emily's eye, and nodded ever so slightly. At the signal, Emily picked up the jar with the fat grey crane fly in. Inside, the insect battered itself against the glass.

'I don't like those things,' said Jenny, in a very small voice.

'You'll like this next bit then,' said Charlie. She wanted to laugh suddenly, and the wind gusted up across the beach towards them, a moaning wail. In it they heard a few distant cries from beachgoers as inflatables were abruptly picked up and flung down the sands. The air felt strange, and the light had turned an odd, sickly yellow. Stormlight, Charlie's nan called it. Charlie lit the first match, cupping her hand around the flame to save it from the breeze, and nodded to Emily. 'Do it now.'

Emily unscrewed the jar and tipped the crane fly out into her hands. Jenny gave a small cry of disgust, and then as she had done before, Emily crushed the insect into the side of the rock. Then, she took the penknife from her pocket and placed it in the pentacle, the blade out and winking in the light. Charlie raised her eyebrows at this – she hadn't told Emily to do that, but it was a neat touch. The first match had burned down to her fingers, so she stubbed it out in the sandy grass.

'A blade for you,' said Emily. 'I need your help, Stitch Face Sue. I want revenge for Louise. And . . . and for me, too.'

Jenny was looking at her feet, her mouth pinched in that way that meant she was trying not to cry. Charlie lit the second match.

'Now it's your turn, Jenny.' Charlie nudged the other girl with her knee. 'Say something to Stitch Face Sue. Ask her for something, while the match is burning.'

'I don't want to.'

Charlie felt a surge of irritation. 'Do it or I'll . . . pinch you.'

'Stitch Face Sue, I want my cousin to stop being so *mean*.'

Charlie rolled her eyes and stubbed out the second match. She was determined not to be derailed by Jenny's attitude. 'God, don't be such a div, Jenny.' When she lit the third match, she held it up over the middle of the pentacle. 'When the third match goes out, Stitch Face Sue will be with us. Just very quickly, for a second, and if you see her, don't make a sound. If she hears you, she might get angry and try to grab you.' She couldn't resist glancing at her cousin and was pleased to see she had gone pale.

They sat in silence, the three of them, watching the match. The wind was picking up, and unseen behind them, dark clouds were rolling in over the sea. A summer storm, with a timing so perfect Charlie could barely believe it. A handful of seconds passed, and then with another gust from the wind, the match flickered out. Charlie happened to be looking at Emily when it did, and she saw her new friend's eyebrows shoot up. She was staring at something behind Charlie, towards the sea.

'There she is!'

Charlie turned. For an instant she saw a figure outlined against the grey sea. She had long unkempt hair, a white nub of a face, and then Jenny was crashing into Charlie's shoulder, tearing her eyes away from the apparition. Her cousin had leapt to her feet and, unbalanced, immediately lost her footing.

'What are you doing?' bellowed Charlie. When she looked back, the figure had vanished.

'I HATE YOU!' shrieked Jenny. 'Why do you have to be so weird?' She was crying. Charlie realised with a lurch that she had pushed it all too far.

'Don't be daft.' She started to get to her feet, thinking she had to calm her cousin down, but Emily was already there. She grabbed Jenny by the arm and gave her a furious yank, nearly causing her to fall flat into the pentagram.

'You ruined it!' Emily's voice was a hot hiss, full of frustration. 'What if she doesn't come because of you?'

But Jenny's crying had taken on a wild, panicked tone. She staggered away and held up her arm; her pink cardigan was a deep crimson at the elbow.

'What—?' started Charlie. She glanced at Emily. The knife had been in the hand she had grabbed Jenny with. *When had she picked up the knife?*

'I'M GOING TO TELL!'

With that, Jenny was pelting away across the field.

They lost sight of her quickly as she headed down towards the promenade, her tow-coloured hair briefly reflecting the baleful stormy light. For a time Emily and Charlie ran after her, but once they got on the road back to the caravan park, they slowed their pace; no use rushing towards what was clearly going to be an unpleasant scene. Charlie risked a glance at her friend's face. Emily's lips were pressed together in a thin line, and her green eyes looked very bright.

'What happened?' she said eventually. 'With the knife?'

Emily didn't look at her immediately. Instead she rubbed the flat of her palm against her jumper, as though wiping off something Charlie couldn't see. When she did look, she smiled hesitantly.

'I'd picked it up again, and then when your cousin got up, I forgot it was in my hand. Did you see her? Stitch Face Sue?'

Charlie kicked a stone off the road and into the ditch that ran alongside it. 'I saw something,' she said.

'Did it look like the woman you saw last night?'

Charlie examined her memories of the last half an hour, but already it was difficult to remember exactly what she'd seen. The light had been poor, and she'd had maybe a second, or a second and a half, to see the figure across the field. There had been long hair, she was sure of that. And hadn't she seen the face too? A rigid mask pierced with stitches. Or was she remembering the figure she'd seen out of the window, and given its face to the person in the field? Her mum had said the person outside had been a dream and her whole family had agreed. Overactive imagination. Natural liar. Staying up too late.

'It did,' she said firmly. 'It was her.'

Emily nodded.

'I was scared your cousin was going to frighten Stitch Face

Sue away. So I grabbed her, and the knife must have poked her. I didn't mean to hurt her.'

Emily's voice wavered uncertainly. Charlie patted her awkwardly on the shoulder. 'I know you didn't,' she said. And then, 'Is that her up ahead?'

They had reached the turn-off for the caravan park, and they could just see Jenny, walking with her head down, one hand clutching her injured arm. She'd clearly not had the energy to run all the way back after all. Just then, the downpour that had been threatening all afternoon began to fall, big fat drops of summer rain.

'We need to convince her not to tell on us,' said Charlie in a low voice. 'Or there'll be sod all chance of us being allowed out together again.'

They sped up, trying to move quietly, but they were still around six feet away from Jenny when she heard them coming. She gave one, startled look over her shoulder and then she was off, pelting around the side of the campsite shop and across the swing park. Charlie and Emily gave chase; although Jenny was a little older than the pair of them, she was still shorter and slighter, and they eventually caught up with her on the edge of the park, just where the woods met the neatly trimmed grass.

'Jenny, stop! We just want to talk to you!'

'No you don't!' Charlie's cousin's face was a glistening mess of tears and snot. She rubbed her whole face with one sleeve, her eyes and nose bright pink. '*My arm hurts.*'

To Charlie's alarm, Jenny's sleeve had a scarlet circle the size of a coffee cup ring. There would be hell to pay for this when she got back to the caravan.

'We're sorry, okay? It was an accident.' Charlie pushed her mop of ginger hair out of her eyes. 'Let me see how bad it is.'

Jenny clutched at her arm. 'No.'

171

'Listen,' Emily stepped forward and put her hand on Jenny's shoulder. The smaller girl seemed to shrink under the weight of it, while Emily's face remained pale and impassive. 'You won't tell, will you? It's really important you don't. Please.'

'Emily,' Charlie said in a low voice. 'She's bleeding. How is she supposed to explain that away?'

But neither of the girls was paying her any attention. Jenny had gone very still, like a mouse that knows a cat is in the room.

'You don't want to get us in trouble, do you, Jenny?' Emily said sombrely.

Charlie almost laughed at that. Jenny was a serial teller, the classic family grass, always ready to shop her cousins if there was even the slightest sniff of something that wouldn't meet parental approval. But to her surprise, her cousin dropped her head, and one pale hand curled around her injured arm as if to hide it.

'I don't,' said Jenny, her voice barely audible under the drumming of the rain on caravan roofs.

'So you won't tell?' asked Emily.

'I won't,' said Jenny, and something about her tiny squeak of a voice made Charlie feel cold.

'You're a good friend,' said Emily, and at that moment a dark shape loomed at them across the grass. Startled, Charlie looked up to see Emily's dad, his face white with fury. All three of the girls jumped as one, and Emily even took a skittery handful of steps backwards. Charlie opened her mouth to make up some explanation when she saw Emily's father glance directly at the blood on Jenny's cardigan. It was like he could smell it.

'What have you done?' He covered the ground between them in one step and had hold of Emily before she could make a run for it, his huge fist closing around her arm like it was a twig. 'What have you *done*, Emily?'

She yanked herself away from him as best she could, but she may as well have been trying to move a car or remove a bear trap. Charlie took a breath, hoping at least to distract him.

'Emily hasn't done anything, we've just been messing about up by the beach and—'

Still holding his daughter by the arm, Emily's father rounded on them. All the usual florid colour had vanished from his face, and with his free hand he pointed savagely at Jenny.

'What happened to her arm?' he demanded. 'How did that happen?'

'It was an accident,' Jenny piped up. Her watery eyes looked oddly defiant. 'I fell over while I was running, that's all.'

Charlie gritted her teeth. It was a poor story. But Emily's dad glared at them both, his nostrils flaring, and then he pulled Emily across the grass. In moments he and Emily were gone.

Charlie and Jenny walked back to their caravan together. The rain had stopped as suddenly as it had started, and the tarmacked road seemed to radiate a tired, humid heat underneath their trainers. Just as the caravan came into sight, Charlie hesitantly touched Jenny's hand.

'You really should let me look at it,' she said. 'See how bad it is. And how much trouble we're going to get into.'

They stopped walking. It was quiet in the park. The late-afternoon rain had chased everyone inside. Jenny, her face still very pink about the eyes, stripped off her dirty cardigan and held it out to Charlie. There was a lot of dried blood on her arm, but the cut itself did not look deep, just ragged and unpleasant. Sensing that Jenny was in a pliant mood, Charlie convinced her to go into the shower block, where they washed her arm in the sink and threw the stained cardigan into a bin.

'You'll have to say you left it at the beach,' said Charlie. 'It's not like they'll check.'

Next, Charlie took off her own jumper and made Jenny put it on, and when they were back at the caravan they spent a furtive half an hour sneaking plasters out of their nan's handbag, until Jenny's arm was carefully wrapped and concealed.

For a time that evening it seemed to Charlie's mother and her aunties that Charlie and Jenny might finally be getting along; they saw all the secret glances and hushed conversations as some sort of private game. For the rest of the holiday, though, they were distant from each other, and when the adults attempted to get them to go to the swing park together, or go rock-pooling, Jenny would absolutely refuse, turning pink and hysterical if they insisted. Eventually, they gave up.

Chapter 25

Now

The next morning I got up early again and went out with my spade. I was in a good mood, and it was a bright, cold day, the woods full of a brittle kind of post-dawn sunlight. *I'll find it today*, I thought. *I've just got a feeling.*

I didn't find it.

In fact, it was looking increasingly likely that the thing I was trying to find wasn't there at all. Had I moved it, then forgotten about it? Had we buried it somewhere else entirely back then?

When I was very small, around seven I think, my auntie's house was broken into. She phoned my mum in a right state, and so we went straight round there to offer moral support. I can remember very clearly how upset Auntie Beverly was, how her eye make-up was smeared all down her cheeks and her nose was red, and I remember my mum in her kitchen, making a cup of tea, rigid with fury. The house itself was a tip, all my aunt's clothes pulled out of her drawers and scattered across the carpet. A few things were broken too. It was exciting, in that way that unexpected catastrophes are exciting to small children, but I also had a clear sense of *violation* – that a space that was supposed to be safe had turned out to be dangerous.

Later, we heard that one of my aunt's neighbours had seen two very large men walking through her small front garden, both carrying big suitcases filled with her stuff. The neighbour had scuttled back inside to call the police, but the Large Men were already long gone by the time they arrived.

Then, a few years later, when I had a lot of time on my hands to think about things, I remembered my auntie's burglary and there, in my little cache of memories about that day, was a memory of the two large men with suitcases. I saw them in my mind's eye, wearing scuffed coats, with bristly, unshaven cheeks. *Bastards*, I thought. And then it took me a good few minutes to remember that I hadn't been there during the robbery and had never seen the men myself. My mind had made that bit up.

This is one of the problems with having an overactive imagination. Real memories can look and feel very much like the things you have made up inside your own head.

Long after the hot summer where everything changed for me, I made friends with a woman who told me that she couldn't remember any of the funerals she had been to. This person had had a fairly hectic and rough childhood, and had lived with her nan and grandad for a time. She was very close to them. But when they died, and her family had funerals, my friend just had a blank space in her memory. As if her brain had looked at how painful that memory was, packaged it up and threw it away, or cast it down into a very dark pit.

We think of memories as simple, but I don't think they are at all. We think that stuff happens to us, and our brain either chooses to record it in our vast vault of memories, or it keeps them in a little side office for a while before dumping them through the shredder. We remember the important things, maybe, and forget what we had for lunch on a wet Tuesday seven years ago.

I think there are darker things lurking in that vault. Creatures that shuffle back and forth, keeping away from the light, and they have their fingers in our memories all the time; mixing them up, replacing them with things that might look very like events from our own lives, but aren't. It's unreliable. It's broken. It's partly, or even mostly, made up. We're all liars.

What I'm looking for might not be there. Once you realise that your memories are unreliable, it changes everything.

Doesn't it?

For the rest of that day Katie and I sat around the caravan, doing very little. She was ploughing through another of the brightly coloured paperback books she had brought, while I had my notebook up at the table, scribbling odd thoughts and possibilities. My mind kept returning to Cheryl Yates and her family, their cold, grey faces as they handed out pamphlets every day.

At that point I became aware of the TV, which was playing a local news programme. Certain words dropped into my head like cubes of ice, making me sit up: *Hithechurch caravan park, 1988 tabloid sensation.* I looked up, feeling abruptly sick. The presenter was looking out from the screen with a sombre expression.

'. . . there has been considerable controversy over the book deal, perhaps fuelling the pre-order sales that have already projected *A Most Dangerous Spell* to be a top ten bestseller on release. Netflix have also announced this week that they have commissioned a ten-part true crime documentary on the incident, which has led Hithechurch council to query whether they can object to filming in the area. So far—'

I snatched up the remote control and jabbed a button viciously. The news programme winked out of existence, to be replaced by Monty Don standing in someone's muddy garden. I glared back at my notes, my face hot with a mixture of shame and fury. I picked out the pamphlet with Cheryl's picture on it, and tried to focus all my attention on that, instead. Where was she? What had happened to her?

Could I help her?

Chapter 26

1960

Having a well-to-do father had its advantages. The business with Nedry and the knife went away after a visit from Dr Grafton, but the incident further soured the relationship between Derek and his father, and one night when he had just turned sixteen, Derek snuck some pieces out of the Archive, packed a bag with clothes, and left his old home behind. He did not see his father, or any of the people who lived and worked in that house, ever again.

Without much thought he headed towards the Kent coast, reasoning vaguely that there would be work on ships, or even a circus; someone somewhere would be willing to pay a boy with a strong back to do some form of work. It was, admittedly, a long way from his dream of being a surgeon, but at that time freedom seemed more important – besides which, since the accident Derek found that his attention span had shrunk significantly, and even small tasks could cause him to fly into a rage. His potential employer also needed to be someone who didn't ask a lot of questions, and luckily for him, in a small town on the Kent coast, he fell in with a family known as the Rushbrooks, and they were very happy indeed to keep their work quiet. In a moment of unusual caution, he told them his name was Harry, not Derek. There was no need for them to know who he really was.

'Harry' started off with simple, innocuous jobs, like tidying the yard and loading the vans, and then came riskier assignments, like keeping a lookout on certain nights outside certain buildings, or driving some boxes out to another town and keeping an eye on them for a while. As Harry grew taller, the Rushbrook family found him a useful sort to have around on some of their more unsavoury tasks, and it wasn't long before his affinity for knives became apparent.

And Harry enjoyed the work. The feeling of pleasure and rage he'd had when cutting Nedry was now something he could find quite regularly, and gradually this became the most important aspect of his life. Over the years he came to know the Rushbrook family very well, and made friends with one of their drivers, a lad from London called Robert McLean. He was trusted by the family and he trusted them. He had Christmas dinners with them, went to their weddings, and even gave lifts to their youngest daughter, a feisty fourteen-year-old called April.

In 1961, when Harry was seventeen years old, a funfair opened in Hithechurch, run by the Stimpson family, who had come from out of town. Very quickly the Rushbrooks moved in on them, ensuring a steady income from the fruit machines and rides, and almost as a kind of exchange Harry began working exclusively for the funfair. He enjoyed it; there were lots of people his own age there, he learned how to fix and maintain the rides, and in the evenings he still did small jobs for the Rushbrooks – jobs that often involved the snapping of bones or the spilling of blood.

And it was there that he came to know Rosalind Stimpson.

Rosa, as her family called her, was a strikingly beautiful girl of sixteen. She had black hair and creamy skin, a natural pink flush to her cheeks and startling green eyes, and she soon became a kind of unofficial funfair attraction herself – boys and young men flocked to the place to get a glimpse of her, and Harry was no different.

And Rosa enjoyed the attention. While Harry steamed with jealousy, she would walk around the funfair or stand leaning against the neat white fence around the carousel, accepting the attentions of her admirers and flatly turning them down. It became something of a competition between the boys of the town; who could get Rosa to hold their hand? Who could earn a kiss from Rosa? Who – and this was spoken of in low voices only – who could get her to lie down and part her legs?

One day, Harry dressed in his best clothes – a pressed shirt, a pair of chequered slacks, leather shoes – and went to see Rosalind himself. She often helped her mother out at the Gypsy Caravan attraction, taking coins and passing out tickets, and that was where he found her. She leaned against the dark green wood of the caravan, licking an ice cream and watching the punters from underneath her thick, dark eyelashes.

'Afternoon, Rosa.' Harry cleared his throat and offered her what he thought of as his most winning smile. He had taken the time to grease his hair into a style he considered fashionable.

'What do you want, Harry?' Rosa spared him one look and then turned her head, apparently finding something much more interesting to watch on the far side of the fair.

'I wondered if you wanted to go for a drive?' He leaned against the caravan too, trying to create an intimate, easy atmosphere. 'We could go up to Folkesholme, go to the record shop there. Got my own car now.'

She tossed her head and narrowed her eyes at him. To Harry they looked like pieces of sea glass, smooth and cold. She took a long moment to look him up and down.

'You think a car makes you more interesting? You're just one of those Rushbrook thugs.' She tipped her head to one side and licked the edge of her cone, chasing an errant dribble of white ice cream. 'I wouldn't be seen dead with you.'

Harry shivered. Watching her lick the cone and dismiss him at the same time made him feel strange; hot and cold, full of fury but also pleasure. Just like cutting did. He thought of the knife he had in his trouser pocket. He smiled, and shrugged.

'Your loss.'

And he walked away into the summer sunshine.

Chapter 27

Now

I couldn't believe I hadn't been there before.

The caves were no more than a twenty-minute walk from the main hub of Hithechurch, putting them somewhere in between the town and Folkesholme. It was mid-morning, a bright, cold day, and the sun was glittering whitely on the steel grey of the sea. The caves were clearly signposted, and some distance away from the highest point of the tide, so that the sand leading up to them was relatively dry. As we paused by the entrance, I took a moment to read the large metal sign printed with safety information. Katie was fidgeting from foot to foot next to me.

'You see that? Safety info – are you reading it?'

She shrugged elaborately.

'Come on, I'm sure the world's best reader can manage it. And if I know you've read it, I'll feel better about taking you in there.'

She sighed, then muttered, 'Keep to the central paths, be careful of slippery surfaces, wear sensible footwear. That okay?'

I nodded. The entrance was wide and low, supported by big, reassuring-looking struts, and the inside was brightly lit with electric lights. Even so, I dawdled a little by the signs, reluctant to lose the blue sky that was currently above our heads. I took out the book I'd bought at the bookshop and flicked to the page I had marked by turning down a corner (if that's not a sign of a diseased mind, I don't know what is). I already knew there wasn't much information there; a few black and white pictures from what I guessed was the late 50s or early 60s (no safety sign then) and a few lines of text suggesting that the caves were a mixture of natural formation and manmade. It also told me that the caves were known locally as the Devil's Honeycomb.

We went inside. Immediately, Katie sped in front, eager to explore, and I called after her, 'Don't go out of my sight, all right?'

She yelled back, the echoes of the place tattering her reply into nonsense.

The place appeared to be empty. As I wandered in, the constant white noise of the sea became pinched off and strange. The place smelled of salt, and chalk, and a ranker metallic smell that I put down to rust, or something like it. There was a waist-high handrail along the path in case you felt uneasy on your feet, and I took hold of it gladly.

The place widened out, and I looked up into the dark craggy ceiling. Somewhere nearby, water was dripping steadily. Bolted to the handrail was another metal sign. This one gave a little more information on the caves. There was a very basic map and a short paragraph on the history of the place. In the 1700 and 1800s, it seemed, these caves had been a popular hiding place for smugglers, like much of the south-eastern coast at the time, and an especially infamous gang had been run to ground here once by angry locals. The smugglers had liked the place enough that they had made the caves their own, excavating extra boltholes and even constructing tunnels that ran from one cave to another, some making it all the way to Folkesholme. I tried to imagine the place lit by oil lamp or candle, and what it would be like to hide here – what it would be like to work your way back into the cliff, deeper and deeper, terrified that someone would find you. You and your gang, crushed into a tiny space, daggers clasped in wet fingers, holding your breath while that great weight of stone and chalk hung suspended above you.

Someone took hold of my elbow and spoke loudly into my ear.

'Take no notice of that, it's useless!'

I swallowed down a shriek and turned to see a middle-aged woman beaming helpfully at me. She had rosy cheeks and she was wearing a black cagoule that looked like it had seen a lot of action. She also had the sort of lightweight rucksack you see on the backs of serious hikers and one of those aluminium sticks to walk with.

'Sorry, did I make you jump?' She squeezed my arm once and let me go. She didn't look sorry at all. 'I keep petitioning the tourist board to update these old information signs, make them a bit, I don't know, jazzier. Geology is my passion. Been all over the world to see different caves, but it's always nice to come home to the ones you grew up with, isn't it?'

She spoke as if poking around dark caves was something everyone did in their spare time, like baking or sunbathing.

'It is?'

'I've been to the Mammoth Cave National Park in Kentucky, which is the longest cave system in the world, did you know that? Makes these caves look piddly. Like mouse holes. It has a limestone strata, capped with sandstone. Beautiful.'

'Okay.' I glanced over her shoulder, but I still couldn't see anyone else around. Perhaps she liked to wait in the caves and surprise people with lectures.

'I've also been to Reed Flute Cave in China – my goodness, that was a trip and a half. Beautiful place. One of the grottos is called the Crystal Palace of the Dragon King, can you imagine? My favourite though is Fingal's Cave in Scotland, the most remarkable hexagonal basalt columns, you really do have to experience it for yourself. Have you been there, dear?'

'No, I haven't, I'm afraid.' I was still struggling to get up to speed with this conversation.

'I'm Pat, by the way,' she beamed at me. 'You'll have to forgive my enthusiasm, but I don't normally see anyone else in here at this time of year. You must really like caves!'

'Just an enthusiastic amateur, I'm afraid.' I forced a smile onto my lips. 'I'm here researching a book on the area, collecting folklore and stories, things like that. The man who runs the bookshop in Folkesholme told me I should check out these caves.'

'Oh, *him*.' Pat's mouth briefly turned down at the corners, and then she seemed to brighten. 'A book! That's exciting – I'm not sure that I've ever met a writer before.'

'Haha, well.' A prickle of embarrassment worked its way up my neck. For some reason lying to Pat made me feel uncomfortable; it was like swearing in front of your nan. 'I'm an enthusiastic amateur there as well, I'm afraid. But the caves are very atmospheric.'

'They're not all that special really, I suppose.' Pat smiled affectionately, as if they were discussing a beloved but dim grandchild. 'Ocean erosion rather than the usual limestone erosion of inland caves, but they've been filled out by enterprising people over the centuries. Lots of history packed away in these little tunnels.'

'I was just reading about the smugglers . . .'

'Yes!' Pat gestured at the path winding away deeper into the cliff. 'Very popular with them. They built tunnels into the cliffs all along here, you know, chipping away in the night. Hair-raising work.'

'I wouldn't fancy it much.'

'It's good stone to make tunnels and rooms in though, very pliable. This whole coast is essentially a honeycomb of them, and they come in very useful.' She tapped her stick against the rocky wall as she said this. 'Did you know there are caves – well, I should say rooms – right up in the sea wall of Hithechurch itself? Built during the Second World War to store ammunitions, supplies, even people when the bombers were going over. All but forgotten about now, unfortunately, and all shut up to the public, although I have petitioned them many, *many* times.' Pat sounded rueful. 'Probably nothing interesting in them now but dust and mess, but I'd love to have a peek, all the same.'

'Why don't they open them up? Wouldn't do any harm to have another tourist attraction around here.'

'I quite agree! But, well, I won't get into it because the whole thing is daft, just a lot of local superstition really, but . . .'

She seemed embarrassed, and it intrigued me. 'What do you mean?'

'I suppose it's exactly what you're after, with your book,' she said, still sounding uncertain. 'They're supposed to be cursed.' She shrugged. 'Curses go hand in hand with caves, you know, but the chambers built into the sea wall were manmade, so it seems extra silly to me.' She shrugged. 'One of them collapsed, you see, while there were people sheltering inside at night. This was during the war. Twenty-odd people, snuffed out like that.' She tapped her stick against the stone again for emphasis. 'Their bodies were never retrieved, so I

187

suppose that rightly it's a tomb. The council doesn't want it getting about – twenty skeletons all bricked up somewhere behind the funfair? Well.' She smiled wryly. 'It'll put people off their chips.'

I thought of Katie, and looked round sharply, but she was still just in sight – I could see her bright blue coat in the gloom. I called out to her, just the same.

'Katie? You all right there?' I turned back to Pat. 'Just keeping an eye on my niece.' I thought about what the man in the bookshop had said about secrets, about places on the coast being full of them. How many dark things were hidden in Hithechurch? 'Did they ever check this place for Cheryl Yates?'

'I believe so, yes.' Pat's face lost a little of its cheer. 'No sign of her.'

'What do you think happened to Cheryl?'

'I'm sure I couldn't say.' She gave me an apologetic look. 'It sounds awful, I know, but I try not to think about these things. There's so much pain in the world, and this isn't the first terrible thing to happen around here.'

My chest seemed to grow tight then, as though someone had reached right through my ribs and was squeezing my heart. I forced myself to nod and smile. *Keep going. For Cheryl.*

'I had heard that some other girls had gone missing, over the years.'

'Yes, gawd, it's all so sad. It always seems to be the girls that suffer, doesn't it?' Pat shook her head slightly. 'There's supposed to be a ghost of a girl that haunts these caves. I suppose that's the sort of story that would be good for your book?'

I nodded. 'Exactly the thing.'

'I'm afraid I don't have any excitingly grisly details. A few people have seen her though – a girl, or a woman I should say, in ragged clothes. They see her on the beach, or even at the mouth of the caves, and then she's gone. The Grey Woman.'

I kept the friendly smile on my face, although it felt painfully false. 'Are these recent sightings?'

'Oh, they go back years, dear. People were talking about the Grey Woman when I was a girl.' Her tone changed then, as she moved back to her favourite subject. 'You know, though, I always thought there might be a way through . . . from these caves to the old war chambers in the sea wall. The tunnels that run up to Folkesholme, they could run all the way back to the Hithechurch sea wall too. I've made unofficial maps over the years . . .' She flapped her hands at this, as though everyone spent their spare time mapping smuggler tunnels. 'But it's a young woman's game really. Some of those passages, you'd have to be a child to get through, really. I still think it's possible though.'

'That sounds like a job for a braver woman than me.'

'It'd put the wind up you, all right.' Pat smiled, and then seemed to remember where she was. 'Oh, 'ark at me. I've got a meeting this afternoon and at this rate I'll be late. Local history society, dear. Let me give you a pamphlet.'

From inside one of the cagoule's many pockets she drew out a sepia-tinted pamphlet and passed it to me. As she did so, I felt an odd sense of dizziness pass through me. This woman was involved in local history, clearly spent much of her life enthusiastically engaged with it, yet she hadn't recognised me. For a moment I felt strange, insubstantial. Perhaps I was just a ghost here after all.

'Come and visit if you like. We have a tiny office on Church Street. We're always looking for someone new to bore to death. I'm sorry, dear, I didn't catch your name?'

'Sarah,' I said. 'It was nice to meet you, Pat.'

With that, she bustled off, and I was left alone in the echoing cave, until to my surprise a tall teenage lad wearing an official-looking coat came round the corner. He looked just as startled to see me as I was to see him; he had a badge on his coat that read 'Devil's Honeycomb Guide – Please Ask For Help'. I nodded at him but didn't invite more contact than that. He looked relieved, and vanished back around the corner to the entrance to the caves. I supposed he'd probably nipped off for a fag and hadn't been expecting any punters today – aside from Pat, who I suspected was his most frequent and dreaded visitor.

I called out to Katie, who came skittering back, her trainers making scrunching noises on the uneven floor.

'Who was that lady?'

'Just a local cave enthusiast. What do you think of it then? Pretty gloomy, isn't it?'

Katie wrinkled her nose.

'I don't like it much. It's cold and spooky. And it smells weird. Can we go back now?'

To my own surprise, I was slightly disappointed. I suppose on some level I had been pleased to find a distraction like the caves and had hoped Katie would be impressed.

'In a minute. I want to have a bit more of a look around.'

'Can I wait outside then?'

I nodded. 'Go on. There's a kid with a badge at the entrance. Go and ask him where the best place to get fish and chips is.'

Once she had skipped off, I wandered towards the back of the caves. Here, the passage grew narrow, eventually splitting off into a fork, both paths of which were carefully signposted, although I noticed that the lights were a little dimmer here – for atmospheric reasons, I assumed. On a whim I followed the left-hand fork, moving slowly over the uneven ground, listening to the odd, heavy silence of the caves, broken with the sound of water dripping somewhere. I found myself thinking of Joseph. I hadn't seen him since our impromptu date. Was he avoiding me? Had he figured out who I was? Or *did he actually like me?*

The thought sounded stupid inside my own head, like a teenage girl mooning over her new boyfriend.

I came to the far end of the passage. On the right-hand side, beyond the handrail, there was a sudden drop, and it was possible to see the entrances of other tunnels leading away, as well as a couple of ledges, dusted with tiny stones and debris. I looked at it, this area that was cordoned off from visitors, and deep inside me something just fell away.

Have you ever missed a step coming down the stairs, and for a second you just plunge forward into nothing? Your heart leaps up into your chest, and adrenaline surges around your body, making your fingers tingle and your teeth fizz. Even though you are safe. Quite safe.

That was how I felt then. I closed my hand around the handrail and truly gripped it for support for the first time. I looked around, behind me, half certain that *she* would be there, her face all ruined and a pair of scissors in her hand, but there was nothing, no one. The lights flickered. Somewhere, outside I assumed, I could hear people speaking in low voices. I sucked in a breath through my teeth and forced myself to look at the small ledge, the little tunnels.

It's just a creepy place, I told myself. *Maybe you're a little claustrophobic.* The idea that I might be afraid of small spaces was in itself sort of funny, given where I had spent most of my life, but there was no question: the caves, or at least this part of them, scared me badly.

I took one last look at the dark section of weathered stone

– why could I remember what they felt like under my hands, the cold stony grit of them? – and I turned around and walked out into the sunshine.

That night I dreamed about the caves, or at least, the dream had the feeling of a cave about it. Darkness, the sound of running water nearby. The ground underneath my feet was shifting and unreliable, and someone was looking for me – someone who was angry with me, and I was afraid of them. Sometimes it was my mother, or my sister.

And then other times it was someone else, someone smaller, following me in the dark.

I woke up from this nightmare at one point, and I heard a light tread outside my room. There was a thin bar of moonlight shining under my bedroom door. Katie must have got up in the night to go to the toilet, that was all, yet when I saw the light change below my door, and knew she had to be standing outside it, a cold terror seized hold of me. I lay in bed, my eyes rooted to that small dark spot.

Go back to bed, I thought. *Please, just go back to bed.*

I held my breath, trying not to picture her standing there, one hand pressed against the thin wood of the door, her hair hanging in her face – and eventually the small dark spot moved again. I let my breath out and closed my eyes.

Chapter 28

July 1988

Charlie stretched her legs out. Next to her, Emily was rolling a yellow plastic skittle between her hands. They were sitting on the grass outside Emily's caravan, and her father, who was hosing down his beige car, stood around ten feet away. Charlie was very aware of the sharp glances he kept directing at his daughter's back – she wondered if her friend could feel them, like hot little needle pricks.

'Why is he washing his car on holiday?' she asked, in a low voice.

Emily shrugged her bony shoulders. She did not move to look at her father.

'He's always washing it. Even though it's a crappy rust bucket.' She *donked* the fat end of the skittle against her knee. 'He went through this phase where he cleaned it all over, inside and out, over and over. He smelled like soap for days.'

'Is he still angry?' Charlie glanced up to see if he was listening to them, but he had a sponge out and was furiously soaping up the windscreen. He had one yellow glove on over the hand that had been bitten by the dog. It was another blistering day, and the skin on his forearms was a uniform pink.

Emily half smiled. 'He's never not angry.' Despite the heat, she was wearing a long-sleeved navy top, faded from the wash. It was a little too big for her and the cuffs came halfway down her fingers. Charlie wondered if the top had originally belonged to her missing sister, Louise. With a sister herself, Charlie was very used to wearing hand-me-downs.

'Listen,' Emily said eventually. 'We need to try again. Soon. Right?'

Charlie pulled some grass through her fingers, not looking at her friend. 'I dunno. After Jenny . . . Maybe we should leave it alone.'

Emily glared at her. 'You want to give up now? When we're so close?'

Charlie shrugged. She thought of the crimson circle on Jenny's pink cardigan.

'We can't stop now,' said Emily. 'We're almost there, I can feel it.'

'I guess.'

'So.' Emily held up her hand and began ticking things off her fingers. Charlie looked up from under her eyelashes at Emily's dad again, but he had his back to them, the muscles in his shoulders furiously bunched together as he washed the car. 'We need to do everything right this time. The *best* and most important gifts. We need to light matches, maybe even a fire, and we need three of us to do the ritual. That definitely seems to summon her. Do you think your cousin would help us again?'

Charlie snorted. 'Fat chance. She'll barely be in the same room as me at the moment. Like I'm some sort of monster.' An unfamiliar pang of guilt moved through her chest.

'We'll have to get someone else then,' said Emily, as though this were the simplest thing in the world.

'Where are we going to do it? I think we've pushed our luck too far with the field by the beach. It's too far to come back to the caravans.'

'The woods,' said Emily. 'The woods here will do. You saw her here, didn't you? On the campsite.'

'Yeah,' Charlie agreed reluctantly.

'Then here will do. Do you have to go back, this afternoon?'

'No. They've gone to the caves.' She paused to pick a daisy, twirling the thin stem between her fingers. It had been a chaotic morning as the family decided who was going to the caves and who was going to the beach. Auntie Beverly had flat out refused to go to 'that dark horrible place', but for Darren and her dad it was one of the highlights of holidaying in Hithechurch and they wouldn't be dissuaded. 'I'm free all day until tea.'

Emily smiled. 'Then let's go to the swing park.'

It was quiet at the small collection of swings, slides and climbing frames in the middle of the campsite. The pair of them wandered about listlessly for a while, sharing a packet of Polos and not saying much. They got on the swings and tried to swing as high as possible, then hung upside down on them, legs twined around the metal chains. The roundabout was inhabited by a family of kids that all shared the same cornsilk blond hair, and they clearly had no interest in playing with anyone else. Eventually they spotted a girl sitting by herself in the shadowy cool spot under the slide. She was reading a battered-looking library book, her head down and her legs stuck out in front of her as though this were a place she regularly hid from the sun. She had dark brown hair that fell long over her shoulders, and she was wearing a pair of frayed denim shorts and a pair of scuffed trainers with rainbow laces.

Together, Emily and Charlie leaned in under the slide, and the girl looked up – not startled, just curious.

'Hey,' said Charlie. 'Do you want to play a game or something? What's your name?'

The girl took a bookmark from out of her pocket and, laying it between the pages, closed her book. Even in the gloomy shadow under the slide, Charlie could see a smattering of freckles across her nose.

'Yeah, all right,' she said. 'My name's Katie.'

Chapter 29

1961

Rosalind Stimpson's reign of beauty did not last much longer.

Around a year after Derek – or Harry, as he was known by then – met her, Rosa slipped and fell while cleaning the inside of the Haunted House attraction. She crashed down a set of crooked steps and an errant nail caught at her cheek, leaving a three-inch gash from the corner of her mouth up towards her cheekbone. The hospital stitched it back up for her, covered much of her head with gauze and sent her home, warning her that if anything, she had been lucky; she could have broken her neck, or her back.

Rosa did not think she was lucky.

The wound healed well enough but it left a scar, and the days of Rosa preening herself in all corners of the fairground were over. Boys stopped asking after her, and unsavoury men took their attentions elsewhere. Harry though, was not dissuaded. To him, the puckered purple scar across her cheek did not look so bad; after all, he had grown up looking at pictures of much, much worse, and he had his own scar, a rigid whorl of dark hardened skin just behind his ear.

At first, Rosa would not see him. She would not see anyone. When it was clear that the scar would not heal any better than it already had, she took to her room and would not leave it. When Harry called round he would be faced with her mother, who would only give him a sour look and tell him to leave. So he began leaving notes for her – simple things, asking how she was and if he might take her out sometime. Sometimes he left a box of chocolates – Dairy Box or Milk Tray – or a bunch of flowers he'd picked himself from the Rushbrooks' overgrown lot.

Then one day, in the spring, her mother stood aside and told him he could go up. For a long moment he was too surprised to move, until the old woman rolled her eyes and walked back down the hallway, leaving him standing in the open door.

'Hello?'

Having made his way upstairs, Harry knocked gently on a painted pink door, and hearing a murmur from within, stepped inside. The room was brightly painted but gloomy, with thick curtains pulled across dirty windows and the place smelled sour – a sick-room smell. Rosalind was sitting up in her bed wearing a nightie with long sleeves, and she held her head up defiantly, glaring at him.

'Well? Come to have a good look, have you?'

He came over to the bed and stood over her, his hat in his hands. She did not turn away from him, but instead pushed out her chin so that her hair fell back from her cheek – he could see the scar clearly, even in the gloom of the bedroom. It was such a small thing really. With make-up, he thought it would be quite possible to cover much of it up. So her skin would not be flawless, but whose was? She was still very beautiful. He sat down on the bed, taking pleasure in being this close to her. He shook his head slowly.

'I am so sorry, Rosa. Your face . . . what a mess.'

She jerked as if he had struck her, and he had to press his lips together to keep from smiling. Rosa had dismissed him before, as if his opinion meant no more than dust in the wind, but now . . . Now she needed him to tell her she was beautiful. What a sweet thing it was to hold over her. Her hand crept up to her face, touching the thin line of the scar as if seeing for herself.

'Is it . . . is it really so bad?'

Harry carefully arranged his face into an expression of pity.

'It hurts my heart to look at you, love. Could the doctors not have done a better job than that? They've butchered you. What a shame.'

Rosa's big green eyes filled with tears, turning them glassy. She drew her knees up to her chest.

'I've been saving up.' Her voice was quieter than he'd ever heard it. She sounded like a girl of ten or eleven, some child whispering in the dark. 'I wanted to go abroad. To America. I wanted to . . . I've read about it in magazines, how you can go out there and some Hollywood producer will see you on the street and ask you to be in a film. I wanted to be a *star*.'

Keeping his eyes on her, Harry shook his head slowly. The tears in her eyes spilled over, tracking silver lines down her pale face.

'Oh no, love. Not you. I'm so sorry.' He put his hand on her knee, feeling the warmth of her through the covers. He thought of her mother, downstairs. He wondered if she was listening. He pictured her in the kitchen, looking up at the ceiling, her sour face twisted with suspicion – and the image made his heart beat faster. *Let her listen*, he thought.

199

'Don't worry, I won't leave you,' he said. He took his hand off her knee and slid it instead under the covers. Her leg beneath the duvet was warm and smooth, and it was the work of seconds to push her nightie aside. 'I know how to make you feel better.'

Chapter 30

July 1988

Charlie, Emily and Katie tramped through the small stretch of woods on the caravan site, each with a backpack full of stolen goods. Katie had a Tupperware pot under one arm, and they were sharing a packet of Fruit Polos. It was after teatime, and under the shade of the trees it was pleasantly cool. Charlie could feel a slight prickle on the back of her neck from a patch of sunburn. She was explaining to the other two about maps, and treasure.

'Why would we need a map to it, though?' asked Emily. 'It's for Stitch Face Sue, we don't need to go and get things back.'

'No, not need as such,' Charlie conceded. 'But what if we all come back here next year, and we dig the pot back up? If it's empty, we'll know she took the stuff we gave her. That would be cool.'

'Or,' added Katie, in her quiet, thoughtful voice, 'she might have left *us* a present.'

Charlie shot Katie a grateful look. Overnight she had got

quite attached to the idea of having a map of the woods with their treasure marked on it, and she wasn't about to be dissuaded now.

Emily shrugged. 'All right, I suppose. Where are we going to bury the things?'

In the end they found a spot in a small clearing, near a couple of large chestnut trees and a fallen trunk. It was, Charlie reasoned, a fairly memorable place, but even so she took out her pink diary and carefully drew a map, each of the biggest trees marked. On a whim, she named the three biggest after them: Charlie the Chestnut, Emily the Silver Birch, Katie the Oak. Once they had decided exactly where they were going to put the thing, Charlie wrote down some rough instructions: *Eleven paces east from the big chestnut tree. Seven paces north. X marks the spot!* She had filched Darren's compass so she could note the directions.

The three of them sat in a circle with the open pot between them. The lid, which had a picture of a cheerful snowman on it, they had put to one side.

From her backpack Charlie pulled out the items she had brought with her: a Yahtzee pad, an old paperback book stolen from the caravan, several boiled sweets, a couple of plastic tokens they used at the funfair and a black hairbrush with a silvery handle, stolen from her sister Carol. She was pleased with the haul, but it was getting harder to find interesting things to take. Emily had suggested they pick items that Stitch Face Sue might especially like, but she was running out of options. Katie pulled a crumpled pick 'n' mix bag from her rucksack, and tipped the contents out on the ground. There were three pink and yellow hairclips, a keyring with a small fuzzy blue teddy bear attached, and a number of long silver pins. Seeing the other girls looking at them, she picked one up and held it between her thumb and forefinger.

'My mum brings her embroidery with her. She likes to work on it in the evenings. Oh, and there was something else.' Katie reached back into her bag and brought out a large pair of sewing scissors, with big orange plastic handles. There was a Dymo label on the outside of the handle that said 'JEANIE'. At the sight of them, Charlie felt uneasy, and she thought of Emily's penknife again. Where had that gone?

'Won't your mum miss those?'

'Oh, she has another pair that she likes better,' said Katie, smiling. She put the big scissors in the pot next to her hairclips and Charlie's boiled sweets.

Emily had been sitting and watching, but sensing it was her turn, she opened her bag and began taking out items. There was a neon-coloured scrunchie, which Charlie noted because Emily's hair was much too short to be held back – perhaps she had used it before she'd had her hair cut short? And then, curiously, a lipstick. It was a light coral pink. Emily took off the top and turned the base so the stick of colour revealed itself. It looked half used.

'This was my sister's,' she said quietly. Charlie glanced at Katie. They had not told her that Emily's sister Louise was missing, only that her dad was a bad man who needed to be punished. But the girl seemed unfazed.

Next, she brought out the manila envelope from her rucksack, the one Charlie knew contained photos of her sister.

'Are you sure you want to give those up?' She had asked the question before she had really thought about it. Emily gave her a dark look she didn't understand, then shrugged.

'It's just a few. I have others. I want Stitch Face Sue to know who she's . . . doing this for.'

'What are they?' asked Katie. It was gloomy in the woods now, and her thick fringe had cast her eyes into shadow.

'Photos,' said Charlie. Emily put the envelope in the pot. Next she brought out a VHS tape. Both girls raised their eyebrows. VHS tapes were rare and expensive things in their world. It seemed outrageous that Emily wanted to bury it in the dirt.

'What's that?' asked Charlie. She crunched a Fruit Polo between her teeth.

'It's Louise's favourite film,' said Emily. '*Stand By Me*. We used to rent it from the shop all the time, and then when she left, no one ever took it back.'

But when she put it inside the pot, Charlie noticed that rather than a label saying *Stand By Me* it had a plain white sticker, onto which someone had scribbled '1987' in thick black marker pen.

Katie put the lid on the pot. Using a couple of brightly coloured plastic spades, they spent some time digging a hole, which was much harder work than Charlie had been led to believe by certain children's books and TV shows. By the time they had finished packing the dirt back in on top of the pot, the woods had got much darker. Overhead, clouds had gathered for the night, and the shadows around them were growing thick and elastic, bleeding into each other.

'What now?' asked Katie.

'Now,' said Emily, 'we draw a pentagram over the grave . . .'

'Grave?'

'Hole, I mean. We draw this big star thing and then we light matches and think really hard about Stitch Face Sue. And that summons her.' Emily rubbed her thumb over her chin. 'And then she does what we ask.'

Charlie shifted where she was crouched. This, she felt, should have been hers to explain. The whole ritual had been her idea after all. And Stitch Face Sue had been her idea, too. Thinking about how she wasn't real felt disloyal, though, and some instinct told her that it was important for Emily to feel she was in control of this.

And Stitch Face Sue was just a game.

Wasn't it?

'Here.' Charlie got her torch out of her bag under the pretence of needing some light on the ground. 'You draw in the dirt, I'll point the torch.'

The weak plastic light fell listlessly against the ground. Emily picked up a stick and began to rake it through the dirt, and at that moment they heard the sound of something heavy moving through the trees and undergrowth. Emily dropped the stick.

'What—?'

A figure came crashing out of the bushes next to them, huge and dark. Katie let out a little shriek, and then the figure swooped down on them, stamping straight into the middle of Emily's half-drawn star. Charlie scrambled backwards, but it was too late. A big hand grasped her by the front of her shirt and yanked her to her feet.

'What are you kids doing out here in the dark?'

A blast of stale beer breath. It was a man, not Stitch Face Sue at all, but a tall rangy man with his hair pushed back from his head in carefully combed lines. He wore a white vest, which even in the dark Charlie could see was stained yellowish at the armpits. It was the man from the funfair, the man who had been painting the brightly coloured van; the man who had chased her out of the slots.

'Get off!'

'Get out of it.' The man from the slots dropped Charlie and glared down at all of them. He was carrying a long rope looped around his other arm, and Charlie felt a sudden jolt of panic. This was a *real* threat. Not something they'd made up for fun.

The girls were all on their feet. Their spades were scattered at their feet like neon litter.

'What are you doing out here, anyway?' the man spat. 'People let their bloody kids roam like tramps.'

'This is our campsite,' said Charlie, feeling the bite of injustice even under her own terror. 'We're on holiday here!'

The man scowled at them and stamped his foot forward, like he was trying to frighten away pigeons. He was drunk, Charlie realised.

'What have you seen? You seen anyone out here?' And then, before they could answer: 'Go on then, get out of it, you little shits, before I give you something to worry about.' He stepped forward again and made a sweeping gesture as if to grab one of them again, and like a spell suddenly broken the girls turned as one and ran, deeper into the woods.

Chapter 31

Now

I was thinking more and more about the missing girl, Cheryl Yates. It began to eat away at me, how this place seemed to be cursed – the events from my childhood, the missing girls, and Cheryl. Can a place be cursed? The man from the bookshop, Mr Kastner, seemed to be hinting that was the case, that Hithechurch and Folkesholme were a kind of vortex where people just went missing.

There's a small library in Folkesholme, and I decided to go there, telling myself it was on a whim. I had a look through stacks and stacks of old local newspapers and microfiche. It was warm and quiet, but I felt so conspicuous I was sure all the blood in my body had relocated to just under my cheeks, and I was certain I was glowing like a lamp. But no one bothered me. I was beginning to think that I wasn't really there, somehow.

Katie, sitting next to me on her own stool, was making short work of a book she'd picked up. The cover had a girl in antiquated clothes, stepping through a door in a garden wall.

'Is this part of the research for your book?' she asked.

'Yeah,' I said, not quite looking at her. 'Libraries are good for research.'

What I found out is that all in all, including Cheryl, eight girls had gone missing in the area of Hithechurch and Folkesholme in the last fifty years or so. I didn't know much about the averages of these things, but it seemed like a fairly high number to me. I took photos of all the girls with my phone, and made notes on their names and their ages when they'd gone missing. The first had been in 1961, her name was April Rushbrook, and she'd been fourteen years old. Then I went to a café on the seafront, a cheap, bleak sort of place with dead flies in the windows, and I began poking around on websites. The internet on your phone, on a little slab of glass you carry around in your pocket. Let me tell you, I'll never get over that.

I sipped weak tea while Katie picked at a slice of cake. Of the eight girls, I could only find concrete news on two of them: Lucy Bunyon, who had gone missing from Folksholme in 1973, had turned up three years later, a runaway who'd made her way to London and had an awful time of it, by the sounds of things, and Jane Mellows, who had been killed by her boyfriend, her body hidden in a stretch of woods somewhere in Kent. The other six were unaccounted for, no further news or updates – like they had simply floated upwards into a waiting sky, like helium balloons someone didn't keep a tight enough grip on. I underlined their names: April Rushbrook (1961), Natalie Price (1975), Alison Smith (1976), Sophie Bennett (1979), Laura Jennings (1984), and finally Cheryl Yates, missing since last summer.

I looked closer at the three who had apparently lived in the area, rather than going missing while on holiday, like Cheryl. One of them, Laura Jennings, had been a local, and she had disappeared in 1984, just four years before my disastrous holiday in Hithechurch. There was an article from 1994 still on a local newspaper's database, marking the tenth anniversary of her disappearance. The photograph of her showed a girl with crimped blonde hair and freckles, and a pair of striking green eyes. She had been fifteen when she vanished, and no one had heard anything of her since. I looked at her photograph for a long time, growing more and more uneasy. Did she look familiar to me, somehow? Had I seen her on the news? It was possible.

According to the article, Laura Jennings still had family in the area – or she did in the mid-90s, anyway. I faffed around for a bit longer on the internet, marvelling at the sort of personal information people left online, and eventually found what I was fairly sure was Laura Jennings' brother, who now ran some sort of second-hand car business on the edge of Folkesholme. It was something to think about.

Katie pushed herself away from the table, balancing her chair on its back legs while she looked at me.

'Did you find out anything interesting?'

'Yeah.' I gave her a quick smile. 'Lots of interesting stuff. Do you want to go back now? There's still some daylight left, you can have a run around.'

We drove back, and once we were inside the park, Katie asked to be let out, so I stopped the car, watching her run across the grass to the swings, her brightly coloured trainers with their trailing rainbow laces the brightest thing in the day. The wind was blowing hard again, so I think that's why I didn't hear Joseph until he knocked on the driver's window. I jumped about a foot in my seat, and opened the window. Surprise was one thing, but that didn't quite explain why my heart was thumping so rapidly at the sight of his face.

'Oh, hey,' I said.

'Hey you.' He smiled, leaning down to face me more directly. 'Not seen you about for a couple of days. I hope you're not avoiding me. Was the curry that bad?'

'Not at all, no, it was great, I . . .' I pushed my hair out of my eyes. 'I've just been busy, you know?'

'Looking after your niece?' He nodded, as though he knew all about looking after rambunctious children.

'She mainly looks after herself,' I said, truthfully enough. He smiled again, looking me directly in the eyes, and I felt that strange sense of electricity again. I said the first thing that popped into my head. 'Anyway. I guess it's my turn to provide dinner? I'm no kind of cook, but maybe we could go out.'

His smile broke into a grin.

'That would be lovely, Sarah.'

Hearing him use that name reminded me what a fraud I was, but otherwise I was giddy with success.

'It's a date.'

Chapter 32

July 1988

The girls ran, helter-skelter, into the trees, deeper and deeper until the foliage was almost too wild to pick their way through. There was a hard nugget of anxiety in Charlie's chest – she had never been this deep in the woods before – but gradually she realised that the fairground man wasn't coming after them. He probably hadn't been chasing them at all. She called to the others to stop, and Katie did, her face looking pale in the gloom. The sun had gone down. She had a long blade of grass sticking out of her hair, so Charlie picked it out and tried to blow a tune on it. Katie laughed.

'What are you two doing?' snapped Emily. She was still crashing through the bushes, her T-shirt covered in burrs. 'There's a way out up here, look.'

They joined her, and Charlie saw that she was right. There was a chicken-wire fence with a hole in it, certainly big enough for kids their age to squeeze through, and on the other side of it was an overgrown field.

'Where is that?' asked Katie. 'It's not the campsite, is it?'

'No,' agreed Charlie, 'I think we must have come out on the other side.'

Emily was already climbing through the hole.

'Shouldn't we go back?'

Emily shook her head tersely. There was a strange electricity running through the girl. Charlie had the strangest idea that if she touched her, her hair would stand on end. She climbed through the hole and helped Katie through after her.

'I want to go to the beach,' said Emily. 'I think that's where we should do it.'

Katie looked nonplussed. Charlie frowned. They'd left the Tupperware pot where they'd buried it, filled with the offerings for Stitch Face Sue. How could they complete the ritual?

'You've still got the matches, haven't you?' said Emily as though she could read Charlie's mind.

They were still in her backpack, so Charlie nodded.

'The fire is the important thing, I think,' said Emily. 'And that there's three of us. Let's go.'

Together they set out across the field, Charlie wondering when it had become Emily's ritual; when Stitch Face Sue had become Emily's to coax and command. A few birds flew up from the long grass, but Charlie couldn't tell what they were; black on black, they vanished into the dark.

In time they came back to the main road, and Charlie realised that the field they were in was just the overgrown field you could see on your right when you walked back to the caravan site. How different things looked when you saw them from another angle. Emily walked across the road and made straight for the ditch on the other side.

'This'll be a shortcut,' she said. 'We want to keep away from the roads.'

212

'How come?' asked Katie, but Emily ignored her. Charlie just shrugged, and the two followed on into the night.

It was a longer walk than any of them expected, but just as Charlie was beginning to wonder if they had managed to get lost after all, they heard the sound of the sea; a huge, shifting, uneasy animal in the dark. It made Charlie think of a visit to the zoo the year before, where they'd watched a bored-looking tiger prowl back and forth in his inadequate enclosure. The tiger could wait forever to get its teeth into you, thought Charlie, and so could the sea.

They walked through fields, passed over more ditches, fences, went over a couple of stiles. It was dark but the sky was clearing out, and the open spaces around them were lit with the hard, glittery luminescence of starlight. They passed through a copse of trees and the sea suddenly spread before them like a dark shifting mass – away to their left were the lights of Hithechurch, looking cosy and welcoming, with a few closer lights from the houses scattered at the edge of the town. To the right, the land gradually rose into the rocky cliffs that led to Folkesholme. Together, they picked their way down through the sandy paths and dunes sprouting long, hardy grasses, until they stood on the beach itself. The tide was out, but close enough that Charlie could see runners of white foam inching their way up the sand.

Immediately in front of them was the dark geometric form of the old outfall. In the starlight it looked black and somehow heavy, like it had been dropped from a great height and embedded in the sand. Charlie knew the outfall well; it was the place where her sister and Darren went crabbing, but at night it looked different. Everything looked different.

'Let's do it there,' said Emily, pointing at the outfall. 'It looks like a big gravestone or something.'

213

'I don't know,' said Katie. 'My mum told me that place is dangerous.'

'It is,' said Charlie. Emily gave her a sharp glance, so she shrugged. 'I mean it's dangerous to be in the tunnel when the tide is coming right in over it – you can get sucked under. My nan saw it happen here, once. A little kid just went, pop, under the water, and the grown-ups had to go in and drag him out. He lost both his shoes. But it's not dangerous now, the sea isn't close enough. Plus we can sit on the tops of the walls, can't we?'

Emily nodded at this compromise, and they headed over, Katie trailing behind slightly. The main slab that lay across the top of the outfall tunnel was mostly covered in sand, but as they walked over it and down the top of the leftmost wall, the sand gave way to grey stone thickly covered in dark green seaweed. The place smelled ripe – it had been years since the outfall had been a proper sewer pipe, but seaweed cooking over the long hot day gave it a rank, salty stench. They came to a wide stone section with fewer barnacles and Emily sat, crossing her legs and patting the stone next to her.

'Come on, let's do it here.'

The girls sat, keeping away from the side with the drop. Sand came up almost to the top of the wall on the other side, but to Charlie's right, there was a sharp seven-foot drop to the ground. She peeked over the side. The sand there was still wet, and she knew from experience that it was thicker and muddier than other sand. It liked to suck your sandals off, if it got the chance. Behind them, the dark tunnel mouth waited, like a hole in space. Charlie turned away from it to see that Emily had her knife in her hand again and was using it to carve a rough pentagram in the seaweedy stone. She twisted the knife and a single spark bounced across the stone, as clear and as bright as a shooting star. *Magic*, thought Charlie.

'That will do.' Emily sat back, and the three of them crowded around the pentagram. Aside from the distant glimmering motion of the sea, everything was very still.

'Who was that man?' asked Katie. 'He seemed really . . . angry.'

'He's one of the people that run the funfair, and the slots,' said Charlie. 'He always seems angry to me.'

'Angry men,' said Emily, with a note of disgust in her voice. 'That's why we're here, isn't it? That's why Susan Cartwright died, because of stupid angry men, and now we're going to send her to get rid of one more. Charlie, have you got the matches?'

Charlie got the box out of her rucksack pocket and took out three matches.

'We light them, one at a time, and each of us says a kind of prayer to Stitch Face Sue. Emily goes last. And then when the last match goes out, Stitch Face Sue will appear, and we can tell her to go and . . . deal with Emily's dad.'

Katie looked sceptical then, and Charlie had a moment of real worry. Emily was taking this all very seriously, and she felt herself torn between the pair of them. This was hers and Emily's game, and yes it might seem daft but . . . she had seen Stitch Face Sue, outside the caravan. She had *seen* her.

'She made a dog bite my dad,' said Emily suddenly, as if sensing that the other girl wasn't buying it. 'Out of nowhere, this dog came and attacked him, blood everywhere, I saw it.'

'All right,' said Katie, in a placating tone. 'Sounds spooky. Let's do it and head back though, yeah? It's getting colder.'

Again, Charlie felt that stab of unease, but even so, she struck the first match against the matchbox. There was a *fizz*, and she held it up, a tiny orange flame in the dark purple shadows of the night.

215

'Susan Cartwright, are you there? We ask for your help again tonight. We know your ghost must be very close, as we are near the anniversary of your death, and sit in sight of your grave.' Charlie cleared her throat. The heat of the match flame was hot against her fingers. 'We've buried offerings for you, and we lit a fire for you.'

The flame was too hot and she dropped it, where it winked out against the seaweed. She turned slightly to Katie, and struck the second match. There was a moment's silence.

'Now you speak,' she prompted Katie.

'Oh, er . . . Stitch Face Sue, we call out to you!' Katie lifted her hands up and waggled her fingers, then laughed. Charlie risked a glance at Emily. The girl's face had gone chalky white under the starlight, and her mouth looked like a line drawn in pencil. 'We call upon your ghostly powers for revenge!'

Katie laughed again, a shrill girlish giggle which sounded as though it belonged at the funfair on a sunny day, not in the darkness of a deserted beach.

'Katie . . .' Charlie started, not sure what she was going to say, and then the match burned her fingers again and she dropped it. 'Shit.'

'Do the third match,' said Emily, her voice very soft. It made Charlie think of Emily's dad, the quiet tension that hovered around him like a cloud. She struck a third match, her fingers trembling just a touch. The small light swam into life, and Emily started talking.

'Susan Cartwright, Stitch Face Sue. I've needed your help all my life. My sister Louise needs your help. Please, I need someone, *something* . . .' The skinny girl with the black hair took a gasping breath inward, and placed her hands directly on the scratched pentagram. 'Come and take him away, Stitch Face Sue. He deserves it, just like your father did, and the pirates who killed you.'

Katie snorted, one hand pressed against her mouth to hold in a bigger laugh.

Years later, Charlie would wonder if Katie laughed then because she knew the real story of Susan Cartwright – that the girl had hidden from the pirates successfully, and survived. She would wonder if the girl had known that Charlie's version of the story was nonsense and was amused that Emily had fallen for it.

She'd wonder about that a lot.

Emily made a noise in the back of her throat, and threw herself forward across the pentagram, slamming her hands into the centre of Katie's chest. Katie, who had been sitting on the side with the drop, gave a strangled kind of cry and went over backwards, her legs and trainers briefly in the air before they vanished, followed a second or so later by a loud crunch. Charlie scrambled to the edge after her, but she was much too late to do anything but look down at the girl, lying crumpled in the mud below.

'Katie? Katie!'

'Shh. She was messing it up,' said Emily.

Charlie stood up, not looking at her friend, and began to run down the length of the outfall, looking for where the sand inside it came up to the edge of the stone wall. Eventually she found the section she thought she could safely jump from, and landed, her knees smarting with the impact. She ran up the inside of the outfall, her trainers sticking and sucking in the wet sand.

'Katie?'

For a terrifying second she couldn't see the girl at all, and she thought that perhaps the sand had swallowed her up already, like the quicksand she had read about in books she got from the library. And then she saw her; a thicker piece of darkness in the shadows, the sole of one brightly coloured trainer turned towards her.

'Katie!'

She got to the girl and stopped. A cold sensation, like being plunged into the sea unexpectedly, moved through her blood. Katie was lying wrong. All of it was . . . wrong. Her eyes were open but her neck was turned at a drastic angle. There were thin trails of blood leaking from her nostrils and ears. The blood looked black.

Charlie swooned on the spot, a rush of darkness at the edge of her vision, and then a cold hand squeezed her shoulder.

'Is she all right?' asked Emily.

'I . . .' Charlie coughed, shook her head. Katie trembled slightly, and made a gurgling noise. One of her hands, lying face up on the dark grey sand, twitched like a dying spider, bone white. 'We have to go and get someone. We have to . . .' She bent down, reached out to touch the girl, then stopped. Were you supposed to move someone who had broken their neck? She thought not, but the idea of leaving her there in the dark, in the wet dark, seemed even worse. 'You stay here. With her. I'll go . . . I'll run to the town.'

'No, look.' Emily bent down next to Katie, her tone very matter-of-fact, and Charlie felt a sudden rush of relief. Emily knew some way to make it better, she could fix it somehow: Charlie had an image of a scene she'd seen on a TV programme once, of a man with a dislocated shoulder having it snapped back into its socket by a doctor. Emily would do something like that. It would be all right.

And then blood began to seep from a sudden gash in Katie's neck. Belatedly, Charlie saw that Emily had her knife again. She had cut the other girl's throat.

This time, the darkness enveloped Charlie fully, but it couldn't have lasted for very long. The next thing she was aware of was Emily shaking her arm brusquely. Her fingers were icy.

218

'Come on,' she was saying. 'I need you to help me move her.'

'What?' Charlie snatched her arm away and got to her feet. Katie was still there, lying in the dark sand. There was blood, but surprisingly little of it. Charlie felt herself swooning again, and pinched her own arm, hard. 'What did you fucking do?'

Emily blinked, as though offended by the language. 'She messed up the ritual, but it's all right I think, because this was the *sacrifice*.' She said it as though this was obvious. 'It works better this way, probably.'

Charlie began to cry.

'No, don't do that. She was dead anyway, you saw that. You *saw it*, Charlie. She was dead, but now she's Stitch Face Sue's.' Emily sounded exasperated, as though Charlie was refusing to go on a scary ride at the funfair. 'We have to hide her though, or we'll both get in trouble.'

'Trouble?' Charlie made an odd choking sound that wanted to be a laugh, and then bile was surging up the back of her throat. She turned away and heaved a small pile of sick into the space by the wall. As she stood there, looking down, she saw that there was a small stream of water curling its way up towards the tunnel. The tide was coming in.

'Hurry up,' said Emily. She grabbed Charlie's arm again and squeezed it. As if from a great distance, Charlie saw that she was still holding the knife in her other hand. 'You've got to help me.'

Chapter 33

1961

In time, Harry moved Rosa into a tiny maisonette on the edge of Hithechurch. He decorated a bedroom just for her and he filled it with mirrors: a huge dressing table like a frosted wedding cake, a full-length gilded mirror that stood by the wardrobe, an oval hand mirror on the bedside drawers. He didn't want her to forget what she was, after all – if she did that, she might realise what *he* was.

Rosa did not work. She did not spend idle time walking the town, or in the shops. Rosa stayed indoors in their tiny maisonette and she was glad to, because it meant that she avoided the nosey stares of their neighbours. It meant that she could hide her face away from the world. The only time she did go out was to the pictures, which Harry would drive her to three or four times a week. There was a grand old cinema in Folkesholme, and Harry took her to every film they showed there, twice if the films starred glamorous women like Doris Day or Grace Kelly or Audrey Hepburn. He loved to sit there in the dark and drink in Rosa's face as she watched her impossible dreams play out on the big screen.

And afterwards they would go home and Rosa would let him do whatever he liked to her, as long as the lights were off. She never made a sound.

These were the happiest days of Harry's life, but gradually he came to realise that things were off kilter with Rosa – something, somewhere, was not right with her, and like a piece of grit inside the soft flesh of an oyster, it was building on itself, growing. He would come home from a day of fixing rides or making deliveries to find her standing in their small square of back garden in just her underwear, her hands and feet nearly purple with the cold. Or on one occasion she smashed all the mirrors in their bedroom, leaving glittery shards of glass embedded in the plush carpet. When he tried to talk to her about what was wrong, she would sob and lock herself in the bathroom.

Finally, on a day when he'd caught her trying to cut off her hair with a pair of kitchen scissors, he sat her on a stool in the kitchen and held her face with his hands.

'Tell me,' he said. 'Tell me what you want.'

Her face in those days was not the showstopper it had once been – not because of the scar on her cheek, which had faded to a faint purple line, but because she was sallow and pale from a lack of sunlight. Her eyes were often bloodshot from crying, and her lips were dry and cracked.

'I read an article in *Hollywood Goss*,' she said. This was one of the magazines Harry bought her, full of chatter and lurid speculation about actors and films. She would pore over them, perhaps imagining herself in the sequinned dresses, walking the red carpet. 'They can do so much these days. Plastic surgeons. Perhaps they could . . . fix me.'

For Harry it was like his father was suddenly standing

221

behind him; he hadn't thought of the old man in years. He didn't even know if he was still alive.

'Rosa, love, that stuff is for the rich, you know that.' He nodded to the grotty kitchen with its blistered lino. 'That's not us, is it? We're not rich, you can see that.'

'But we could save up.' From the way her voice became brighter, he could tell that she had been thinking about this for a long time. 'Put a little aside until we have enough.'

'No, love.' He took the scissors away from her and put them back in the kitchen drawer. 'Let this idea go.'

But that night he dreamed of the wax model again. Rather than in his father's study, they were in the bedroom with the mirrors, only they were all broken. The wax model stepped from shard to shard, reflecting his raw, red flesh into a thousand points of bloody light, and when Harry bent down to listen, he whispered in his ear with his scratchy, insistent voice.

And when he woke up, Harry knew what they had to do.

Chapter 34

July 1988

'Listen to me.'

Charlie looked down at her wrist where Emily was gripping it so tightly it hurt. Her friend had been speaking but she hadn't heard any of it; she kept losing track of what was going on, as though her attention was fading in and out like a poor radio signal.

'What?'

Emily shook her arm. 'Help me move her, all right? We have to hide her.'

'*Hide* her?' Charlie pulled her arm away. 'No, we have to, I don't know, call the police, an ambulance.' The sudden thought that they hadn't run to get an ambulance straight away hit her in the gut, and the edges of her vision went dark again.

'Don't be stupid,' said Emily. 'I already told you. She's dead. There's nothing we can do about it, but if we get caught here then you and me are in huge trouble. My dad will kill me, and you'll go to prison. Is that what you want?'

'How can we hide her?' Charlie asked. Her lips were numb. 'They'll know it was us.' She hurriedly corrected herself. 'They'll know we were with her.'

'They don't know anything. Come on. We can't put her in the sea, we won't be able to carry her in far enough. And we'd get soaked.' Emily turned her back on Charlie and marched back to the still form lying on the wet sand. She pushed her sleeves up and bent down to take a hold of the dead girl under the armpits. 'Come *on*.'

Charlie joined her, the thin currents of water swirling around her trainers. The tide was coming in faster now. She took hold of Katie's ankles, and the two of them began awkwardly to drag her towards the mouth of the tunnel. It was pitch black in there, and the thought of leaving Katie in there . . . of even taking one step into that thick darkness . . . Charlie's grip slipped, and Katie thudded onto the wet sand.

Emily hissed at her, so she leaned down and got a better grip. Tears were rolling down her face. It took them around fifteen minutes to get her up the length of the outfall, with frequent stops as she got too heavy for them – Charlie would never have guessed that any girl could be so heavy, especially one as slight as Katie. By the time they got to the mouth of the tunnel, Charlie felt weak in her very bones, a deep hard sickness in her chest weighing her down. Katie's hair had fallen over her face, so that Charlie could only see her mouth. Her lips looked dark and strange. The ring of blood around her neck was black under the starlight.

'Do you have your torch?'

Charlie looked up to see Emily glaring at her. She shrugged off her rucksack and with trembling fingers she wrestled the cheap plastic torch out and passed it to Emily, who turned it on and directed the beam into the outfall tunnel. The light was narrow and weak, but it revealed a dark cavern filled with broken stones, thick fat slabs of seaweed, and huge clusters of barnacles and mussels. A pale crab the size of Charlie's hand scuttered away from the light and was lost.

'We'll put her behind those rocks there,' said Emily.

'This is stupid,' said Charlie. 'She'll be found.'

'Not if we hide her. Not if you shut up and help me.'

In the end, they dragged her into the tunnel and squeezed her into a nook in the piles of stones, then laboriously picked up rocks and piled them on top of her. Charlie fell back at one point, exhausted and shaking. How long had they been gone from the campsite? It felt like a hundred years. She watched as Emily took handfuls of seaweed and wet sand and piled them on top of Katie's body. They had left the torch on top of one of the rocks, sending its beam across the tunnel, and every now and then Emily would walk in front of its light, her pale face caught in its watery luminescence. She looked tired, and dirty, but she also looked calm, even bored.

When Emily was satisfied they had hidden Katie's body as best they could, she made Charlie walk down the beach to the edge of the sea, and there they washed their hands and shoes in the cold surf. Charlie held her hands up to her face, trying to see if they were clean. She had scuffed her knuckles against the rough rocks and now they stung viciously from the salt.

'We have to make a promise,' said Emily then. They both stood up to their ankles in the roiling surf. Charlie could feel the tide tugging at the sand under her shoes. 'More than a promise. We have to swear an oath. Not to tell anyone. Okay?'

Charlie nodded, not looking at the other girl. Emily grabbed her shoulder and shook it.

'You have to promise! My dad will *kill* me, Charlie. He'll kill me, you know he will. Do you want to get me killed, too?'

It was like a dagger in her heart. Charlie shook her head,

forced the two words out of her lips like they were jagged stones.

'I promise.'

'Stitch Face Sue will come for you if you tell,' said Emily, and she smiled. Then she put her arms around Charlie and hugged her tight, while Charlie stood very still, her arms straight by her sides.

When they turned to go, they stopped again, abruptly. Some distance away a man was standing on the shore, watching them. It was too dark to see much of him, but Charlie could see the rope hanging from his hands.

'How long has he been there?' hissed Emily.

Charlie opened her mouth, but nothing would come out. She felt firmly in the grip of a nightmare, and she was shaking so badly her teeth were chattering. Emily yanked her arm again, pulling her back towards the outfall and away from the man.

'But what—'

'It doesn't matter,' Emily said, brightly enough. 'He didn't see anything. He didn't. I'm sure of it. Now let's go.'

Chapter 35

Now

I woke up in the night, the stink of that old outfall thick in my nose, the sandy mud sucking at my shoes. Gasping with panic I fought briefly with the covers, and then I came back to where I was: the horror of the outfall was decades ago, and I was in a narrow caravan bed with a cheap mattress. My room felt much too dark – too much like that cave at the end of the outfall – so I got up and went out to the front door. It was a still, freezing night, the tips of the grass already white with frost. My breath puffed into little clouds of vapour.

'I'm all right,' I said aloud. 'I'm okay.'

When I turned back around, Katie was standing in the shadows of the front room. She had wet sand in her hair, and her shirt was dark with blood. When I see her she usually looks the way she did when we first met: a lively girl with rainbow laces in her trainers. And then sometimes she looks like this.

'Oh I'm so glad *you're* all right,' she said, with all the sarcasm of the teenager she would never grow up to be.

I covered my face with my hands.

I sat up for the rest of the blisteringly early morning, making myself cup of tea after cup of tea, compulsively eating plain digestive biscuits, until a weak sort of sunshine dabbed dirty fingers at the caravan windows. I knew I should go back to the woods, but I was beginning to think I could dig up every inch of those ratty woods and never find that Tupperware pot. Could someone else have found it, not known what they were looking at, and chucked it away? Or, an even worse thought, had Emily somehow already found it? It would be just like her to cover her tracks.

'What are you doing?' asked Katie as she watched me put my shoes on. Her hair was still wet and sandy.

'Going for a drive around Folkesholme. Do you want to come?'

Katie shrugged one shoulder. It didn't really matter either way. She was always with me.

It was a shitty day for a drive. The clear sky overnight which had led to the early frost was gone, shunted out by tall grey rain clouds, and as I drove the windscreen wipers swept back and forth, fighting against the sort of freezing, driving rain that January does so well. The fields and country roads were lost in a grey static of miserable weather, so I kept my eyes firmly on the road, my hands gripping the wheel with white knuckles, until eventually, I came to the outer edges of Folkesholme. This was the less picturesque bit – no view of the sea here, but plenty of those big shops with massive car parks that seem to cluster just inland of seaside towns. I drove in looping circles for a while, slightly lost, until eventually I came across a tatty-looking car dealership. There was a stretch

of open tarmac dotted with nondescript cars, and a tempo-
rary-looking one-storey building with lots of peeling stickers
in the window. The sign said '**Carl Jennings Second-Hand
Cars**' in comic sans font. There was a small open garage next
to it.

I parked up, wondering if a salesperson would appear to
sell me a car, but when I'd been sitting there for five minutes
listening to the thunder of rain on the roof, I got out and
scampered across to the small building. I saw through the
windows there was no one in there, and instead popped my
head in the garage. A man in overalls was leaning in the open
bonnet of a blue car, and he turned to me, smiling. He had a
tanned face, lots of crow's feet clustering around his eyes, and
curly, greying hair.

'I didn't think anyone would be out on a rotten morning
like this. Can I help you?'

'Are you Carl Jennings?'

'One and the same.'

'Hi, yeah.' On the way there I had wondered if I should
pretend to be interested in buying a car, but faced with this
man in soiled overalls and the quiet, rain-swept car lot I found
I didn't really have the energy for it. 'This is going to sound
weird, but I wondered if I could ask you about your sister.
Am I right in thinking your sister was Laura Jennings?'

His face fell. I could imagine Katie at my elbow, her lips
twisting with distaste. *You just take good cheer everywhere
you go, don't you?*

'She is my sister, yeah.' He pulled a rag from his pocket and
wiped his hands, although they didn't look all that dirty to
me. 'Why do you want to know?'

'I'm a journalist.' This came out of nowhere. I couldn't get
enough of pretending to be a writer, it seemed. 'I'm writing
something on the recent disappearance of Cheryl Yates. You've

229

heard about her, I expect? I wanted to write about some older cases too. Ones that people might have forgotten about. Which is outrageous, if you ask me.'

I told myself this could almost be true. I wanted to find Cheryl. I wanted to help her, somehow; one small tick in a life of bad marks.

'Aye, that girl. Same age as Laura. Come in. I don't have much to say, but it's warmer up the back.'

I followed him further into the garage, where at the back was a small trestle table with a kettle, a box of teabags and a blue glass sugar bowl with a teaspoon sticking out of it. There was a little radio set on the table, quietly playing talk radio. He flicked the switch on the kettle and sat down in one of the chairs.

'Cup of tea?'

After all the tea I'd drunk in the early hours I wasn't much in the mood, but I thought it might make me look more like a journalist. I imagined that journalists were always on the lookout for free drinks. I nodded and sat down in the other chair. When the kettle boiled he poured the water over a couple of teabags, and sighed. He didn't offer me any sugar.

'What did you want to know?'

'First of all, what was Laura like?'

He shrugged. 'She was a normal fifteen-year-old girl. A little bit wild, maybe. She went out a lot, which used to drive our mum spare, because she was so pretty, see. It got her a lot of attention.' He paused, and pulled a wallet out of his back pocket, then extracted a photo, which he passed to me. It was a tiny passport photo and it showed a girl with heaps of crimped blonde hair tied into two bunches with neon pink hair ties. A silly hairstyle more suited to a kid much younger than her, but she paired it with a lot of quite grown-up make-up and a shimmering top. Looking at it, I felt a pang of something

230

deep in my heart. The photo said 'child of the 80s' so clearly it hurt.

'She had boyfriends?'

'What girl doesn't at that age?'

I didn't, I thought, but then the circumstances were rather different.

'I imagine the police asked about them, at the time?'

Carl Jennings snorted. 'The police? They barely asked anything at all. She was just a silly girl to them, someone who'd run away from home. She'll be back in a week, when she gets hungry, they said. It was because we were poor.' He picked up the teaspoon and dumped a heaped spoonful of sugar into his tea. 'No dad. Mum was bringing us up by herself, and she did what she could, but kids then, they ran wild, no telling them anything. I was the same, really.'

I thought of me and Emily running through the woods at night, picking our way down to the beach. People seem to have forgotten, but you didn't keep a close eye then. Not really.

'You were her older brother?'

'Three years older, just at that age where we wouldn't be seen dead together.' He smiled, not looking at me, clearly thinking of old memories. 'If she were still alive . . . if she were still here, she'd be fifty years old. Fifty! And when I remember her she's this mouthy girl who smelled of bubble-gum all the time. Hubba Bubba. Do you remember that? Mum was always pulling empty wrappers out of her pockets.'

I nodded. I felt cold for some reason, and I shoved my hands deeper into my pockets. Why did that little detail worry me?

'What happened the day she disappeared?' I asked.

Carl Jennings sat back in his chair.

'It was a school day, but Laura wasn't at school. She didn't fancy it. I was free of it by then, so I was down the pool hall – there used to be a decent one in Folkesholme, with a bar in it that would serve you even if you weren't old enough. Gone now. I think it's a Costa Coffee. Anyway, it was autumn, dark early, you know, and she came wandering into the pool hall at about three o'clock and it was already gloomy out. She'd been into Hithechurch with her mates – they liked to hang around the funfair there, although they all said they were too old for rides – and then come back on the bus, but she hadn't wanted to go straight home, so she came in to see me. Get a drink out of me, more like.'

'Did she seem . . . okay?'

He shrugged again, shook his head. He put the photo back into his wallet like he was annoyed with it. 'She said she thought she was being followed. By a black van. That's why she hadn't gone straight home, she said, because she didn't want whoever it was knowing where she lived.'

'Bloody hell.' I cleared my throat. 'I didn't read anything about a van.'

'No, well, you wouldn't,' Carl Jennings said tersely. 'Police took no notice when I told them.'

'What happened after that?'

'She asked me to get her a drink, but I wouldn't.' Carl ran a hand through his curly hair. 'I said I didn't have any money for more drinks, and I didn't, but . . . She left after that, said she was going home. And I never saw her again.'

'I'm sorry,' I said.

He took a deep breath. 'I always think, what if I'd asked one of my mates there to lend me the money for a drink? She'd probably still be around now, wouldn't she?'

'So to your mind, there's no chance Laura just ran away?' I said it carefully, wary of an outburst.

'Nah.' Carl Jennings didn't seem angry, just deflated. 'She was flighty and got up to mischief, but she liked the comforts of home too much to just, I don't know, run off to London.

232

She was a tiny thing but she could put away her dinner.' He coughed, and I realised he was getting emotional. 'Mum used to say feeding us was like feeding a pair of gannets.'

There was an awkward pause as I waited for him to regain his composure, and in it I finally tuned in to the radio. They were talking about the book again. Emily's fucking book.

'. . . *several victims' rights groups have petitioned the publisher to cancel the contract for* A Most Dangerous Spell, *but in an unusual move Pine Cone Press have revealed some of the details of the contract, stating that the author's fees are going to charity and it is in the public's interest to know the full story of the Hithechurch murder of Katie Hennessey. Regardless of the controversy, or perhaps because of it, pre-order sales of the book have—'*

'Can you believe that?' Carl Jennings cut in, gesturing at the radio. 'One of those kids making a mint out of that poor girl's murder? You can't tell me that little witch isn't getting something out of it.'

I grimaced, my heart trying to burst out of my chest. 'Oh, I'm sure she is.' *She's getting the chance to drag me through the dirt.*

'It shouldn't be allowed.' Jennings shook his head. 'You ask me, they both should have rotted inside forever.'

I thanked him for his time and left.

On my way back to Hithechurch, I stopped by a newsagent and spent some time looking through the local newspapers for the one I'd seen in Joseph's shop. I eventually found it at the back of the pile, the big fat headline shouting at me: BEACH GIRL STILL MISSING SIX MONTHS ON. I skimmed through the article to find the bit I had been looking for – police were asking about blue vans seen in the area. A black van following Laura Jennings, thirty-odd years ago. A blue van seen around the time Cheryl disappeared. Thirty years was a long gap.

Thirty-five, I corrected myself. Could a blue van, seen on a dark autumn night, be mistaken for a black one? Did people really keep the same van for that long? Just another aspect of ordinary life I knew nothing about.

I went to the till and asked to buy a bottle of vodka from behind the counter. The shop assistant gave me a look, and asked for ID. I blinked in surprise.

'Shit, sorry, I don't have anything on me.'

I left without the vodka but found a supermarket round the corner staffed by people with better eyesight and I stocked up. Back inside the caravan, I drank a rum and Coke, letting the burn of the alcohol warm me up. I felt woozy almost immediately – I was starting to see why people were so keen on booze.

Did I think the two missing girls were connected? Maybe. Could I go to the police about it?

I snorted to myself and tipped back the rest of my drink. In the corner, half hidden in shadow, Katie glared at me.

Chapter 36

Now

The next day was bright and sunny. I wanted to get out of the caravan so I went on a brisk walk around the site, pausing at the little shop. Joseph looked like he'd been nodding off at the counter, but he sat up straight at the sight of me and grinned.

'There's a sight for sore eyes.'

'Hello.' I felt both intensely embarrassed and proud of myself. 'Are you up for getting some food this afternoon?'

His face fell. 'Ah shit, I can't today. I've got to drive up to that big B&Q and get some stuff in to fix the fence.'

Abruptly, I felt sick. What was I doing? Of course he wasn't interested in spending time with me. I took half a step backwards, hoping a dark hole would open up in the floor and swallow me.

'Oh, uh, no worries . . .'

'But,' seeing the look on my face, he came around the counter, 'I will definitely take a rain check on that, okay? There's a café in town, if you fancy it. Do you like quiche? They do a great slice of quiche.'

Despite myself, I laughed. 'I'm not sure I have strong feelings either way about quiche, but yeah, that sounds great.'

'Text me,' he said. 'We'll work out a time when I'm not doing something so bloody tedious, yeah?'

When I left the shop I went back to the caravan. Perhaps Joseph did want to spend time with me after all, which was great, but I still felt like I wanted some company. I took out my phone, and on a sudden impulse I texted Watkins, asking if she wanted to meet up for some chips or something. When it was done I put my phone down on the table and glared at it, feeling sick again. Katie sat opposite me, leaning her head against the smudged caravan window.

'Oh that's sweet,' she said. 'Do you think you've made a friend? Do you think she wants to be friends with you?'

'That's not entirely impossible, you know.' I thought of Joseph. Except, of course, that Joseph didn't really know who I was. 'I've had friends before.' The phone remained silent.

'Yeah, and look how that ended up,' said Katie.

And then the phone dinged. I tried not to snatch it up too obviously, but I couldn't hide my relief at the answer: Watkins was happy to meet up – she was free right now.

I drove out of Hithechurch again and into Folkesholme, parking the car in a car park half covered in sand, and walked up to the beachfront. Without having to talk about it, it seemed to me that we were both avoiding Hithechurch itself, and that was fine by me. I met Watkins on the promenade, which was fairly busy for a weekday in January. A lot of older people, wrapped up in scarves and puffy coats, were sipping hot chocolates and lattes bought from a fancy coffee vendor. We queued up at a burger van for a bag of chips each, and I slathered mine in salt and vinegar. We found an empty bench and sat on it, looking out across the battered blue steel of the sea.

Watkins was as twitchy as ever, and I noticed that she kept

looking up and down the promenade, her eyes moving constantly. For a few seconds I was amused, and then I realised that she was probably worried someone would see us together in public – someone who would recognise me for who I was. My stomach seemed to drop to somewhere in my knees, and I tried desperately to rally some of the good feelings the sunny weather had given me.

'I'm glad for some sunshine at last,' I said inanely. 'There's something to be said for the bleakness of the seaside in January, but it is possible to have too much of it.'

'Yes,' said Watkins, although she didn't sound at all sure. 'Listen, have you found it yet?'

I frowned slightly. 'No, sorry. I am looking, but . . . I don't know. Maybe someone else dug it up, maybe it's lost. It was a long time ago.'

'Oh. I thought, when you messaged me, wanting to meet up, that you must have good news.'

My stomach sank a little lower. 'I just thought it would be nice to get out. With some company.'

A small silence grew between us then. I suddenly didn't want my chips anymore, and Watkins had barely touched hers. What had I been thinking? Katie was right. Why on earth would Watkins want to be friends with me? Why would anyone? I cleared my throat. To my horror, my eyes had filled with tears and the light reflected from the sea was dazzling me. Desperate to distract myself, I said the first thing that came to mind.

'A girl went missing along this stretch of the coast last year. I've been looking for her. Sort of.'

Watkins turned to look at me, startled.

'What?'

'Her name's Cheryl Yates. She was on holiday here, and it sounds as though someone snatched her from the beach.

237

I looked into it, and it turns out several teenage girls have gone missing from this area.' Talking about this, I felt better immediately. This was something I was *doing*, not something I *was*. 'I don't know what the average number of missing people is from a small seaside town, but it seems like a lot to me.'

'What do you mean, you've been looking into it?'

I shrugged. 'There's so much information you can find out just from the internet these days. And I've spoken to a few people around here – you know, just casually. These girls going missing – it goes back decades. That's odd, isn't it? And Cheryl's family think that the police aren't bothering themselves because she's a teenager. I just think, maybe I could help. That it would be a good thing to do.'

Gradually I realised that Watkins was staring at me like I was insane. Her eyes, behind her huge watery-lensed glasses, were very wide.

'This is what you've been doing?' It was the loudest I had ever heard her voice.

I opened my mouth, with no idea what I was actually going to say, and then to my astonishment I saw that Watkins was crying. She dropped the chips on the bench and stood up.

'Hey, wait – what's wrong?'

She began to march off down the path, winding her way through the cocooned old people with their hot drinks, and I scrambled to catch up with her.

'Hold on. I'm still looking, I *told* you that . . .' Once I was close enough I looped my arm through hers and turned her to face me. Her face was flushed and wet, and the look she gave me wasn't sad or angry – it was terrified. I dropped her arm like it was made of white hot metal, and several things suddenly dropped into place. It was the combined expression of fear and misery that did it; I had seen that face before, many years ago, only she hadn't been wearing glasses and the hair had been different, but this was a perm, and a recent one at that . . . And people always look slightly odd in Polaroid photos.

'Fucking hell,' I said, my heart thundering in my chest. 'You're Emily's *sister*. You're *Louise*.'

She pulled a hanky from her pocket and rubbed her mouth and nose with it. She looked around at the people passing by. 'Shit,' she said faintly. 'Shit shit shit.'

I took a step back. 'Christ, what is this about? What are you playing at?'

'Listen.' She lifted her glasses and wiped her eyes. Now that I could see it, the resemblance to Emily was impossible to miss. A cold hand walked down my back, and I thought I could hear Katie laughing, somewhere close. 'Let's go down onto the sand. It's quieter there and we can talk.'

'I'm not sure I want to go anywhere with you.'

'I'm sorry. Please. Just five minutes.'

Down on the sands it was very still. There were a few people walking their dogs in the distance, but mostly we were alone, with only the sound of gulls overhead for company. Watkins, or Louise, as I now supposed I should call her, had pulled herself together a little.

'When I was a teenager, I ran away from home. I couldn't live in that house anymore, with those people. That family was poison.'

'Your dad?' I asked. I'd chucked my chips away and had my hands deep in my pockets. 'He scared me too.'

She glanced at me briefly and then pulled a hand through her hair, pushing it out of her face.

'I was gone and safe for months, but after what happened with you and Emily . . . I went back home, to help look after

239

my mum. It was all awful, but I thought, at least they won't let her out. They *can't* let her out. Shows what I know.'

'Did you go and see her while she was in prison?'

'Once or twice.' She grimaced. 'Mum wanted me to go, said that it would do Emily good, but she was just the same in there as she was on the outside. It's very hard to explain to people what it feels like to be afraid of your little sister.'

'I think I can probably understand.' She glanced at me, a shadow of a smile on her face. 'So where did you get my contact details from? That can't have been easy.'

'Easier than you think,' she said, and shrugged. 'I gave your lawyer's assistant a lot of money for it. Sorry. I couldn't think what else to do.'

'Bloody hell. You can't trust anyone these days.' I laughed a little to myself. I should probably have made a note to complain to my lawyer, but big conversations with my legal representation felt like something I should be avoiding. 'So, you don't work for Pine Cone Press? You're not an editor.' I was thinking of the gloomy little house, and how there hadn't been a single book on display.

'No.' Louise sighed. 'I've watched this book deal happen from Emily's side of things. I've spoken to her agent too, although very carefully, when Emily isn't around.'

'Where is she?' My insides suddenly felt like they were made of ice.

'Don't worry, nowhere near here. She was given a flat up north, very much inland. She hates the south now, and the sea. I had thought that when she was out of prison she would . . . hide away. That's what I would have done. Keep my head down, stay out of trouble.' Louise's mouth turned down at the corners, and I thought she might start crying again, but she seemed to pull herself back from it. 'But instead she came out with this book idea, this determination to shove some of the

240

blame off her and onto you. And it's more than that. She wants *sympathy*.' Louise frowned, and then, in a gesture that surprised me, took hold of the sleeve of my coat and tugged it. 'That's why you have to find whatever it is she wants to stay hidden. You can't be distracted by this other stuff, okay? It's very sad about the missing girl, but . . . You're the only one who can do this. And apart from me, you're the only one who really knows what . . . what she's like. You have to stop her.'

I felt cold, and strange. From somewhere up the beach, a dog was barking excitedly.

'I know,' I said. 'I know I do.'

Louise gave me another watery smile. She looked relieved. 'Thank you. I know you can do it.'

Chapter 37

July 1988

Charlie woke up late the next morning, the sun already blazing in through the window. Normally one of her relatives would have been in to chase her out but instead she could hear them all talking in low voices beyond the bedroom door. She got up, pulled on some fresh clothes – the clothes from the night before she had shoved far under the bed – and went to listen at the door.

Her mother's voice, warm and uncertain. 'It wouldn't be the first time a kid has stayed out all night,' she said. 'They'll find her, probably fallen asleep somewhere.'

'Asleep? Outdoors?' Charlie's nan's voice was sharper, louder, clearly impatient. 'Don't talk daft, Jill, honestly. Probably messing about on the beach and drowned. What they were thinking, giving her free rein, I don't know.'

Charlie opened the door an inch. She felt sick. How could they know about Katie so quickly?

'There's police out there now.' Her grandad was by the window, peering out through a net curtain. 'Looking all around the campsite, they are.'

'They thought she was with her cousins,' continued Charlie's nan, her voice still full of acid. 'They *thought* she was running around with them. What sort of people don't *check*?'

'You can't have a go at them for that, Mum,' Charlie's mother was saying tersely. She was buttering toast while she spoke, slapping a knife across a charred piece of bread. 'They're on holiday, for Christ's sake. We all are. You know what kids are like, running all over the place at all hours, could easily have been one of ours.' At that moment she looked up and saw Charlie, and her gaze softened. 'Crawled out of bed, have you? Come and have some toast.'

Charlie took the offered plate, but didn't move to touch the toast. She slid around her relatives to go and sit on the edge of the seating area.

'What's happening, Mum?'

'Nothing to worry about, love.' Her mother spared her a worried glance, pushing a lock of red hair behind her ear. 'Just a girl who's turned up missing. They'll find her soon enough.'

Abruptly Charlie realised that Jenny was sitting opposite her, clutching one of her plastic ponies in her lap. She was silent and pale, and her eyes behind her thick glasses were huge, moon-like.

She knows, thought Charlie. *Somehow she knows what happened.*

And that was almost it. She put the plate down on her lap, feeling like she was about to shatter into pieces. She would open her mouth and tell her mum what had happened, all of it, and then they'd all hate her but at least it wouldn't be her problem anymore, at least this huge weight in her chest would be gone. She opened her mouth, and there was a quick knock at the flimsy door. Charlie's Aunt Marj opened it, then seemed disappointed.

'It's your friend, Charlie,' she said over her shoulder.

Emily was standing in the doorway, smiling up at them. She wore a yellow sundress, which contrasted badly with her sallow skin.

'Don't you look pretty today?' said Charlie's mum, before turning back to Charlie. 'Go on then, but don't go far, okay? I want you to stay within sight of the caravan today.'

For a long moment, Charlie didn't move. Jenny, at the sight of Emily, had got up and walked back through the kitchen area towards the bedrooms, but no one was taking any notice. Emily caught Charlie's eye, and raised her eyebrows.

'Mum,' Charlie said, not quite looking away from Emily, 'I don't feel all that well, actually . . .'

'Some fresh air will do you good.' Her mum plucked the plate from her lap, picked up the piece of toast, took a bite out of it, then passed the toast back. 'Go on, take it with you. I don't need you under my feet today.'

Defeated, Charlie plodded out of the door and followed Emily outside to the corner of the caravan. She glanced back, to see if her mum, or any of the adults, would restate the warning about wandering off, but they were already back to their discussion in the kitchen, and no one stopped her and Emily as they walked up towards the shower blocks. They sat in the shade of the small red-brick building, knees drawn up to chins. Charlie dropped the toast in the dirt.

'They're looking for her,' Charlie said eventually, unable to keep it in any longer. 'They know she's gone.'

Emily shrugged. 'Course they do. Most parents would notice their kids not being home for bedtime.'

'But . . .' Charlie didn't know how to express what she was feeling. It was as though there was a nest of snakes in her gut, but Emily looked calm. Bored, even. 'Emily . . .'

'We only really knew her for one day, didn't we?' said Emily.

'We wouldn't know where she went, or what she got up to. No one saw us with her.'

'That man,' Charlie hissed. 'He walked right into us, after we buried the Tupperware pot. And he was on the beach too. He could have seen all of it.'

For a long moment, Emily didn't say anything. Charlie watched the girl's face closely, looking for a sign of guilt or panic, but there was nothing. She looked blank. She looked dangerously like her dad.

'It was dark,' she said eventually. 'I don't reckon he saw anything much, just three little kids in the dark. I bet we all looked the same to him, and what was he doing out there anyway? No, I reckon that's all right.'

'All right,' Charlie repeated hollowly. 'Nothing is all right.'

'And she's not *here*,' continued Emily, as though Charlie hadn't spoken. 'She's on the beach. They won't think to look there for ages, because the caravan site was the last place she was seen. It's good that we buried that pot when we did.'

'It is?'

'It has our stuff in it, doesn't it? My stuff, your stuff, and . . . her stuff.'

Charlie shivered. The pair of scissors Katie had brought had been her mother's, they even had her bloody name on them – and there had been the keyring, the little blue teddy bear attached to it. All stuff that was obviously linked to Katie.

And the pot. The pot was hers too. She had brought it from her own caravan.

Emily continued to speak, apparently oblivious to Charlie's anxiety.

'They won't find it,' she said confidently. 'I think Stitch Face Sue will come tonight. She'll come for my dad. She has to, because we gave her everything she could want.' She turned and smiled at Charlie. Her dark green eyes were too bright and wet, like she was holding back tears. Charlie looked down at her feet.

'They'll find out,' she said in her smallest voice. 'They'll find out. We should tell—'

'No.' Emily grabbed her arm and squeezed it, sinking in her fingernails until Charlie squirmed. 'We made an oath, remember? We just have to wait. Stitch Face Sue will come, and everything will be all right.'

Charlie shot to her feet. For a wild second she was on the verge of telling Emily everything: that Stitch Face Sue wasn't real, of course she wasn't, Charlie had made it all up; the real Susan Cartwright had survived, no pirates had torn her guts out and no vengeful ghost with a pair of scissors haunted Hithechurch. But then she remembered the figure she had seen outside the caravan window at night, her long ragged hair, her butchered face. The crane fly Emily had killed stuck in her hair like a Christmas bauble.

It was too much. She turned away from Emily and ran off, not looking back when the girl called after her.

Charlie wandered, her arms slack by her sides. It was a warm day again, with a company of small white clouds making stately progress across the huge blue basin of the sky; another perfect beach day on a holiday where the weather had been almost suspiciously good. Charlie's head, though, was full of dark, wet memories. With no conscious thought, her mind presented her with a parade of agonising images: Emily's hand slapping the graffitied stone; Katie's trainers in the air as she fell backwards off the outfall wall; the long dark stretch of the deserted beach at night. Emily said: don't tell, be quiet – but how could she when everything inside her head was so loud?

She had wandered to the edge of the strip of woodland.

Here she stopped, not wanting to get too close to the place where everything had started to go wrong, when she saw two policemen, walking into the woods further down. Although they walked slowly they had serious expressions on their faces. They carried long metal sticks, and as she watched, one of them used the stick to move a section of bush out of his way. One of them called, his voice low.

'Katie? Katie Hennessey?'

They were searching the woods, which meant they could find the pot. How deep had they buried it? Not especially deep, because the ground had been too full of stones and roots to dig very far with their plastic spades . . .

The spades!

For a dangerous second, Charlie felt faint. When the man from the funfair had surprised them, they had grabbed their rucksacks and ran, but none of them had stopped to pick up the brightly coloured plastic spades they'd been using to dig.

Without pausing to think about what she was doing, she slipped into the woods, her head down, looking for one of the paths. When she found it, she followed it instinctively, taking care to keep one eye on the woods to her left; she didn't want to run straight into the policemen looking for Katie. She went too far at first, into a thicker part of the wood that was entirely unfamiliar, and she had to double back, carefully retracing her steps. Eventually she only found the place where they'd been because the spades were so brightly coloured: she caught a glimpse of neon pink and green through the trees, and there they were, still muddy from the night before.

Charlie gathered up the spades and held them tightly to her chest. She stood, looking down at the forest floor. She recognised none of it, she realised with a start. In the daylight, and approaching it from the wrong angle, the place looked completely different, but the pot had to be around here some-where, just beneath her feet.

Could she dig it up, hide it again, somewhere better? She took a step forward, one spade clasped in her right hand, but at that moment she heard a voice calling.

'Katie? Katie!'

It was a woman's voice. Charlie looked up to see a figure moving through the trees off to her left. She caught only a brief glance – a woman with brown hair and her arms crossed over her chest, like it was cold. It had to be Katie's mum.

Charlie crouched low, and moved away, putting a good distance between her and the searchers. There was no time to retrieve the pot. She'd have to hope they wouldn't find it. She'd have to hope she could sneak out and come back later.

When she was out of the woods, she threw each of the plastic spades under a different caravan, and went into the shower block to wash her hands.

Chapter 38

Now

It was another bright morning, and I got up and dressed on a kind of autopilot, my mind full of all sorts of dark things.

Katie watched me from where she sat, on the edge of the dining table.

'Why are you here, Charlie?'

'We're having a little break by the seaside,' I said mildly. 'Relaxing. Having some quiet time with my favourite niece. Researching a book about local folklore, a little personal project of mine.'

'Try again,' she said. I cleared my throat as I shrugged on my coat. It didn't feel as icy, but rain was always just around the corner on the coast.

'I'm here because Emily has written a book.' Just saying it made my mouth turn down at the corners. 'And she's made the whole thing look like it was my fault. Like I was the *monster*.' My hands, chasing the zip on my coat, were trembling. 'So. I need to find something that will show everyone . . .' The zip caught, and I yanked it up viciously. 'Who the monster actually was.'

'Why are you pretending?' Katie asked. She was kicking her legs back and forth under the table. 'You're always just pretending.' Then she tried a different tack. 'Do you think that if you help this other girl, Cheryl, it will undo what you did to me? Or is it just a handy way of distracting yourself?'

I didn't answer this. I left her there and got in the car. About ten minutes into my drive to Folkesholme, I saw that she was sitting in the back seat, her face turned to look out of the window.

Mr Kastner was exactly where I had seen him last, wearing exactly the same orange corduroy trousers, only the book was different: he'd moved on to *The Little Friend*.

'That one's my favourite,' I told him, and he looked up and smiled.

'Really? It seems to be too long and meandering for most people.'

'I've had a lot of time on my hands lately,' I told him, truthfully enough. 'You know you said lots of people go missing in seaside towns? I wondered if you'd looked into it any further than that.'

From my pocket I pulled out my phone and found one of the articles I'd bookmarked. It was about April Rushbrook, the first girl on my list. She'd vanished in 1961, and she had a paltry couple of inches in a local newspaper, which said she'd gone missing earlier that year and hadn't been reported missing for two days. Mr Kastner took it and peered at it, bringing the phone very close to his thick glasses.

'Oh, this is interesting. Did you know about the Rushbrooks?'

'No.'

'Well.' Mr Kastner leaned back on his chair, then nodded to the stool next to the counter. I perched on it. 'The Rushbrooks are a big and sprawling family. A notorious *crime* family. Notorious for around here, anyway.'

'In Kent?'

'You'd be surprised. The Home Counties have a seedy under-belly, you know.' He sounded delighted by the very idea. 'But the Rushbrooks were small fry really, in the grand scheme of things. They were known around here for burglaries, moving stolen goods, dealing in antiques they shouldn't rightly have had their mitts on, that sort of thing. And they lived right in Hithechurch town, or at least they did in the 60s and 70s.'

'April was only fourteen when she disappeared. I doubt she had much to do with it.'

Mr Kastner shrugged one shoulder. 'Either way, the police won't have troubled themselves too much, will they?' He tapped the screen with a slightly overlong fingernail. 'Two days before the family reported her missing. It clearly took a while for them to be worried enough about her to do anything.'

'I suppose. What do you think happened to her then? Last time I was here, you told me that the coast was . . . a weird place, with lots of secrets.'

'Most likely, she ran away. Local girl, not on holiday down here, she was probably bored stiff of the place. Or the Rushbrooks annoyed someone they shouldn't have, and the girl was collateral. She would be, what? In her seventies by now. There is someone you should talk to, though. Bob McLean, old chap, still drinks most afternoons at the Black Horse pub. He was one of the drivers for the Rushbrooks, back in the day. He might have known April.'

'A driver?'

'You've got to move stolen goods around somehow.'

'So he would have driven a van?'

'I expect so. Go to the Black Horse, it's in Hithechurch. He's in there so often the old sod has his own stool.' Mr Kastner smiled.

'I will, thank you. How do you know all this stuff?'

'A keen interest in local history,' said Kastner. 'Speaking of which, I put something aside on the off chance you would come back in. I thought it might have some useful information for your book.' He leaned down, opened a drawer in the bottom of the counter and pulled out another slim volume. It was titled *Hithechurch and Folkesholme: A History*. It was £8.99.

'Thank you,' I said, feeling vaguely chagrined. Clearly I would never be able to visit this bookshop without buying something.

'Cash or card?' asked Mr Kastner.

The Black Horse was your classic local pub, looking down on its heels. There was an old man smoking a fag outside, next to a shed that promised 'fresh cockles and muscles, straight from Folkesholme Bay', although it was shuttered up that day. Inside, it was gloomy and largely charmless – three fruit machines were providing what there was of the atmosphere, and the tables were sticky and tattooed with circular glass marks. I got there just after four, so the place had only been open an hour or so, but already it had a small collection of men, presumably sitting at their usual seats. A couple of them were younger guys, leaning their heads close together over tall pints of lager, and they gave me an appraising look as I walked in, which I was careful not to notice.

There was one old man on a stool at the bar. He wore a crisp white shirt and a black waistcoat, and on the bar itself, to my delight, rested a genuine black pork-pie hat. The bar lady was a large woman in her sixties with a smart platinum dye job cut into a bob, and when she raised her eyebrows at me I asked for a rum and Coke. And then I stood at the bar, sipping it, wondering what on earth I was supposed to do next. Part of me wanted to bolt for the door.

'Another pint, Bob?'

The bar lady was already pouring it. I glanced at the old man on the stool as if I'd only just spotted him, shifting my face into an expression of pleasant surprise.

'Bob McLean?'

The old man turned to me stiffly. His hair was white yet his eyes were very clear, watchful. He cocked his head to one side, like a bird that's spied a worm.

'Who's asking?'

'My name's Sarah,' I said. Just out of the corner of my eye, I saw the two lager drinkers turn to watch me. I was acutely aware of how loud my voice was, even against the whirr and clatter of the fruit machines. 'The man who runs the bookshop in Folkesholme was talking about you the other day.' I found I wasn't especially worried about dropping Mr Kastner in it. 'I'm writing an article about missing girls in the area.'

I caught the bar lady giving me a sharp look.

'The bookseller told me you might have met April Rushbrook, back in the day. I just wondered . . . what she was like.'

'He told you that, did he?' Bob McLean had a strong London accent and a voice that sounded like it had been dragged through gravel.

'Sorry.' I gave him my most disarming smile. 'I don't mean to drop this on you out of nowhere. I'm writing an article about Cheryl Yates, the girl who disappeared last year, and some other girls who have gone missing on this part of the coast. April Rushbrook is the first one on my list. I wondered if you might share what you remember of her?'

'I might,' he grumbled back. 'If you buy me a drink.'

I gave his untouched pint of bitter the bar lady had just passed him the tiniest glance, then shrugged. 'What would you like?'

The cheeky sod ordered a double whisky, from the best

bottle they had behind the bar. When he'd taken a good gulp from it, he turned to face me finally, folding a pair of hands like shovels in his lap.

'What do you want to know?'

'Did you know April Rushbrook? It would have been a long time ago now, I understand.'

He nodded, looking at a spot over my right shoulder. I imagined the two lager drinkers behind me, looking back. Were the Rushbrooks still a powerful family around here? Or perhaps Bob just gravitated towards the scariest local people.

'I knew her, yeah.'

'What do you remember about her?'

He shrugged. Despite his age, it was easy to see how he had once been a large, powerful man.

'She was a kid. She got under our feet sometimes.' He shrugged. 'Like any fourteen-year-old.'

I had a sudden burst of respect for journalists, who managed to get information out of people like this. Mr McLean clearly had no intention of telling me anything useful. He picked up his glass of whisky, had a good sniff of it, then had another good gulp, finishing it off. He pushed the glass towards the bar lady.

'Another one of those. Put it on this girl's tab.'

I did my best not to wince.

'Anything else you can remember about her? About the day she went missing?'

'It was nearly sixty years ago, that's the main thing I remember about it,' he said, and I caught the slightest hint of laughter from behind me. I nodded, as though this were a useful observation, and then I pushed up the sleeves of my jumper, revealing a small, ugly tattoo on my left forearm. If you were feeling generous you could say it was of a rose, but it was also clearly the job of an amateur, hammered in with a hot needle and an ink substitute that had faded significantly. I saw McLean look at it, and he did that odd, bird-like head tilt again. His eyes flicked up towards the lager-drinking men, and the atmosphere in the room seemed to settle a little.

'Yeah, well. Did a bit of driving for the Rushbrooks, here and there. They had their fingers in a lot of pies back then, and it kept me good and busy for a while. When April went it took the wind out of them a bit. Which isn't surprising, if you ask me.'

'Did the family think she'd run away?'

He leaned back on his stool, considering the idea. 'Nah, I don't reckon they did. April, she was a good kid. For them, I mean. You had a hard job getting her into a classroom, like, but she was more than happy to help out with the family business.' He paused, clearing his throat in what was almost a chuckle. 'You know what I mean by the family business, girl?'

'I suppose I probably do,' I said.

'Yeah well. There's always jobs for people willing to use a bit of elbow grease, get their hands dirty. She was a likely girl, was April.' He sighed suddenly. 'I gave her a lift in my van sometimes and she did not stop talking. Gawd, that girl could talk. She never struck me as the type to run away. She was the apple of their eye, more like.'

'You drove her around sometimes? In a van?' A small prickle of excitement moved down my spine.

'Yeah. Like I said, I was the driver.'

'Do you remember the day she vanished?'

He paused then, taking a more careful sip of his whisky.

'I don't know if I do, rightly. It was different then, you see; you didn't keep such a close eye on your kids. These days, families know where their children are twenty-four hours a day, but then? Then it wasn't so unusual for kids to wander off for a couple of days, come back when they were bored. Did it myself a few times. Well, everyone thought that April was off on a jolly somewhere, never thought nothing of it, until . . . well. I remember her family being reluctant about going to the police. They put the word around, checking in with some old rivals they had up in Essex, but nothing came of it. April just didn't come home one day.'

'Is there anywhere you thought April might have gone in particular?'

'There's all sorts of places when you live in a place like this. Get a lift to Margate maybe, or Broadstairs. Before she disappeared, April was helping out with the new funfair here. I mean, it was new then, of course.' He grumbled out another chuckle. 'There's a photo, behind the bar, actually. Of the day it opened.' He turned back towards the bar. 'Diane, love, can you pass us that picture of the fair?'

There was a number of framed black and white photos on the wall behind the bar, as well as some framed newspaper clippings. The bar lady plucked one off the wall and passed it to Bob McLean. He looked at it for a moment, nodding, before passing it to me.

'You can just see April on the left there. She had ribbons in her hair to match the bunting. Not that you can tell, in that photo.'

The framed picture was a newspaper clipping. The date said it was from July 1960, the year before April went missing, and the headline read SPARKLES FUNFAIR LIGHTS UP HITHECHURCH TOWN. It was possible to recognise the carousel in the background where I had watched Katie ride a frightened-looking horse a few days earlier. I could also see the crooked house, and there was a big slide that had since vanished. Arrayed at the front of the fair were a bunch of people wearing old-fashioned clothes, smiling awkwardly, some of them holding sticks of candyfloss.

On the far left was April, a tall girl for her age, her dark hair tied back with silk ribbons. Of all the people in the photograph, she was the one who looked happiest to be there. She was grinning widely and had one hand posed jauntily on her hip. She was, like Laura Jennings, strikingly beautiful.

The landlady leaned across the bar and held out her hand for the framed picture. I took one more look at it, trying to memorise the faces; there was a tall, wiry-looking young man who wasn't smiling so much as squinting – he looked vaguely familiar, but I have found that often people in old photographs give me that feeling, as though they are relatives that have slipped my mind. The bar lady cleared her throat pointedly. I slipped my phone out of my pocket and took a quick photo of the clipping before handing it back.

'So, you're writing about these missing girls, are you?' said Bob, fixing me with a speculative look.

'Yeah, just trying to nudge memories,' I said. I finished off the last of my rum and Coke. I had a sense that Bob wasn't going to tell me much more. 'Cheryl's been missing for six months now, and the police don't seem to be getting anywhere with it. Can't hurt to get people thinking about her again.'

Bob McLean nodded, but I got the distinct impression he knew this was horseshit. I thanked him for his time, paid my bar bill, and made my way out. Just before I closed the door behind me, I caught a look being exchanged between him and the lager drinkers, and I saw the bar lady shaking her head.

Chapter 39

Now

'I just wanted to say I'm sorry for how I reacted before. Again.'

Louise was looking down into her coffee as she spoke. She looked paler than the last time I'd seen her, and the cream Arran jumper she was wearing was a bad choice; it made her look like an especially wan ghost. But she sounded calmer, at least, and I found I was glad to see her.

'I think, given everything both of us have been through, we can be forgiven for the occasional extreme reaction,' I said. I thought of Katie, her slight form following me around all my life. The café was a Starbucks that had once been a bank or something like it; the space around us was vast, and a cool grey light filtered in through the huge old windows.

'What's it been like? Since you . . . you know.'

I immediately felt tense, but I forced myself to relax. *Have a normal conversation, like a normal person.*

'Mostly it's been lonely. My parents aren't around anymore, my sister has her own family now and, well, she just doesn't have the time for me really.' I laughed a little. 'Christ, that all sounds really sad, doesn't it? What do I have to complain about, really? It could all be a lot worse.' *At least I came out of that summer alive*, is what I wanted to say. 'Mostly I feel like the world jumped ahead this huge amount and left me behind, and now I'm trying to figure out stupid things like do I really need a fancy mobile phone if there's no one to call me. Wow, that sounds even worse.' I cleared my throat. 'What about you? Is Watkins actually your surname? Did you get married?'

Louise fiddled with a packet of sugar. Someone in the far corner of the café was talking very loudly into their phone, and a sudden burst of laughter made us both jump.

'No. Watkins is actually my boss's surname – I often have to book tables in restaurants for her, so I just . . . used that one. Secretarial work. Or more like a personal assistant, I guess. It's quiet, straightforward. She helps people find venues for pop-up shops.'

Seeing my blank look, she laughed quietly.

'They're like temporary shops, set up in places that have usually been empty for a while. It's a useful way to get some good marketing for a small business, plus it makes the high street look busier.'

'Blimey,' I said.

'It's satisfying, to help out these little businesses, plus the opening of each one is kind of like a small party. I like it. And no one really *looks* at a secretary, you know? You're never the person someone has come to see, and I find that reassuring. I'm basically invisible.' She smiled, and I noticed how tightly stretched her skin was around her mouth and eyes. Had she actually lost weight since I'd seen her last? 'There was always such chaos when I lived at home with my family. With Emily.'

'What was that like?' I couldn't quite keep myself from asking the question. 'I only knew her for that summer. You lived with her for years.'

259

'Volatile,' she said immediately. 'It was like living in a house full of landmines. She . . .' Louise stopped, took a long sip of her coffee. 'Our father was an angry man. And when I was younger I was less inclined to be quiet, especially about things that annoyed me. So we fought. A lot. Mainly what I remember is a feeling of tension, all the time. Like constantly waiting for a loud noise to happen.'

'And what about Emily?'

Louise hunched her shoulders over her coffee and her already soft voice became something close to a whisper. I found myself leaning forward to hear her.

'After I ran away, I thought a lot about how Emily was born into that angry household, and raised by it. Did you know that kids who grow up in a house where the parents are always fighting get marked by it, forever? It's to do with how your brain is still forming, and the stress signals constantly being sent to your brain actually start to *change* the pathways, so that your brain thinks being stressed is normal. Like being in the middle of a fight all the time is normal. When I think of Emily in my mother's womb, I imagine her being awash in all this poison and I think, of course she is the way she is, she's a creature born of . . .' She trailed off. 'I'm not making excuses for her.'

'So you ran away?'

'I just got to a point where I thought, if I stay here, with them, it will kill me.'

'She told me once that she was sure your dad had hurt you. She couldn't believe that you would leave her on her own.'

A series of expressions passed over Louise's face then, and I felt a stab of guilt. I apologised, and she shook her head.

'It's fine. I guess I just forget, sometimes, that even when she was a little girl, she could be so duplicitous.' She took a deep breath and shook her head slightly, as if stepping away from some precipice. 'Look, I also wanted to say about this Cheryl girl. It's a good thing to do, I think. Why shouldn't you look for her? It can't do any harm. I'm sorry I was so weird about it.'

'I feel like if I can unearth one tiny thing, it will open the whole case up, and then maybe Cheryl's family can know some peace. Christ knows I've not contributed much good to the world so far.' I laughed nervously. I felt vulnerable again. 'And something about Hithechurch definitely stinks. I know it's not just me having bad memories of the place. And don't worry, I am still looking for the pot.'

'If that book is published, she will feel vindicated,' added Louise. 'And I just couldn't bear it if that happened. I know she's my sister, but I can never look away from what she did. And I don't think she should be able to, either.'

'I couldn't agree more.'

Louise smiled, and it made her look younger, hopeful even.

'Do you want another coffee?' she asked. 'I've got nowhere to be.'

After another hour or so we went our separate ways. I promised Louise that I would let her know if I had any news about the buried pot. As she walked away down Folkesholme High Street, I watched her for a moment and felt an odd wave of warmth towards her. She had been through so much and it obviously cost her a lot to even talk about Emily, but none-theless she was trying to stop her sister from doing more harm. It was admirable.

I turned up the collar of my coat against the freezing air and started to make my way back to my car. Before I drove off I got my phone out. I had successfully spent time with another person – and I had managed to talk about small things, like a normal human. Surely, I was on a roll. I punched in a message to Joseph and sent it off, feeling pleased with myself.

What about that quiche you promised me? xxx

Chapter 40

1961

When Harry showed Rosa the Archive for the first time, it was clear that she didn't know what to think. She sat with the black and white photos spread over her lap, and her face was very still. He had the idea that he had frightened her somehow.

'What is all this? Why are you showing it to me?'

He sat next to her on the bed. Seeing the old photos was like seeing old friends.

'Because this was what I was supposed to do,' he said. 'But then I had that stupid accident, and it made my father lose all faith in me. But he was wrong. I think you are my second chance, love – to show him. To show everyone what I'm really capable of.'

And now that he was thinking about it, the idea was impossible to get out of his head. In the years since Nedry, his work with the Rushbrooks had given him plenty of opportunities to use his knives, but these had all been frantic pieces of work carried out in dark alleys or in gloomy basements. As satisfying as they had been, none of these instances had involved any *finesse*. Here, then, with Rosa, was a chance to prove that he was able to live up to his father's dreams after all. Already his mind was full of the things he would need to find to work on Rosa: surgical thread, scalpels, something to knock her out with, or at least keep her still. Just the idea of having those tools close to hand made his heart beat faster.

'I don't know, Harry.' Rosa made to pass the photos back to him. 'I'm not sure it's such a good idea . . .'

'Rosa.' He pushed her hair back and tipped her face up to the light. She made a small sound of distress as the scarred side of her face was exposed. 'It's already decided, love. I will help you. You'll see. Don't you want to be beautiful again?'

Chapter 41

July 1988

Charlie lay awake into the early hours that night, watching and listening for the rest of the family to settle down and go to sleep. It took a long time.

The adults always did stay up long after the kids had all been forced to bed, but that day there had been a different, uneasy atmosphere hanging over them all. They talked intently at each other, or stood at the windows looking out, pulling the net curtains back, and when the kids asked questions they got long, introspective looks followed by the sort of reply that suggested the adult hadn't been listening in the first place. That night they had all been up talking late, and Darren and her grandad had been out after dark with torches, having a last look for the missing girl. Eventually they gave in, one by one; last cups of tea were drunk, the tiny TV set was turned off, and finally the crack under Charlie's door went dark. The lights were off.

She lay there for at least another hour, staring at the ceiling and willing herself to get up.

When she heard the first chorus of snores from the pull-down beds in the living area, she slipped out of bed and pulled on some clothes. She picked up her bag, which already had her torch and her diary in it. Creeping to the door, she pushed it open an inch and looked out.

The kitchen area was in darkness. She could see a sliver of light bouncing off the kettle, and the big soft mound where the dining table was during the day – at night, it was flipped over to become another double bed, shared by her nan and grandad. Grandad was the perpetrator of the snores.

Moving as quietly and as smoothly as possible, Charlie snuck through the kitchen into the living area. Here, the sofa areas had been turned into beds, and there were more relatives to avoid. At that moment, someone to her right grunted and turned over – it was too dark to see who it was – and Charlie froze for a long moment, her heart thundering in her chest.

The worst bit was opening the door. She turned the lock as slowly as she could, then pushed the handle down even slower, her eyes on the various sleeping forms in the room around her. The tap in the kitchen was dripping. Every sound seemed agonisingly loud. When she finally stepped out into the dark, still night, for a few seconds she stood rooted to the spot – leaving the caravan had been so stressful she had almost forgotten what she was doing it for.

She grabbed one of the spades leaning against the caravan – it was Darren's, with a grown-up wooden handle – and she set off into the dark.

The campsite at night was still and quiet, the big sodium path lights making everything look pale and watery, as though the whole place was caught underwater. The grass was slightly damp and she stayed on it, creeping from caravan to caravan, doing her best to stay in the shadows. When she got to the woods' edge, she almost lost her nerve entirely and went straight back; the woods were a thick black curtain hanging at the edge of the park. The idea of walking into that darkness willingly made her throat feel tight and strange. She opened up her diary, got her torch out, and looked at her own directions.

You know where it is, really, she told herself. *You've just got to be brave for a few minutes, and then once you have the pot . . .*

And then, what? Charlie hadn't thought that far ahead. All she knew was that the pot would tell the police that they had been together, all three of them, Charlie and Emily and Katie, and then they would *know*. And then it would all come out, and her family would know, and the world would know, and worst of all, her mother would know.

Charlie pointed the torch ahead of her and stepped onto the dirt path. She tried to imagine how the place looked during the day. She tried not to look at the busy dark at every side, or the twigs and branches that seemed to leap at her every time she moved the torch. Once, she thought she saw a figure standing off to her right – someone small and grey and watchful, her hair full of sand – and Charlie almost dropped the torch.

'It's nothing,' she told herself. 'There's *no one there.*'

It was easier to find it, this time. The small clear patch, the disturbed earth. She could even see the imprint of her own trainers in the dirt. Propping the torch on a rock to light the area as best she could, Charlie began digging, and the plastic shovel hit the Tupperware lid almost immediately. They had barely buried it at all.

When she dragged it out and saw the cheerful picture of the snowman on the lid, a strange shaky feeling came over her. She sat awkwardly in the dirt and felt, for the first time in her life, that she didn't understand what her body was doing. Presently she touched her trembling hands to her face and realised she was crying.

'I'm sorry,' she whispered to the pot. 'I'm sorry I'm sorry I'm *sorry*.'

Time seemed to pass in a jump then. Abruptly Charlie was lying on the ground, and the woods were full of a greyness that hadn't been there before. She got to her feet, feeling dazed. Her mouth was full of the bitter, coppery taste of pennies, so she spat into a bush. Shakily, she wrestled the pot into her rucksack, pushed the diary in on top of it, picked up the spade, and gradually made her way back to the path that led out. It was still dark, but there was a softness to the shadows that made her think she had been in the woods longer than she'd intended. Suddenly it was very easy to remember every scary story she'd ever read; stories where people on the other side of the world appeared to their relatives at their moment of death; stories where cars drove past women wearing white shrouds; stories where a girl dies and becomes an avenging creature, something that stalks the woods with a pair of scissors.

In the semi-dark, all of these stories seemed very plausible.

The edge of the woods was just in sight when the darkness reached out a hand and curled it around her throat. Charlie gave a strangled yelp, and then another hand closed over her mouth. A pale, ragged face came close to hers, close enough that she could smell the wretched fetid breath that escaped from between long, yellowed teeth; the old sweat and mould smell of the tattered clothes she wore. Charlie could see stitch marks marching along the side of the woman's nose, the skin there puckered and pink and twisted.

'Shh,' said Stitch Face Sue. Her voice was slightly slurred. 'If you're not quiet she'll cut your tongue out, won't she?'

In one compulsive movement Charlie jerked the spade up and cracked the hard plastic shovel into the side of the woman's head. It wasn't a hard blow, but Stitch Face Sue let go of her immediately, and so Charlie ran, blindly out of the woods and into the caravan site. There was a noise behind her, the sound of something moving heavily through foliage, but she didn't look back or stop to see what was happening. She ran on and on, her mind entirely blank, until eventually she realised that she had left the caravan site and was in the road. On the other side were the fields she and Emily and Katie had walked through to get to the beach before. Belatedly she realised that at some point in the last few minutes she had wet herself. She choked out a sob, and jumped down into the ditch and up the other side. She'd also dropped the spade somewhere.

'You're all right,' she whispered. 'It's okay. You're all right.' She looked over her shoulder, but from what she could see the road behind her was empty. To the east, the sky was a little lighter than it had been, but overhead the cold pinpricks of stars were still watching. She walked on, across the fields, until she could hear the sea again. 'You're okay, it's all right.'

For a long time, she wandered across the sand, her arms slack by her sides. Years later, a doctor would describe to Charlie the symptoms of severe shock, and for a moment she would almost remember that night – the long periods of blankness, the taste of salt in her mouth. But mostly it would stay hidden, lurking behind the more memorable, sunlit impressions of that particular holiday.

She thought about digging a hole in the wet sand with her hands, but the idea of leaving the Tupperware pot there, in that vast flat space, felt too vulnerable, even if it was buried. She thought about just throwing it into the sea, but she knew she wouldn't be able to throw it far enough, and besides, the tide was in. When it went back out again, how could she be sure it would take the pot with it? What if it wrestled the pot open somehow, and everything that was inside it would be scattered up and down the beach, just waiting for people to find it.

Eventually she realised she was standing opposite the entrance to the caves. At night they were locked up, with a barred gate pulled across. A bright yellow sign, lurid in the gloom, hung on the front of the gate: CLOSED, STAY OUT. Charlie wandered closer.

It was shut and locked, but the cave entrance was an irregular shape, leaving a slim gap on the left-hand side. Not a big enough gap for an adult to get through, or even a teenager, but Charlie had always been on the shrimpy side, and when she crouched and shifted herself through the gap, she only got a small scrape on the back of her arm where it rubbed against the bare rock. Inside, the place was lit with low emergency lights. Charlie got her torch out anyway and clicked it on. Bare grey walls loomed all around her, and they made her think of the face of the woman who had grabbed her – *grey and craggy like her flesh . . . don't think about it, don't think about it* – so she aimed the torch down, at the path, and walked into the next cave, and then the next. All around her the sound of dripping water echoed, and there was a smell . . . a chalky, wet smell. Something like salt, but also like rot. And underneath that, a smell that was almost familiar, like dirt.

In the back of her mind she knew this was wildly dangerous. That she could fall down an unseen drop, or simply get lost. But she was also thinking about hiding places. About tiny spaces that might not be explored for years. There could be a hole, she reasoned. A deep enough hole, and no one would find it.

After an unknowable period of time, she came to an area that had a chest-high fence across it, and beyond a sharp drop there was a narrow ledge, that led to an even smaller hole, completely dark. There was a ledge at right angles to it, far too small for anyone adult-sized to climb across, but . . .

Charlie stood and looked at it for a long time. Her heart was beating fast and light, and she was more frightened than she'd ever been in her life, possibly even more so than when they'd hidden Katie's body, but part of her had come to believe that if she could just get rid of the Tupperware pot, if she could just hide it well enough, then she could banish Stitch Face Sue, and everything she had brought with her. That she could make the whole problem go away. The thing needed to be hidden. After all, hadn't Stitch Face Sue appeared again as soon as she dug it up? Charlie had to do it.

She had made up a monster and it had come to life. It was eating her alive. Now she had to stop it.

Charlie put the torch on the floor, with its beam of pale light pointing out across the drop to the section of cave she wanted to get to, and then she made sure her rucksack was firmly on her back, straps over both arms. She clambered up over the fence, slid along to the narrow ledge and climbed across it, her teeth biting into her lower lip the whole time. Once she was across she crouched for a time on the lower ledge, breathing hard. Although the climb had been easy, she felt close to passing out, so she pinched her arm, hard. The rotten chalky smell was stronger now, pressing dirty fingers down her throat.

Then she turned and looked at the hole.

It was black. Black like a solid thing, like the outfall tunnel, and there could be anything in there. Spiders, crabs. Another hand, reaching out to touch hers . . .

Charlie unzipped her rucksack, pulled out the pot, and

pushed it into the hole. She pushed it as far as she could, and then she knelt by the hole and put her whole arm behind it, pushing it even further. She felt it dragging over small stones and grit, and then suddenly it was gone. There was a thump, from somewhere deeper inside, and she realised it had fallen somewhere. Gone. It was gone.

'There,' she said, aloud. 'It's gone, it's gone, now leave me alone.'

The next morning, Charlie's family woke up to find her curled on the floor of the caravan living room, her trainers covered in wet sand, her trousers smelling of urine. It was their first clue that something was very wrong.

Chapter 42

Now

With everything that was going on I could say that I'd forgotten about Joseph and my suggestion we go out for food, but that would be a lie. In truth, I'd been thinking about him quite consistently, both excited to see him again and deeply embarrassed that I was excited at all.

The café where we'd agreed to meet for lunch was exactly the sort you get on the coast. It was run by old ladies, and all the tables had tablecloths, and the counter where you paid your bill had a doily on it. Joseph and I were two of only five customers, the others being old dears who were clearly regulars. We sat at the window table and grinned at each other like fools. I suppose you could say it was a date.

'What do you do around here, in January? Through the winter, I mean? It must be dead quiet.'

Joseph shrugged one shoulder. He looked cheerfully out of place, with the silver piercing in his eyebrow and his rough, workman hands.

'There's always some nonsense needs doing on the site,' he

said. 'Grass cutting, drains cleared, maintenance. Most of the caravans on the site have signed up to my uncle's *caretaker service*.' He smiled lopsidedly. 'Which basically means you pays your money, and you get this idiot tidying up your caravan before you or your guests arrive. I clean the place, make sure they've got little cartons of milk in their fridges, that sort of thing. I'm dead glamorous, aren't I? Cleaning bogs, stocking up on groceries.'

I grinned at his joke, but I felt an odd surge of emotion. What was it like, I thought, to have a good, simple job? With no terrible past hanging over you? Joseph thought nothing of it, but I found it admirable.

'You're a useful man to have around,' I said.

I had ordered a cheese and pickle sandwich, and at that moment one of the elderly owners brought it over, along with a big slice of homemade quiche Joseph had asked for. On the side of my plate were a handful of crisps and a few optimistic morsels of salad. I looked up at the waitress to say thank you and found that she was looking down at me oddly, as though I'd said a rude word. She hovered just a second too long, and then was gone.

'So, do you spend all your time writing?' he asked. 'Or do you have a less glamorous job you're not telling me about.'

I nodded. I'd had time to think about this.

'I'm a librarian,' I said. 'Only a junior one. I think that makes me more glamorous than you, right? What's more glamorous than dust and books.'

I had decided this was a safe bet. I had spent a lot of time in at least one library, and had had a lot of time to read books. And it was just boring enough I thought it unlikely he would ask too much about it.

The sandwich was good. We chatted a little longer, and I was just starting to fiddle with the dessert menu when I saw

273

the brightly coloured funfair van draw up on the opposite side of the road, with its slightly wonky depictions of the latest Marvel superheroes. A tall figure stepped out of the cab, moving slowly, before walking around the van on the road side to reach the back doors. I stopped hearing what Joseph was saying.

Joseph followed where I was looking. 'Ah, there's old Harald,' he said. 'Still working in all weathers, poor old sod. Been here forever, from what I've heard. Cut him open and he's probably got Hithechurch written through him like those sticks of rock. You should talk to him about your book.'

Despite the cold weather, Harald was wearing a blue dress shirt with the sleeves rolled up, a pair of brown braces looped over his shoulders, and no coat. His grey hair was carefully combed back from his forehead.

'The slots man,' I said out loud. Joseph gave me an odd look, so I smiled. 'I remember him, I think, from when I had holidays here as a kid.'

'You've been close to him all along, you know,' said Joseph. He must have seen something in my face then, because he rushed to explain. 'I mean, he lives on the caravan site most of the year. He's in this really old model that's been there since god was a kiddie, and he's got all sorts of sheds and what have you set up around it.'

The Ranch. I turned back to the window just in time to see Harald heading into the funfair with a big cardboard box in his arms. I thought of how he'd stumbled over the three of us in the woods on the night everything went to shit – and the figure on the beach, a rope in his hands. I couldn't be *sure* it was him, not truly; it had been too dark. And yet . . . At that moment my brain made one of those funny leaps brains do sometimes, where a few unrelated things suddenly drop into place. I got my phone out, and after a bit of scrolling, brought up the photo I'd taken of the newspaper clipping at the Black Horse.

'Here,' I showed it to Joseph. 'Do you think that's him, there? The young bloke in the middle.' I tapped my finger on the face of the tall, wiry-looking man.

'Huh. Could well be.' Joseph had finished his quiche by then and was chasing a few crumbs around with his fork.

'This girl here you see, the one on the end, she went missing here years ago, in the 60s. Like Cheryl Yates did.'

Joseph looked up at me then, and there seemed to be more in his gaze than I was expecting. I wondered if I'd made a mistake.

'It's just funny you see, because—'

'Charlotte? Charlotte Watts?'

I turned around automatically, already cursing myself for doing it but unable to stop, and two of the old ladies who ran the café were standing there in their aprons, looking like woeful children from a fairy tale.

'I knew it,' spat one of them. 'I bloody knew it.'

'What?' I cleared my throat, trying to arrange my face into something resembling polite confusion. 'You must have me confused with someone else.'

This was my fault. I had become so used to not being recognised, to pretending to have a normal life, I'd forgotten that such things were impossible for me. I can never escape who I really am.

'How dare you.' The woman who had brought over our lunch took a bold step forward and rapped her fingers on the table sharply, like she was a teacher demanding our attention. She had small blue eyes and they were watery with some strong emotion. 'How dare you set foot in here. What are you even doing in Hithechurch, you monster?'

'Here, hang on,' said Joseph, leaning back from the table.

'You think you can just dye your hair and waltz back in here?' She gestured at my head, and inwardly I winced. One of the problems with having bright ginger hair is that if you dye it a darker colour, when the roots start to grow through they are very, very obvious. 'Why are you even out? You should have been locked up for life!'

'I knew it was you,' put in the second old woman. 'Knew it as soon as you walked in the door. I could never forget your face. And to think you would come here now, when that *other* one has her face plastered everywhere because of her disgusting book—'

'Now then.' Joseph stood up, and that seemed to quiet them briefly. I think they had forgotten he was there. 'I don't know what you two are on about, but this is my friend Sarah, and you are both being very rude.'

They both moved a step or so away from the table, darting glances at me and then back at Joseph.

'Sarah?' said one of them, and I felt a trickle of relief. They hadn't been sure, after all.

Joseph pulled a ten-pound note out of his pocket and left it on the table. He turned to me, and cocked his head at the door.

'Come on, let's go get an ice cream. Somewhere friendlier.'

We walked back to the campsite and raided the shop for ice creams, which we ate in Joseph's back office. Like his tiny kitchen, this was a small cosy room with a desk and an old portable TV, a big comfortable office chair and a wooden chair with a busted cushion. There was a cupboard with its door standing open, which appeared to contain a variety of rakes and spades, and on the back wall, behind the desk, was a board nailed with hooks, on which several sets of keys dangled. He let me sit in the comfy office chair while I ate my Feast.

'You do seem to make friends wherever you go,' he said. He was sitting on the wooden chair, making short work of a Twister.

'Ice cream in January is a good idea,' I said, then, 'I don't know what that was all about. I suppose I just have one of those faces. My mum always said that I did.'

'Yeah well, locals,' said Joseph, as if that explained everything.

'Speaking of which, that old guy, Harald – he really lives here? On the campsite?'

Joseph shrugged, and chucked his empty lolly stick in the wastepaper bin. 'He sometimes disappears for a little while. He keeps himself to himself though, never asks me for anything. I think he's one of that generation of older men, you know, who've grown up taking care of themselves and would rather die than ask for help. His caravan has never been rented out, so I suppose he doesn't need me to stock up on milk and teabags for him.'

'Do you still have a key?'

Joseph cocked his head at me then. I shrugged.

'In case he has a fall, or something. He's getting on a bit.'

'Oh yeah, I guess so.' He nodded to the board behind my head. 'Never had to use it. He's a tough old buzzard. I expect I'll be in my grave long before he croaks.'

At that moment, we both heard the rattle of the shop door as someone tried to get in. Joseph had shut up the shop for our 'date'. He rolled his eyes.

'You wouldn't know there was a bloody sign on it saying "Closed", would you? I don't know why I bother, no one ever reads it . . .' He got up and left the small office, and I heard him walking across the shop floor, calling out to whoever was waiting there. *All right, all right, keep your knickers on . . .*

I swung the office chair around and looked at the wall. The back of my neck immediately started to prickle, but the opportunity was just too good to miss. I scanned the keys, seeing

277

that most of them were neatly labelled with numbers, which was of no use to me. Then, on one of the lower hooks, I saw a few keys that looked older, less used. They appeared to be the same sort of key, but their labels were handwritten. One of them had a plastic fob with the single letter 'H' written in black marker. I glanced back at the door, but I could still hear Joseph talking to the customer. Was it the right key? I had no way of knowing. Was it worth a chance anyway? I thought so.

I plucked the key off its hook and put it in the front pocket of my bag.

When Joseph came back, complaining lightly about people running out of cooking oil, I found I couldn't stay so close to the rack of keys so I came around to the front of the desk and sat on it; I felt oddly sure he would look at me and see guilt all over my face.

Instead, though, he came over to the desk too, and he smiled lopsidedly at me.

'I've had a good afternoon,' he said.

'Me too.'

And despite everything, it was true.

Chapter 43

July 1988

Charlie had been put on the caravan steps, where her mum could keep an eye on her. The general consensus was that she had been staying up too late, being 'overstimulated' and not eating properly, which was leading to some especially vivid nightmares. It was yet another peerless sunny day. Behind her in the caravan, her family prepared for the expected day at the beach, but they were all moving a little slower, their usual enthusiasm somewhat dampened.

Charlie looked down at her bowl of Coco Pops, which were rapidly turning into a brown sludge. Every now and then her hand would move up to touch her neck, although she wasn't conscious of it.

'Here, turn that up, will you?' said Charlie's nan, shouting over the general hubbub. A second later, the radio that was always on in the mornings got louder, and an odd hush came over her family.

'—not the first disappearance, but police are keeping an open mind. Katie Hennessey's family say they thought she was out playing with her cousins in the campsite park, but it was later realised that the girl had wandered off at some point. Katie is white, with brown hair and blue eyes, around four and a half feet tall. The police are asking that if anyone has any information or believes they may have seen Katie, to call—'

All the adults behind her were talking at once now, and she heard her aunt say that the police were searching all of Hithechurch, and were even said to be looking around Folkesholme. Her grandad put in that there were police gathered at the entrance to the site, and he thought it likely they were checking people's car boots as they left. Charlie thought of the outfall, that dark space right up the end where kids weren't strictly allowed to go, the place where they had shifted heavy rocks and piled sand until Katie's face had disappeared from view. Abruptly she tipped her breakfast into the bush next to the caravan. She couldn't even entertain the idea of food.

'That's a waste,' said Emily cheerfully as she stepped around the caravan into view. 'I'd have eaten those for you. I'm never allowed chocolatey cereal.'

'What do you want?'

A flicker of confusion passed over the girl's face, and then she shrugged. 'Do you want to come over? My dad's out and my mum's having a lie-down, so we can sit in my caravan. There are some ice lollies in the freezer.'

Charlie looked down at her hands. It was hard to look at Emily; every time she saw her delicate features she remembered how her face had looked when she'd pushed Katie off the wall.

'I'm not allowed to go out. Not on my own. Mum wants me to stay in sight today.'

Emily stood on tiptoes and peered into the caravan behind her. She smiled.

'Look at them, they'll never notice you're gone. Besides, you won't be on your own, will you?' Emily beamed at her, and there was a hard glitter to her stare that Charlie hadn't noticed before. Had it always been there? She wasn't sure. Suddenly she felt it would be a bad idea to say no to her.

Charlie stood up, wiped her hands on her shorts, and followed the girl. The interior of Emily's caravan was quiet; the curtains were drawn, making the living-room space dim and overly warm. There was a powerful smell of soap, floral and cloying. Emily went to the fridge and pulled a couple of strawberry split lollies from the tiny shoebox-sized freezer and passed one to Charlie.

'My mum's going to go spare when she realises I'm not there,' Charlie said, wondering if she could leave soon. Emily shrugged. 'Why is your mum lying down? Is she sick?'

'No, not really. She was just listening to the radio and then she said she had to go and have a lie-down for a while. She does that a lot.'

To Charlie's horror, Emily went to the door beyond the narrow kitchen space and pushed it open with her foot. Inside, her mother was lying prone on the bed, the covers thrown on the floor. On the bedside table were two brown pill bottles and a glass of water. Emily's mother had her head turned away from them, her long dark hair spilled carelessly across the pillow. One sandal dangled from the end of a foot.

'Look, she's sound-o.' Emily didn't bother to lower her voice, and when Charlie gave her a startled look, she smiled. 'She's a deep sleeper. Come on.'

They sat cross-legged on the living-room carpet, eating their ice lollies. The front door was open, and through it Charlie could see the grass that was beginning to turn slightly brown. It made her feel better that the door was open, but even so, Emily's presence next to her seemed to crackle and

281

seethe. *I shouldn't be here*, she thought. *I should stay away from her.*

Emily, though, seemed oblivious. She was chattering on with an ease and carelessness that Charlie found staggering.

'. . . Anyway, I think it'll be tonight.'

'What will?'

Emily licked a blob of ice cream from the back of her hand.

'That *she* comes. I don't think she'll send a dog for him this time. I think she'll come herself, and then he'll be sorry. For Louise, for everything.'

Charlie shook her head, hardly able to believe what she was hearing.

'Emily, what are you on about? Aren't you at all worried about . . . what we did?'

'What we did is what we had to do, wasn't it? We know that she wanted a life . . .'

'Did we?'

'. . . because of the crane flies. It'll be fine. Stitch Face Sue will come, sort out my dad, and no one will ever know. It'll be perfect.'

Before she realised she was doing it, Charlie was up on her feet. The last bit of strawberry ice slipped off the end of her lolly stick and onto the carpet.

'Perfect?' Her voice sounded strangled and weird to her own ears. She gulped down a breath. She was close to crying again. 'You are a nutter, Emily, and I hate you! My mum is going to find out and then she'll h-h-hate me and it's all your fault!'

Emily, who had also leapt to her feet, looked as though she'd been struck.

'What?'

'You're an idiot! Stitch Face Sue *isn't real* and you hurt Katie for nothing and I hate you!'

Emily flew at her. Charlie could usually hold her own in a fight, but Emily was fast and vicious. The girl grabbed fistfuls of her ginger hair and yanked it hard enough that tears sprang to her eyes. Charlie thumped her hard in the chest, over and over until she let go briefly, but then they were rolling together, crashing into the sofa. Emily's hot little hands closed around her throat, and abruptly Charlie was terrified. She screamed, a high, panicky sound that surprised Emily enough that her arms went slack. Charlie took the opportunity to kick her firmly in the shins.

'What are you two doing?'

The voice bellowed across the both of them, and they jumped apart, Charlie half falling against the sofa. Emily's father was in the doorway of the caravan, blocking out the light, but even though his face was in shadow Charlie could see that he was furious, his big pink face dotted with sweat. His eyes seemed to bulge from their sockets.

'Answer me!'

Charlie got up, looking warily at the space around him. She desperately wanted to get out of the caravan, but that would mean squeezing past him. Emily was glaring at her dad, her hands in fists at her side.

'Nothing!' she shouted back. 'I wasn't doing anything!'

He took a few steps into the room. Charlie scuttled back, terrified. Of course he would be angry about Emily bringing her back to the caravan. He was angry about everything. But then he glanced at her, and the look on his face, she realised, was worried.

'What are you doing with that girl, Emily? Where's your mother? Why isn't she watching you?'

Emily shook her head violently, then, to Charlie's shock, began smacking herself across the face with both hands. The slaps made hard, flat noises in the small space.

'Nothing!' Each word coincided with a smack. 'I! Wasn't! Doing! Nothing!'

Her father crossed the room in one stride and grabbed hold of Emily's arm, yanking her hand away from her face. He spared Charlie another glance. There was spittle on his lips.

'Get out.'

Charlie was glad to obey, but as she moved to the door Emily began to shriek again.

'She's coming for you!' she screamed. She paused, gasping in a breath, then actually laughed. 'You're gonna get what's coming to you, you're gonna get justice!'

For a horrible moment Charlie thought she was screaming at her, but then she saw how Emily was flailing at her father, kicking and biting and scratching like a wild thing. He pulled her up by her arm, shaking her briskly.

'What are you talking about?' he said sharply. 'Emily, you will answer me right this minute.'

But Emily just laughed. Charlie slipped out of the door and ran, the sounds of their fighting echoing in her ears as she fled. When she got back to her own caravan, she was relieved for a handful of seconds to see that no one was standing on the steps looking for her. Then, as she walked into the small living space, she saw why. Her Auntie Marj was sitting on the sofa dabbing her eyes with a tissue, and her grandad was standing with his arms crossed, shaking his head.

'Oh Charlie, love,' said her mum. She looked as though she'd been crying too. 'They've found that poor little mite. All washed up on the beach.'

Chapter 44

Now

I told Joseph I could walk myself back, not because I didn't want his company, but because I wanted to have a good look at the Ranch. I wound my way through the caravans, noting how I'd never really forgotten the way, until I turned a corner and saw it. The clouds overhead had moved on so it was a clear evening, the ghostly presence of the moon giving everything a kind of silvery glow. The big, rambling caravan stood in the midst of its various additions and extensions, and for once I forced myself to look at it properly – not as a scared child would, or even a distracted adult.

The first thing I noticed was that the lights were on inside the main part of it. The windows were covered in heavy curtains or pieces of cardboard, but here and there an orange kind of light slipped through, as though the fires of hell were burning somewhere inside –

Stop it, I told myself. *The last thing your imagination needs is more exercise.*

There was a string of old fairy lights leading from the

caravan to one of four sheds and what looked like a massive chest freezer peeked out the open door of one. Parked up to one side was the van; the same van I'd seen the old man driving in Hithechurch town. The brightly coloured images of super-heroes on the side and the twinkly fairy lights should have given the place a kind of charm, but it didn't. In fact, it seemed to do the opposite. The longer I stood looking at the place, the more uncomfortable I felt. I thought of the key in my bag, that might or might not fit the lock to this caravan.

It doesn't matter anyway, I thought. *Because the lights are on and he's home. Go back.*

But I didn't, not straight away. I circled around, trying to get an idea what all the sheds and containers were for. I chose the shed that was furthest from the caravan and gave the door a very gentle tug, but it was locked. There was a slim gap left by the warp of the wooden panels, so I pulled out my phone and used the torch function to get a very limited peek at what was inside. At first I saw nothing at all, and then I angled the light down and saw a number of large white cylindrical containers. They made me think of the various bits of equip-ment my grandad had used to brew his own beer, but when I looked closely I could see the labels. Vaseline. Huge, surely industrial-sized buckets of Vaseline. Next to them were other odd things: plastic containers of latex gloves, a large pair of bolt cutters, and, perhaps weirdest of all, a big Tupperware pot containing plastic hair curlers, like the sort my nan used to use. I stood for a moment, trying to figure out what any of it meant, but the truth was, for all I knew this stuff – apart from perhaps the curlers – could have legitimate uses when it came to taking care of a funfair.

The back doors of the van were open. It looked empty inside, save for a pile of what looked like old carpet and rags. I lit up my phone again, casting the light about. It was all dirty-looking and stained, and something about that made me uneasy. There was a smell, too . . .

Without really thinking about it, I picked up one of the rags and the smell increased tenfold. I gasped, suddenly panicked, because the smell was salt and rot, mould and earth. It was the smell of worms and ruin. It was the smell of *her*. I dropped the rag, took a few steps back.

'Do you remember now?' asked Katie. She was at my side suddenly, her face in the gloom small and round, and tipped up to watch me closely. She narrowed her eyes. 'Do you remember, Charlie?'

'No,' I said. But I did. 'No I fucking don't. Leave me alone.'

'You have to remember it, idiot.' She took my hand and squeezed it, digging her half-moon fingernails into my flesh. A light came on in the Ranch, and a curtain twitched, and then I was running. I didn't stop until I got to the door of my own caravan, and for a moment I clung on to the handrail that led to the door, my head swimming.

'The caves,' I said aloud. 'The fucking caves.'

Later, I sat at the small dining table opposite Katie. I had made hot chocolate, and added a big slug of whisky. It had made me feel tired, and slow, but somehow that was comforting. At that moment I felt like I could stay in that caravan forever, within its reassuring cocoon of warmth and silence.

'I moved the Tupperware pot,' I said. 'That's why I can't find it in the woods. Because it's not bloody there. I moved it and I never told anyone. Not even . . .'

Not even Emily.

I had hidden the pot in the caves, but if you'd asked me a few days ago I'd have told you that until recently I didn't even know there were caves there, let alone that I'd ever been in them. Like I said before, memories can't be trusted. Those little gremlins that take your memories and copy them down, but copy them down slightly differently – perhaps they also lose things, too. Like my friend who couldn't remember any of the funerals she had been to. This piece of your life is too hard to look at directly? Not to worry, we'll put it where you'll never find it again.

'You didn't forget what you did to me though,' said Katie.

'No, but I was made to relive that, wasn't I? Over and over.' I laughed shakily. 'No one could ever let me forget that.'

My mind was full of what had happened the night I had snuck out, decades ago. The whole thing was still very fractured, a tapestry with lots of holes in; the individual threads made up of images, sounds. And smells. The smell of Stitch Face Sue that was also somehow the smell of the caves. And the smell in the back of Harald's van.

'None of this makes sense,' I said. '*Stitch Face Sue was not real*. I made her up.'

Katie shrugged. 'You made me up too. But I was real, wasn't I?'

'That's of no use whatsoever,' I said. But I kept thinking of that cold hand closing around my throat, the rough rasp of scarred skin against my own. Something had happened that night, but what? *Who* was it who grabbed me in the woods? And who was to say that what I was remembering now was real, or accurate? I picked up the hot chocolate and downed the last of it, even though it was still slightly too hot. The whisky sent a pleasant numbness out from the depths of my belly.

'I'm going to get drunk now,' I said.

Chapter 45

July 1988

Despite the strangeness of the atmosphere in the campsite, Charlie's family continued their usual holiday routine: a morning at the beach, home for showers and lunch, and dinner at one of the small restaurants, beers and wine and ice cream for afters. It was late when they all walked back together to the campsite, along the road with no streetlights, the fields a sea of unformed darkness on either side. It was a clear night and the stars overhead were very bright. Charlie walked in her own tiny pool of silence, her eyes on her feet while the conversations of her family continued above her head; would the good weather hold, who wanted to play cards when they got in, how the steak and kidney pie at the restaurant hadn't been up to its usual standard. Eventually, the word 'police' floated over her head, and Charlie looked up, startled. They were inside the campsite now, nearing their own caravan, but everyone had stopped to watch a gathering on the grass. There was a police car, its lights flashing bursts of blue across the shower block wall and the faces of the gawkers. Two policemen were standing with Emily's father, talking in low voices.

'Now what do you suppose that's about?' said Auntie Marj, and Charlie's grandmother tutted at her impatiently.

'What do you *think*?'

Charlie watched, her eyes wide. Emily's father was shaking his head, his lips pressed together so hard his mouth seemed to disappear. The policeman shrugged, and gestured at the back door of the car, which was standing open. Emily's father turned around and looked at the crowd watching, as if to memorise their faces for future reference, and then he got into the back seat of the police car.

'Well,' said Charlie's nan, sounding oddly satisfied. 'I'm not surprised at all. I never did like the look of him.'

Chapter 46

1961

From the very first cut, Harry knew that it was going wrong.

Blood welled up and poured freely as he made the incision, so much blood in fact that almost straight away he couldn't see what he was doing, and when he attempted to absorb some of it with the towel, the fabric was immediately sodden, leaving crimson streaks wherever he moved it. His father's archive was spread out around him so that he could refer to it, but when he glanced at the detailed notes and photographs they seemed to shiver and blur before his eyes. In desperation, he made another cut, trying to keep it smooth and straight. His hands, he realised too late, were trembling.

'Fuck. *Fuck.*'

He ploughed on, cutting and slicing until he could lift away the piece of skin with the scar on it, although the scar itself was lost under a sheet of blood. The skin wasn't thin and pliant, like he was expecting, but ragged and untidy, and pieces of fatty tissue clung to the underside of it – that, he knew, wasn't right, and as he put the skin down on the clean plate

291

his heart skipped a beat: he had forgotten that he needed to cut the skin to be transplanted first, so that could go in the place of the scarred skin. For a long moment he was still, the room spinning around him as he stood in a sick panic. *How could he have forgotten that?* He glanced up and caught his own reflection in one of the many mirrors. Instead of a skilled, imperturbable surgeon, he saw a teenage boy with blood on his hands and face. He had stripped down to his vest and braces for this *surgery*, and his own face was white with horror. He did not look like his father. It was impossible to think that he and his father existed in the same world.

A butcher, he thought, remembering the basement where he had cut Nedry. *That's what I am.* His free hand reached up to touch the hard whorl of scarring behind his ear, and it seemed to him that he could hear a whispering from all the dark shadows in the room.

At that moment, Rosa moaned, her head moving slightly under the belt strap. Her eyelids fluttered dangerously.

'No, my love.' He took another towel and wiped some of the blood away from her mouth. 'You need to sleep a little longer.'

Regardless of what he was, he had to finish the job as best he could. He picked up the already bloodied scalpel, and went back to work.

Chapter 47

Now

So, what did I do now? That was the question.

The pot wasn't where I had thought it was. The pot was in a place that I had little chance of accessing. I was, at least, relieved that I no longer had a reason to go back into the strip of woods on the campsite; remembering what had happened there the night I had moved the Tupperware pot had made me deeply reluctant to ever revisit.

The next day I went out into the cold miserable morning with my thickest coat on, my hood pulled up over my head. I'd noticed in the mirror as I brushed my teeth that my roots really were growing through; a little hint of ginger fire clinging close to my scalp. The air was damp but it wasn't quite raining yet, and the smell of the sea was sharp in the air, like being half underwater already. I made my way to the Ranch via a circuitous route, not wanting to bump into the old man or Joseph, and when I got close I hung back slightly, peering round the corner of one of its neighbour caravans. The collection of sheds and tents and awnings looked especially drab, wet with the melted frost of that morning.

'So,' I murmured. 'Anyone home?'

The windows still had their curtains drawn at the back of the caravan, which was the side I was facing, so I retraced my steps slightly and came back to it from the other direction. From here, I could see the front door and the wider windows of the living area. Here, at least, a pair of curtains had been pulled back, and through a yellowed set of net curtains I could see the dim luminescence of a lamp – I wasn't the only one to think it was too dark this morning.

I wanted to know more about Harald, because he had been there. He was, in his own way, one of the minor players from that particular haunted summer, and it worried and intrigued me that he was still here, in Hithechurch. Why I thought everyone should have upped and left after 1988 was beyond me, but still, something about it itched. It itched even more when I considered that he also had a tenuous link to April Rushbrook, the girl who had gone missing in 1961. Both he and April had been working at the fair – April not in any official capacity, maybe, but it seemed likely that they'd known each other. For a moment, I considered going up to the caravan and knocking on the door, trying out my whole 'I'm researching a book' routine.

I would say I was getting comfortable with lying, but we all know that's always been my greatest skill.

'You're not going to do that, though,' said Katie, from a space somewhere behind my left ear. 'You're going to break in.'

I thought about it. 'That would be a really stupid thing to do.'

'Exactly,' said Katie.

I must have been standing there for a good twenty minutes

before I acknowledged that I was waiting for him to leave. Eventually, the dim light in the window vanished, and a few seconds later, the door opened. I moved back, pressing myself flat against the neighbouring caravan, then peeked around the corner. Harald glanced around, and his gaze was as dull as the sky above him. His chin was slightly whiskered, as though he hadn't shaved in a few days. And then he got in his jauntily coloured van and drove off.

I stood there for a few moments in an agony of indecision. When I had been a kid, the Ranch was known for the people coming and going from it at all hours. We had assumed, back then, that it was all part of the same family, although now I wondered if it had simply been connected to some of the Rushbrooks' less legitimate work. It did not look like the place was filled with people now. And if there was someone still in the caravan, he wouldn't have turned the lamp off, or locked the door, would he? That seemed like a reasonable assumption. And besides, the key I had stolen from Joseph might not even be the right key. I could always just go and try it. And if it didn't fit, oh well. And if it did . . .

I made myself count to sixty, just in case the old man had forgotten his lunch and suddenly appeared back round the corner, and then I walked over to the front door of the caravan. I knocked loudly on the door a few times, but no one answered, and I couldn't hear anyone inside moving about. I got the keys out of my bag, willing my shoulders to relax, and I pushed the key in the lock. It fitted, and when I turned it, I heard the soft *chonk* as the door unlocked. So.

'So now what?' asked Katie. I pushed the door open.

My first impression was of the dank stench of clothes left to go mildewed, of things that had been washed, perhaps, but then not aired properly. It was dark inside and the carpet under my boots was threadbare and very worn just inside the door, where a doormat should be. I stood for a few seconds, just listening, but the place was silent – I could hear a blackbird outside, the sound of it loud in my ear, while the caravan seemed to sit in its own pool of quiet. Dirty cups and bowls on the table, washing-up left in the sink, discarded clothes here and there. Everything about it said older man, living alone. And then my eyes lifted to look at the walls . . .

My fingers clenched around the key. Where other caravans might have chintzy wallpaper, this place had a hectic, discordant collage. Someone – Harald, I had to assume – had cut out pictures from magazines and posters and newspapers, and pasted them on every spare inch of wall. I crept closer and peered at them; they were all pictures and photographs of women. Women with perfectly made-up faces, fresh and youthful, their mouths glistening with pink or red or purple lipstick, their eyes glittering below smoky arches of eyeshadow. All fashions were represented, and I realised with a gradual sense of wonder that the pictures went back years, decades even. I saw nude lip gloss and ombré hair dye, but I also saw the coral blusher and icy blues of the 80s, the pale pink lips of the 60s, and the Farrah Fawcett flicks of the 70s.

'What on earth . . . ?'

It must have been the work of years. Some of the clippings were faded and yellowed, while others were still glossy and bright. I followed the collage across the living-room walls into the tiny kitchen area, and here some of the images had peeled with the steam thrown up from the cooker, but they still continued, all the way to where the doors for the bedrooms began. Here I stopped. On the floor by a second outer door was a big orange toolbox, and I was reminded then of the tall, sturdy figure of the slots man from my childhood, the handyman at the funfair – the man, possibly, who had stood on the beach and watched me and Emily wash our hands in the sea. Was he really the person who had so painstakingly cut out hundreds of pictures of glamorous models and stuck them to his walls? It seemed deeply peculiar.

'What are you doing here?' asked Katie, her voice little more than the rapid beating of my own heart.

I didn't know. Did I really think Cheryl Yates might be here?

It was about then that the other smell hit me. A deeply unsavoury kind of funk, quite different to the mouldy scent I'd noticed when I'd entered. I held my breath for a moment, listening again for any kind of movement beyond the bedroom door.

'Hello?' My voice came out in a squeak, so I cleared my throat and tried again. 'Anyone in there?'

No reply. Using the very tips of my fingers, I pushed the door and it swung open, and inside, lying on a narrow bed in the middle of the room, was a dead body.

I jumped as though someone had pinched me and I skittered backwards, but then I stood very still, in a half-crouch. My heart was thundering in my chest like something that needed to get out, but I made myself look again. *Look properly, you idiot*, I thought. *We all know you have a talent for seeing what isn't really there.* I came a few steps forward and blinked into the gloom.

The pasted pictures from the caravan's living space continued on the walls in this room, although they were broken up with five or six different mirrors, their surfaces dusty and smeared. There was a narrow dressing table, its surface crowded with big glass jars and plastic pots, which were also thick with cobwebs. Sitting on top of one of the big jars of Vaseline was a bobbin of dark thread, a silver needle sticking from the side of it. The curtains were drawn.

The bed had a thick eiderdown over it, and under the eiderdown was . . .

I bit my lip, hard enough that I tasted a coppery tang of blood in my mouth.

An ancient-looking woman lay in the bed. She wore a nightdress with long sleeves decorated with lace, and her hands lay face up, her fingers curled into claws. Her bony wrists looked raw and utterly fleshless, and her nails were long, and as yellow as autumn leaves. Lips had drawn back from long teeth and the bony angles of her face were covered in a thick layer of night cream. At first glance I had seen all that white and assumed I was looking at a skull, but it was certainly night cream, or some sort of moisturiser. From where I stood I couldn't see her eyes, only the dark sockets of shadow where they should be.

The smell of rot in that tiny room was overwhelming.

I moved towards the bed, my face frozen into a grimace, and I forced myself to look more closely at her chest. The nightgown came right up to her bony neck, and although I watched intently, I did not see her chest move.

This is not Cheryl. This is something else.

I'd read about things like this before. Usually involving reclusive people, people who weren't quite able to let go, or face life without a loved one, so they kept the corpse on hand, in a room no one else went in. There was the woman who'd surrounded her mother's dead body with hundreds of air fresheners, or the old woman who'd had her husband's embalmed body dug up and moved to their home, so she could be closer to him. And there was Ed Gein, the infamous Wisconsin serial killer who'd missed his dead mother so much he'd decided to make a kind of giant mother-shaped sleeping bag out of bits of other dead women . . .

Stop it, stop it.

I was close enough now to see her face more clearly. The woman's mouth was open, and inside I could see the twisted dry thing that was her tongue. Her eyelids were little wrinkled pouches, and her hair – which was mostly missing from the top of her head – was a snowy white.

She can't have been dead all that long, I thought. *Or she's been embalmed somehow?*

There was something smeared over what passed for her lips. I peered closer, my curiosity briefly overriding my disgust. It looked wet, almost, and red . . .

The second I realised it was lipstick was also the exact moment that the ancient dead woman lurched up from the bed, her eyes suddenly open and staring. One claw-like hand closed around my forearm, and we both screamed. I felt the fetid warmth of her breath crawl across my cheek.

'Fuck!'

I leapt back, breaking her grip easily enough, and crashed into the dressing table behind me. Jars and tubs clattered and rolled onto the floor.

'RAAAAAAA!'

She had sat up, her head lolling on her neck like it was too heavy for her, her hands still laying face up on top of the duvet.

'Fuck, shit, I'm sorry,' I said, backing towards the door with my hands up in front of me. 'I thought this place was empty.'

'HUUUUU!' The noises she made increased in ferocity, and thin lines of drool began to run over her lower set of teeth. As the bedcovers fell back, I saw that there was a belt across her waist, securing her to the bed.

'I'm sorry!' I backed out of the door, my skin attempting to exit the caravan before me, and just as suddenly as she had lurched to life, the ancient woman sagged back, her eyes turning confused, hurt. The noises she had been making became stifled 'rurs' and 'guhs'. I crashed backwards, almost tripping over the orange toolbox, and ran for the door, suddenly completely certain that Harald would appear in the door before I could get there, and I would be trapped between him and the horror in the bedroom.

I made it out. The cold morning air was like a slap to the face, and I slammed the door behind me, wild-eyed. What the fuck had I been thinking?

Chapter 48

July 1988

The rhythm of their holiday had changed entirely.

Now, the radio was on constantly, and Charlie's grandad went out early in the morning to pick up a copy of the local paper. Her Auntie Beverly also went out early, but it was to do a slow and observant circuit of the caravan site, gathering gossip from the other holidaymakers. Everyone was tense; voices were subdued, thoughtful. Only Charlie's cousin Darren and her sister Carol seemed unaffected – they rattled and sulked around the caravan as only teenagers could, complaining about their curtailed plans and repeatedly opening the fridge door. Charlie found herself following her mum around. If she was sitting on the sofa, she would sit next to her. If she went outside for a fag, Charlie would make sure she was out there too.

It was while she was outside observing one of these fag breaks that she saw Auntie Beverly coming back from her patrol. Despite the heat of the day her arms were crossed tightly over her chest, and Charlie could tell she had some new piece of information. She bubbled with it.

''Ere, give us one of those, will you?'

Charlie's mother offered her a cigarette from the packet, and lit it with her lighter. For a few seconds Beverly puffed intently.

'Well,' she said eventually. 'What I've heard is that the girl's cousins saw her hanging around with some other kids. The day before. You know.'

Sitting on the grass some feet away, Charlie felt the ground underneath her shift, become uncertain; her own personal earthquake.

'So?' said her mother. 'The kids all hang out together here.'

Beverly was not to be put off. 'They think that's who she was with when she disappeared though. Two girls of the same age.' Beverly rolled her fag between her thumb and forefinger. 'I spoke to this woman who's staying three caravans down from the Hennesseys. She's not letting her kids out at all now. She says it's a classic ruse by child abductors. They send in harmless-looking kids to act as a lure, and then when they've got the victim somewhere isolated . . .' She flicked the ash onto the grass.

'What about the man they took away? Emily's dad,' said Charlie's mum. 'I noticed bruises on that kid a few times.' She seemed to remember Charlie was outside with them, and lowered her voice. 'You can tell what sort he is.'

Although her head was down, resting on her knees, Charlie felt their attention fall on her.

'We should see how she's getting on, the kid,' said Beverly in a musing tone. 'Charlie's thick with her, isn't she? Maybe we should go and check on them.'

'Bev,' her sister's voice was rueful. 'You are outrageous.'

'Just to see how they are.' Beverly dropped the fag end and squashed it under her sandal. 'You want to come and see your little friend, Charlie? You can't sit moping around here all day.'

Charlie looked up. Both her mother and her aunt were looking at her speculatively.

'You've been under my feet all morning,' her mother said eventually. 'Go with Beverly.'

Charlie got to her feet. 'But—'

'Good girl,' said Beverly brightly. She stepped over and took Charlie by the arm. 'Won't take five minutes.'

Propelled by her aunt, Charlie walked away from the caravan. She did not want to see Emily again. She didn't have any idea how Auntie Beverly knew where Emily's caravan was, but her aunt was the sort of person who seemed to just come by knowledge in secret ways; she knew when Darren had tried smoking, or who had broken the ugly vase in Nan's living room. When they got there, to her surprise Charlie saw that the caravan door was open, and Emily's mother was outside, leaning against their old car. She didn't lean casually; she looked stiff and unnatural, like a broom left against a wall.

'Hiya,' said Beverly brightly. Emily's mother looked startled. 'Charlie wanted to come and see Emily, so I thought I'd tag along. Just to check how you're doing.' Charlie's aunt had arranged her face into an expression of kindly concern. When Emily's mother didn't respond, she offered her a fag from a packet in the back of her trousers. 'I'm Beverly, by the way, Charlie's aunt.'

'Katherine,' said Emily's mother. She took the offered cigarette then held it in her fingers, as if she didn't know what it was for.

'Need a light for that?'

Katherine shook her head slowly.

'So, how are you doing?'

'Fine.' Katherine picked at a tassel on her skirt. 'Just waiting for John to come back. He'll be back soon.'

'Will he?' asked Beverly. She lowered her voice to a just-us-friends tone. 'They must be getting desperate, right, the police? If they're just taking random people away? Don't you think?'

Katherine turned her head, her long dark hair falling across her face. At that moment, Emily appeared at the open door. She spotted Charlie and grinned widely.

'There you go.' Beverly gave Charlie a little shove. 'Go and play with your friend, okay?'

For a long, elastic second Charlie considered turning her back and running, just running out into the park, but her traitor feet carried her over the grass and up the small steps into their gloomy living room. Behind her, Auntie Beverly started in on a new approach: 'Did the police tell you anything? Where are you all from?'

'Did you see?' said Emily, once they were out of earshot. 'He's *gone*. They took him.'

Charlie said nothing. The other girl looked as happy as Charlie had ever seen her. She wore clean white shorts and a pink spaghetti-strap top. Her shoulders glistened with sun cream.

'I told them, didn't I?' she went on happily. 'I thought, Stitch Face Sue needs some help, that's all, she needs a way to get him on his own. I told the police that I had seen him with a little girl. That he was holding her arm, really hard.' She laughed. 'It was so easy.' There was no sign on her face of the fight they'd had the last time they'd seen each other.

'They believed you?'

'Of course they did, the police always believe me.' Emily grinned. 'Do you want an ice lolly?'

Charlie glanced at the open door, an oblong of summer hanging in the shadows of the caravan. It felt like every time she tried to get there, she was dragged back into the shadows with Emily.

'Emily, I'm scared. What we did was . . . so terrible. I can't think about anything else.'

'But my dad—'

'I don't care about your dad! I don't care about you, you weirdo! I just want, I just want . . .' Tears sprang into Charlie's eyes. 'I just want to go home, I just want to be okay again!'

Emily had gone very still. Just then to Charlie she looked like a doll, something with loose limbs and dead eyes. She remembered the last time she had seen Emily, how the girl had started hitting herself, the flat clapping noise of her open palm meeting her cheek, over and over.

In the silence that followed, the voices outside rose, and distinct among them was a male voice, sounding terse. Emily's head snapped towards it, and Charlie ran to the door.

It was Emily's father.

He looked ruffled and annoyed. His hair was untidy, and there were distinct sweat stains at the armpits and on the back of his dark shirt. He was glaring at the two women standing by his car, while Katherine, Emily's mother, had covered the lower part of her face with her hands. Charlie looked at her aunt; she had taken a step backwards, her expression wary.

'What are you doing here?' This was from Emily, who had followed Charlie to the door.

Emily's father smiled his cold shark-smile.

'I had an alibi, didn't I? You little idiot.' In the sunshine, the gold cross at his neck winked and sent arrows of fiery sunlight towards them. 'All accounted for, every hour, multiple witnesses. It just didn't add up. In the end, *they* were apologising to *me*. Very sorry they ever listened to you. I should get them to take you away for biting me, you little animal.'

Emily screamed, shoving past Charlie so violently that she fell from the steps into the dirt, scraping her knees. She heard her Auntie Beverly shout something then, but it was all drowned out by Emily – the girl had run to her father and was tearing at his clothes. The noises she made were guttural, strange; the

305

sounds of a trapped animal finally ready to gnaw its own leg to pieces to escape.

Charlie got to her feet and ran.

Perhaps things would have been different if the police officer Charlie had seen had been a man. Perhaps then she would have been too scared, or too intimidated.

Instead, when she rounded a corner towards the swing park, she saw a young woman in a police uniform. She was talking to some teenagers by the swings, and her hair, which was cut into a neat bob, was red. This also seemed like a sign of some sort – a darker red than her own, but close enough to seem safe. And suddenly all Charlie wanted was some semblance of safety.

The teenagers spotted her first, raising their eyebrows at the kid with the pink face, her eyes still streaming with tears. The police officer turned, and an expression of concern moved over her face. It only made Charlie cry harder.

'What is it, love? What's happened?'

Charlie gasped in a breath. 'I have to tell you something. I have to tell you w-what happened to Katie Hennessey.'

Later, but not much later, Charlie was escorted back to her caravan by the police officer. Her mother was still standing outside, talking now with Charlie's nan, but they both looked up as the policewoman approached. Charlie saw the changing expressions on her mother's face – confusion moving to surprise, moving to dread. She saw her mother look more closely at the policewoman's face, her posture, and then, like her blood was draining away into the dirt, her face turned an ashen cream colour, like the wall of the caravan behind her.

It was an image Charlie would remember forever.

Chapter 49

Now

Church Street, it turned out, was the road that ran parallel to the seafront, but the building I was looking for was further down the road than I'd ever been – there had been no gift shops or ice-cream parlours this far down when I was a kid, so we had never bothered. The morning had turned wet, big gusts of salty-tasting wind barrelling across the pavement, getting my hair damp despite my hood. I stood looking at the little brass plate screwed into the brick wall, covered in water droplets.

Hithechurch Historical and Geological Society, EST. 1968

It sounded quite grand, and I was half considering turning back as I rang the doorbell, but it opened almost instantly, revealing the woman I had met in the caves, a pair of yellow Marigolds on her hands.

'Oh bloody hell, look at you,' she said. 'It's pissing down, get in.'

I stepped over the threshold reluctantly, too aware of the rainwater positively leaping off my jacket onto the carpet. The place was homely and smelled of polish. There was a wooden side table with a rotary phone on it just inside the door, and a stack of cardboard boxes next to that, full of pamphlets like the one she had given me.

'Pat, isn't it?' I said. 'We met the other day.'

'Of course,' she said, waving me into a room off the hallway which seemed to be an office of some sort. There were two desks covered in papers, with two more rotary telephones. 'I'm sorry, love, but I've quite forgotten your name. It was in the caves, wasn't it?'

'I'm Sarah,' I said. It was always a relief to say that name aloud, before anyone got the wrong idea. Or the right idea. 'I had a quiet morning' – an image of the old woman in Harald's caravan swam before my eyes and I had to clear my throat – 'uh, and I was just wondering about the caves. I'd like to know more about them.'

'You have come to the right place!' Pat beamed at me and snapped off her Marigolds. 'Do excuse me, it's my week on the cleaning rota.' She gestured to the desk nearest the front window. 'Take a seat, that's the geology desk. I'll just get us a cup of tea.'

While she vanished back into the corridor, I sat down on the chair facing the desk. I could see maps and more pamphlets, and something that looked like a poster made by a child. On the plastic desk tidy there were several brightly coloured furry things with googly eyes – they each had a silky tag printed with things like 'greetings from Wookey Hole' and 'I have been to Smoo Cave'. I heard the kettle boiling in another room nearby.

Pat poked her head around the corner. 'Milk? Sugar?'

'Just milk, please.'

She vanished again.

I looked around some more. The other desk was partly

hidden under towers of history books. Along one wall was a huge bookcase and cabinet, with more books and other odd artefacts. I had half decided to get up and have a closer look when Pat came back in the room carrying two mugs, one of which she set down in front of me. She took the seat on the other side of the desk.

'So.' She sipped her tea and looked at me over the brim of her mug. She seemed pleased to have an excuse not to do the dusting. 'The caves?'

'Yeah,' I summoned a rueful smile. 'I guess I've just got a bee in my bonnet about it, you know? It's probably the weather being rubbish, but I can't stop thinking about the other caves you mentioned. The tunnels. The ones that aren't open to the public.'

Actually I was thinking about the hole where I had wedged the Tupperware pot, where it had fallen out of sight. Perhaps there was a chance it had dropped into another cave, another part of the tunnel.

'And,' I added, 'I kept thinking about the curse.' I laughed a little, embarrassed. 'I love stuff like that. Creepy local history. I'm writing a little book, I'm sure I must have mentioned it? About local folklore. Weird or scary stories, things like that.'

'You should talk to my colleague, Erin,' said Pat, nodding at the other desk. 'She loves all that stuff too, the gorier the better. My husband says we've both got morbid imaginations, too interested in dark places and old secrets.'

'You should tell her,' said Katie, suddenly next to me, 'how that sort of thing gets you in trouble.'

'How big is the cave network?' I asked. 'The one tourists don't get to see.'

'Here . . .' Pat unearthed a map from her desk and spun it round to face me. It didn't make much sense to me, but she began poking at sections of it with her finger. 'See, the blue

309

sections are the Hithechurch caves currently open to the public. Now, you see this red section?' She traced it for me. The red section seemed intertwined in places with the blue; in places, they crossed over. 'The bit that isn't opened yet. Don't worry – in this instance red doesn't mean dangerous. It's just a bit of a mess, to be honest with you, loads of junk and rubbish has accumulated over the years, and, well, clearing it up is a slow process. When you don't have much funding, anyway.' She sniffed. 'The local handyman is doing what he can with it. Do you see how far along it goes? There are little pockets all along Hithechurch seafront. Some of it, we think, has to be manmade.'

I looked closely at the map, willing it to make sense to me. 'Is it possible to have a copy of this?'

'It would be my pleasure.' She picked up the map and took it to the photocopier in the corner of the room. She opened the top and stared down at the various buttons for a moment, her eyes narrowed.

'Do you ever open to other people? I'd love to see this other cave system.'

'The plan is to open it to everyone eventually.' She put the map face down and closed the lid. She pressed a few buttons, an uncertain expression on her face. When she looked up at me though, she smiled. 'How long are you here for, dear?'

'Just a few more days.'

'Perhaps we can arrange something for you. Here.' The photocopier whirred into life and spat out several sheets of paper. 'Bloody thing. I only wanted one.' Pat took one piece of paper and passed it to me, then folded the rest on her desk. 'I hope you get some use out of it.'

At that moment, there was a rattle at the front door, and I heard heavy footsteps coming up the hallway. I put the picture down and looked up in time to see Harald lean into the doorway, one dirty calloused hand curled against the frame. He was looking right at me.

'Oh there you are, Harry,' said Pat merrily. 'This is Sarah. You wouldn't mind showing her around the secondary cave system this afternoon, would you? Isn't it nice to have someone in town interested in local history?'

Chapter 50

For the duration of their trial, Emily Elizabeth Haynes and Charlotte Watts were referred to as Child A and Child B, respectively. Due in no small part to a huge tide of public feeling on the case, they were both tried as adults in an adult court. It was put forward by the judge that children of ten years or older could reasonably be expected to know right from wrong, or at least 'mischievous behaviour' from acts of violence that could cause lasting damage and trauma. So it was that Charlie found herself in a courtroom, sitting in the dock away from her parents, perched on a raised chair so that she could see over the barrier. They were tried for murder and abduction.

It did not go well for Child A or Child B.

The tabloid press had a field day, going after both families with typical singlemindedness. Photographs of Katie were plastered all over the front pages, photographs that showed a happy, patient kid devoted to her younger siblings. One particular image, of her planting a kiss on the top of her

312

brother's downy head, became the picture that lodged in people's heads during the trial, while the stark mugshots taken of Charlie and Emily became equally infamous.

Charlie sat through it all in a kind of daze, her fingers clasped so tightly in her lap that they were bone white. Journalists present at the trial described her as 'seemingly catatonic'. In contrast, Emily had to be restrained. She screamed at the court at large, beating her small fists against the dock. She shrieked that her father was the one who should be going to prison. Her usually pale face was constantly flushed, and, to Charlie's quiet horror, she continued to shout about the imaginary friend who she believed she had been 'summoning' during their 'ritual'. The journalists present described her as 'deranged', 'remorseless' and clearly dangerous, while the defence pleaded that she was undoubtedly mentally ill. The court of public opinion didn't care much either way, and eventually both children were found guilty of murder and sentenced to be detained 'at her majesty's pleasure' for a period of no less than twenty years, with the understanding that if they should ever see the light of day again it would be under extremely close observation. A petition by one of the leading tabloid newspapers saw the sentence raised from twenty to twenty-five years.

In the secure unit where she was housed, Charlie learned quickly to keep herself to herself. She had nightmares every night – she was back inside the outfall, but she couldn't find the way out. Emily was there too, talking in a low voice. Or she would dream about Stitch Face Sue, a huge pair of scissors in her hand. In these dreams she was cutting the legs off crane flies, thousands of them, so that their delicate grey legs scattered so thickly over her ragged skirts they seemed to make their own lace. Stitch Face Sue would chop and chop and chop until it was her own fingers she was snipping off. Snip snip snip.

Charlie would be visited once a week by her mother and father, and then eventually, just her mother. Charlie came to dread these visits – the woman who visited her did not look like her mother. Her cheery red hair had gone grey, and her face was slack, joyless. It looked like she was wearing a mask. The other members of her family did not visit.

The years passed, and when she turned sixteen, Charlie was moved to a larger prison. In this broader population, she began to hear whispers about Emily – information carried along on the hungry gossip pipeline that was the prison system. Emily had gone to another secure unit, designed to house young people and teens with serious behavioural problems, but she had proved to be too volatile. In the first six months she had attacked both her social worker and one of the other patients. She was moved, and reassessed. They diagnosed her with a number of personality problems. When Charlie heard that, she laughed.

Also in the year that she turned sixteen, two ten year old boys abducted and murdered a boy of two, and once again the Hithechurch case was in every newspaper – they would feature in a paragraph on the end of every story about the murder, asking what had happened to the country's young people. In the wave of sorrow and fury that followed, Katie's parents and supporters waged a successful campaign to once again have Charlie and Emily's sentence extended. Charlie, looking at the headlines, found it hard to care about her own freedom.

On one of the visits with her mother, when they had run through all their usual topics of conversation, Charlie found her mouth opening and a question about Emily coming out. They sat in silence for a few seconds, both equally stunned by it. Eventually Charlie's mother shifted in her seat and tucked a lock of grey hair behind her ear.

'How is *she* getting on? Why would you want to know

that? You want to put that little witch far from your mind, Charlie.'

Charlie shrugged. 'I'm curious, that's all.'

'Well, she's not keeping her head down, like you are.' Her mother leaned forward over the table, lowering her voice. 'They moved her to another prison, again. It was all over the papers again, all of it.' She leaned back, and Charlie could see that her hands were trembling. Her mother, father and sister had all been moved from their home and given new names, due to fear of vigilante attacks. Charlie could well imagine how they had felt to see the Hithechurch child murder making headlines yet again. 'She's still violent.'

Charlie was taken in to have an assessment, some twenty years after the murders, and the doctors seemed kind, and pleased with her, but the idea of being outside was terrifying. She told them about her nightmares, about the panic attacks that shredded her because some small sound or smell had reminded her of the beach, and so they all nodded, made notes, and looked vaguely disappointed.

A few years after that, the nightmares began to fade. Charlie had made a few close friends in prison, and she began reading books again – a trickle, at first, and then she was in the prison library all the time. She got a tattoo. She still cried at odd moments, or found herself gulping with terror in the middle of a perfectly normal afternoon, but she also found herself thinking about what it might be like to be able to walk down to the shops, or sleep without the sound of hundreds of other women, snoring and snorting. Public opinion was changing too, with a greater emphasis on rehabilitation entering the conversation. A documentary about a similar case in Sweden, where a child of seven had killed a schoolfriend in a play-ground, won several awards. In the documentary, it explained how the child had been given help and anonymity rather than being locked away, and the boy had grown into an apparently well-adjusted adult. Charlie's lawyers quietly started an appeal process.

It was around this time that she heard from another inmate that Emily had apparently turned her life around. She had become deeply involved with some weird church, the sort of religious organisation that saw rehabilitation of the worst in society as part of their mission. Charlie had listened to this news with a faint frown. She remembered that Emily's father had worn a tiny gold crucifix around his neck.

Then, when she was preparing for her next parole interview – with the hope that she might have a chance at some limited freedoms – she received a letter in the post. The header informed her that it was from the Church of the Shining Hill, but the letter was blank. Or almost blank.

In the wide open space of paper, someone had carefully drawn a crane fly in grey pencil.

Charlie failed her next assessment for release, too.

Then, one day, some thirty years after the summer of 1988, she had a new visiting request. Charlie looked at the name on the slip for a long time, and when she asked about it she was told the person was a lawyer. She could say no, if she liked.

When she walked into the visitors' room that day, she saw an attractive, tanned woman with loose curly hair sitting at her table. She wore a dove grey skirt suit, with a silver pin in her lapel.

'My name is Becky Waller, Miss Watts. I'm here on behalf of a mutual friend.' Her smile was dazzling, decades of exemplary American dentistry behind it. 'Do you mind if we have a chat?'

'A mutual friend? That doesn't seem likely.' Charlie glanced around the room. It was a wet grey day in November, and it was largely empty. 'I don't have many of those that aren't in here.'

'Our client, Emily Haynes, has recently—'

Even Charlie was surprised at the surge of feelings that name caused. She slapped her hand flat on the table between them, and the woman flinched, just a bit.

'That – she is *not* my friend.' Charlie choked back a strangled laugh. 'What are you doing here?'

Becky Waller folded her hands together on the table. 'Miss Watts, you may or may not know this already, but Emily is due for release near the end of this year.'

'I had heard that, yeah. Funnily enough, I get out of here soon, too.' In the end, with Charlie's 'mental instability' worrying the shrinks and Emily's violent behaviour over the years, they had ended up serving roughly the same amount of time.

'During her time in prison, she has been writing a memoir.'

'What?'

'An account of her life,' continued Becky.

'Yes, I know what a fucking memoir is.' Charlie took a quick breath. 'What's it got to do with me?'

'She has found a publisher for the book. Now, as you can imagine, that has thrown up a number of legal and ethical questions, and subsequently the terms of the contract include certain measures – that any profit Emily might make from such a book go to a charity for victims of violence, for example. Emily has happily agreed to these stipulations. She feels a great deal of remorse for what happened when she was a child.'

Charlie bit her lip. 'I find that hard to believe.'

'She feels that it is important that people know the truth of what happened that summer. She sees it as a kind of public service.' Becky shifted in her seat, her eyes dropping from Charlie's to look at the tabletop. Charlie had the sudden idea

317

that she was uncomfortable with the whole thing. 'And she also wanted you to know that she was going to tell her story – which is why I am here.'

Charlie leaned back from the table. A freezing shard of ice had lodged in her chest, the cold radiating out through her arms, her throat, her stomach. She thought of the letter she had received before, the sketch of a crane fly in the middle of a blank page.

'Christ. She's still a monster.'

Becky looked taken aback. 'She is doing you a courtesy, Miss Watts. Giving you time to come to terms with it. Giving you time to . . . inform your family. The Hithechurch child murder will be in the news again.'

'A courtesy!' Charlie did laugh this time. 'Is that what you really think? She wants to torture me, you idiot.'

Becky Waller nodded once, then stood up, straightening her blazer and brushing an invisible piece of lint from her sleeve.

'Believe what you like, Miss Watts. Either way, Emily wanted you to know. She's telling her side of the story.'

Chapter 51

Now

I agreed to meet Harald later that afternoon on the beach by the old deckchair kiosk. I found myself there after lunch; the wind had picked up, whipping the dry sand along the beach at tremendous speeds, so that I could feel the grains stinging the side of my jeans. I turned my face away from it, and saw him coming, a tall, wiry form, dark against the pale sand.

'Are you going to ask him about the old woman in his caravan?' asked Katie.

'About the living corpse?' The wind snatched the words from my lips. 'Not easy to drop that into conversation, is it?'

I was more worried than I wanted to admit. I could hardly have backed down from my request in front of Pat, and I did want to get a proper look at these other caves – just in case they gave me access to what I had lost – but part of me believed that Harald would know just from looking at me that I had broken into his home. That more to the point, he would look at me and see Charlie Watts, a girl with a very dark history indeed – just as the old women in the café had done. There

319

was no Joseph to bail me out here. But when Harald reached me, he didn't look at my face for long, and he gestured wearily, as though I was a boring distraction in a long day of boring tasks.

'Thanks,' I said, speaking up over the wind. 'I really appreciate this.'

He grunted and led me up to where the caves began. We were a short distance away from where the official Hithechurch caves had their entrance, and I could see why I had missed this second set; they were hidden behind a small row of brightly coloured wooden buildings that, in the summer, sold ice cream and hot dogs, and then again, behind those, was a small group of scruffy storage buildings. There was a low fence, and then behind that, a somewhat rusted-looking gate leading into the cliff face. He unlocked it, and we stepped inside.

'Can you believe I never knew these were here?' My nerves were making me sound extremely chirpy, so I cleared my throat and tried to tone it down a bit. 'Is it safe, this part of the cave network?'

He made a low grumbling noise in his chest as he roused himself to speech.

'Safe enough. Full of crap, as you'll see, but safe.' He reached up and flicked on a lamp that was hanging from a beam above us. As the yellow light leapt into life, I saw a livid scar just behind his ear, mostly hidden by hair. The further in we walked, the more lamps we clicked on, and I could see what he meant about the rubbish. There were piles of refuse all over – things that had obviously been dumped there, like glass bottles, plastic crates, even an old portable television, and things that had been blown in by the weather over the years; newspapers, crisp packets, soft drinks bottles. Looking at it all, I had to wonder what Harald was actually doing in the caves, since it didn't seem like he had spent much time clearing them out, and as

320

if he could sense what I was thinking, he met my eyes for the first time, his eyebrows drawn together in a scowl.

'It's a lot of work,' he said. 'You wouldn't believe the stuff that people have left in here over the years. It's a bloody thankless task.'

I thought of Pat, so cheerful and pleasant. I found it difficult to believe she hadn't thanked Harald for his labours. Nonetheless, I smiled and nodded.

'Do you mind if I have a look around?' I pulled the photocopied sheet out of my rucksack. 'I have a map and I want to match it up with the caves.'

'You're used to caves, are you?'

'Oh yes. I was saying to Pat earlier, it's one of my passions. Poking around caves.' The ludicrousness of this lie made me want to laugh, but Harald didn't seem to find it so outrageous. 'This is a real thrill, seeing some that aren't open to the public yet.'

Harald shrugged. He went to a toolbox resting on a nearby rock and retrieved a large black torch from it, which he passed to me. It had a bright yellow rubber grip on the handle.

'Take this. Be sure to keep an eye on the floor, and on what's at head height too. Very easy to brain yourself walking around these caves. Shout if you need help.'

I took the torch and I wandered, eager to get out of his line of sight. I turned a couple of corners and I was on my own, although I listened carefully as I moved; it wouldn't do to have Harald sneaking up on me here. As I walked, my torch trained ahead of me, I saw that the walls had been scribbled on – bright dashes of colour, the dark scrawls of tags. I've always had a fascination for graffiti – you see a lot of it in prison, just as an entirely random example – and I let my light dawdle across the whorls and jagged lines, looking for words I recognised, phrases, images.

321

the red wolf hunts
Tom 4 Lanie
Matt Haberly sux cocks!
Bango Skank woz ere

The further in I went, the weirder the graffiti became. Some of them seemed oddly childlike, the sorts of things you might expect to see scribbled in rainbow crayon on a piece of paper stuck to someone's fridge. There were stick figures of men and women; sea birds, wings outstretched; big looping hearts and the inevitable phallus. One of the images looked like a man with a dog's head, and I grimaced at that before turning another corner. Maybe teenagers broke in here to smoke joints or get drunk. It seemed a likely spot.

I looked again at the map, willing myself to make sense of it. Following my route from the entrance, it looked like I was now in the section of the caves that ran right alongside the main Hithechurch system. A little further ahead, I should come to the place where the red and blue sections overlapped.

I walked on, the torch scouting ahead. Eventually a fissure opened up to my right, and I paused to look at it. This wasn't the section I wanted – that was all to my left – but something about it caught my eye. It was a tall, thin rent in the rock, tall enough for a person to get through, although it would have been a tight squeeze. Making the prospect even less likely was a pile of garbage that seemed to half fill it up. I ran my torch beam over it, illuminating old clothes, tin cans, an old broken bucket. It almost looked as though the garbage had been placed there deliberately.

Curious, I edged closer, and realised that there was a very faint breeze coming through the gap. And then, I heard voices.

I jumped back, oddly panicked. It had to be Harald, muttering to himself somewhere behind me, or perhaps some odd trick of echoes was bringing me the voice of someone on the beach or in the town.

When I turned away, Katie was waiting for me.

'What was that?' she asked.

'I don't know. It's not what I came for.'

For the rest of the way, I followed her.

She was a slim shape in the gloom, sometimes no more than a disturbance in the shadows. Sometimes I would catch a portion of her face in the torchlight, as white as paper, as she turned to give me an impatient look.

Eventually, we came to a section where the ceiling seemed to drop suddenly, and the ground to slope. I paused and examined my map again. This looked like the place; one loop of blue intercepting a loop of red. Katie only had to bend her head to get under it, but I would have to go on my knees. A sick feeling unfurled in my chest. The portion of this mini cave I could see was entirely black, a darkness so thick it looked like a solid thing. I crouched and waved my torch around. There was a lot of rubbish back there, too.

'What are you going to do?' said Katie. She was already in there, peering out at me. 'Come all this way and then not take the last steps?'

For a long second I couldn't answer her. Her face, hidden in the shadow of the rocks; the smell of the caves; the gritty feeling of sand under my fingers. It was all giving me a very bad feeling. I thought of the outfall, the crabs running from our clumsy footsteps, the rushing sound of the tide coming in.

'It's probably not there at all,' I said. My voice sounded very faint, like I was a ghost in the caves myself. 'It's stupid.'

She didn't answer that. I shoved the map back in my bag and got down on my knees, one hand awkwardly holding the torch. As I began edging forward, I could feel the cool damp of the caves sinking into my trouser legs. The smell here was mostly of garbage, and periodically I found myself holding my breath, but then, some tension in me seemed to ease. I was here. I was dirty and damp. I may as well do a decent job of looking for the thing. The idea that Harald might come after me and find me crouched down inside the space made me work faster, but even so it took a long time, and the further in I went the harder it was to move. The stone ceiling pushed down and down, until I could feel it scraping against my scalp every time I moved. I was sweating too, and could feel it gathering under my arms and down my back.

'Bollocks,' I hissed. 'This better be worth it.'

And then abruptly there was a space above my head. I stopped moving, and aimed my torch directly up. I couldn't make out much, but there was definitely a small chimney-like space in the cave ceiling here, a hole that perhaps led directly to the official Hithechurch caves.

I looked down again, and there it was. The Tupperware pot, so filthy it was a mottled orange and green, but I could see a tiny patch of the original image – a snowman's black coal eye winked out at me from the dark.

'Well, fuck me.'

I grabbed it and scrambled backwards out of the narrow space. Now that I had what I had come for, the idea of being wedged into the tiny cave was unbearable and as I stood up in the wider space and crammed the pot into my rucksack, my skin was prickling all over with horror. Suddenly more than anything I was desperate to get out of there, to see daylight and the blameless grey sky stretching over everything.

On my way back towards Harald, though, I paused again by the tall fissure in the rock, the one where I had heard sounds. There were still noises coming from there, a strange keening sound, and then knocking . . .

All sounds in here are strange, I thought. *I could be hearing anything.*

When I found Harald again, he was by the entrance. I watched as he looked me up and down, a frown creasing his face. I could see him thinking about asking what I'd been up to in there – there was dirt on my knees and hands, and I smelled like garbage – but I also saw him dismissing the idea. I was of no interest to him. He had no idea who I was, after all.

'You done?' he said.

'Yeah,' I said, and then realising that I actually was, I smiled. 'I suppose I am.'

Chapter 52

Now

I went up onto the promenade and sat for a while on one of the benches. I felt dirty, but mostly I felt elated. Against all the odds, I had found the bloody thing, and according to Louise, the contents of the pot would bring Emily's book deal – and her new, shining, undeserved life – crashing down around her ears. I also felt a little shaky, and as I sat there on the bench I grinned to myself like an idiot. Soon I could go back to my own fresh start, back to the quiet and unassuming life of Sarah Hewitt – Sarah, who had never done anyone any harm. While Emily would have to live on with the world knowing she was a monster.

'She won't be able to paint over the truth now,' I said aloud. Katie was sitting at the far end of the bench, her face hidden by a curtain of brown hair. 'She's going to dredge up the past only to end up condemned by it. Ha.'

Katie still said nothing.

'What's up with you?'

She turned to look at me. There was sand in her hair, and

a smudge of blood on her chin. Her eyes looked entirely blank.

'Fine. I know someone who will be pleased, anyway.' I got out my phone and texted Louise. I only had to wait a handful of seconds for her reply – I wondered if she'd been watching her phone, waiting to hear from me.

That's incredible news! I would like to see it, if that's okay? :D

She texted an address in Hithechurch where we could meet, and that gave me a moment of uncertainty – I thought we were avoiding the town – but I was too excited to worry about it, and I thought it likely she was too excited to mind either. I picked up my bag and turned my back on the sea. At least I wouldn't have to go and get the car.

I was surprised to find that the address was an empty shop, down one of the quieter roads branching off Hithechurch main street. The windows had been soaped over and there was a pile of post on the mat, but I figured it had to be one of the properties her boss was using for a 'pop-up' shop, as weird as that sounded to me. The door was unlocked and a bell jangled as I stepped inside.

'Hello? Louise?'

Inside, the place was a little spooky. There was an old dust-covered desk at the back of the room, next to a doorway covered by a beaded curtain, and there were a few mannequins standing propped up against the walls. It was gloomy but I could see that there was a light on in the room on the other side of the beaded curtain.

'Hello?'

The place smelled of old clothes and dust. I glanced behind me to see the soapy windows; the light they let in was diffuse and tired. A second later, Louise stepped out through the beaded curtain. My first thought was that she looked stiff, like a child being forced to take part in a nativity play when they'd rather do anything else but that. For once her cheeks were flushed rather than pale. I smiled and held up the Tupperware pot.

'Bingo!' I said, then felt slightly foolish. 'You won't believe where it turned out to be in the bloody end. This is the thing we buried, all those years ago. Can—'

'You should go.' She cleared her throat and repeated herself. 'Go *now*.'

'What? I just—'

But she spoke over me, her words tripping over themselves.

'Charlie, *go*! I couldn't do anything about it, I had no choice, you have to—'

When the figure stepped out through the beaded curtain and came up behind her, I assumed it must be her boss, here to check out the property, and then I saw the face more clearly. There was a roaring noise in my ears.

'Great job, sis,' said Emily. She moved so she was standing so close to Louise that she could rest her chin on the older woman's shoulder. She was grinning, her eyes very bright indeed. 'You made yourself useful for once. It doesn't quite make up for leaving me in the shit all those years ago, but it's a start.'

'I . . .' At the sight of Emily my throat had turned entirely dry. Her dark hair was long and elegantly styled into loose curls, and she was wearing make-up, a warm coral pink lipstick that made her eyes look greener. Her coat looked expensive too, and my brain gave me a single confused thought: *how can she look so well when she is so clearly unwell*. And then I saw that the hand that curled at Louise's throat was holding a long knife, and all other thoughts left my head.

328

'You can put the pot down on the desk,' she said. 'Or do you think I won't hurt her?'

Louise had closed her eyes tightly and her lips were trembling.

'What are you doing? Are you out of your mind?'

Emily grinned all the wider. 'I'm not the one still holding on to that while a woman with a knife tells her to give it up.'

I walked over to the counter and put the pot down on it. My body felt numb. Emily nodded to the front of the shop, so I took a few steps back.

'There. All done.' Emily nodded. 'Thank you, Louise. And there's just one last thing you can do for me.'

Her arm made a sudden jerking motion, and at first I couldn't quite process what I was seeing. Louise sank forward, her knees dumping her on the floor, and a dark red curtain fell from her throat. I saw her hands grasp at her neck, instantly becoming covered in blood as she tried to hold in what her sister had released. Emily stood over her, the knife dripping.

'She's your *sister*!'

'Really? Because I think she had forgotten that,' said Emily. She looked up at me with those sea green eyes and decades fell away. We were back together in the outfall, the smell of blood and salt in my nose and the world had just broken into pieces. Between us, Louise was gurgling on the floor. 'Sisters don't leave sisters in a house with a monster.' There was blood on her coat, so she shrugged it off and folded it over one arm. Slowly I reached into my pocket and brought out my phone. Emily laughed, a cheerful, childlike sound. 'What are you going to do, Charlie – call the police? Don't worry, I already did that, about five minutes ago. I told them that the notorious child-murderer Charlotte Watts was in Hithechurch, revisiting the scene of her crime, and that she had blood on her hands. I love, by the way, that you've been asking questions about that Cheryl girl. How do you think that's going to look to the police when they find you here? With the body of the sister of the woman you hate most in all the world?'

'You . . . you wouldn't.' I was dimly aware that I was swaying on my feet. There was a good chance I might pass out at any moment. 'You're not supposed to be here either.'

'I didn't give them my *name*.' Emily rolled her eyes like I had made a bad joke. 'God, you're an idiot.'

'It's been you all along, hasn't it? The text messages. The fucking *letter*.' The sense that I was going to faint suddenly increased, so I pinched the skin of my wrist viciously, and the pain brought me back a little. It would be incredibly unwise to be unconscious with Emily in the room.

'I looked for it myself already,' said Emily. She jabbed the knife in the direction of the pot. 'Couldn't bloody find it. And it was dangerous to be here. So Louise helped me. Not that she had much choice, of course. She was always so scared of me, even when I was little.' She looked down at her sister, who was now lying very still. A dark pool of blood was eating up the dusty floor. And then, cutting through the silence like a knife, came the high wailing warble of a siren. Emily smiled.

I ran for it. I crashed out of the shop with Emily's laughter in my ears, and I ran blindly down the street, trying to head away from the sound of the sirens. I got round one corner and then another, and found myself in a slightly down-at-heel residential street. The road was empty of cars and I could see no one around at all. My heart hammering in my chest, I slipped into a narrow passage between houses that was lined with large green and blue bins and got my phone out.

'*Fuck.*'

I was thinking of Katie, the shape of her on the sand, in the dark; I was thinking about how I hadn't gone for help. Because I was scared of Emily, but also because I was scared of what would happen. With numb fingers I punched 999 into my phone and held my breath while I was connected.

'Ambulance please.' For a horrific handful of seconds I couldn't think what the address had been, and then the knowledge dropped into my head like a gift. '89 Boswell Road, the old clothes shop. It looks closed but someone in there has been hurt, please hurry up.'

I disconnected the call and bent over at the waist, dragging in big gulps of air.

'What are you going to do?'

Katie was a quiet grey presence next to me. Black spots were popping in front of my eyes, but gradually they began to fade as I got my breath back.

'I don't know. *Christ*. Louise is probably dead. I've got to assume that Emily knew I was staying at the caravan, so I can't go back there. My car is there too. I need to get out of Hithechurch somehow.'

'Do you?'

I looked at her, the girl who wasn't there, and she looked steadily back at me.

'You have an idea,' she said. 'And you won't get another chance to see if you were right. You'll have to go quickly.'

'If I get caught . . .'

'Does that matter?'

In the distance, I could hear sirens growing closer. 'No,' I said. 'I suppose it doesn't really.'

Chapter 53

Now

I ran to the caves.

My clothes still smelled of them, and there could hardly be a more appropriate hiding place. It would be like hiding in a Famous Five story, like the smugglers who had once hidden their barrels of rum and spice. I didn't let myself think about it too closely. The day was creeping into the afternoon by then, and what there was of the yellow January daylight was being rinsed from the sky with ominous dark clouds.

Harald had locked the gate again when he'd left but it was old and rickety, and when I threw my whole weight against the bars the thing snapped instantly, causing me to stagger awkwardly a few steps before I came to a stop. I pushed the gate shut behind me and hurried into the deeper caves. Once inside, I walked as far as I could in the dark and then I clicked on one of the hanging lamps. The smell of garbage and salt, and the distant roar of the sea surrounded me. I stood, panting.

Katie was there. She stood some way off, where the very edge of the lamplight met the shadows.

'Well,' I said. 'What a fucking idiot I am.'

I expected her to agree, but instead she shrugged. 'Come on,' she said. 'You have to be deeper in.'

'Perhaps Joseph can help me . . .' The words hung in the air, awkwardly. 'I'll have to walk. I can do that. Spend the whole night walking. Get a bus from somewhere, or a train.' When Katie didn't answer, I felt a tremor of impatience. 'What do you suggest, then?'

She shrugged her narrow shoulders. In the dim light, I could see that her jumper was sodden with sea water, and a limp strand of kelp was tangled in her hair.

'You have to go deeper *in*,' she said again.

From somewhere outside, I heard the brief *woop-woop* of a police siren. It sounded far away, but I reminded myself that within the caves, noises were bound to be distorted. I pulled my rucksack more securely onto my back and headed further into the caves, the dank salty scent of them closing around me again as it had before. Katie moved ahead of me, her hands closed into fists at her sides – she, at least, seemed quite certain of where she was going.

I was beginning to panic. The police would get to the beach soon enough, and then surely it wouldn't take them long to figure out where I was. If I was lucky, they might assume I had run straight into the sea – or, more likely, I realised with a lurch of horror, they would spot the footprints I'd left in the sand and follow me right into the caves.

'Shit,' I hissed. 'I'm a fucking idiot.'

Katie wasn't listening. We had reached the tall fissure in the stone I had noticed before, the one that was largely plugged up with garbage, and she had stopped next to it. As I watched, she stretched up onto the tips of her toes and touched the very top of the garbage pile with her fingers. There was a gap there.

'Oh.'

It was a disgusting idea, but I was out of options. Grimacing, I began to yank the garbage out of the hole – black bin bags, an old supermarket wire basket, some sort of plastic kids' toy shaped like a large cheery dog. To my surprise, it all fell away quite easily, and the space beyond, although dark and stinking, was largely clear. I flicked on the torch function on my phone and hurried inside, before leaning out again to pull some of the garbage back into place behind me. Perhaps the police would miss the hole in the dark or decide I couldn't have gone that way. It was worth a try.

Inside the fissure, it quickly grew much too narrow to be comfortable. I took off my rucksack and held it in my hands, and then even turned sideways to scrabble through, but soon enough I could feel cold damp rock scraping against my back and pressing on my front. The slippery feeling of panic I had been nursing in my chest took a sudden leap up my throat.

'I can't do this.'

I remembered all the grisly stories I'd ever read about people getting trapped underground; kids getting lost in the crypts under Paris, miners trapped under a rockfall. No way out, slowly starving or suffocating . . .

'Keep going.' I couldn't see Katie anymore, but she was still ahead of me, somewhere.

I reached out with my right arm, groping in the dark. It did feel like there might be a bit more space beyond the bottleneck I was squeezing through. There was no longer enough space to hold my phone up, so I pushed it into my trouser pocket, closed my eyes against the dark and squeezed through the tight gap.

Someone on the far side took my hand and yanked it, hard.

There was no room to scream. I was there in that tiny space with someone else – Not Katie, but a flesh and blood person. I passed through the bottleneck and they grabbed me and hugged me close to them in the dark. I tried to wrestle free but their grip only tightened, and a cold bony hand slid up the back of my neck into my hair. The face that was pressed next to mine felt rough to the touch, rippled and strange. The smell was there too, the smell of *her*, and I knew who it was. After all these years, Stitch Face Sue had come to claim me.

'No!'

The grip on my hair tightened, and the person holding me yanked my head back. Belatedly I realised that there was light coming from a source I couldn't see. The woman who had grabbed me had long grey hair, hopelessly matted and tangled, and she wore a long, shabby dress that came right down to her wrists and ankles. Her face, such as it was, was a mass of livid scar tissue. Wet eyes glared out at me from a pair of shadowed eye sockets.

She opened her lipless mouth, but no words came out. Instead I got a blast of her breath, which was sweet and rancid at the same time.

Bubble-gum, I thought, in the midst of my panic. *Her breath smells like bubble-gum.*

With her hand still in my hair, she dragged me, kicking and shrieking, out into a wider space. There was a confusion of stacked boxes and piles of old newspapers, and then we appeared to be in a corridor with red-brick walls. There were electric lights screwed into iron sconces. I was busy trying to pull her hand away from my head, but every time I struck her I only hurt myself; she seemed almost to be made of iron and steel wire, no flesh on her at all. Ludicrously, I thought I could hear music playing somewhere, very distantly.

'What the bloody hell do you think you're playing at?'

The voice was loud and male, and at the sound of it Stitch Face Sue's grip on my hair loosened. I yanked myself free; there were strands of my dark hair caught between her skeletal fingers. I turned around just in time to see Harald rounding the corner. He gave me an unmistakable double-take.

'What are *you* doing here?'

I backed away, blathering something about getting lost, but in seconds he had reached me and grabbed hold of my arm. He dragged me further down the corridor and abruptly shoved me through a door into a room, where I fell to the floor. Stitch Face Sue appeared at his shoulder, looking down at me with wild eyes. And then to my shock, he turned to her, his eyebrows raised.

'And *you*. You've caused enough trouble for today. Get back in there.'

'You can *see her*?' I said, painfully aware of how mad I sounded.

Harald just glared at me. Stitch Face Sue walked sedately into the room, and only then did I scramble to my feet – just in time for Harald to slam the door in my face. I heard a bolt rattle home and I threw myself against it anyway, too desperate to think straight.

The woman came up to me, her bony hands curled underneath her chin. She was looking at me so closely, as though she recognised me from somewhere.

'No no, it 'on't do,' she said then. Her voice was croaky and somehow rusted. She spoke slowly and carefully, trying to get the words past her mangled lips. 'Your *thace*. It 'on't do at all.'

Chapter 54

1961

There were a few weeks where Harry was sure that Rosa would die.

He had disinfected everything, he had carefully cleaned the wounds and bandaged them, but still a fever took hold of her and the infection rampaged through her body. Once or twice he was almost frightened enough to take her to the hospital, but each time he remembered his face in the mirror, white and spattered with blood. If anyone else saw what he had done, it would end badly for him. Through the Rushbrooks he got hold of a variety of pills and drugs, painkillers and antibiotics mostly, and when they seemed to make little difference, he asked for the services of one of their tame doctors – the sort of shady men who knew how to stitch up bullet wounds and weren't inclined to ask questions.

When the doctor arrived he stood on the doorstep for a moment, wrinkling his nose and leaning away from the sick-room stench of their home. He was a small, rat-faced man with great twists of dark hair on the backs of his hands, a fact that annoyed Harry for some reason. When he ushered the doctor into the room where Rosa lay, the little man turned to Harry and narrowed his eyes.

'What happened to her?'

'None of your concern. We pay you to fix people, don't we? So fix her.'

The doctor went over to the bed and murmured a few words to Rosa, although if she replied, Harry didn't hear it. He began to unwind the bandages, and the hot smell of illness and infection increased. It made Harry's heart beat faster. How had it gone so wrong?

You're still learning, the wax figure whispered in his ear. *You think everyone gets it right on their first attempt? You think your father did?*

When the doctor had removed all the bandages, he stopped, his hands still holding the filthy strips of material. He sat staring at Rosa's face for so long that Harry took half a step into the room, suddenly furious.

'Are you just going to sit there?'

The doctor looked at him then, and Harry was shocked to see a mixture of disgust and anger on the little man's face.

'Please leave the room and let me work. That is all I will say to you, sir.'

The doctor made three more visits to Rosa over the next week, and whatever it was that he did while the door was shut and Harry waited in the hallway, it worked. Her fever broke, and gradually her strength returned. During her fever Harry had taken all the mirrors out of the bedroom, and once she was back to herself it was the first thing she noticed.

'Where have all the mirrors gone, Harry?' She was sitting up in bed, her dark hair brushed back from her face.

'The doctor told me to take them down, love,' he lied. He

forced himself to look her in the eyes and smile. It was important not to let his eyes wander. 'Some sort of superstitious
thing, I think. He was a funny little chap, wasn't he?'

Rosa did not smile back. He could sense some of her old
defiance in the way that she held herself, in the way that she
stared at him without blinking.

'Show me what you did, Harry.'

Later, when she had worn herself out, Harry sat on the living-
room settee with the old newspaper he had saved spread across
his knees. Rosa was sitting on the floor, leaning against the
sofa; this was where she had fallen after she had thrown herself
at him, smashing her fists over his chest and shoulders. She
was still breathing heavily, her head so low that her long hair
hung over what was left of her face.

'Listen,' he said into the heavy silence. 'I've been reading
about these other procedures that they've been doing. In
America, like. Taking . . . taking parts of one person's body
and using it to fix another.' He held up the paper, but she
didn't look at him. 'They did it in America in the 50s with a
heart. Can you imagine that? And what I think is, I think it's
got to be so much easier to do it with skin than an organ.'

In his head, the scratchy, whispering voice of the wax model
kept up its quiet, insistent refrain. *You can do this. It's what
you were meant to do. You will make Rosa right again.*

When Rosa spoke, her voice sounded different; broken. He
had the sudden persuasive idea that what she had seen in the
mirror had pushed her out of her own mind into a stranger,
darker place.

'Yes,' she said, and she laughed. 'Why not? Find me a new
face, Harry.'

Chapter 55

Now

'It's your face she's talking about.'

It was another voice, younger, female. I had initially taken the place to be a kind of storeroom, but it looked more like a place where old junk was left to rot. Storage boxes were piled up all over, and fruit machines stood dark and ominous in the corners, like sentinels. The whole place smelled of the slots – old coins, warm electronics, cigarette smoke. There were no windows. And in the far corner was an odd sort of den, a space filled with blankets and cushions, a small dressing table with a mirror, and an ancient-looking television set with a bulky VCR sitting underneath. Sitting amid the blankets with her knees drawn up to her chest was a teenage girl. Her face was round and solemn and very pale, and her features looked soft, almost swollen; she had been crying. Her hair was a brassy kind of blonde, shining under the single light bulb, and she had it brushed sharply back from her face and secured in a purple scrunchie. She wore a heavy jumper, a corduroy skirt, and thick, white tights.

'I'm sorry – what?'

'Your face,' the girl repeated. Stitch Face Sue had moved back into the shadows of the storage boxes and having her behind me was making the skin on the back of my neck prickle. 'You're too old.'

'Well that's rude, I . . .' Knowledge washed over me like freezing water. 'Cheryl. You're Cheryl Yates!'

The girl blinked slowly at me. She shuddered.

'Can you pass me the water? It's on the side there.'

I looked to where she was nodding. On the dressing table there was a beaker of water. I passed it to her and Cheryl gulped down the water greedily.

'You're alive,' I said, somewhat needlessly. 'Bloody hell.'

'Sorry.' She put the beaker down next to her, empty. 'I just had lunch, and it has drugs in it. They make me feel woozy, so it's hard to concentrate.'

'Drugs? What are you doing here? You've been here, what, six months? What happened?'

Cheryl shifted on the blankets, and I saw that her ankles had been bound with plastic ties. There was a smudge of brownish blood on her tights where the plastic had rubbed a hole.

'Six months? I don't know. I can't see whether it's day or night. I kept screaming but no one ever came. I miss my mum . . .' Her voice grew thick, and I watched her visibly bring it under control. Tough kid. 'I think we must be underground somewhere, right?'

I remembered the music I thought I had heard, out in the corridor. 'The sea wall, we're inside it. By the funfair.'

I knelt then, next to her. I hesitated, then put my hand on her arm. 'Was it her?' I asked in a low voice. I tipped my head towards Stitch Face Sue. 'Has she hurt you?'

Cheryl looked appalled. She glared at my hand until I removed it.

341

'Her? Of course not. Look at her. Look at what they did to her!'

'What?'

I looked back at Stitch Face Sue. She was standing in the corner, her head down so that her long grey hair covered her face. I forced myself to look at her. She was real. Not a thing made up by an overimaginative child. She was a real person, a flesh and blood woman, and clearly something very bad had happened to her.

'Who is she?'

'I don't know,' Cheryl replied. 'She doesn't say much. And I don't think she remembers. The drugs in my food . . . they do it to her too, but she's been here much longer than me. A lot longer. I think it's made her forget. Over time.' She blinked and I could almost see her fighting the drugs. 'Listen, you have to help me!'

'Yes.' I stood up and made a quick circuit of the room. The door had not magically unlocked itself, there were no windows hiding behind the boxes. There was no obvious way out. I went and sat next to Cheryl on the blankets. 'My name is Charlie, Cheryl. It's going to be okay. Who's doing this? That old bastard Harald, okay. Anyone else? You said "they".'

'Harry,' said Cheryl quietly. 'That's what *she* calls him. He doesn't say much. He just waits, I think, to be told what to do.'

'She? Who's she?'

I heard the crash of a door slamming somewhere, and then the clatter of what sounded like high heels on a concrete floor outside. I could hear the low rumble that I already knew was Harald – or Harry – speaking, and then an answering voice that was louder and sharper. The effect on Cheryl was electric. She scrambled towards the dressing table, moving awkwardly with her bound feet.

'I forgot!' she gasped. 'I forgot to do it at lunch! Quick, help me!'

'Help you what?'

She stabbed a finger at a large glass jar on the dressing table, so I passed it to her. She tore the lid off and stuck her hand in it, bringing out a fat handful of what looked like moisturiser. Quickly she began dabbing it all over her face and neck, and I noticed as she did so that her hands were shaking.

'Three times a day,' she said, and there was a weird singsong quality to her voice that I didn't like at all. 'Three times the charm.'

The bolt rattled on the door and it swung open.

Chapter 56

Now

The lights in the corridor were brighter than the single bulb in the junk room, so for a couple of seconds I couldn't make out who was at the door, but I stood up anyway, prepared to rush them, or try to shove them out of the way. The person who came in first was shorter than Harry, and their silhouette confused me – they looked too big at the head, too thin at the waist.

I cleared my throat. 'Who are you?'

The figure stepped into the light, Harry close behind. She was wearing a large black sun hat with a white ribbon – that was the thing that had confused me – and a silky kimono-style dressing gown, cinched tightly at her minuscule waist. She had pretty little silk slippers on her feet, too. Her face was lost in shadows.

'One might ask you the same question.' Her voice was plummy, slightly hoarse. Behind me I could hear Cheryl making small noises of distress. The hairs on the back of my neck stood up. 'Where did this one come from, Harry?'

'Through the hole, my love,' he said. He sounded different when he spoke to this woman; a wheedling, subservient tone that was very unlike his usual gruff indifference. 'Laura caught her there.'

'Right, that's enough of this freak show,' I said loudly, taking a step forward. I hoped to bluster my way out. 'I know who you've got here, all right? And you're letting her out, right now.'

The woman chuckled throatily. Harry came to her side, and I saw that he was carrying a knife. It wasn't a knife you used in the kitchen – this was something you used for darker jobs, things that didn't get done in the daylight.

He's an old man, I reminded myself. *All you need to do is get past him.*

But it's a funny thing. Thinking about it with no knives in front of you, you might think that a man wielding a knife isn't that scary. It can't get you unless you get close. It's not a *gun*, after all. Yet when you're standing in a dimly lit room, with only one way out and a terrified teenager behind you, it's funny just how dangerous it can seem, that knife. And I had seen what knives can do, after all.

I gritted my teeth and stood rooted to the spot.

'Shall I get rid of her, Rosa?'

'Let me see her first.' The pair of them came into the room and although I drew away from them, Harry caught me by the arm and then the blade was cold against my throat. Part of me, the part that controlled my arms and legs, seemed to go into hiding.

'Take her to my dressing room,' said the woman, 'the light is better in there.' Harry, still holding the blade to my throat, walked me out of the room and back into the corridor. I did my best to look around, to try and get an idea of the layout of the place, but within seconds I was in another room. This one was smaller and cosier than the junk room. Like Harry's caravan, the walls were covered in pictures of women, glamour shots from fancy magazines, even film posters. There was a dressing table against one wall, which had a string of lights around the mirror. The table was cluttered with lipsticks, half-used tubes of foundation, a dirty palette of glittery eyeshadows. Harry sat me down in the chair, and the woman he had called Rosa stepped up behind me. The big sun hat still hid her face in the shadows, but her long hands curled around my throat, tipping my face up into the light.

'Oh no,' she said eventually. 'Goodness me no. You're what, forty? I had thought, perhaps . . . You are just short. Very slight, for a woman your age. You should take better care of your skin.'

'Who are you?' I said. 'Why did you take Cheryl?'

She let go of my chin and tugged sharply at my hair instead. 'A natural redhead. That is something at least. Once you've grown all this awful dye out I will be able to make a very fine wig.'

'Why have you taken Cheryl? What happened to you?'

'Oh, you know what happened. It happens to all of us.' The woman's awful hands curled around my face, framing it, forcing me to look directly into the mirror. 'All us women, anyway. Your body betrays you. It gets older, you lose who you are.'

'That makes no sense at all,' I said. 'You're out of your mind.'

She was quiet for a moment, and behind her, Harry looked away. When she spoke, her voice was low and unspeakably old.

'There was an *accident*.'

I strained my eyes to look up, trying to get a glimpse of what was hidden underneath her hat, but the pressure on my face increased. I thought about trying to break the mirror, trying to grab a shard of glass. But I didn't think I could do it before Harry reached me.

'I've just been taking back what was taken from me, that's all,' said the woman.

'You,' I said loudly, 'are out of your fucking mind.'

She dropped my head abruptly and strode away. Harry dragged me back up from the dressing-table chair, then before I knew it I was back in the junk room with the other two. He gave me a good shove, so that I half fell into some boxes, and when I had straightened up I saw the woman was talking to Cheryl again, her face still hidden under the huge hat.

'Sweetheart, your face looks a little greasy. If you'd put on your creams when you were supposed to, it should all be absorbed by now, shouldn't it? What do we say? Three times, every day, after every meal. It's not hard, is it?'

In the corner by the door, I saw that Stitch Face Sue, or at least the woman I had thought was Stitch Face Sue, was crouched down with her arms over her head. Her long grey hair hung over her face, hiding it.

'Leave her alone,' I said. 'You lunatic.'

'Now then, that's enough of that.' The woman moved back towards the door, and I finally got a brief look at the lower half of her face. It looked white and oddly wet somehow. Her lips were a bright, hectic red, inflamed and puffy-looking. 'Harry does so love to play with his knives. Perhaps I should let him play with you for a while.'

Harry grunted in an amused way.

'Come on.' The woman swept back to the door. 'We have things to do.'

The door clanged shut, and then they were gone again. I stood with my heart pounding, cursing myself. First Emily, and now this nightmare. How was it possible I had fallen from one horror into another?

347

'It's the routine,' said Cheryl quietly. I went and sat next to her on the blankets. 'I have to wash my face a certain way, every day. She has him bring in a basin of water for it, every morning, and these different lotions, to clean my face. And there's different creams for different times.' She nodded to the dressing table, where several pots of moisturiser clustered next to the dirty mirror. 'I have to do it every day, or . . . There's a mask at night too, a mask I have to wear that's made of paper, with a thick cream underneath. I hate it. It stinks, and melts and slides off down my neck in the night.' Her face crumpled, and I thought she would cry, but instead she wiped angrily at her eyes with the heel of her hand. 'I can't cry,' she said then, an angry note in her voice. 'If I cry it makes my eyes red, damages the skin. That's what Rosa says.'

'But why?' I said. 'Why is she making you do all this?'

Cheryl didn't answer immediately. She looked down at her hands, and abruptly I realised how young she was. A kid who had been stolen from her family and kept in a dark room for months, terrified out of her mind. A strange mixture of panic and fury threatened to close up my throat.

'When I was brought here, before, I was kicking and screaming and carrying on, and the man, Harry, kept hitting me to get me to be quiet, but Rosa told him to stop it, because he might damage me. She said to him, "I've got something better to keep her quiet, haven't I?" and they dragged me into this other room and it . . .' She stopped, made an odd choking noise, then shook her head. 'The room was full of faces.'

'What?'

'Har'est,' said Stitch Face Sue from the corner of the room. 'She har'ests your thaces. It's where all aye sisters go.'

'What does that even mean?'

Cheryl would say no more, though, and she wrapped her arms around her knees and put her head down. She was shaking now, shaking with a bone-deep horror, and I felt terrible for making her talk about it at all. I stood up, rubbing my hands on my trousers. I was the adult here. I was the responsible one. I thought that Katie might appear then, to mock me, but she had been curiously silent since I had passed through the cave.

'There has to be something in here we can use.' I began to move around the room, sliding my hands over the old fruit machines and the storage boxes.

'There's nothing,' said Cheryl, her voice muffled. 'I already looked.'

'What's in these boxes, though?' I yanked the top off the nearest one, praying for a handy crowbar or flamethrower, but instead I found pot after pot of moisturiser. In the next one, big tubs of Vaseline.

'Don't bother,' said Cheryl again. 'They're all like that.'

'All right.' I moved to the fruit machines, examining them for parts that could be torn off, perhaps, made into a weapon somehow, but I could see nothing obvious. The other woman, the one with the ruined face, watched me through the gaps in the curtain of her hair. 'There has to be something.'

Finally I stopped in front of the old television set. I stood frowning at it, hands on my hips.

'We could smash it.' I had no idea how cleanly a television screen would break. Would they hear the noise, and come running? I might not have long to find a good long piece of glass. 'Would that work?'

The other woman got up and came over. She was looking urgently at Cheryl, and wringing her bony hands together.

'Um, Laura would prefer it if you didn't break the television,' said Cheryl. 'It's all we have. They let us watch it. Or watch tapes on it, anyway.' She nodded to a small pile of VHS tapes by the video recorder. 'Sometimes Harry brings us a new film.'

349

'Laura. Her name is Laura?'

Cheryl nodded. I was getting an idea now of the full scale of this horror show. But there was something else, too. I shrugged off my rucksack, which I had completely forgotten, and unzipped it. Inside were the contents of the pot I had given to Emily: a teddy bear keyring, a brown envelope of photos, a plastic hairband, an old VHS tape – and Katie's mother's pair of sewing scissors.

'You emptied the Tupperware pot,' Katie said wonderingly, into my ear. '*You gave her an empty pot.*'

She never asked for the contents, did she?

Katie laughed.

Chapter 57

Now

The scissors, obviously, were the prize.

I sat down next to Cheryl and cut the plastic ties around her ankles, which was rather harder than I was expecting. Although the pot had kept the scissors from falling apart entirely, they were still fairly rusty and not as sharp as they had once been. Eventually the blades snapped through the plastic and Cheryl's feet were free. She rubbed her ankles briskly, and I tried not to look at the scabs that had crusted through her laddered tights. It felt like a small victory.

It was around then that I noticed that Stitch Face Sue – Laura, as it turned out – had crept closer to Cheryl's den of blankets and was sitting just on the edge of them. She was looking, quite intently, at the VHS tape I had unpacked from my rucksack.

'She wants to watch it,' said Cheryl. 'It's her favourite thing to do, watch videos.'

'Is it?' I put the scissors down next to my leg. I wanted them close. 'Laura? It's Laura, isn't it?'

351

The woman turned her head towards me, although her eyes – which were a startling green, now that I looked – didn't venture higher than my shoulders.

'How long have you been here, Laura?'

A cold feeling was growing, somewhere in my chest. I thought of what Cheryl had said, about a room full of faces. About the woman saying she was simply taking back what had been stolen from her.

'Laura, do you remember where you were before this place?'

'Don't,' Cheryl said urgently. 'She gets upset if you ask her about it.'

I kept my eyes on Laura. 'Do you remember your last name, Laura? We can watch this in a minute' – I tapped my fingers on the VHS tape – 'but I'd like to know who you are. What do you remember?'

The woman hunched over herself, wrapping her long thin arms around her body.

'I don't know,' she said, in her strange, slightly slurred voice. 'Don't know.'

'It's been years, hasn't it? Lots of years. You've grown up here.' I stopped, briefly silenced by the sheer horror of that. This room, with those two monsters as your prison guards. 'Stuck in this place.'

'No,' she said then, surprising me. 'I go out. Son'tines, I go out. To the eech. The eech.' She shook her head, clearly frustrated about trying to get the words out. 'Trees. I see trees.'

'She isn't locked in here all the time,' said Cheryl quietly. 'I think they've decided there's no harm in her, anymore, because . . .' At this she met my eyes and touched a finger to the side of her head. *They think she's crazy.* 'When they took me at the beach, Laura was there. But she was hidden, under a tarp.'

'Laura, can you tell me any more?'

The woman was fiddling with her pocket, and I saw a small flurry of chewing gum wrappers fall out. I remembered the sweet smell of her breath in the cave.

'Laura, do you remember your brother Carl?'

She jumped as though I had pinched her, and when she looked up at me her eyes were very wide and full of pain. When was the last time anyone had said that name to her? I felt like I had hurt her, shamed her somehow.

'I'm sorry . . .'

She was crying, holding her long fingers up to her face and sobbing through them. She rocked back and forth, making garbled sounds through her ruined lips.

'I *told* you,' said Cheryl, and she sounded close to crying now too.

'All right, I'm sorry. I'm sorry, Laura.' I picked up the VHS tape and crossed over to the old television set. I pushed the tape in the slot and took the remote off the top of the TV. There was a whirring as the tape started playing, and on the screen there was a flutter of jumping pictures. Laura had grown quiet the moment the TV had come on, and when Cheryl spoke, she sounded genuinely curious.

'What is it?'

'I don't really know,' I said. I went and picked up the sewing scissors again, one eye on the junk-room door. 'It's supposed to be *Stand By Me,* a film from the 80s. River Phoenix is in it. Uh. If you know who that is.'

'Sure,' said Cheryl. 'Joaquin Phoenix's brother, right?'

At first I thought it wasn't going to work at all. There was a burst of static noise, and the picture jumped and wobbled all over the place. I kept looking back at the door, trying to think what I would do when Harry and Rosa came back again. I would have to rush them with the scissors and hope I gave us enough time to get out. What was there beyond this corridor?

I assumed there were the caves that Pat at the Historical Society had talked about – the cursed ones, I realised wryly – but there also had to be a way out into the funfair.

'This is so retro,' said Cheryl.

I turned back to see that the picture on the screen had settled down. It had clearly been filmed on some sort of handheld camera, and it was trained on a living room at Christmas. There was a big blue tinsel Christmas tree, a sofa of beige velvet, and orange and brown wallpaper. Cheryl was right, it was very retro. And sitting at the bottom of the Christmas tree, next to a pile of shiny presents, was Emily. Smaller, and younger, but unmistakably her – her dark hair was a shiny bowl around her head, and she was wearing pyjamas. There was an older girl sitting next to her, beaming at the camera. *Louise*, I thought. Her mouth opened, but I couldn't hear what she was saying.

'How do I turn this up?'

Cheryl leaned over to the TV and turned the volume knob, and out of the static and the years came Louise's voice. She was saying something about a selection box and the person holding the camera – Emily's father, I realised with a shudder – laughed.

The Christmas clip ended abruptly, taped over with something else – a scene of a child's bedroom, posters of New Kids on the Block and Bros on the walls. Louise and Emily were there again, and this time the camera was steady, resting on a table or a desk. The two girls were holding hairbrushes and singing a song together over music playing from an old boombox. The older girl was laughing and acting up for the camera, showily throwing her pretend mic from one hand to the other and swishing her long hair back and forth like she was Kylie Minogue. I wondered if the ambulance had reached Louise in time, and my throat grew tight. Next to her older sister, Emily looked small and pale and awkward.

'Who are they?' asked Cheryl. 'Do you know them?'

'No,' I said. 'I don't think I know them at all.'

In the video, Emily tried to copy her sister and throw the hairbrush from one hand to the other, but she missed, and the brush clattered onto an untidy dressing table, knocking a bottle of perfume onto the floor. Louise gave a snort and then bellowed with laughter, bending over with the force of it. Emily went rigid, and I recognised the look of fury that passed over her face – it made me feel cold, even thirty years later.

'What a weird little kid,' said Cheryl.

'You don't know the half of it,' I said.

Louise continued to laugh, and Emily suddenly leapt on her, tiny fists flailing. There was a scream, shouting, and then Emily's father lurched into view. I only saw a brief image of his white shirt and tanned forearms and then he was lifting Emily, kicking and screaming, into the air. Louise had gone very pale, and when she came closer to the camera, clearly meaning to turn it off, the expression on her face wasn't angry or shocked; it was sad, and oddly resigned. The picture flickered again.

The next scene on the tape was of a small back garden on a bright summer's day. The camera was moving around, much lower to the ground than it had been in the previous clip. Louise was in the video again, but she seemed unaware of it; she was lying on a sun lounger in a white swimsuit and shorts – there was a book folded over her knee. The camera edged closer and closer, very slowly, as though whoever was holding it was creeping up on the sunbathing girl. When it was right up to her shoulder, a small hand crept into view holding a plastic bottle with a nozzle cap. The hand squeezed, and a bright arc of red liquid squirted out over Louise, splattered all over her shorts and swimsuit like a burst of arterial blood. Behind me, Laura made a strangled noise in her throat, and

355

Cheryl grabbed at my sleeve. On the video, Louise had scrambled to her feet and was looking with horror at the red mess all over her clothes and skin.

'Is that blood?' asked Cheryl.

'No,' I said, too quickly. 'I think it's hair dye, something like that. I recognise the bottle.' I'd used something like it not too long ago myself, after all. But even so, the video made me uneasy. There was an undercurrent here that went beyond the usual antagonism between siblings. The videos continued, and we saw more incidents like it – always with Louise as the victim, and Emily's violent temper on display. It gradually became clear that Emily herself was filming some of it, as though she wanted to keep a record. We saw one incident where Emily waited outside her sister's bedroom in the night, and then bit her leg when she ventured out to the bathroom. We saw her bring in mud from outside and put it under her sister's pillow; we saw her push a birthday cake onto the floor – carefully iced with 'Happy Birthday Louise!' In one video clip that turned me cold, Emily crept into her sister's room while she was sleeping with a pair of scissors, and cut away big chunks of her hair in the dark.

'I don't like this,' said Cheryl. 'I think we should turn it off.'

'Yeah,' I said, although I didn't.

I thought of the photos in the brown envelope. Emily had told me that her father beat her sister up, that they had taken photos together as 'proof' of what was happening to her. Now, thinking back on those Polaroids with Louise's black eyes and split lips, they seemed to take on a different meaning. Had Louise looked defiant in those photos, or afraid? Who was she afraid of?

In the last clip, the camera sat at a very low angle on the landing carpet. It was possible to see the top of the stairs, and there was a light on below somewhere, while the landing itself was in darkness. After a little while, Louise appeared on camera, and paused at the top of the stairs, turning her head as if she had heard something.

Go back, I thought, suddenly filled with dread. *Get back in your own room and shut the door.*

Emily stepped into frame, carrying something that glinted in the light. I saw the look of horror that passed over Louise's face, and then I was on my feet, reaching for the television's power button. There was a ripping sound and a shriek and then the picture *plinked* into black again as my finger jabbed at the off switch.

A child with a knife attacking her sister. No wonder Emily didn't want this video getting out.

Chapter 58

Now

I put the tape back in my bag, and Cheryl put on a video of some cartoons. They seemed to calm Laura down, and she sat placidly on the blankets again, her hands folded neatly in her lap. I was thinking about Louise, terrorised by her sister. Had she survived the attack in the shop? It didn't seem likely.

'Cheryl,' I said, 'I'm going to get you out of here.'

She smiled wanly, and I remembered what she had said about the drugs.

'Do they put something in all your food?'

She shrugged. 'I think so. I always feel tired after I eat, and sometimes just really heavy, like I can't lift my arms or legs. For ages I didn't eat anything at all, I wouldn't touch anything they gave me. But I was so hungry. I thought I was going to starve.'

I had already checked my phone, which, for all the signal it was getting, may as well have been a very expensive brick, but I spent some time inching my way around the room, holding it up to the ceiling or next to the crack under the door. The bars never even flickered, and my battery was low. I put it away.

'They come in here three times a day? To give you food, and make sure you've . . .' I nodded at the dressing table. For some reason, I didn't want to talk about her daily skincare routine, or what it implied.

'Yeah,' said Cheryl. She looked tired, the skin under her eyes bruised and delicate. 'It's usually him, Harry, who brings in the food, but Rosa comes every now and then too. She gets a torch and shines it on my face. She tells me I have to drink five bottles of water a day, but it makes me want to pee all the time, and there's just the bucket.' She curled her toes inside her stained tights. 'Laura drinks it for me, if she's here.'

'All right,' I said, trying to sound upbeat. 'According to my phone, it's just after six, so they should come back in the evening with your dinner, right? We just have to wait until then.' I didn't say what I intended to do when they came back, and Cheryl didn't ask. On the dusty old television screen, Top Cat was harassing a policeman. I sat down on the edge of the blanket, where I could watch the door.

They didn't come back that evening.

I kept the scissors with me, stuck into my coat pocket, and periodically I would touch my hand to them, and look at the door. I thought I'd be able to get them out pretty quickly if I needed to. I pulled out the map of the cave network and looked carefully at the place where the sea wall caves began, but there wasn't a lot of detail – the organic, wandering lines of the caves straightened out into neat squares in this area, and that was all. I couldn't see any obvious way out.

I have spent a lot of time in small spaces, with company and without, so I thought I would be uniquely experienced to deal with being shut up in the junk room, but as the hours passed I began to notice things. To dwell on things.

I noticed the smell of urine from the bucket by the door. I thought about the lack of windows, about the slim crack under the door which was the only place air was getting in, and how there were three of us in there, merrily breathing away. I thought about where the room was, hidden away inside the sea wall, tons of rock above us. I spent some time considering how Cheryl had been stuck here for months, how I had assumed she was dead. Everyone would think I was dead, too, eventually, if I didn't get out. I thought, then, of Laura, of the girl who had gone missing in 1984. The world thought she was dead too.

'Laura,' I kept my voice low, friendly. 'A little while ago you mentioned your sisters. Who were they? Carl was your brother, but who were your sisters?'

Cheryl shot me an alarmed look. Laura, who had been turning a videotape over and over in her gnarled hands, shook her head slightly.

'I thought I saw you once, when I was a kid.' I made myself smile. 'It certainly looked like you – out of my caravan window. But now I think it can't have been, because you were still a kid then really, only just an adult, but this lady, she looked . . .' I thought of the swaying figure in the night, a dead crane fly in her hair. 'She was older, I think. Could she have been one of your sisters, do you think?'

'She doesn't like to talk about it,' said Cheryl, although she too was watching Laura closely.

'Laura?'

The older woman hung her head. If I was right, if she was Laura Jennings, then she would be around fifty years old now. She had suffered decades of this madness, of being drugged and imprisoned and . . . whatever it was they had done to her face.

She lifted her head, so that her pointed chin poked through the curtain of her hair.

'Alison,' she whispered.

Alison Smith, who had gone missing in 1976. I felt sick. Was that who I had seen through my window, all those years ago?

'Where is Alison now?'

The woman got up and went over to one of the unplugged fruit machines. She slipped her bony fingers into a small gap near the bottom of the unit, and after a bit of poking around, pulled out what looked like a thick piece of card. She brought it over and placed it very gently on the carpet in front of me. Cheryl scooted next to me to look over my shoulder.

The card had been protecting a number of old photographs, each of them very creased and slightly faded, as though they'd been kept in a wallet for years or handled every day.

'So we didn't 'orget,' said Laura. 'This.' She tapped her bony fingers across her face, then pointed at Cheryl's. 'Our *thaces*.'

Carefully, I separated the photos with a single finger. One, the oldest-looking one, was a black and white photo taken in someone's back garden. There was washing on the line. In the middle of the photograph was a tall girl of around thirteen or so – her hair was dark and glossy and tied back with ribbons, and she grinned merrily at the camera. I thought of the newspaper clipping I had seen in the Black Horse, of the girl at the opening of the funfair. *That photo would have been taken just above us, somewhere*, I thought, my flesh creeping. *When April Rushbrook vanished, she was down here, carefully hidden away.*

The second photo was also black and white, taken on the beach, with the sea a thin white line in the distance. This girl was posing with a spade next to an older boy in swimming trunks. On the back of the photo, someone had written

361

'Folksholme '66'. The third photo was a little colour passport photo of a girl with a gap in her teeth, her hair carefully styled into the big lazy flicks that were fashionable in the 70s. The next one I looked at for a long time. It was a colour photo and it showed a vivacious girl with frizzy blonde hair and green eyes, leaning against a pool table, the cue held as if she was about to hit someone with it. Laura. Laura Jennings.

'This is you, isn't it, Laura?' I said, tapping the photo. 'I'm glad to see you, you know.'

There were three more photos, all more recent looking – two were photo booth photos, one showing a girl with freckles and long, poker straight hair. In the other, a girl with thick eyeliner and black lipstick glared out at the camera. Her hair was a mess, and there was a gauntness to her cheeks that worried me. The last was a photo of a pair of girls standing in front of the Millennium Dome, of all things – judging from their wide-legged jeans, it was the early 2000s.

'I never saw these,' said Cheryl quietly. 'She never showed them to me. Where are these girls now?'

I couldn't think of an answer that wouldn't be alarming, so instead I got out my phone, where days ago I had taken photos of missing girls in the library. I scrolled through the names and pictures, matching them up to Laura's creased photographs. April Rushbrook, Natalie Price, Alison Smith, Laura Jennings. I couldn't see Sophie Bennett in any of Laura's pictures. Perhaps she hadn't had any hidden away in her purse when she was taken. I wondered if that was still something kids did. I thought of the slick phone in my fist, filled with electronic images, and thought that they probably didn't. And there were the other unidentified girls too. Girls who had run away from home perhaps – I looked again at the girl with the gaunt cheeks – and just slipped through the cracks. I had only looked for girls that had gone missing in or near Hithechurch after all. Who knew how far Harald had been with his van?

'What happened to these girls, Laura? Where did they go?'

I picked up the photo of April Rushbrook. If she was still alive, she'd be in her seventies. She would be . . .

The photograph dropped from my fingers. The Ranch. The old woman strapped to the bed. I felt dizzy suddenly and cleared my throat. I looked around for the bottle of water, but Laura, I realised, was trying to say something.

She picked up the photos of Natalie Price and Alison Smith. Making sure she had my eye, she shook her head slowly.

'Sore,' she said, and tapped her scarred face again. 'Too sore. Sick, hot, and then . . .' She shook her head again.

'And Sophie?'

Laura looked away. I wondered if Cheryl had caught the significance of any of this – somehow, I hoped not.

'She was here with you?'

Laura nodded sadly. 'Here, and they took her away. Didn't come back.'

I pressed the back of my hand to my mouth. He was butchering their faces. How easy would it be to cut something you shouldn't? It was a miracle any of them had survived the procedure, even without the risk of infection.

'We have to get out of here,' I said hoarsely. 'I'm getting you both out of here. Somehow.'

Chapter 59

Now

We sat for a time, not speaking. Now that she had revealed them, Laura seemed pleased to have the photos to look at again, and she sat gazing at them. I wondered what memories she had left in that fractured mind. I knew I had to use the scissors the next time Harry or Rosa came in the room – it was the only chance we had. If I didn't, if I held on, waiting for some other stroke of luck, they could find the scissors and take them, and that would be that. And I couldn't leave Cheryl and Laura in this room for a second longer than necessary. To distract myself, I turned to Cheryl and smiled.

'You know, I met your mum the other day.'

'You did?' Almost instantly, the girl's face crumpled. She wiped impatiently at her eyes again. 'Is she okay?'

'They're looking for you,' I said. 'Every day, they're still looking, your whole family. They haven't given up.' *And neither have I*, I thought, closing my hand tighter around the scissors in my pocket. 'You'll see them again soon.'

'Were you looking for me then? Is that why you met my

mum?' She blinked several times, and then said incredulously, 'Are you a *police* officer?'

That surprised a laugh out of me. 'No, I, er . . .' The truth was much too complicated. 'I was looking for lost things, and I found you.'

At that moment the door bolt clattered back, and I scrambled to my feet, my hand going back to the scissors in my pocket. Laura snatched up the photos and put them back in their hiding place, while Cheryl threw the blankets over her legs. The door swung open, and Harry came in with his knife held out in front of him. Rosa stood behind him, hidden in the shadows.

'I don't like it,' Harry said. He seemed to be speaking to Rosa. 'Having them all in here together. It causes trouble. Like it did before.'

I felt paralysed again by the sight of the knife. All at once, the rusted scissors in my pocket seemed ridiculous. I couldn't imagine them cutting paper, let alone flesh.

'Perhaps you're right. They get agitated, and then poor Cheryl will get stressed. And stress is the last thing we want to see on that beautiful face. Stress can cause lasting damage.' She stepped around Harry, and I realised she wasn't wearing her sun hat, and the brutal light of the bare bulb lit up her face like she was in the middle of a stage, waiting for her turn to sing. Her eyes peered out from behind a stiff, leathery mask, a hard crusted thing with holes for her nostrils and mouth. Grotesquely she had applied thick red lipstick to the squirming things that were her lips, and powder across the rigid bumps of her stolen cheeks. She was a fright mask, a thing from a tomb, a fun-house mirror gone horribly wrong. And yet she stood with such pride, one hand over her jutting hip, and her hair – clearly a wig, I realised a second later – fell in luscious brown locks over her shoulders. I gaped.

And then, I laughed.

I don't rightly know what came over me then. There are some things that are so bleak, so horrific, that there is no sane response.

Cheryl looked at me in shock, while Harry only looked confused. Rosa cocked her head at me.

'What is so amusing?' Her tone was icy.

'I think,' I said, reaching up to wipe away a tear from the corner of my eye. My hand was shaking. 'I think stress is the least of your problems, love.'

The features underneath the mask twisted with fury, and I saw something, some sort of fluid, leaking down her neck. Another gust of hysterical laughter curled up inside my throat, but I swallowed it down.

'Harry,' she said, still glaring at me. 'We'll take our dear Cheryl now. I've waited long enough, I think.'

Harry lurched forward and this was it: I had no more time. I brought the scissors out and rammed the point into his back as he passed me, just under the shoulder blade. He bellowed, a mixture of fury and pain, and Rosa hissed like a scalded cat, backing out into the corridor. I yanked the scissors free again, although it took a lot more effort than I was expecting, and I stumbled awkwardly over the blankets.

'Cheryl!' I yelled. 'Laura! Run, for fuck's sake!'

Harry was already turning on me, his teeth bared in a snarl, and I didn't even see the knife move. There was a ribbon of hot red pain across my midriff that seemed impossibly large: it felt like he had simply sliced me in half. I slashed with the scissors again and this time I caught him across the eyes, and he turned away from me, screaming.

Get out get out get out. Katie in my ear, cold and distant.

Time becomes a little fractured here.

I got out into the corridor, Cheryl ahead of me, dragging

me by my sleeve. It was a confusing place, too dark and too bright at the same time. There were doors, which we opened, but each one seemed to lead into another storeroom. No way out, and somewhere, nearby, Rosa was screaming.

'We probably want stairs,' I mumbled to Cheryl. It was hard to speak above a whisper, for some reason. 'We're under the fair.'

I looked down at my hands and they were red with blood. A powerful pulse of panic moved through me, making it hard to think clearly. *She killed Katie*, I thought. *We killed Katie and her blood is on me.*

'Which way?' wailed Cheryl. 'I don't know which way to go.'

We opened another door, and this one was different. It was clean and white and strange, and there were things on the walls. Faces. This was where Laura's sisters were. The preserved pieces of them, anyway. Cheryl had fallen against the door jamb, sobbing. I grabbed her arm and hauled her up, ignoring the ripple of agony this caused across my stomach.

'Nearly there.' I sounded ludicrously chipper to my own ears. 'Just a little further.'

It felt as though the warm life of my body was leaking away. My shirt and trousers were hot and sodden – almost steaming, it seemed, with my life – while inside everything throbbed with pain.

We passed another room, where the door stood open, and somehow, Rosa was in there already, and so was Stitch Face Sue. She had her scissors back, and she was cutting Rosa up into pieces – each part that fell off was dry and old, like an autumn twig, or a piece of jerky. Rosa was howling, but Sue looked peaceful, determined. Like she was finally getting around to a job she had been waiting a long time to do.

'Is that real?' I said out loud, although I wasn't sure who I was asking. '*Is that real?*'

I turned away from that terrible sight to see Laura in front of me, leading us to another door. *She isn't Stitch Face Sue*, I thought then, *she isn't a monster at all. Just a woman damaged by them.*

The door opened onto stairs, and a shaft of dirty morning light. We went up, and out.

Chapter 60

Now

We came up into the back room of the slots in the funfair, and let ourselves out through a fire escape. The sky was a pale luminous grey and there was no one around at all, and for a second I thought that we had walked out into an empty world – as though we had escaped the hell of the caves only to wander into a weird kind of limbo. Cheryl was crying steadily but silently, tears tracking down her face and soaking into the collar of her jumper, while Laura clung to her hand and looked around, wide-eyed. We headed for the gates, which were standing open slightly, and walked out into the street. Still, we could see no one.

'It must be very early,' said Cheryl. We had lost track of time, that was all.

'Come on,' I said, 'let's get as far away from that place as possible. Up the road. I don't want to be in sight of it.'

We limped our way up the street, and once the funfair slipped away around the corner, I pulled my phone out and passed it to Cheryl. I left a big smear of blood on it, but it still had a little battery left.

'Call the police,' I said. 'Keep walking up this road, okay, even if I stop. There's a building on the right here, somewhere, has a gold plaque on it. Says "Historical Society", something like that. Wait there, for the police. The ladies in there are nice.'

'What about you?' Cheryl looked horrified.

At that moment, a car drew up around the corner and stopped. I froze, sure it would be Harry, come to drag us back, but it was Joseph who leapt out of the car. He sprinted over to us with his eyes wide.

'Christ, Sarah, what happened? The police have been all over, looking . . .'

'Joseph.' I felt like I could cry at the sight of him. 'Get this girl to the police, can you? It's Cheryl, Cheryl Yates, okay? She needs to get home. And this is Laura. She'll need help too.'

Joseph looked thunderstruck. 'Good god, Cheryl? *Cheryl?*'

'She was under the bloody funfair all along, can you believe it?' I laughed, out of breath. Joseph had pulled out his own phone and was dialling 999.

'Stay with Joseph, okay, Cheryl? He's a good guy. He'll get you home safe.'

'Don't go.' Cheryl grabbed my arm. 'You need to go to hospital!'

Very gently, I removed her hand and patted it. Laura was watching the three of us with bright interest, as though this were vastly more interesting than any of her videotapes.

'I just need to see the sea.' I couldn't bear the thought of Cheryl seeing me handcuffed. She had seen enough villains for one lifetime. 'Don't worry about me.'

I pulled away from them and lurched, almost drunkenly, across the road. Somewhere, in the distance, I could hear sirens.

Joseph called after me again, but I ignored it. I wanted to go and look at the sea.

The sand was cold and gritty under my fingers. The sirens were louder. I imagined Cheryl getting into the back of a police car, imagined a kindly policewoman giving her a blanket, a Mars Bar. I imagined the faces of her family when they got a phone call, later on this morning.

I felt fine. Just tired, really. The sun was a pale disc in the distance, and I marvelled at it. Had I ever been able to just look at the sun before? There must, I reasoned, be a layer of cloud between me and it, something that was diffusing its power. That was all. The surf crashed and swept away, crashed and swept, over and over.

For something to do, I opened my rucksack and pulled out the book I had bought from Mr Kastner, the one about local history and folklore. It took a bit of flipping backwards and forwards, but eventually I found the page on Susan Cartwright, with its story of pirates and wreckage and bravery. It was, it turned out, not a piece of local history at all, but a story written in the 1950s by a pulp writer called Roberta Thorne, who had lived in the area. It had been part of a collection of stories about the sea, something Thorne specialised in, and one or two had been made into films by Hollywood. Hithechurch, seeing a chance for some free publicity perhaps, welcomed the fictional story of plucky Susan Cartwright with open arms, selling copies of the book in local gift shops, alongside sticks of rock with scarecrows on the wrapper.

Not only was there never any Stitch Face Sue, there never was a Susan Cartwright either.

I like to think that Roberta Thorne was like me – a born liar who couldn't resist a grisly tale. Aren't all writers born liars? I think they probably are. I left the book on the sand next to me, bloody fingerprints all over the pages. I could see Katie, I realised, further down the beach. Her hair was flying about in the wind, and she was walking with her hands held out to either side of her, like she might at any moment hop up into the air and soar away, like a seagull. She was coming towards me, but slowly, very slowly.

I raised my hand to wave at her, and smiled.

Chapter 61

Now

Sarah Hewitt didn't last long after all. The press were beside themselves with the discovery of Cheryl and Laura – not to mention the surprise appearance of Emily Haynes – which meant that both my real name and my new name were splashed all over the front pages for weeks. Laura is in a home now, getting the help she needs and regular visits from her brother, and Cheryl is back with her family too. Harry survived the damage I did him with the scissors, although I understand that he doesn't see too well out of his right eye anymore, and I can't say that worries me much – I imagine he doesn't have a lot to look at in prison, anyway. Rosa was found in the rooms underneath the funfair, dead from an apparent heart attack, and Emily . . . Emily is back where she's supposed to be, paying for what she did to Louise.

I have moved away again, to a city this time, and I have a brand new name, which Joseph claims suits me, although I'm not sure I believe him. Cheryl knows it too – she asked if she could keep in touch with me, and so I get emails from her every now and then. I read them over and over until I have them memorised, these little snapshots of teenage life, full of school and boys and exams, and I wonder if I'm reading them for me, or for the other girl who lost any chance of that life back in 1988.

I don't see Katie anymore. Katie is gone, back to wherever bad memories are supposed to stay. Sometimes I miss her, and when that happens I grab Joseph's hand and suggest we go for a drive somewhere, or to the cinema.

You can't walk with ghosts forever.

Acknowledgements

When I was a kid we spent our family holidays in a caravan on the southeast coast, in a little town called Dymchurch. Some of my earliest, and happiest, memories are of those holidays: hectic fried breakfasts cooked in a tiny kitchen, seats that became beds, playing garden bowls on the grass outside, chaotic games of forty-forty around the campsite with my cousins. None of those holidays ever ended in murder, thankfully, although obviously I have drawn a lot from them while writing *Games for Dead Girls*. So first and foremost, thank you to my family for those days we spent on the beach and in the amusement arcades, playing Yahtzee and eating strawberry bonbons and toffee-crumble ice creams. And I suppose I must also thank the grumpy old woman who worked in the slots who did indeed once chuck my entire family out (allegedly because I was running around unsupervised, your honour); and thanks also to my nan, for flicking the V's as the old woman watched us leave, a gesture that has inspired a certain attitude in my family ever since.

Huge thanks must go to my editor at HarperVoyager, the brilliant Natasha Bardon, whose edits, notes, and comments were always a pleasure – this book is so much better because of you. Gratitude also to the great team at Crooked Lane, who have made me feel so welcome and kept me plied with enthusiasm – Faith Black Ross, Melissa Rechter, and Madeline Rathle, thank you.

I can never praise my wonderful agent enough. A true force of nature, an endless source of wisdom, and a tireless advocate; without Juliet Mushens, there would be no books from me at all. Thank you, darling.

I don't know if you've noticed, but it's been a weird few years, and I wouldn't have made it through them without a bunch of exceptionally brilliant people who have provided more support than perhaps they are even aware. Thank you, Andrew Reid and Adam Christopher for the late night and/or early morning bitching sessions; big love to the Onesies for the much-needed escapism and innuendo; enormous thanks to everyone at Herne Hill Books and Clapham Books, you super stars; and thank you to every reader who has ever got in touch to say how much they've enjoyed one of my books – these are the things that keep me coming back to the page.

Lastly, all my love and gratitude to my partner, Marty, who makes me laugh every day, keeps me sane, and has an unerring ability to provide a gin and tonic at exactly the right moment. Love you, moof.